About the Authors

Lucy King spent her childhood lost in the world of Mills & Boon when she really ought to have been paying attention to her teachers! But as she couldn't live in a dreamworld forever, she eventually acquired a degree in languages and an eclectic collection of jobs. Now writing full time, Lucy lives in Spain where she spends time reading, failing to finish crosswords and trying to convince herself that the beach really is the best place to work!

Rachael Thomas has always loved reading romance and is thrilled to now be a Modern author. She lives and works on a farm in Wales, a far cry from the glamour of a Modern story, but that makes slipping into her characters' world all the more appealing. When she's not writing or working on the farm she enjoy photography and visiting historic castles and grand houses. Visit her at www.rachaelthomas.co.uk

Sara Orwig lives in Oklahoma. She has a patient husband who will take her on research trips anywhere from big cities to old forts. She is an avid collector of Western history books. With a master's degree in English, Sara has written historical romance, mainstream fiction and contemporary romance. Books are beloved treasures that take Sara to magical worlds, and she loves both reading and writing them.

Red-Hot

COLLECTION

May 2018

June 2018

July 2018

August 2018

Red-Hot Affairs

LUCY KING

RACHAEL THOMAS

SARA ORWIG

MILLS & BOON

Published in Great Britain 2018
by Mills & Boon, an imprint of HarperCollins*Publishers*
Red-Hot Affairs © 2018 Harlequin Books S.A.

The Crown Affair © Lucy King 2011
Craving Her Enemy's Touch © 2015 Rachael Thomas
A Lone Star Love Affair © 2011 Sara Orwig

ISBN: 978-0-263-26726-6

09-0818

MIX
Paper from
responsible sources
FSC™ C007454

This book is produced from independently certified FSC™ paper
to ensure responsible forest management.

For more information visit: www.harpercollins.co.uk/green

Printed and bound by
CPI Group (UK) Ltd, Croydon, CR0 4YY

THE CROWN AFFAIR

LUCY KING

To my parents

CHAPTER ONE

'OH. MY. God,' Laura muttered, her fingers tightening around her binoculars and her breath hitching in her throat at the sight that met her eyes.

Her heart skipped a beat and her entire body flushed with a heat that had nothing to do with the warmth of the early summer sun and everything to do with the view.

Because, wow, what a view...

There, approximately two hundred metres away, across a lush green field and over a drystone wall, in one corner of the extensive grounds of the manor house, was a man.

Standing with his back to her, bending down and hauling a hefty log onto a stump. Wearing nothing but a pair of jeans, heavy-duty work boots and a rather impressive tan.

Whoever he was, he was dark-haired and tall. Broad-shouldered and fit. The muscles of his shoulders and back twisted and flexed as he hammered the axe down on those poor helpless little logs, displaying such strength and control that every inch of her began to tingle.

When he moved round the other side of the stump and lifted the axe high above his head, the tingle turned to full-blown lust. For a brief frozen moment, in sharp definition, there was the most magnificent chest she'd ever seen. Tanned. Lean. Sprinkled with a smattering of dark hair that narrowed down his taut stomach and vanished tantalisingly beneath the waistband of his jeans.

Ignoring the little voice in her head telling her she really ought not to be doing this, Laura pressed the binoculars closer and bit her lip, largely to stop herself whimpering.

She'd never whimpered in her life, but if ever there was an occasion to start, this was it.

She could make out every rippling muscle. Every one of his ribs. Her fingers itched to trace the dips and contours of his body. What would he feel like beneath her hands? What would it feel like to have all that strength and control on top of her? Underneath her? Inside her?

At the bolt of desire that burst deep inside her, Laura's temperature went through the roof. The breath shot from her lungs and her heart practically stopped. A weird kind of fizzing sprang to life in the pit of her stomach and she clutched at the curtain before her balance vaporised and she nearly toppled out of the window.

Good Lord, she thought dazedly as stars spun around her head. She was fantasising. Ogling. Virtually salivating. Since when had she started doing *that*? She dragged in a shaky breath. Crikey, maybe she really *had* gone off the rails.

Letting the binoculars dangle from the leather strap hanging around her neck, Laura sagged against the wall and willed her breathing to steady and her heart rate to slow.

Now, of all times, when she was by herself and inches from an open window with a ten-foot drop to the ground, would really *not* be a good time to faint.

Which was precisely why she ought to unwrap herself from the curtains, back away and pull herself together.

Besides, quite apart from her precarious position, she had no business ogling men, however hot. After the traumatic collapse of her last relationship she'd sworn off the whole lousy lot of them. And even if she had been in the mood, voyeurism had never been her thing. It was sneaky. It was reckless.

And kind of thrilling.

Laura swallowed and blinked to clear her suddenly blurry vision. Oh, for heaven's sake. That little thrill currently whooshing around her body could stop it right now. She was interested in the house, that was all.

For the six weeks she'd been living in the village the manor house had been as silent as the grave, and her frustration at not being able to take a look inside had reached such a peak that if she weren't such a law-abiding person she'd have contemplated a spot of breaking and entering.

So when she'd heard the sound of splintering wood coming from the other side of the village earlier this morning she'd barely been able to believe her luck. Grabbing her binoculars, she'd raced upstairs, wrapped herself in her curtains and scouted the landscape for the source of the noise.

Quite what she'd been expecting she wasn't sure, but it certainly hadn't been a sight as enticing as this.

As the thrill returned, more delicious and more insistent than before, Laura paused mid-unwrap, nibbled on her lip and frowned. She'd always appreciated beauty. Had always admired structure. Which was why she'd become an architect. Now here was the finest animate example of both she'd seen in a long time and given the current sorry state of her love life it was unlikely that she'd ever get the chance again.

Her heart thumping with illicit excitement, she edged closer to the wall, huddled deeper into the curtain, and fished her binoculars out from beneath the heavy fabric.

How could another second or two hurt? After all, it wasn't as if he could see her, was it?

Matt swung the axe high above his head and froze.

There it was again. The flash.

Once. Twice. And then intermittently, like a sputtering light bulb. Like a beacon. Or like the sun glinting off a pair of binoculars.

Hell.

He thwacked the axe down on the log with such force that the blade scythed through the wood like a hot knife through butter and lodged in the stump.

Something hard and tight settled in the pit of his stomach. Couldn't they leave him alone for *one* measly second?

Ignoring the stinging in his muscles and the sweat trickling down his back, he bent down, picked up the two halves of the log and hurled them onto the pile.

One last weekend of peace. That was all he wanted. One lousy weekend of privacy before he embarked on a role he wasn't sure he was entirely prepared for, and life as he knew it turned upside down.

Matt grabbed the bottle lying in the grass, sloshed water over his head and flinched when the ice-cold liquid hit his burning skin.

Hadn't he provided the press with enough stories recently? They'd been hounding him for weeks, ever since it had been announced he was the long-lost heir to the newly restored Sassanian throne. They'd been camping outside his London house and tailing him wherever he went. Shoving tape recorders and cameras in his face at every opportunity and demanding responses to questions about his private life he had no intention of ever answering.

By and large he'd played his part. Given interviews. Posed for photographs. And borne it with remarkable, if grim, tolerance. But by following him here, to the house in the Cotswolds he'd almost forgotten he owned, they'd crossed the line.

As irritation escalated into anger, Matt shoved his hands through his hair and pulled his T-shirt over his head.

Enough was enough. No way was he just sitting back and letting some miserable lowlife hack gawk at him all weekend. To hell with the consequences. He was going to go round, grab that pair of binoculars and wind the strap round their scrawny neck.

Ah, that was a shame, thought Laura, biting her lip as she watched that magnificent chest disappear beneath a swathe of navy cotton.

If she had control of the world, a man like that would be consigned to a life of naked-from-the-waist-up log-chopping. On permanent display. As a gift to the nation or something. And if she had control of the world, she'd rewind time and hit the pause button at the exact moment he'd taken that impromptu little shower.

Despite the heat simmering in her veins, Laura shivered as the image slammed into her head. Utterly transfixed, she'd followed the rivulets of water trickling down his chest and hadn't been able to stop herself trembling with longing. The powerful lenses of her binoculars had picked out every glistening drop clinging lovingly to his skin and her breath had evaporated all over again.

Even now, when he was all covered up and striding across the lawn towards the house, as if the hounds of hell were snapping at his heels, she felt as if she were on fire. Tiny flames of heat licked along her veins. Her skin sizzled. Her stomach churned.

He disappeared inside the house and Laura blinked and felt a sharp pang of loss.

The unsettling shock of such an intense reaction snapped her back to her senses. She blinked. Rubbed her eyes and pulled herself together.

Right, she decided, unwinding herself from the curtain and setting the binoculars on her dressing table. That was quite enough of that. She'd indulged for far longer than was wise and she had things to do.

So no more thumping hearts and trembling limbs. No more tingling in inappropriate places and erratic breathing. And definitely no more fantasising.

Tucking a notebook and pencil in the back pocket of her shorts and slinging her camera over her shoulder, Laura pulled her shoulders back and headed downstairs.

If she was going to wangle an invitation inside what appeared to be a near perfect example of early seventeenth century architecture, she had to be charming, determined and above all, strong of knee.

One of the first things Matt had planned to do once installed on the throne of Sassania was open up the press and grant the country's journalists more access to information.

Now, he thought grimly, eyes down as he strode along the path in the direction of the binocular-toting hack, he wasn't so sure. Now he'd like to abolish it altogether and string up the entire lot of them. Starting with the one he was about to tear a strip off.

'Good morning.'

At the sound of the voice a few feet in front of him, Matt skidded to a halt and his head snapped up. His gaze rested on the woman blocking his path smiling blindingly at him and for a second his mind went blank. All thoughts of journalists and Mediterranean island kingdoms evaporated; if someone had asked his name he'd have been stumped.

As his gaze automatically ran over her he felt the ground tilt beneath his feet. Blood roared in his ears and fire surged through his veins. His chest contracted as if he'd been walloped in the solar plexus, and for one horrible moment Matt wondered if he was having a heart attack.

But then as suddenly as it had started, it stopped. The ground settled, his head cleared, his lungs started pumping and his heart rate steadied.

Keeping his extraordinary reaction firmly behind the neutral expression that had helped him make billions, Matt shoved a hand through his hair and forced himself to relax.

No doubt it was the unexpectedness of her that had caused his violent reaction. The sudden interruption to his train of thought. That was all. It couldn't possibly have had anything to do with the mass of blond hair, the big cornflower-blue eyes or the wide smile. Or, for that matter, the set of killer curves encased in the skimpiest shorts and tightest T-shirt he'd ever seen.

Because that would be as disconcerting as it would have been unusual. He'd never been distracted by a woman, however beautiful and however well packaged, and he didn't intend to start now.

Reminding himself what he was supposed to be doing, he gave her a brief nod and the flash of an impersonal smile. 'Good morning,' he said, taking a step to the right to weave past her.

Which she mirrored.

Matt frowned. 'Excuse me,' he muttered, and took a step to the left.

Which she blocked, too.

He rubbed a hand along his jaw and stifled a sigh. Once might have been an accident. Twice was deliberate.

Matt bit back a growl of frustration. This was precisely why up until now he'd chosen to live in a penthouse in an exclusive apartment block in the centre of London, where none of the neighbours knew each other and no one was interested in wasting time on idle chit-chat. Everyone kept themselves to themselves and just got on with their own lives.

Here, however, out in the country, things evidently didn't work like that. Whoever she was, she clearly wanted to chat. While he didn't. Nor did he have the time to tango from side to side like this all morning.

Toying with the idea of clamping his hands round her waist and hoisting her out of the way, Matt dipped his eyes to the narrow strip of bare flesh between the hem of her T-shirt and the waistband of her shorts.

He wondered what it would feel like. Smooth. Silky. Warm. Undoubtedly. And what would it taste like? At the thought of his mouth against the skin of her stomach, moving lower and lower to see what *she'd* taste like, his mouth went dry and his pulse leapt.

Hmm, he thought, shoving his fists in his pockets.

Perhaps putting his hands on her wasn't the wisest course of action. Conversation, polite but brief, it would have to be. Assuming he could speak, of course.

'Are you all right?' she asked, her brow creasing in concern.

Matt gave his head a quick shake to dispel the lingering fuzziness and cleared his throat. 'Fine,' he said. 'Why?'

'You went very pale for a second.'

'You startled me.'

Her smiled widened and his temperature went up a notch. 'I'm sorry,' she said. 'I thought it would be safer to alert you to my presence rather than wait for you to barrel straight into me.'

At the thought of his body colliding with hers, of having all that softness and warmth plastered against him, a bolt of desire kicked him in the gut. A vision of the two of them tumbling down onto the grass, limbs entwined, mouths jammed together, hands everywhere, slammed into his head and his heart nearly leapt out of his chest.

So much for trying to kid himself that his reaction to her was simply shock. Shock had never given him an erection harder than granite.

Great. Scorching attraction. Just what he needed.

Matt's jaw tightened. 'I was deep in thought,' he said, finally drumming up some of that steely control he was supposedly so famous for and hauling his body into line.

She tilted her head to one side. 'I could tell. And not about anything good by the looks of things.'

'Not particularly.'

'That's a shame.'

'Is it?'

She nibbled on her lip and nodded. 'I think so. Especially on a day like today.'

'What's so special about today?' Apart from being the day he thought he might be losing his mind.

'Well, for one thing, the sun is shining, and, this being Britain in May, that's a cause for celebration. Plus the flowers are beautiful and the air smells heavenly.'

Were they? Did it? Matt had been too wrapped up in his thoughts to notice. Now his thoughts had been scattered to the four winds. Forget the flowers. Forget the air. *She* was beautiful. *She* smelt heavenly. And her mouth was something else. 'Really?' he muttered, trying not to imagine what it would feel like crushed beneath his.

She nodded. 'A day like today should be all about lying on the grass, reading the papers and drinking rosé,' she said, giving him another wide smile that had his control threatening to unravel all over again, 'not marching around and glowering at the ground.'

At that timely reminder about where he was and what he was supposed to be doing, Matt pulled himself together. This was ludicrous. If the people of Sassania could see the state of him now, they'd have thought twice about their decision to reinstate the monarchy.

'Unfortunately I don't have time to read the papers or drink rosé,' he said sharply. And as for sprawling over the grass, well, the less he thought about that the better. 'So, if you'll excuse me…'

She stuck out her hand. 'Laura Mackenzie.'

Matt resisted the urge to grind his teeth. 'Matt Saxon.' He took her hand and ignored the leap of electricity that shot up his arm. 'Look, is there something I can help you with?'

'I hope so.' Her voice sounded a little hoarse and she ran her hand over her hip as she cleared her throat.

Matt frowned. 'If it's directions you're after I'm afraid I won't be of much use.' He spent so little time in the area he'd had to programme his satnav just to get here.

She shook her head and the sun bouncing off her hair, dazzled him for a second. 'I'm not after directions.' She shot him another smile that made his stomach contract. 'In fact I'm after you.'

For a second Matt couldn't work out what she was talking about. 'Me?'

She nodded and a chill, as if the sun had disappeared behind a cloud, snaked down his spine. The lingering trace of desire fled and his body tightened for an entirely different reason.

Why would she be after him? How did she know who he was?

Unless she'd been watching him.

As suspicion slammed into him his pulse began to race. She couldn't be...

He ran his gaze over her again, this time skating over the curves and the clothing. This time his eyes clocked the camera slung over her shoulder. The corner of a notebook and the pen sticking out of the back pocket of her shorts. The hopeful, eager look on her face.

The chill running through his body turned to ice. Oh, damn. It appeared she was.

His gaze trailed back up and he scrutinised her features, comparing them against the bank of journalistic faces he'd filed away over the past few months. But he drew a blank. Whoever she worked for, he thought grimly, she was new.

Stamping down hard on something that felt suspi-

ciously like disappointment, Matt hardened his heart.
Why was he surprised? Why was he disappointed? Once
again life was simply proving that some people were
only out for what they could get.

'I'm glad we bumped into each other,' she said.

He just bet she was. 'Why?'

The smile faltered and her eyes widened a fraction
at his tone. 'I was on my way to see you.'

'Were you?' he drawled as a strange sort of numbness
seeped through him.

'You've come from the manor house.'

'I have.'

Matt shoved his hands in the pockets of his jeans and
rocked back on his heels, deciding to wait and see to
what lengths this one would go to wangle an interview.
Her outfit was certainly designed to kill.

'Nice place.'

'Thank you,' he said coolly.

'Fabulous detail on the gabling.'

'Really.'

'Absolutely. And beautiful—er—grounds.'

'Naturally.'

'Are you the gardener?'

Matt frowned. The gardener? Hah. 'I'm the owner.'
As if she didn't know.

Her eyes widened. 'Oh.' And then she gave him a
smile that had the ground beneath his feet tilting all
over again before he could tell it not to. 'Well, that's
even better.'

'Of course it is.'

She frowned and blinked. 'What?'

Oh, she did the innocent thing very well. 'What do
you want?' he said.

Laura's smile faltered. 'If it's not too much trouble,

I was wondering if I could come over and take some photos. Of your house,' she added.

Too much trouble? Matt's jaw clenched. The complete and utter gall of the woman.

'It would only be for a second,' she added, as if sensing his reluctance. 'You know, just a few shots. If you wouldn't mind…'

Matt's tenuous grip on his patience snapped. 'Yes, I do mind, and no, you can't.'

The smile slid from her face and she recoiled as if he'd slapped her. For a moment she just stood there, staring at him in shock, her face draining of colour so fast he thought she might be about to pass out.

Matt steeled himself against the brief stab of guilt and the flash of distress in her eyes and told himself not to be so idiotically soft.

What the hell had she expected? That he'd welcome her into his house with open arms? That he'd *want* to be photographed lounging on the sofa in his drawing room? That he'd roll over and offer her a double-page spread of the new ruler of Sassania 'at home'?

If she really thought that, she could think again.

Laura blinked a couple of times and then pulled her shoulders back. 'Oh. Right,' she said blankly. 'Well. Sorry to have bothered you. Enjoy your weekend.'

Like that was a possibility now.

As she gave him a vague nod and turned to walk back in the direction she had presumably come from, Matt's hand shot out and clamped around her upper arm. 'Not so fast.'

CHAPTER TWO

WHAT the hell?

Laura felt Matt's fingers dig into her arm and went rigid as alarm flooded through her.

Well, alarm and a whole lot of something else. But alarm was what she decided to channel at that particular moment. Because he might have eyes the colour of dark molten chocolate and thick brown hair that her fingers itched to thread through. He might have a voice that made her think of whisky and honey and warm nights in front of a fire. And he might have a body that she longed to get her hands on.

But he was clearly a psychopath.

All she'd wanted was a bit of a snoop and a few lousy shots of his house, for goodness' sake. Anyone would think she'd been after his soul.

'Ow,' she muttered, wincing and trying to wriggle away from beneath his fingers.

His grip loosened and she pulled back and rubbed her arm where her skin burned. If she had any sense whatsoever she'd be spinning on her heel and racing back to the safety of her cottage. For although she'd been drooling over his house for weeks, at no point had she considered the fact that its owner would be anything other than congenial and cooperative.

Hah. How wrong could you get?

Laura glanced up to find him glowering at her and nearly swooned at the fierceness of his glare. Whatever his problem was, and he clearly had many, she wanted nothing to do with it. She had enough problems of her own. The biggest one at the moment being the treacherous way her body appeared to respond to him.

When he'd taken her hand she'd nearly leapt a foot in the air from the jolt of electricity that shot up her arm. And then when he'd looked her up and down, so thoroughly, as if he could see right through her clothes, every inch of her body had burned in the wake of his gaze. The heat that had whipped through her when she'd been ogling him through her binoculars had been nothing compared to the scorching heat that was thundering through her now.

In the face of such blatant hostility her reaction to him was perverse.

What exactly was it about that penetrating stare of his that pinned her to the spot? Why were her insides going all squirmy and quivery? And more importantly, why wasn't she taking advantage of the fact that he'd released her, and running off just as fast as her size sevens would carry her?

That was what the old Laura, the one who avoided confrontation like the plague and never said no, would have done. And despite the assertiveness course she'd recently completed, there was enough of the old her still floating around to make her long to run and bury herself under her duvet.

But scarpering in the face of confrontation wasn't an option any longer, was it? Laura squared her jaw. No. Now she dealt with stuff. Or at least that was the idea. Up until now she hadn't had the opportunity to practise.

Channelling everything she could remember from the course, Laura took a deep breath, stuck her chin up and returned his glare. 'What do you want now?'

'Who do you work for?' he snapped.

She blinked and inwardly flinched. 'That's none of your business.'

'What?' His eyebrows shot up.

Laura bristled. 'Well, who do you think you are hauling me around and demanding to know who I work for?' She tilted her head and shot him a defiant stare. Her tutor would be proud. 'You know, your small-talk skills leave a *lot* to be desired.'

Matt's face tightened. 'I'm not interested in small talk. Do you or do you not work for *Celebrity* magazine?'

Laura frowned. Maybe the mushrooms she'd eaten for breakfast had had a touch of the magic about them, because this conversation had her baffled. 'Of course I don't. Currently I don't work for anyone.'

'Freelance?' he snapped.

Made redundant, but there was no way she was going into that. 'On sabbatical.'

'Right,' he drawled, clearly not believing her for a second. 'Then why were you watching me?'

Uh-oh. Laura's mouth opened. Then closed. And then to her dismay she felt her cheeks begin to burn. 'What makes you think anyone was watching you?' she said, aiming for a blank look in the hope that it would counteract the blush. If asked, she'd attribute *that* to the heat.

Matt raised an eyebrow. 'Well, let me see,' he said dryly. 'How about a pair of binoculars glinting in the sun and pointing straight in my direction?'

Oh, rats. Laura's heart plummeted. So much for thinking she'd been discreet. She shouldn't have pushed her luck and indulged for so long.

Her brain raced through her options and she realised depressingly that she had no choice but to confess. Since she'd already told him she'd come looking for him she couldn't even bluff her way out of it.

She ran a hand through her hair and straightened her spine. 'OK, fine. But technically I wasn't actually—'

'I'll ask you one more time,' he said flatly, his eyes narrowing. 'Which scurrilous rag do you work for?'

Which scurrilous rag? Laura's hand fell to her side and she blinked in confusion. What on earth was he talking about? Perhaps she ought to suggest he get out of the heat. What with all that bending and twisting while log-chopping, the sun must have gone to his head. Something had certainly gone to hers and she hadn't even been in the sun. 'I don't work for a rag, scurrilous or otherwise,' she said. 'I'm an architect.'

A flicker of surprise flashed across his face and then vanished. 'That's one I haven't heard before.'

Laura's hackles shot up. 'It's not a joke.'

'You're absolutely right.'

'Why would you think I was a journalist?'

'I don't think, I *know* you're a journalist.'

Her mouth dropped open at the scorn in his voice and she had to dig deep and drum up the techniques to Embrace Confrontation to fight back the temptation to quail. 'You're insane.'

A muscle in his jaw hammered. 'So explain the binoculars.'

Laura planted her hands on her hips and glared at him. 'I was about to when you interrupted me.'

Matt's expression took on a 'this'll be good' kind of

look and indignation simmered in her veins. Why the hell was she bothering? Oh, yes, the house.

Laura tightened her grip on her manners. 'I was going to clarify that I wasn't actually watching you.' Much. 'I was really eyeing up your house.'

He stared at her. 'My house?' he said, his brows snapping together. 'Why?'

'Because it's the best example of seventeenth century architecture I've ever seen. Certainly round here.'

'That's not uncommon knowledge,' he drawled.

Laura couldn't help bristling at his sceptical tone. 'Undoubtedly,' she said tightly. 'However I have more than a passing interest. I specialise in the restoration and conservation of ancient buildings, and I've been coveting yours for weeks.'

'Is that so?'

Matt folded his arms across his chest and stared at her. For so long and so intently that she began to drown in the heat of his gaze. She might be churning with indignation, but that didn't stop her head swimming, her knees turning watery and her stomach fluttering. Laura silently cursed her treacherous body and hoped to God he couldn't see the effect he was having on her. 'Absolutely,' she said with a coolness that came from who knew where.

Matt tilted his head. Raised an eyebrow. Gave her a lazily lethal smile that zoomed down the entire length of her body and curled her toes, and quite suddenly her skin began to prickle.

'If you're an architect as you say you are,' he said, leaning forwards a fraction and lowering his voice, 'prove it.'

Prove it? *Prove it?*

For a moment, all Laura could hear was what sounded

like the faint hum of a tractor somewhere in the distance. But that could well have been the blood rushing in her ears.

'What?' she said, giving her head a quick shake. Presumably she'd been so distracted by the muscles of Matt's arms flexing as he crossed them she must have misheard. Been hypnotised by his eyes or something. Or maybe he just had a truly warped sense of humour and was joking. Because what kind of man went round accusing random strangers of being something they weren't and then demanding they prove it?

'If you expect me to believe you're an architect and want nothing more than access to my house, prove it.'

Laura blinked and stared at him. Nope. Gorgeous forearms and mesmerising eyes aside, she hadn't misheard. And he wasn't joking. That he meant what he said was etched into the stony expression on his face.

Her pulse raced. What exactly was his problem? Was he on some sort of lord-of-the-manor power trip? Was he completely paranoid? And frankly, did she even want to venture inside his house when he was obviously one pane short of a window?

The rational side of her, the one that was seething with indignation, pointed out that she had no need to continue this idiotic conversation. It was a balmy Saturday morning. She had plenty of things to be getting on with. Like finding a job and sorting out her catastrophe of a life. She really didn't need this kind of headache, and no mansion was worth this amount of hassle.

However, the professional part of her, the one that had recently been so ruthlessly dismissed, so flatly rejected by the company she'd worked for, clamoured for the opportunity to justify her abilities.

The two sides battled for a nanosecond but the sting of rejection was still so fresh, the wound still so raw, there was no contest.

Laura pulled her shoulders back and stuck her chin up. He wanted proof? Then he'd get it. More of it than anyone not fascinated with old buildings could possibly want.

'Fine,' she said, hauling out her notebook and studying the notes she'd made over the past six weeks. 'From my preliminary investigations I'd say your house was probably built some time between the late sixteenth and early seventeenth centuries. The main structure has two storeys and, I believe, an attic.'

Possibly with a mad relative in occupancy to accompany the one who inhabited the rest.

'It's built out of squared and dressed limestone,' she continued, 'and has a stone slate roof. I believe it used to be a quadrangle, but it's now "h" shaped with wings projecting forwards right and left of the central gabled porch. The right hand wing has been substantially rebuilt at the back. I'd say in the mid-nineteenth century.'

She paused to take a breath and glanced up from the pages to find Matt staring at her, a slightly stunned expression on his handsome face.

Good. That would teach him to leap to absurd conclusions and engage in all that sceptical eyebrow raising. And she had plenty more where that came from. She hadn't even begun on the windows.

She arched a challenging eyebrow of her own. 'Would you like me to go on?'

Matt frowned. 'No. That's fine.'

Stuffing the notebook back in her pocket, Laura pulled her camera off her shoulder and switched it on. 'Then perhaps you'd like to see some pictures?' she said.

'I have one hundred and thirty photos of Regency Bath. I could take you through each one of them if you like. In great detail. I'm very thorough. And extremely enthusiastic. Honestly I could talk about them for hours.'

The frown deepened. 'Some other time perhaps. I'm convinced.'

Bully for him. 'I'm so glad,' she said witheringly, hauling her camera back on her shoulder and shooting him a cool glance. 'So why would you think I was a journalist?'

'Experience of binoculars.'

'Are you really that newsworthy?'

His mouth twisted into a wry smile. 'I have been.'

She racked her brains to place his face, but drew a blank. He probably dated supermodels or something. Poor old supermodels. 'Who are you?'

'Ever read the papers?'

Laura shook her head. 'Not often. Too much doom and gloom. Unless you've appeared in *Architecture Tomorrow*, I'm unlikely to have heard of you.' So there.

'How refreshing.'

Now she was naïve as well as everything else? Wow, he really knew how to make women feel special.

'How patronising,' she fired back, before she could remind herself that he still held all the cards and she was supposed to be being charming and polite.

Matt didn't say anything. Just looked at her steadily with those dark eyes of his until the urge to kick herself became almost impossible to contain.

Rats. Had she gone too far? Been *too* demanding, and blown it? Laura caught her lip and frowned. Damn, that assertiveness course had a lot to answer for.

Then the glimmer of a smile hovered at his mouth

and the tension that she hadn't realised she'd been feeling fled her body. 'It appears I owe you an apology.'

Phew. Thank God for that. She hadn't blown it. 'It *appears* you owe me an apology?' she said, her eyebrows lifting a fraction as she gave him a broad smile.

He shrugged and shoved his hands in his pockets. 'More than one probably. You'll have to bear with me, though, I'm a little rusty.'

That was the understatement of the century. 'An apology would be good,' Laura said, deciding to capitalise on his obvious unease and press home her advantage. 'An invitation to take a look around your house would be better.'

Invite her to take a look round his house?

The faint smile tugging at Matt's lips vanished.

That was absolutely out of the question.

Apart from the invasion of his privacy, with his judgement so skewed and his behaviour so unpredictable, who knew what might happen once she was inside his house and within stumbling distance of a bed?

Matt frowned as his mind raced. He was usually so measured. So careful in his decisions. He never went off the rails. Never made mistakes. So why now?

Maybe the memories the house held were more unsettling than he'd thought. Maybe the stress of the past six months had got too much. Maybe he was cracking up.

Because why else would he have leapt to the wrong conclusion and rushed over here? Why else would he have completely overreacted and lashed out at her? And why else would he be finding it so hard to keep his hands off her?

The flush of colour in her cheeks, the flashing of her

eyes and the heaving of her breasts made him want to behave in the kind of prehistoric way that he doubted would go down well with a twenty-first-century woman. Even when he'd thought she was a journalist and had been burning with fury, he'd still wanted to throw her over his shoulder and cart her off to the nearest bedroom.

Which was never going to happen. Even if he'd wanted to explore the attraction that sizzled between them he didn't have the time and really didn't need the complication.

Ignoring the sliver of regret that pierced his chest, Matt set his jaw and pulled himself together. A tower of strength, that was him. Rock hard. Implacable.

Above all, he was absolutely not cracking up and it was about time he proved it. Giving Laura a polite smile, he hardened his heart. 'I'm afraid that's completely out of the question.'

Oh.

Laura's smile faded and her shoulders sagged a little at Matt's flatly delivered response. A flood of disappointment washed through her and a lump formed in her throat. Dammit, she could have sworn he'd been about to agree to her request. She'd thought she'd had it so in the bag.

But as she stared up at him, taking in the rigid expression on his face and his unyielding stance, it was blindingly obvious that Matt had made his decision, and it was equally clear that nothing she said would make him change his mind. He looked unforgiving, unbending and as immovable as granite.

She swallowed back the lump and inwardly shrugged. Ah, well. She'd tried. That was the main thing.

She'd given it her best shot and been defeated. Matt clearly valued his privacy and definitely wanted to be left alone. He'd made his decision and she'd respect that. So her curiosity would remain unsatisfied, but that didn't matter. There were plenty of other equally interesting houses she could visit if she felt like it. It really was no big deal.

She was on the point of turning on her heel and leaving when her conscience suddenly decided to wake up and demand to know what the hell she thought she was doing.

Hang on a minute. She froze as her head began to pound. Was she really going to give in just like that? After all she'd been through? After all the self-analysis she'd done? After all the money and energy she'd spent on that course?

What was she? A wimp or a warrior?

Feeling determination begin to course through her, Laura stiffened her resolve. Hadn't she vowed to banish her inner wimp and embrace her inner warrior?

She had. At length. So no way was she going to let the wimp win.

This wasn't about the house any more. This was about her, and the promise she'd made to herself to shuck off the old Laura and embrace the new.

Matt might be standing there like Everest, but he was still a man, flesh and blood just like anyone else. Well, not *quite* like anyone else, she thought, letting her gaze roam over him and feeling her temperature rocket, but he was bound to have an Achilles heel somewhere. All she had to do was find it.

She'd get what she came for. By whatever means possible.

* * *

Why wasn't she spinning on her heel and going?

Matt watched the emotions play across Laura's face and his frown deepened. He'd made it perfectly clear his answer was no, so why was she still hovering there?

More to the point, why was *he* still hovering there? Just because she was running her gaze over him didn't mean he had to stay until she'd finished, did it?

'Oh,' she said, her teeth catching on her lower lip as she finally lifted her face and batted her eyelids up at him.

Oh, no, Matt thought, steeling himself against the nugget of guilt that suddenly started tugging at his conscience. He was *not* going to be swayed by the disappointment swimming in the big blue eyes shimmering up at him. Or distracted by the wet red pout of her mouth.

No way. The guilt and the desire could get lost. He pulled his hands out of his pockets and dragged them through his hair. Dammit, this was precisely why he should have been the one to leave.

'Please,' she said, looking up at him from beneath her lashes, the pout curving into an enticing smile.

Matt's gaze dropped to her mouth before he could stop it and he was thwacked by a vision of those lips roaming over his body, her hair fanning out and tickling his skin as she moved down him, her hands stroking everywhere. At the force of the desire that slammed through him his mouth went dry and his head swam.

And for the life of him he couldn't remember why letting her loose in his house was a bad idea.

'OK,' he heard himself say. 'Sure. Why not?'

'Great,' she said, the disappointment vanishing from her eyes and her smile switching from enticing to strangely triumphant. 'Lead the way.'

Why not? *Why not?* God. He was definitely cracking up. Wishing he could give himself a good slap, Matt muttered a 'Follow me,' turned on his heel and marched off.

CHAPTER THREE

WELL, that had been something of a surprise, thought Laura, resisting the urge to punch the air and setting off in Matt's wake instead. Having never employed such wily tactics before, she hadn't really expected the pout and the eyelash flutter to work. But while she might be faintly stunned that they had, Matt, judging by the merciless pace he set as he stalked along the path, was fuming.

By the time they reached the front door of the house Laura was hot, panting and, without doubt, hideously red in the face. Matt, on the other hand, hadn't broken a sweat.

If she was being brutally honest, her current breathlessness wasn't *entirely* due to the unexpected exercise. She'd trotted along behind him, her gaze fixed to his lithe muscular frame as if magnetised, and her body had begun to hum with something other than adrenalin. The easy way he moved and the purposefulness of his stride had her thinking about all the other things he might do purposefully and easily, and her head had gone all fuzzy. She'd scraped her hair back into a messy ponytail in the faint hope it might cool her down but it hadn't worked.

'Where would you like to start?' he snapped, dropping his keys onto the console table and whipping round to face her.

With the removal of his T-shirt ideally, Laura decided, totally distracted by the rippling muscles in his forearms as he crossed them over his chest. First she'd slide her hands beneath it and draw it over his head. Once she'd dealt with that she'd run her hands down his torso and tackle his belt. Then she'd undo the buttons of his jeans, hook her hands over the waistband and ease them down over his hips before pushing him down onto a deep soft sofa that was bound to be lurking somewhere around the place. And then she'd sink to her knees and—

'Laura?'

Laura blinked and hurtled back to reality. God. She was doing it again. At the heat that rushed through her, her cheeks began to burn even more fiercely.

For the first time since she'd decided to become an architect she thanked God for the eighteenth century window tax that had bricked up thousands of windows and ultimately led to dark halls across the country. Including, to her eternal gratitude, this one.

'Yes. Sorry.' She blinked and swallowed and gathered her scattered wits. The house. He was talking about the house. Of course. 'The—ah—attic, I think,' she said. As far away from Matt and his disturbing effect on her equilibrium as possible.

'I'll take you to it,' he said, heading for the stairs.

What? Alarm knotted her stomach. He was planning to accompany her? Laura shivered at the thought. With him watching her every move she'd never get anything done.

'No,' she blurted out.

Matt stopped, turned and stared at her in surprise. As well he might.

'I mean, it's fine,' she added hastily with a quick smile. 'I'm sure you have things to be getting on with and I should be able to find the attic. Top of the house, right?'

'Where else?'

He stared at her, his eyes narrowing as if trying to work out if she was entirely trustworthy, and, what with the unorthodox methods she'd employed to inveigle her way inside his house, she couldn't entirely blame him.

'Well, quite.' Laura swallowed hard and tucked a tendril of hair behind her ear. 'Look, Matt,' she said, giving him what she hoped was a reassuring smile, 'I really do work better alone. And I promise not to run off with the silver.'

Matt frowned and then shrugged. 'Fine. I'll be in the library if you need anything.'

Oh, for God's sake, Matt thought, scowling down at the report into Sassania's fishing quotas that he'd been trying to work on and shoving it aside. How long did getting a few photos take? The house wasn't that big, but Laura had been up there for an hour at least. She couldn't have found *that* much of architectural interest, could she?

Something banged right above his head and Matt winced. Perhaps she had. Judging by the sounds of scraping furniture and the hammering on walls that had been coming from various parts of the house, Laura was taking the whole place apart.

While part of him reluctantly admired her thoroughness and determination, another, more persistent part of him had spent the past hour wondering whether her enthusiasm and passion for her work carried over into other areas of life. Like sex.

An image of her lying on his bed, naked, her hair spilling all over his pillows, her long tanned limbs tangled in his sheets, her eyes all slumberous and inviting, slammed into his head yet again and his body stiffened painfully.

Matt shoved his hands through his hair and ground his teeth in frustration. This was ridiculous. He was a sensible rational man of thirty-three, not a hormone-ridden adolescent. So why was he finding it so hard to concentrate? Why had he spent the past ten minutes reading the same page of that damned report with still no idea of what it was about?

It hadn't been *that* long since he'd had sex, had it? He cast his mind back and tried to remember the last time he'd had a woman in his bed. Was it six months ago? A year? Surely it couldn't be longer than that, could it?

Matt frowned. Even if it was, there was no need to panic. He'd been busy. That was all. And it wasn't as if he *needed* sex. He'd gone far longer without it and had survived perfectly well.

Footsteps echoed down the stairs. His blood rushed to his head and he pushed himself away from his desk and leapt to his feet. He needed to get out, before he did something really rash like bundle her back upstairs and demand she show him the architectural features of his bedroom.

He'd go and chop what was left of those logs. The release of hard physical work after spending months in stifling meeting rooms had worked earlier. It would work now. Just to be on the safe side he'd stay out there until she'd finished. If he ran out of logs, he'd fire up the lawnmower.

And there was another benefit of his strategy, he thought, identifying the sound of a camera clicking coming from the drawing room and striding across the hall. Laura could let herself out. Once he'd told her where he was going he need never lay eyes on her ever again. And then maybe, just maybe, his body would stop twitching and aching and straining, and he'd regain some sort of equilibrium.

Good. Excellent. It was a brilliant plan. With every step he took he could feel his head clearing and his sanity returning.

Until he got to the doorway. Where he stopped dead.

As he'd figured, Laura was in the drawing room. What he hadn't allowed for was that she'd be investigating the fireplace. With her back to him, on her knees. With her legs spread and her bottom in the air.

His gaze dropped, automatically zooming in on her bottom, and as his blood rushed to his feet and his body began to pound with lust the breath whooshed from his lungs and his brilliant plan turned to dust.

Laura sensed Matt's presence a nanosecond before she heard it. The nape of her neck pricked, her pulse skipped and goosebumps sprang up all over her skin. And then she caught the sharp exhalation of breath and the muttered oath, and with utter horror the picture she realised she must be presenting flashed into her head.

Barely a minute ago she'd walked into the drawing room and immediately spied the ornamented fireback of the fireplace. She'd rattled off a couple of photos before hunkering down to take a closer look. As a result she was on her hands and knees, face to the stone and bottom to the air.

Oh, God. A cold clammy sweat broke out over her entire body as mortification flooded through her. It was so not a good look. Heaven only knew what Matt must be thinking.

Desperately seeking to claw back some kind of dignity, Laura clambered to her feet as elegantly and quickly as she could.

Which would have been absolutely fine had she not been tucked inside a four-foot-high fireplace.

Realisation came way too late.

As did Matt's shout of warning.

With a sickening thud her skull cracked against solid seventeenth century stone. Her yelp of shock ricocheted around the fireplace. For a second she could feel absolutely nothing. Could see nothing but a fuzzy sort of blackness dotted with stars. Could hear nothing but the hammering of her heart.

Then as the blackness faded an excruciating pain shot the entire length of her body and spread throughout her limbs. She let out an agonised gasp. Her stomach churned and sent a wave of nausea rolling into her throat. Her knees buckled and she crumpled. She screwed her eyes tight shut and braced herself for more unimaginable pain.

Which didn't come.

How strange. Where was the agony? Where was the shock?

Faintly bewildered, Laura just hung there for a second, suspended by two bands of steel that had come from who knew where and snapped round her waist. Come to think of it, what exactly was the solid thing she was pressed up against and why was her body suddenly zinging with electricity?

Her heart beginning to pound even faster, Laura gingerly opened her eyes. And found herself staring straight up into Matt's, so close, so dark and so focused on her that she nearly saw stars all over again.

When he'd caught her he'd evidently had to clamp her to him. Now every inch of her body was plastered up against his and awareness fizzled along her nerve endings. She could feel the tension in his muscles as he held her. She could feel his heart banging against the palm of her hand. The intoxicating scent of him enveloped her, seeped into her head and made her dizzy.

He was so close she could see flecks of gold in the brown of his eyes. So close his mouth was barely an inch from her own. The lingering traces of pain and shock receded and slow drugging desire began to hum in the pit of her stomach.

Laura's pulse leapt. Her lips actually tingled. All she'd have to do would be to lift her head a fraction and she could put an end to the speculation and find out exactly what he tasted like. Perhaps she could blame it on concussion, because, Lord, it was tempting.

But it was also just not on, Laura reminded herself, dragging her gaze from Matt's mouth and fixing it firmly on the wedge of tanned flesh exposed by the V of his T-shirt.

The only reason she was in his house was because she'd guilt-tripped him into it. He didn't really want her here and, as was clear from the scowl on his face, he wasn't exactly ecstatic about having had to jump to her rescue.

A kiss from her would be about as welcome to him as UPVC windows were to her. No doubt about it.

Unfortunately knowing that wasn't apparently enough to stop a deep sigh of longing escaping her lips.

Heat rushed to her cheeks in the silence that followed.

God, she really hoped Matt hadn't caught that. And she really hoped he couldn't feel her swelling breasts and hardening nipples press against his chest.

But as his arms tightened around her any hope she might have had that he hadn't noticed her reaction to him evaporated. Her heart skipped a beat. Her eyes jerked up and met his just in time to catch something flaring in the brown depths. Barely a flash, but it was enough to set her heart galloping and her head spinning. And then she felt another part of his anatomy flaring and the bottom fell out of her stomach.

Oh, good Lord.

It wasn't just her. He felt it, too. Laura's heart thumped. Judging by the impressive evidence swelling against her hip, Matt was as attracted to her as she was to him. His head was moving forward. His eyes were darkening as they roamed over her face, lingering on her mouth before sweeping back up to meet hers.

For a split second delight shot through her and then quite suddenly panic elbowed the delight aside and thumped her squarely in the chest. Her nerves started to twist into a tangled mess.

Oh, God. If Matt did want her as much as she wanted him then she ought to leave. As soon as possible.

Because if he did make a move and kissed her, she'd never be able to resist. One thing would lead to another and another and another, and before she knew it she'd be back where she started, assertiveness course or no assertiveness course.

It would be even worse if he *didn't* kiss her. Because then the danger was that what with her highly unstable behaviour of late *she'd* be the one to make a move.

Either way the outcome would be a disaster of epic proportions.

So why wasn't she pushing him away? Why was she letting him get closer?

Time seemed to skid to a halt and Laura couldn't move. Matt's hand came up to cup her face and her skin burned as if he'd branded her. Anticipation thundered through her and her bones melted. When he slid his hand up and threaded his fingers through her hair Laura couldn't help lifting her face. Couldn't stop her breath hitching and her lips parting.

God, who cared if she couldn't resist? If this was wrong, why did it feel so right? Her gaze dropped to his mouth and her heart hammered. Desperation to taste him clawed at her insides and she had to bite on her lip to stop another whimper of need escaping.

'It doesn't look as if you need stitches,' he murmured, 'but you'll have quite a bump.'

What?

Laura froze. The whimper died in her throat. For a moment bewilderment besieged her brain. And then clarity dawned and she went scorchingly hot.

Agh. The bump on her head couldn't possibly be any bigger than the one she'd just had crashing back to reality.

What on earth was the matter with her? How could she have got it so wrong? Thank God Matt had drawn back before she'd lost patience and grasped the initiative.

At the thought of just how massive a fool she could have made of herself mortification roared through her and made her cheeks burn. God, was there *no* hope for her?

Suddenly desperate to get away, Laura wriggled in his arms and pushed against his chest. When his arms loosened she stepped back. And nearly collapsed all over again.

'Steady,' he said, putting his hands on her shoulders and keeping her upright.

Laura summoned strength to her watery limbs, shook herself free and forced herself to meet his gaze. 'Look,' she said with a calmness she really didn't feel. 'Thank you for catching me and everything, but you must be busy and I've imposed quite long enough. I think I should go.'

Ten minutes ago Matt would have been first in line to agree. Now, with lust ricocheting around him so violently it made his head spin, he wasn't so sure.

He could still feel Laura in his arms, all that warmth and softness crushed up against him. Her scent, something light and jasminey, was still floating around inside his head. The memory of the smoothness of her cheek beneath his palm and the silkiness of her hair winding round his fingers made his hands itch to touch her again.

When she'd looked up at him with those extraordinary eyes of hers, her mouth parting and her breathing shallow, practically inviting him to kiss her senseless, it had taken every ounce of control he possessed not to do exactly that. Quite apart from the fact that he'd decided he really couldn't go there, she'd just banged her head. She might well have concussion.

Matt gritted his teeth and fought back the desire to haul her into his arms. Maybe he'd banged his head, too. Maybe *he* had concussion. What else could be causing this pummelling urge to disregard his common sense, throw caution to the wind, drag her down to the sofa and sink himself inside her?

It would be utter madness. He was about to disappear off to another country. He could promise her nothing even if he'd wanted to.

But it would also be fantastic. Dynamite. It would certainly beat chopping logs the whole weekend. It *had* been too long since he'd had a woman in his bed and who knew when the opportunity would next arise? Who knew when he'd have the time?

Desire pounded through him and his control began to unravel.

'Matt?' she said with a sexy kind of breathiness that had him envisaging her saying his name in a whole lot of other ways.

At the images that spun through his head, the last vestiges of his resistance crumbled and Matt gave in. He wanted her. She wanted him. Why shouldn't they go for it and to hell with the consequences?

Ruthlessly ignoring the little voice inside his head demanding to know what on earth he thought he was doing, Matt tilted his head and gave her a slow smile. 'I think you should stay.'

CHAPTER FOUR

STAY?

Oh, goodness.

Laura hadn't thought it possible for her heart to beat more rapidly than it had when she'd been draped in his arms, but she'd been wrong. It was now galloping so fast she feared it might leap out of her chest.

The atmosphere had turned electric. Something about the way Matt was looking at her made every hair on her body leap to attention and quiver. The intensity of his gaze, the tension in his body and the smouldering smile… A lethally attractive combination that made her stomach lurch. God, if she wasn't careful she'd be in so much trouble.

'For what?'

Matt shrugged, but his eyes glittered with intent. 'Lunch. The afternoon. Whatever.'

Lunch she could do. The afternoon would probably be manageable, too. It was the whatever that concerned her.

'I can't,' she said a little hoarsely, and cleared her throat.

'Why not?'

'I have plans.' That sounded good.

'Cancel them.'

'No.' Excellent. Firm and uncompromising, that was the thing.

'Why not?'

'I'm on sabbatical.'

'From lunch?'

'From everything.'

'Why?'

No way was she spilling out all the details of her disaster of a life. 'I have my reasons.'

Matt's eyes darkened. 'I'm not suggesting you give up your sabbatical altogether. Just take a quick break.'

He ran his gaze over her and her body burned in the wake of its trail. Her breasts swelled. Her nipples hardened and molten heat pooled between her legs. Desire whipped through her and she had to fight not to tremble.

A one-night stand. That was what he was suggesting, wasn't it? How disgraceful. How offensive. And, what with the lust hurtling around inside her, how completely and deliciously tempting.

'That's outrageous,' she breathed, sounding less than convincing.

'Is it?'

'I might be concussed.'

'Are you?'

'Well, no, I don't think so, but that's not the point.'

'Then what is?'

'We barely know each other.'

'So?'

'I don't do that sort of thing.'

'Neither do I.'

'Then why me? Why now?'

A muscle ticked in his jaw and his eyes burned with desire. 'Because of this,' he muttered fiercely, closing the short distance between them, wrapping her in his arms and slamming his mouth down on hers.

Laura didn't have time to protest. Didn't have time to resist. Because the minute his lips touched hers what little rational thought she had left shattered. Fire licked through her veins. Beneath his mouth she moaned. Wound her arms round his neck and threaded her fingers through his hair. Pressed herself closer, parted her lips and felt her entire body soften.

When his tongue slipped into her mouth, seeking hers, finding hers, her knees buckled. If she hadn't been locked in his arms she'd have crumpled to the floor.

Sensation after sensation cascaded over her. Matt slid his hand over her waist, stroked it up her side and cupped her breast. Laura shuddered as his thumb brushed over her straining nipple and arched her back.

Drowning in pleasure, she sank into his kiss. No one had ever done this to her before, she thought dazedly. No one had ever turned her bones to water with nothing more than a kiss and a caress.

And she wasn't sure she'd ever done this to anyone, either. Matt was kissing her as if it were his sole mission in life. So focused. So damn good. His mouth seemed to have been made for hers. She fitted his hands perfectly. He would fit her perfectly.

A wave of lust rolled over her and she couldn't stop herself tilting her hips and rubbing herself against the rock-hard length of him.

Her control began to spin away and, totally unsure of whether to be scared witless or tumble him down onto the sofa, she gave in to the pleasure.

When Matt finally lifted his head, she could hardly breathe. Unlocking his arms from around her, he took a step back, his eyes blazing and his breathing jerky.

At the sudden absence of his support, his heat, Laura shivered and swayed for a second.

'That's why,' he said, drawing in a ragged breath and shoving his hands through his hair.

Laura blinked and touched her lips with trembling fingers. 'That's why what?'

'Why you.' His eyes, still dark and unfathomable, gleamed. 'As for the why now, well, I have the entire weekend free.'

Ah. 'I see,' she said a little shakily.

'You know,' he said, looking at her as if he wanted to devour her all over again, 'I really think you should cancel those plans of yours.'

Burning up beneath the heat of his gaze, Laura suddenly couldn't remember why she'd mentioned the non-existent plans in the first place.

Her heart skipped a beat. Oh, heavens. She wasn't seriously contemplating what he was suggesting, was she? She'd be mad to agree. She barely knew him. It was insane. She didn't do one-night stands. Had never wanted to. She preferred to date, assess and evaluate before leaping into bed with someone.

But where had that sensible, cautious approach ever got her? Dumped, that was where. Relationships sucked. Relationships belonged to the old Laura. Why shouldn't one-night stands belong to the new?

Besides, to have someone want her with this intensity, this hunger, when she'd been so recently rejected by someone she'd been with for years…

Her self-esteem, which had taken such a battering, was already rocketing. And to want someone quite this badly, when she'd thought she'd never be interested in anyone ever again, was heady stuff.

Her breath caught.

Standing in front of her was the most devastatingly gorgeous man she'd ever met. Who for some reason appeared to fancy her rotten. Would it really be so bad to go for it?

Suddenly sick and tired of evaluation and analysis, Laura made up her mind. 'How long are you here for?'

'I'm leaving tomorrow.'

'Are you planning to come back any time soon?'

'No.' His eyes bore into hers, burning with desire but offering nothing, apart from an afternoon of unimaginable pleasure.

Laura's heart pounded. That did it. No mess. No threat of entanglement in another debilitating relationship. Just the promise of hot sex and maybe lunch. 'OK, then.'

For a big man he moved surprisingly fast.

Even though she was ready for it, had been waiting for it, sort of knew what to expect, nothing could have prepared her for the sheer force of the desire that slammed through her at the feel of his arms whipping round her and the touch of his mouth to hers. The floor beneath her feet rocked. Her entire body buzzed with sensation.

Now that she made the decision to go for it, it was as if a dam had burst deep inside her. Any inhibitions she might have had fled.

His hands settled on the bare skin of her back and the electricity that flowed through her made her nerve endings jump.

She pressed herself closer, rubbing her aching breasts against his chest, needing the friction to provide some sort of relief.

As he explored her mouth with his tongue, Laura

slipped her hands beneath his T-shirt and ran them over the muscles of his back, pushing the fabric up. She felt him tense and break off the kiss for a second while he pulled the T-shirt over his head and tossed it onto the floor. Then his hands were at the hem of her top and seconds later it joined his.

Somewhere deep in the recesses of her mind she thought she ought to be faintly embarrassed at getting naked with someone she didn't know. Or at her desperation to have him inside her at the very least. But with his mouth sliding over her jaw, her neck and then down over the slope of her breast, Laura couldn't feel anything except the mindless pleasure sweeping over her.

Cupping his hands under her bottom, Matt lifted her and she wound her legs round his waist as he carried her to the nearest available flat surface. He set her on the edge of a table and began to push her back.

Laura's blood roared in her ears as she eased back but then she caught something out of the corner of her eye and went still. 'Wait.'

Matt jerked back and frowned down at her. 'What?'

'We can't do this.'

The blood drained from his face and his features turned grim. 'Are you serious?'

'Deadly.' She paused and caught her lip. 'At least we can't do this *here*.'

'Why not?'

Laura glanced down at what she was perched on and then back up at him. Poor Matt looked as if he were about to explode with frustration. 'This is a solid mahogany Regency breakfast table. It must be worth thousands.'

Matt let out a sharp breath and his expression relaxed. 'Then it was built to last,' he said, planting his hands either side of her and setting his mouth to the side of her neck.

'It was built to have breakfast on,' Laura said, putting a hand on his chest and nudging him away. 'Not wild uncontrollable sex.'

He lifted his head and one corner of his mouth hitched. 'Wild uncontrollable sex, huh?'

'You promised.'

'Did I?'

Laura nodded. 'Not in so many words. But these kisses of yours suggest a lot. I'm expecting combustion at the very least. And if we stay here I won't be able to concentrate.'

'Well, we can't have that,' he murmured. 'I doubt the insurance would cover sex-induced fire damage.' Pulling her upright, he glanced around. 'Do you have any such concerns about the sofa?'

Laura wound her arms around his neck. 'Is it flame-proof?'

'I should imagine so.'

'In that case,' she said, smiling up at him, 'none at all.'

'I can't tell you how glad I am to hear it.' He scooped her up and strode over to the sofa.

Setting her on her feet, he unclipped her bra and let it drop to the floor. 'These hot pants are going to haunt my dreams,' he said roughly, dragging them together with her knickers down her legs.

'You want me to apologise?' she breathed as she kicked them away.

'I want you to want this as much as I do,' he said, stripping off the rest of his clothes and tumbling her onto the sofa.

'I do,' she said, drawing in a shuddery breath as she

ran her gaze over him. God, his body was every bit as incredible as she'd imagined. Muscled, powerful, lean and tanned.

And any minute now it was all going to come down on top of her. Her gaze dropped to his erection and for a second she went dizzy. 'Oh, I *really* do.' She bit her lip to stop herself whimpering. 'More probably.'

'I doubt that's possible,' Matt said tightly.

Laura let her gaze wander up him, over the dips and ridges of his chest, the strong tanned neck and the square jaw and into eyes so dark they were almost black.

She swallowed and delicious anticipation began to thunder through her. Matt was radiating so much tension, looking as if he was having to battle so hard to cling on to his control that she wondered with a thrill what would happen when it snapped.

God, she thought with a tiny surge of satisfaction. Going for what she wanted was great. The sense of power it gave her was awesome. Who knew?

Lifting her arms above her head, Laura arched her back and batted her eyelashes as she smiled up at him. 'Why don't you come down here and join me and we can figure it out?'

'Just so you know,' he murmured, lowering himself on top of her and bearing his weight on his elbows, 'I always win.'

'I'm sure you do,' she said softly, loving the feel of his body trapping hers. Look where she was. But that didn't mean she couldn't at least try. 'You know what I'd really like?'

'What?'

She lifted her face and looked straight into his eyes. 'I'd like you inside me. Right now.'

She felt his heart thump. Saw his jaw clench. Felt his

whole body tighten. Aha. Who was winning now? 'Is that right?' he murmured, staring down at her but not moving an inch.

'It is,' she said softly.

'I'll bear it in mind.'

Oh. That wasn't the outcome she'd hoped for. 'Please…' she breathed, batting her eyelashes and smiling up at him.

His erection leapt. Feeling a tiny stab of triumph, she tilted her hips against him and let out a sigh of longing.

Matt growled. 'You,' he said, his mouth tugging into a faint smile, 'are irresistible.'

'I know,' she said smugly, and then gasped as his mouth landed on hers.

Hot and demanding, it began a devastating assault on her senses. His tongue drove into her mouth, tangling with hers, pushing her to the edge of reason. His hands settled on her arms above her head and then slid down her body, making her burn and tremble.

He dragged his mouth away from hers and dropped a trail of scorching kisses along her jaw and down her neck. Her head fell back and she moaned. His mouth moved lower, lower, until it closed over her aching nipple and she nearly leapt off the sofa. But he was pinning her down with his weight and all she could do was succumb.

Frankly why would she want to do anything else? Laura clutched a cushion with one hand. Grabbed his head with the other as he sucked, stroked, licked and nibbled and she started to lose it. Great waves of pleasure began to roll over her. Desire drenched her and she ached with the need to be filled with him.

'Please, Matt,' she breathed, no longer conscious of what she was saying. 'I don't think I can bear it.'

His mouth still on her breast, Matt swept his hand down over her hip, round, covered the triangle of hair at the top of her thighs and slid a finger deep inside her. Laura groaned and felt her inner muscles tighten around his finger. He pressed her clitoris with his thumb and her breathing shallowed as she felt herself begin to break apart.

No, she cried silently, clinging on to her control, she didn't want it to be like this.

She wanted him, all of him, all that strength pounding into her.

She wanted him to lose control the way she was about to.

'Are you going to make me beg again?'

'Would you?'

'If I have to. But I'd probably hate you for it.'

Matt let out a ragged breath. 'I wouldn't want that,' he murmured.

'Then help me out here,' she said desperately, dimly aware that he was leaning down and fumbling around on the floor. The sound of a packet tearing, the rolling on of a condom barely registered.

Every inch of her was aching, desperate with need. Biting her lip, she felt him pushing her knees apart, felt him nudging at her entrance and then thrusting forward, up, deep.

Laura gasped. Matt stopped. Waited a second for her to adjust. And then he pulled out of her, caught her mouth with his and drove back into her. A sob of pure pleasure rising in her throat, Laura wrapped her legs around his waist, threw her arms around his back and kissed him with every drop of desire she was feeling.

Her nails raked over his skin. His muscles strained with the effort of restraint.

But she didn't want restraint. She burned for release. Tearing her mouth from his, she breathed, 'More,' into his ear and lifted her hips.

Matt went utterly still. His eyes blazed and then he began to move. Harder, faster, deeper, driving her higher and higher, making something inside her coil tighter and tighter until he thrust one more time and sent her hurtling over the edge. Laura shattered into kaleidoscopic ecstasy. Wave after wave of pleasure poured over her as she convulsed and trembled. Her heart hammered. Her blood roared in her ears. She felt Matt's whole body tense. Heard him groan and then felt him pulsate deep inside her and it was enough to set off a series of tiny aftershocks of ecstasy that took her breath away all over again.

It was quite a few minutes before she got her breath and her senses back. As she drifted back down to reality after the most exquisite orgasm of her life she felt a great grin spreading across her face. Wow. If she'd known all casual sex was as hot as this, she'd have tried it long ago.

Or at least been a damn sight more assertive in the bedroom.

One softly breathed word and Matt's steely control had unravelled. Still cocooned in the warmth of his arms, Laura felt like purring with pleasure. She'd have to remember that in the future.

And then she froze. Her heart thumped. Uh-oh. The future? That didn't sound good. That sounded as if she wanted a repeat. Lots of repeats in fact. Repeats that went way beyond one afternoon.

To her horror she could feel her body softening, heating, getting ready for more just as soon as possible.

'Laura?' Matt's voice cut through the hazy fog in her head.

'Hmm?' She wasn't entirely sure she could speak and not just because his chest was crushing her lungs.

He lifted his head and looked down at her, his eyes unfathomable. 'Are you all right?'

'Fine,' she muttered, thinking she was anything but.

God, she was such an idiot. Had she really thought she could get rid of her old self that easily? That one two-week course, albeit a highly intensive one, could undo the habits of thirty-one years? What a pillock.

If she didn't get out of here this very moment she'd find herself being sucked in by Matt and the incredible orgasms he appeared to be able to give her and she'd end up wanting more. Which was most certainly not part of the deal she'd made with either herself or him.

Laura swallowed and fixed a smile to her face. 'Couldn't be better,' she added lightly.

Matt frowned. 'Are you sure?'

Agh. This was so not a conversation she wanted to be having with him still hard and deep inside her. 'Absolutely.' She nodded, gave him a quick smile and prodded at his shoulders. 'Would you mind?'

'I rather think I would,' Matt said flatly, manoeuvring them to shift himself onto his back and pulling her on top of him.

The blast of cold air that hit her back made Laura shiver. 'Could you let me go, please?'

His arms fell from her waist, and she eased herself off him. Aware that his eyes were following her every move, burning into her skin, Laura fought the impulse to leap back on top of him, and set about retrieving her clothes. She swiped up her underwear and her T-shirt and dragged them on, trying not to respond to the way they scratched over her already highly sensitised skin.

Her shorts, however, lay beneath him. Laura bit her lip. Sprinting back home without them would encourage curtain twitching gossip she definitely didn't need. 'Can you shift a bit?' she said, trying to yank on the inch of fabric she could see.

However Matt didn't budge. Apart from shooting his hand out to wrap itself round her wrist.

'Laura, what's going on?'

'Going on?' she said, her eyes jerking to his. Only minutes ago his eyes had been blazing with passion but his whole demeanour was stonier than granite. 'Nothing's going on.'

'So why the hurry?'

'I have to get going.'

'A little too wild and uncontrollable, huh?'

She stamped down on the blush that she could feel blooming inside her. 'Not at all,' she said, aiming for a nonchalance she didn't feel. 'I really do have to go. Like I said, I have plans.'

Matt released her, sprang to his feet and yanked on his jeans. 'Right,' he said, his voice ice cold and devoid of emotion. 'Sure. Then I guess you don't want lunch.'

With him standing there looking so gorgeous and rumpled in just his jeans, all Laura could think of was how much she did want lunch. With Matt as the main course. 'Some other time perhaps,' she muttered, and legged it.

CHAPTER FIVE

THREE weeks later, Laura had just about managed to wipe Matt and that incredible afternoon from her mind. But it had been one of the hardest things she'd ever had to do.

For days afterwards she'd wafted around in a kind of dreamlike state, not entirely sure whether the whole thing had actually happened or if it had simply been a product of her imagination. It had been so amazing, so mind-blowing and, up until the moment she'd panicked, everything she'd imagined it would be.

Ruthlessly blocking out the way they'd parted, or rather the way she'd scarpered, she'd wallowed in the memories of the hour before, and as a result had got very little done.

If it hadn't been for the call from the headhunter a week ago she'd probably still be at it. Wandering round her house with a dreamy smile on her face, putting the milk in the bathroom cabinet and the toothpaste in the fridge.

To think that she might have missed out on the opportunity of a lifetime just because she'd been too busy drifting around in a daze...

Laura went cold and shuddered. It didn't bear thinking about. And neither did Matt. Not any longer. Now she had to focus on her career. Her savings wouldn't last for ever and daydreaming wouldn't pay the bills.

This job, however, would not only pay the bills, it would also get her life firmly back on track.

The opportunity to head up the restoration project on the isolated island of Sassania was a dream come true. The country had been closed off to the outside world for years. As the result of a recent coup, the dictatorship had been overthrown and the borders had been thrown wide open.

The island had some of the finest examples of Baroque architecture in the world. Palaces and monuments she'd only ever read about. Palaces and monuments that were currently in a terrible state of repair and needed restoring.

Ideally, by her.

She'd emailed her CV to the headhunter virtually the moment she'd put the phone down, and to her delight had received a reply the next day inviting her for an interview.

Which was why she was now in London, taking her best friend out for dinner in return for a bed for the night before catching her crack-of-dawn flight in the morning.

'So how is life in the country?' said Kate, plucking the umbrella out of her cocktail and taking a long slurp.

Dragging herself away from dusty palaces in tiny Mediterranean island kingdoms and back to trendy London restaurants, Laura picked up a fat juicy olive from the bowl and glanced across the table. 'Quiet.'

'I can imagine.'

No, she couldn't, but there was no way Laura was going to elaborate on what she'd been up to. Not when she'd just managed to stop thinking about it. 'How's the world of corporate law?'

Kate took another sip of her cocktail and sighed with pleasure. 'Yum yum. You know, the usual. Nutty hours, problems galore and clients with egos the size of planets. I don't know why I do it.'

'Because you love it.'

Kate grinned. 'I guess I do.' She tilted her head. 'Don't you miss all this?'

Laura glanced around the place Kate had suggested for dinner. A brand-new London restaurant that had shot to the top of the uber-cool lists the day after it had opened.

Against the deep red silk lining of the walls hung enormous canvases by some on-the-up artist. Tiny chandeliers hung above every one of the slate-grey tables, casting flatteringly low sparkling light over the clientele. Model-like waiters who were far too sultry and hip to ever crack a smile whizzed around with plates of food that looked beautiful and made her mouth water. The chatter was low, buzzing and probably far more sophisticated than she was.

Not all that long ago Laura had spent many of her evenings and weekends in places like this. Now she felt a bit like a foreigner.

'Not really,' she muttered, slightly perturbed by the realisation.

'I don't know how you can bear it,' said Kate with a tiny shudder. 'I mean, no shops, no bars and all that greenery.' She wrinkled her nose. 'It's just not natural.'

Stifling a smile at the irony, Laura shrugged. 'I muddle along.'

'But that's my point,' Kate said. 'You don't have to

muddle along. I mean, I know things went a bit pear-shaped, but why you had to run off to the country is beyond me.'

A bit pear-shaped? 'Yes, well, when your life implodes as spectacularly as mine did you can end up doing all sorts of out-of-character things.'

'You could have come and stayed with me.'

Kate sounded a little piqued, and Laura gave her a smile. 'I know. And I did appreciate the offer, but it was something I needed to sort out on my own.'

Plus Kate would have given her heaps of advice, which she'd have insisted Laura follow, and Laura would have been too wiped out to argue.

But not any more. No more taking the easy way out. No more falling in with other people's wishes all the time. If her afternoon with Matt had taught her one thing it was that going for what *she* wanted for a change could achieve some pretty spectacular results.

Not that she was thinking about him of course, she reminded herself, picking up a menu and letting her gaze drift over the other diners. The restaurant was packed with some seriously beautiful people. Not a hint of last year's fashion, nor an un-touched-up root in sight. She was surprised they'd let her in.

And to be honest she was kind of dreading the bill. Laura resisted the urge to slap herself on the forehead with her menu. She'd done it again, hadn't she? Gulped back a knot of panic when Kate had suggested this place, and said, yes, sure, why not.

Why, oh, why hadn't she been firmer, and told Kate they'd be going to the little Italian around the corner from her flat?

Feeling her spirits tumble, Laura's gaze bobbed across the room. She bet none of the people here was quite so feeble. No. They'd all be decisive and in charge. They wouldn't flounder around and let others ride roughshod all over them.

And then her eyes snagged on a broad back and dark head and her heart practically stopped.

Oh, Lord. That looked just like Matt.

For a second Laura went dizzy. Then her heart began to gallop and heat whipped through every inch of her body. What was he doing here? Would he see her? Would he come over? What would she say if he did? What would she do if he *didn't*?

Her chest squeezed. Her mouth went dry. Oh, God. If he did come over she wouldn't just have to deal with him. She'd also have to deal with Kate, whose razor-sharp instinct would instantly pick up on the atmosphere, and who'd wring out every tiny detail and then hammer Laura with a barrage of 'what were you thinking?'s and 'but it's so unlike you's.

Laura took a deep breath and forced herself to calm down before her head exploded. It would be fine. She was a mature sensible adult who'd been through far worse. She'd simply channel the inner Amazon she was sure was lurking somewhere inside her, and be strong.

Nevertheless when all six foot plus of him got to his feet she caught and held her breath. Her pulse thundered. The blood rushed to her feet. He turned. Gave her a glimpse of his face.

And disappointment walloped her in the stomach.

It wasn't Matt.

Letting her breath out before she fainted, Laura blinked and turned her attention back to the menu. Of course it wouldn't have been Matt, she told herself sternly. That would have been too much of a coincidence and she didn't believe in coincidences.

She frowned and scanned the dishes. The weird sensation whirling around inside her wasn't disappointment. It was relief. That was all.

'Quiet?' said Kate. 'Hah! I knew it. So who is he?'

Laura froze and glanced up. The gleam in her friend's eye looked far too knowing for her liking. 'Who is who?' she said deliberately vaguely.

'The man that's put the weird look on your face.'

Laura's heart lurched. 'That's not a man,' she muttered. 'That's the dim lighting.' She squinted at the menu. 'In fact I can barely read this. Maybe I need glasses.' She held it up to the beautiful but fairly useless light that hung above the table.

'Rubbish,' said Kate.

'I definitely need a dictionary.'

'You look as if you've just had the fright of your life.'

'Well, I haven't.' Except perhaps at the prices. 'Whatever you're thinking you're wrong.'

'No, I'm not. I'm a lawyer. I'm known for my tenacity and trained to notice things.'

But not, apparently, the waiter who, with exquisite timing, was hovering at their table ready to take their order.

Laura looked up at him and gave her saviour a wide smile. 'I was wondering…what is the *rouget*?'

'Red mullet, madam.'

'Thank you. And the *poêlée de châtaignes*?'

'Pan-fried chestnuts.'

There were two pages of dishes. With any luck by the time she'd got to the bottom of the second page, Kate might have got bored and moved on.

Hmm. Or perhaps not, she thought as Kate swiped

the menu out of her hands and beamed up at the waiter. 'I'll have the lamb and she'll have the sea bass.'

Huh. Laura waited until he'd melted away before scowling at her friend.

'What?' said Kate, arching an eyebrow.

'I'm perfectly capable of ordering for myself.'

'I know, but I have a feeling there's a story to be told and we don't have all night. Besides you always have sea bass'

Laura stiffened. 'Maybe I was thinking about trying something different.'

Kate gave a little snort of disbelief. 'You were stalling. And when have you ever tried something different?'

Laura bristled. Was she really so boringly predictable? 'That's not fair. I do try different things.'

'Like what?' Kate's eyes zoomed in on her.

Like jumping into bed with scorchingly hot neighbours. Not that she intended to use *that* as an example. 'Fine.' She shrugged as if she couldn't be less bothered, and took a sip of her drink. 'I don't. Boring and predictable, that's me.'

Kate's blue gaze turned piercing. 'I think you lie.'

'Think what you like.'

'Come on,' said Kate, adding a wheedling smile to the penetrating stare. 'I know something's up and it's got "man" written all over it. I'm not going to give up until you tell me so you might as well give in now and get it over with.'

Not for the first time, Laura could see why Kate was so successful at what she did. Dogs and bones sprang to mind. Stifling a sigh, she weighed up her options. Denial and a battle with Kate's formidable persistence, which would last all evening, or half an hour of interrogation, which would be sharp but probably short and would allow her to enjoy the rest of her sea bass.

Hmm. If she wanted to be on top form for tomorrow she didn't have much of a choice. 'OK,' she said, bracing herself, 'you're right.'

'Aha.' Kate grinned in triumph. 'I knew it.' She signalled for two more drinks and sat back. 'You'd better tell me everything.'

Ten minutes and two cocktails later, Laura had finished her rundown of almost everything, and was now watching her friend with faint amusement. She didn't think she'd ever seen Kate lost for words before. She was sitting there, her eyes wide and her jaw almost on the floor. Even the arrival of their food didn't snap Kate out of her state of shock.

Laura decided to leave her to it and tucked in. Popping a forkful of fish in her mouth, she sighed in appreciation. As annoyingly hip as the restaurant was, the food was spectacular.

'Well,' said Kate, eventually pulling herself together and regaining the ability to speak.

'Your lamb is getting cold,' Laura pointed out.

'Sod the lamb,' Kate said, still looking on utterly shell-shocked. 'Let me get this straight. You ogle. You engage in confrontation. You stand your ground. And then you have sex with a man you've only just met.'

'Yes.' Laura took another mouthful and decided that for all the benefits of the countryside, it didn't do food like this.

Kate's mouth opened then closed. 'To be honest I don't know which part of the whole thing I'm more shocked by.'

'I thought it was time for a change.' Hah. Who was predictable now?

'Have you seen him since?'

'No.' She'd known he'd stayed the rest of the weekend but he'd kept himself to himself. Not that she'd been keeping a special eye out or anything.

'Do you intend to?'

'Absolutely not. It was a one-night—afternoon—stand. Non-repetition is kind of the point.'

There was another long silence as Kate absorbed this information. 'Who are you and what have you done with my friend?'

'Ha-ha.'

'I knew moving to the country was dangerous,' Kate muttered, picking up her knife and fork and attacking her lamb. 'You're unhinged.'

Undoubtedly. But that had happened long before she'd met Matt. 'If I am,' said Laura darkly as the image of her ex-boyfriend in bed with his secretary flashed into her head, 'it has nothing to do with geography.'

Kate gave her a sympathetic smile. 'No, well, I suppose I can see why you might need a bit of an ego boost. Lying cheating bastard.'

Laura couldn't help smiling at the disgust in Kate's voice. 'Yup.'

'You know, I still can't believe he did that. To you of all people.' Kate shook her head in bafflement. 'I mean, you're one of the most easy-going people I know.'

'Too easy-going apparently.'

'What?'

'Paul said that I was partly to blame for his affair.'

Kate's jaw dropped. 'The cheek,' she muttered. 'How did he work that one out?'

'He said I was too acquiescent. That if I'd stood up to him a bit more, been a bit more demanding, he might have thought twice about bonking his secretary.'

'The complete and utter snake.'

Laura caught her lip between her teeth and frowned. 'But maybe he did have a point. He kept calling me babe, and not once did I tell him not to even though I hated it.'

'It used to make me wince.'

'Me, too.' Laura grimaced. 'Anyway I've had time to think about it and, you know, I *have* been a bit of a pushover.'

'Rubbish.'

'So why do I end up giving the old people in the village lifts left, right and centre?'

'Because you're a nice person.'

'Huh.' Laura frowned. 'I have a backbone of rubber. Well, not any more.'

'So what's the plan?'

'I've already put it into action.'

'So I can see.'

'Not that,' she said, batting back a blush. 'The minute I moved to the country I enrolled on an assertiveness course.'

Kate's eyebrows shot up. 'Wow.'

'I know.' Laura nodded. 'We learned to Embrace Confrontation, Say No With Confidence and to Go For What *You* Want.'

'So you embraced confrontation and went for the afternoon of hot sex that you wanted.'

'Quite.' Something kicked in the pit of her stomach.

Kate grinned. 'I can't imagine there was a whole lot of saying no, either with confidence or without it.'

'Not a lot.' Just rather a lot of breathy yeses.

'Well, I'm not sure about the rest of it, but that's one way to get a lousy ex out of your system.'

'That's what I thought.'

Kate tilted her head and looked at Laura with something resembling admiration. 'Reckless. Totally out of character. I like it.'

Laura felt a shiver run down her spine. 'So did I.' She nibbled on her lip and frowned. Up until the point she'd panicked and fled. That had been cowardly.

'I'm so envious.' Kate sighed. 'Remind me why you aren't going to see him again.'

Laura shrugged. 'It wasn't like that. The temporariness of it was what was so appealing.' Well, one of the things. 'We didn't exchange numbers.'

'I'm sure he'd be in the phone book. Have you Googled him?'

'Of course not.' She hadn't given in to the temptation yet and she didn't intend to.

'Why not?'

'I don't want to see him again.'

'That's nuts. Great sex isn't something to be dismissed lightly.'

'It hasn't changed anything,' said Laura firmly, before she started agreeing with Kate and waving goodbye to all her good intentions. 'I'm still off men. And I need another relationship like I need a hole in the head.'

'But you're always in a relationship.' Kate frowned.

'Exactly. And look what happens. I get smothered. I lose sense of my own identity and allow myself to get walked all over. And ultimately get hurt.' She shrugged. 'I've had enough.'

'Well, I think you're mad.' Kate sniffed.

Laura smiled. 'Actually I've never felt saner in my life. Which is just as well if I'm going to get this job. Now, let's have pudding.'

CHAPTER SIX

HE'D been right about those damn hot pants, thought Matt grimly, glancing at his watch and noting he had five minutes before his meeting with the finance minister to discuss exactly how deep the corruption that had burrowed into pretty much every governmental department went.

They *did* haunt his dreams. As, to his intense irritation, did Laura.

It was bad enough that the minute he crashed into bed there she was, her hair fanning out over his cushions, her eyes shimmering and glazed with desire as she stared up at him and saying 'more' and 'please' in that breathy desperate way she had.

It was bad enough that he woke up pretty much every morning, aching and throbbing and twitching with desire.

But what was really driving him nuts was the lack of control he seemed to have over his thoughts while he was awake.

She kept popping up, shooting smouldering smiles at him, and the memory of the way she'd exploded and shuddered in his arms would slam into his head and his train of thought would derail and his body would react with annoying inevitability.

Like now.

Feeling uncomfortably hot and growing painfully hard, Matt scowled, got up and stalked over to the window.

Quite why Laura should be taking up so much of his head space when she'd been just a one-night stand and when he had plenty of other things to occupy his mind was baffling.

OK, so the way she'd run off like that had hardly been flattering but it wasn't as if he'd intended on seeing her again, was it? She clearly had issues and that wasn't his problem. And yes, the sex had been incredible, but it had been three weeks ago. He really ought to have got over it by now.

Matt threw open the window and inhaled deeply. He'd have liked a nice icy blast of around minus five to relieve the hot achiness of his body. But unfortunately Sassania was in the Mediterranean not the Baltic, and this being early summer all that drifted in through the window was a soft balmy breeze.

Stifling a groan of frustration, he yanked open the top buttons of his shirt and made a mental note to get someone to investigate the air-conditioning options. Then at least he'd be able to control the temperature, if nothing else.

He was just about to turn back to grab his laptop and head off to his meeting when he heard the rap of heels on stone and caught a movement out of the corner of his eye.

Something, he had no idea what, made him pause. Made him train his focus on the woman walking across the patio.

For some reason his breathing faltered. The floor beneath his feet lurched. His pulse jumped. She was walking away from him, and he couldn't be sure, but that looked just like Laura.

Matt blinked and gave his head a quick shake. No. That was nuts. It couldn't be Laura. Because what would she be doing in *his* palace on *his* island? It was his feverish imagination working overtime, that was all. Lack of sleep, too, probably. And this damn stifling heat.

Nevertheless something about the way she moved had his eyes narrowing and awareness prickling his skin. Maybe it was the graceful sway of her hips. Or maybe it was the way she suddenly reached up to tuck a lock of hair behind her ear. She might be wearing a nifty little suit instead of a T-shirt and hot pants, but those curves looked very familiar.

As she stopped and turned to say something to the security guard accompanying her Matt caught a glimpse of her face and any lingering doubt fled.

His head swam for a second. His heart pounded. Hell. It *was* Laura.

He ran a hand over his face. Rubbed his eye and pinched the bridge of his nose. Then frowned.

What on earth was she doing here?

Had she come to apologise?

Had she decided she wanted more than just a one-night stand?

Or had she come to see what she could get out of their brief liaison?

She wouldn't be the first, Matt thought, his mouth twisting into a cynical smile as he shoved his hands in his pockets and watched her gazing at the pillars and arches of the colonnades that surrounded the patio.

Several of the women he'd known in the past had got in touch to suggest that if he was ever on the lookout for a queen they'd be more than happy to occupy the position. And more than willing to provide heirs.

If Matt could have been bothered to reply he'd have told them they were wasting their time. Marriage and children did not feature on his agenda. He'd been engaged once and look what a disaster that had been. No. His jaw tightened. He wasn't even cut out for a relationship, let alone anything more, so anyone who hoped otherwise could think again.

But if any of his suspicions were correct about Laura's presence on Sassania, why hadn't she asked to be led straight to him? Why was she now shaking the hand of his culture minister?

Matt frowned as his mind raced. Then the brief conversation he'd had with Giuseppe Ragazzi about the state of the country's public buildings and the urgent need to restore them flashed into his head and realisation dawned.

Oh, damn. His heart sank. Laura was here for the job.

With the arrest of the former president on his mind at the time, he'd agreed to the request to hire an architect without really thinking about it. Now, he thought, his jaw tightening, he ought to have paid more attention. Imposed certain conditions, at the very least. Such as not engaging the services of one Laura Mackenzie.

No way could she be given the job. If she got the job she'd be there. In the palace. All the time. Screwing up his concentration and messing with his head. What with everything else going on, he did *not* need that kind of complication.

Laura held her breath. She'd done everything she could. She'd answered all the questions she'd been asked confidently and correctly. Outlined the vision she had for Sassania's public buildings. Talked passionately about the career she loved, and clarified the reasons for her redundancy.

Now she was waiting on tenterhooks while Signore Ragazzi flicked through her portfolio with agonising thoroughness.

She wanted this job so badly. Apart from the fact that the idea of working on something she'd drooled over at college made her chest squeeze with excitement, it was such a prestigious project.

If she got it, she'd be made. Her battered professional pride would recover and she'd have her pick of jobs. Her former employers would read the sensational series of articles she'd write for *Architecture Tomorrow* and shake their heads at their stupidity in getting rid of her quite so speedily.

But if she didn't… Where would that leave her?

The worries she'd managed to keep at bay crept into her head. What if Signore Ragazzi didn't like her work? What if they'd had thousands of other applicants, all of whom had more and better experience than she did? What if she wasn't up to the job? What if—?

Oh, for goodness' sake. Releasing her breath before she passed out, Laura gave herself a quick shake and pulled herself together. What was the point of working herself up into a state? She'd take whatever decision he came to graciously and professionally, and face the consequences later.

Nevertheless when Signore Ragazzi closed her portfolio and looked up, she had to sit on her hands to stop them from whipping up and covering her eyes. Which was a good thing because if she'd had her eyes covered she wouldn't have been able to see the wide smile he gave her.

Hope flared in her heart and her ears buzzed. Surely he wouldn't be smiling like that if he was going to say thanks but no thanks.

'Signorina Mackenzie,' he said, and her breath caught. 'I'm delighted to inform you that you have the job.'

The words took a couple of seconds to register. But when they did Laura felt like punching the air. Would it be completely inappropriate if she hurdled the desk, leapt into his lap and gave him a big kiss? Hmm. Perhaps. Just a little. Instead she settled for a grin. 'I do?'

He smiled and nodded. 'You do.'

A bubble of delight began to bounce round inside her. 'That's fantastic,' she said, thinking that was quite an understatement.

He opened a drawer and extracted a sheaf of papers. 'We think so. To be honest, you're the only person we've called in for an interview, so the outcome has never been in doubt. The only obstacle we had foreseen would have been your lack of availability.'

He pushed the document across the desk and Laura glanced down at it, faintly stunned. 'Oh.'

'I've seen your work before. The Church of St Mary the Virgin?' She managed a nod. 'I particularly liked your sense of balance.'

Crikey. She'd never felt less balanced. 'I'm so glad,' she murmured.

'We'd like to begin with the palace.'

'Of course.' Excitement clutched at her stomach. She'd studied every fabulous inch of the palace. Pored over photos and reports. Salivated over the flying buttresses and crumbling gargoyles and idolised every one of the six thousand windows. No amount of books and papers could get across the smell of the place, the vitality of the stone and the feel of the warm breeze on her skin when she'd stood outside the gate, the same warm breeze that must have caressed these walls for centuries. Walls that were now crumbling and collapsing.

'When would you be able to begin?'

Right now would be fine with her. Or would that seem a little desperate? Not to mention totally impractical. She'd come with only her passport and her toothbrush. She was going to need a lot more than that. 'In a week?'

'Excellent.' He beamed at her. 'I'll arrange for a suite to be made up for you.'

'Thank you.'

'If you'll just sign here…'

He handed her a pen and Laura felt thrills scurrying through her. She'd done it. She'd actually done it.

Well, of course she had, she told herself as she floated back down to reality and worked her way through the contract. Her personal life might be a bit of a disaster, but she'd always been good at her job.

'Will you excuse me?' said Signore Ragazzi, cutting across her musings and picking up the phone, which had just started to ring.

He could strip and dance round his desk naked if he felt like it, Laura thought, finally getting to the last page and signing on the dotted line. She was busy wondering where would be the best place to start. The public rooms undoubtedly. Then the private areas. The gardens… Oh, the possibilities were endless and she lost herself in them.

It was only when she heard her own name that her ears pricked.

'Yes, sir. Signorina Mackenzie has just accepted the position.'

Laura's heart swelled with pride. She'd do the best job she could. Achieve the sort of result people would talk about for years, long after she left. After centuries of decline the palace deserved it. After all she'd been through, *she* deserved it.

'Oh.' At the tone of his voice for some reason her nerve endings tensed. 'I'm afraid I can't retract the offer, sir.' His voice dropped. 'She's just signed the contract.'

Laura snapped her head up and stared at him. Someone wanted him to retract the offer? No, that couldn't be possible.

Signore Ragazzi fell silent, went red and swivelled round in his chair so she couldn't see him. 'Nor can I rip it up,' he added, his voice now dropping so low she had to strain to listen.

Rip it up? Who the hell was that on the other end of the line, and why did they not want her to have the job? What had she done to cause such offence? Had there been some sort of mistake and the job already been given to someone else? Laura's chest squeezed at the thought that she might have had her dream snatched from her at the very last minute.

'No, sir... Yes, sir... I'll see to it immediately.'

Signore Ragazzi swivelled back and gave her a smile too bright to be genuine.

Laura clasped her hands together in her lap to stop them from flapping. 'Is there a problem?' she asked, bracing herself for the answer to be yes and for him to laugh and tell her it was all just one big joke.

'No, no,' he said, gathering up the contract she'd just

signed in an effort, she suspected, to avoid eye contact. 'Just one more tiny formality.'

'Oh.'

He smoothed his hair, pushed his chair back and got up and indicated that she should do the same. 'If you wouldn't mind coming with me...'

'Of course,' Laura murmured, her heart beginning to thud. What on earth was going on?

The feeling of trepidation as she followed Signore Ragazzi didn't abate. In fact it swelled to such proportions that she barely noticed the busts on pedestals lining the corridor. Or the old masters hanging on the walls. The only thing hammering at her brain was that something didn't feel right.

Signore Ragazzi stopped in front of a pair of huge gilded doors and knocked. Laura's heart banged with consternation.

'Come in.'

At the sound of the voice from deep within, all the hairs at the back of her neck leapt up and her stomach clenched.

Something *wasn't* right.

Because if it hadn't been utterly impossible, she'd have sworn that that was Matt's voice coming from the room.

But it couldn't be Matt because that would be crazy. What would he be doing here?

No, Laura told herself, pulling her shoulders back, going through the doors that Signore Ragazzi held open and entering the room. First she'd thought she'd seen him in that restaurant in London. Now she imagined he was here? Hah. This was precisely why she'd vowed to have nothing whatsoever to do with men. They messed up your head. She was far better off sticking to inanimate

objects like the crumbling cornice and the chipped re-
liefs that adorned this room.

Wow, she thought, her alarm momentarily vanishing
as she looked up at the ceiling. Faded and dilapidated
it might be, but it was still a magnificent room. And,
she noted, letting her gaze drop and scan the space, an
empty one. She hadn't noticed Signore Ragazzi melt
away. Perhaps she'd imagined that 'come in', too.

'Hello, Laura.'

The deep lazy voice behind her nearly made her jump
a foot in the air. Her heart lurched. She swung round
and at the sight of the man leaning against the bookcase,
his gaze pinned to her, the breath shot from her lungs.
Shock and disbelief slammed through her.

Oh, good Lord. It *was* Matt.

Bewilderment clamoured at her brain. Her head
went fuzzy, her blood zoomed to her feet and her vision
blurred. Laura flung her arm out and grabbed on to the
nearest thing to stop herself swooning.

The nearest thing happened to be Matt. For a second
she clutched at his arm. But the feel of his muscles
brought the memory of that afternoon careering back
and she went dizzy all over again.

Jerking back, Laura dragged in a breath and willed
the room to right itself.

No need to panic. There was bound to be some rational explanation for Matt being here. At this particular
moment she couldn't imagine what it could possibly be,
but she'd figure it out somehow.

Just as soon as her heart rate slowed and her breathing
returned to normal. Which would happen a lot quicker
if he didn't look quite so gorgeous. Wearing a pale blue
shirt with the sleeves pushed up to his elbows and light
brown chinos, he looked rumpled, incredibly sexy and

oddly at home. His face was more tanned than when she'd last seen him and the lines around his mouth and eyes a little sharper, but if anything they just made him even more attractive.

Heat pooled in the pit of her stomach and began to spread through her body. Extinguishing it with a determination she hadn't known she possessed, Laura ran her palms down her skirt and fixed a neutral smile to her face. 'Matt,' she said as coolly as she could, as if she weren't completely clueless as to how to proceed. 'How lovely to see you again.'

'Quite.' He didn't look like he agreed. 'How's the bump?'

Laura blinked and tried not to think about the circumstances that had brought about the bang to her head or the consequences. 'Fine. How was the rest of your weekend?'

'Pleasingly uneventful.'

Oh. So he clearly hadn't spent any time drifting around in a daze. 'What are you doing here?'

'I live here.'

Right. Laura's mouth opened and then closed. She couldn't begin to work out where to start. Was he here for a job, too? 'Village mansions a little on the small side?'

The ghost of a smile played at his lips and Laura had the uncomfortable feeling that he knew everything while she knew nothing.

'It comes with my job.'

'What do you do?'

'Usually?'

How many jobs did he have? 'Yes.'

'I buy ailing businesses, turn them around and sell them for a profit.'

That didn't make things any clearer. 'Is that why you're here?'

'In a way.'

Laura frowned. 'But you were the "sir" on the other end of the line.'

Matt nodded. 'I was. Would you like to sit down?'

'No, I'm fine.'

'I think you should sit. You look a little pale.'

Was it any wonder? Laura thought, sinking into a leather library chair before her legs gave way. Baffled didn't begin to describe the way she was feeling. 'How did you know I was here?'

'I saw you from the window.'

So that would account for the weird tingling that she'd experienced while she'd been walking across the patio. The twitchy feeling that had made her stop and ask the security guard about mosquitoes.

'I don't get it,' she said, her eyebrows drawing together a fraction. 'I've just been contracted to restore the palace. Why does it have anything to do with you?'

Matt moved round to sit on the edge of the huge partners' desk. 'It's my palace.'

Maybe the state had given it to him in payment or something. Laura blinked but it didn't make her brain hurt any less. 'I'd have thought it would belong to the king.'

'It does.'

His expression was unreadable, his eyes unfathomable. Which was a shame as she could really do with a little help here. Absolutely nothing was making any sense.

If the palace belonged to the king and it also belonged to him, then that would mean that Matt was the king. Her brain might be about to explode but she could work that much out. And if he was king what had he been doing in Little Somerford? What had he been doing smouldering at her, tearing off her clothing and taking her to heaven and back?

God, it was a good thing she was sitting down.

'Who exactly are you?' she said, not at all sure she wanted to have the horrible suspicions flying around her head confirmed.

'You know who I am.'

'I thought I did. I thought you were Matt Saxon.' She gave a little shrug as if it didn't bother her one way or the other. 'It looks like I was wrong. Silly me.'

'You weren't. I am Matt Saxon. I happen to also be King of Sassania.'

Ah. There it was. Proof that she hadn't been going mad. At least not within the past five minutes.

Laura gulped, completely unable to unravel the swirling mass of emotions rolling around inside her. Maybe it would be best to stick to facts. 'Since when?'

'Three weeks ago.'

'Before or after we...' she broke off and went red '...you know...?'

'The coronation took place the Monday after the weekend when we...er, met.'

He gave her a little mocking smile and her cheeks flamed even more.

And then out of the tangle of emotions, indignation suddenly broke free and fuelled through her. How dared he laugh at her? It was all very well for him, perched there being all high and mighty. She was the one who was totally wrong-footed and struggling to get her head round what was happening. She had every right to be confused. And to demand some answers. 'And you didn't think to mention it?'

His eyebrows shot up at her sharp tone. 'Why would I? We didn't exactly stop to engage in small talk.'

Damn. That was true.

Matt tilted his head and shot her a quizzical glance. 'Did you really not know who I was?'

Laura scowled at him. 'I really didn't.'

'No, well,' he said, lifting himself off the desk and moving to sit behind it, 'I doubt the coronation was covered in *Architecture Tomorrow*.' Like that was an excuse. 'However if you remember I did suggest lunch, and if you hadn't run off quite so speedily I might have mentioned it then.'

Laura's eyes narrowed. Oh, he was clever. Turning it around so it was her fault. 'I'd like to believe that, but somehow I don't.'

Matt gave her a quick grin that curled her toes. 'We'll never know now, will we?'

Unfortunately not. 'What were you doing in Little Somerford?'

'Escaping the press.'

No wonder he'd flipped when he'd thought she was a journalist. He was gorgeous, young, rich and royal. A paparazzo's dream. And she hadn't had a clue. She really ought to broaden her reading horizons.

'And you got me instead.'

'Briefly.' The grin faded and his mouth twisted.

Hmm. Laura bit back the urge to apologise. Any previous notion she might have had of apologising had long since disappeared beneath a blanket of confusion, indignation and something that felt suspiciously like hurt. 'You sound peeved,' she said coolly.

He raised an eyebrow. 'Well, the speed with which you fled wasn't particularly flattering.'

A smidgeon of guilt elbowed its way through her

indignation. Laura shrugged and ignored it. 'We had a quickie. It was no big deal.'

His eyes glittered. 'If it was no big deal why did you run?'

'Like I told you at the time, I had plans.'

'Right.'

He fixed her with a gaze that had her squirming in her chair until she couldn't stand it any longer. So much for thinking she might have had the upper hand. Matt made one formidable opponent.

'OK, fine,' she said, throwing her hands up in exasperation. 'I guess I panicked.'

'Why?'

'I'm not entirely sure,' she said, forcing herself to look him in the eye. 'It was kind of intense. For me, at least. I don't know. Maybe for you it's like that all the time.'

'Not all the time,' he muttered, looking less than thrilled by the admission.

At his obvious discomfort Laura suddenly relaxed. 'It was kind of amazing, wasn't it?'

'Hmm.'

Matt regarded her thoughtfully and she bit her lip. It wasn't his fault she'd been spooked. He didn't know about the battle she'd had with herself. And now it seemed that fate had decided they were going to have to work together. Unless she cleared the air the tension that simmered between them would soon reach an unbearable level. 'I'm sorry I rushed off like that.'

He shrugged. 'It really doesn't matter. I put it out of my mind weeks ago.'

'Oh,' she said, stamping down on the perverse disappointment that he could dismiss it quite so easily.

'Well, that's good, seeing as we're going to be working together.'

Matt's gaze jerked to hers and his eyebrows shot up. 'You don't really think you can stay, do you?'

Laura went very still and felt her face pale. 'What do you mean?'

He leaned forwards and clasped his hands on the desk. 'I appreciate the fact that you've been given the job, and I realise there's nothing I can do contractually, but in the light of our recent history don't you think it would be wise if you refused?'

What? Refuse? He wanted her to give up the job she so badly needed? Over her dead body. Sticking her chin up, she fixed him with a firm stare. 'No.'

For a second there was a stunned silence. Matt looked as if she'd slapped him. Clearly no one had ever said no to him before. Well, that was tough, thought Laura, folding her arms over her chest and crossing her legs. Her days of endless people pleasing, of always acquiescing, were over.

'No?'

'Absolutely not,' she added, setting her jaw and glaring at him just in case he still didn't get the message. 'I'm not going anywhere.'

Matt's brows snapped together and he shoved a hand through his hair. 'There's a conflict of interest,' he said tightly.

'Then you leave.'

'Don't be absurd.'

'I'm not the one being absurd,' she said coolly. 'Yes, I agree that the situation is far from ideal but I want this job. And you need an architect. The palace is falling apart and bullet holes are so last century.'

His jaw tightened. 'I don't mix business with pleasure.'

'Neither do I,' she fired back. 'Believe me, the last
thing I'm looking for is a repeat of that afternoon.

'Nor am I.'

'Then I really don't see that there's anything to worry
about.'

'Don't you?' he said, dropping his gaze and letting
it slide over her body.

Heat began to pour over her. Desire flared to life
but she banked it down. Right now her work was more
important than anything else. She was *not* going to let
it go. For anything.

'I,' she said pointedly, 'am perfectly capable of sepa-
rating business and pleasure. I,' she added, 'should be
able to control myself. Besides there is nothing you can
do to make me go.'

His gaze dropped to her mouth and stayed there. His
face darkened, his eyes took on a wicked gleam and
Laura swallowed. Her heart lurched and a ball of nerves
lodged in her throat. OK, so for all her fine words if Matt
jumped to his feet, stalked round his desk, hauled her
into his arms and kissed her she'd probably be through
the door in seconds. But after loftily declaring that he
didn't mix business with pleasure she had to hope he
wouldn't put her to the test.

But why was he so desperate to get rid of her? Anyone
would think she'd been stalking him. And what was all
that hostility about? Surely he couldn't be *that* annoyed
she'd run off?

'Look,' she said, 'you must be busy and the palace
is huge. Our paths need never cross.' Thankfully.

Matt sighed, got to his feet and gave her one last glower before picking up his laptop. 'Just make sure you stay out of my way.'

CHAPTER SEVEN

THIS was getting ridiculous, Matt thought, struggling to pay attention to what his advisors were saying. He was in the middle of a discussion about the huge gaps in the public accounts and all he could think about was what Laura was up to.

He hadn't laid eyes on her in the two weeks since she'd been hired. Not that he'd been looking out for her especially. No. He'd had far too much to do. But it did seem odd. The palace might be big but it wasn't *that* large.

In a weird way her absence simply made him more aware of her presence. Which didn't make any sense at all.

Maybe it was the knowledge that he'd overreacted again and undoubtedly owed her another apology. Snapping at her like that to stay out of his way, snapping at anyone for that matter, wasn't how he chose to behave.

But then since he'd met her a lot of his behaviour had been uncharacteristic. If it carried on much longer his reputation for being tough and uncompromising would lie in tatters.

What was it about her that set him so on edge? Why did he have this niggling feeling that she was some kind of a threat? A threat to what exactly? In his experience threats came from rival bidders for a company he wanted and from despotic former presidents with their hands in the till. They did not come from curvy blond-haired blue-eyed architects.

Matt shoved his hands through his hair and let out a growl of frustration. Whatever the hell was going on, it couldn't continue.

He'd start with the apology. The sooner he got that out of the way, the better. And then he'd take the opportunity to find out a little more about her.

Something about the sabbatical she'd claimed she was on, the way she'd avoided his eyes when she'd mentioned it, had been gnawing at his brain. Whatever it was, she was working for him and he should get to the bottom of it.

And that was another thing, he realised suddenly. His company employed dozens of permanent staff and he'd always made a point of getting to know every one of them. Now Laura was on his payroll and what did he know about her? Apart from what she felt like in his arms and wrapped around him, precious little.

Matt ignored the bolt of heat that gripped his body and set his jaw. In fact that was probably what had been bothering him. The non-observation of formalities.

'Sir?'

He snapped his head round to his secretary who was sitting on his right and refocused his attention. 'What?' he said, and added a quick smile to mitigate the sharpness of his tone.

'I hope you don't mind my asking, but is everything all right?'

'Fine. What does Signorina Mackenzie do for lunch?'

The only indication that Antonio Capelli was surprised by a question about lunch in the midst of a conversation about corruption was a double blink. 'I believe she takes a sandwich to the rose garden.'

A sandwich? Matt's jaw tightened. No one could survive on a sandwich. 'What time?'

'One-ish, I believe. Would you like me to check?'

'No, that's fine. Where's the rose garden?'

'Past the kitchen gardens. Before the lake. There's a gate in the hedge.'

'Thank you.'

Matt made a move to get to his feet but Antonio leaned forwards and said, 'The advisors are waiting for your comments.'

About what? Oh, yes. Now that he'd fixed the Laura problem he snapped his attention back to the discussion with thankfully familiar ease. 'How much is missing?'

'Approximately fifty million,' said one of the finance advisors.

Pushing his chair back, he stood, planted his hands on the table and said, 'Trace the money. I suggest you start with Switzerland. When you find out who's responsible, arrest them.'

Laura finished off the last of her cheese sandwich and brushed the crumbs off her skirt. Breathing in the heady scent of roses, she sighed with pleasure. She'd stumbled on this little slice of heaven the day she'd arrived back with all her things, and, absolutely certain that it was one place Matt, or anyone else for that matter, would never visit, she'd made a habit of having lunch here, followed by half an hour of sunbathing before getting back to work.

The weather was gorgeous, the work was absorbing,

and Matt and his disturbing effect on her composure were nowhere to be seen. What could be better?

Laura stood up, unzipped her overalls and pushed them down to her waist. Then she lay down on the grass, closed her eyes as the sun hit her bare skin and basked in the warmth.

This was so the life...

She was in the middle of a particularly lovely day-dream in which she was picking up a RIBA European award for her work on the palace when she heard the squeaking of the gate.

Her heart jumped. Her ears pricked. And caught another squeak. Swiftly followed by a sharp intake of breath and a muttered curse.

Her pulse racing, Laura jackknifed up. Grabbed the sides of her overalls and clutched them to her chest. She twisted round. And nearly passed out.

Matt was standing just inside the gate, frozen to the spot, staring down at her, his face set, but his eyes blazing.

Laura swallowed and felt a raging blush hit her cheeks. Too late to hope that he hadn't seen her semi-naked. OK, so she was at least wearing her bra, which was something to be thankful for, but the muscle hammering in his jaw and the tension in his body told her that he'd seen more than enough.

'You scared the life out of me,' she snapped, aiming for control by channelling her mortification into accusation.

'Next time I'll knock,' he said hoarsely, turning away so she could get her clothes in order.

'At least this time I'm not in danger of banging my head,' she muttered as she thrust her arms into the sleeves and whipped up the zip. Just passing out with overheating. Matt creeping up on her had better not become a habit.

Springing to her feet, Laura gave herself a quick shake and forced herself to calm down. 'You can turn round now,' she said lightly. 'I'm decent.'

More than decent, actually. Her nipples might be annoyingly as hard as pebbles, but the shapelessness of her overalls revealed nothing of the way her body responded to him, thank goodness.

Now all she had to do was sidle off, bury herself in work and find somewhere else to have lunch because, judging by the hamper hanging from his hand and banging against his knees, Matt had decided to appropriate this spot and frankly, with thousands of other heavenly spots in the grounds of the palace it wasn't really worth arguing over.

'Right. Well. I'll—er—leave you to it.'

'Don't go.' Matt flashed her a smile and her stomach flipped. Awareness whizzed through the entire length of her as, unable to help herself, she ran her gaze over every gorgeous inch of him, from the top of his thick dark hair right the way down, past the T-shirt and jeans down to the flip-flops.

She paused and blinked, not sure she'd heard him correctly. 'What?'

'My being here isn't exactly a coincidence.'

Laura frowned. 'Did you want something?'

'I came to see if you'd like some lunch.' He strode towards her and set the hamper beside the table.

'I've already had it.'

'Have some more.'

'I'm not hungry.'

'Fine, you can keep me company while I have lunch,'

he said, folding himself into the chair on the other side
of the table and waving that she do the same.

Hmm. 'I need to get back to work.'

'Later.' He gave her a quick smile. 'Indulge me.'

Her stomach swooped. 'Do I have any option?'

'Not a lot,' he said, his eyes glinting with amusement
and turning her head inside out. 'According to the re-
cords, disobeying the king used to result being thrown
in the dungeon.'

'Charming.'

'Not in the least,' he said cheerfully. 'It's damp and
crawling with vermin. You wouldn't like it.'

Probably not. Although she was pretty sure it would
be less uncomfortable than having lunch with Matt when
her common sense had gone AWOL. 'Wow,' she said,
arching an eyebrow and crossing her arms. 'Absolute
power and blackmail. That's quite a combination.'

'I like to think so.'

Laura tilted her head. 'I thought I was supposed to
be staying out of your way.'

He glanced at her for a second and then grinned.
'That was one of the things I wanted to chat about.'

Now he wanted to chat? She narrowed her eyes.
'Don't you have better things to do? Like a country to
run?'

'Even kings need to eat. And I thought we could get
round to some of that small talk you mentioned.'

The small talk they'd been too busy getting horizontal
and naked to bother with…

Laura's insides tangled into a mass of longing and
frustration. Why was she always on the back foot with
this man? What was it about him that had her feeling
totally at sea? And more importantly why hadn't the two

weeks she'd spent staying out of his way done anything to reduce the effect he had on her?

She nibbled on her lip. Maybe small talk *was* the way forward. If she could get him to reveal a bit about himself, maybe he'd turn out to be hideously arrogant, irritatingly patronising and possibly insanely boring. If she was really lucky, he'd also expose a couple of nasty habits. Like interrupting her. Or dismissing her opinions as if batting away a fly. As her ex had had a tendency to do. Hah. *That* would certainly put her off.

Laura sat down and gave him a cool smile. 'What would you like to talk about?'

Matt leaned down and took a bottle and a couple of glasses out of the hamper. 'It's occurred to me that the apologies I owe you are beginning to stack up.'

Oh. Damn. Not that hideously arrogant, then. She lifted a shoulder. 'Are they?'

He pulled the cork out, filled the glasses and slid one across the table to her. 'First of all, I never apologised for jumping to the conclusion you were a journalist.'

He'd made up for it in other ways, Laura thought, drawing the glass towards her, and then wished she hadn't as her cheeks went red.

'And then when you turned up here, I overreacted.'

She took a sip of wine and felt the alcohol slide into her stomach. 'Why?'

Matt frowned. 'I'm not sure.'

Hah. As if. She'd never met anyone less unsure of themselves. 'Let me guess,' she said with a flash of perception. 'You thought I was here to see you.' He stiffened and she felt a jolt of triumph. 'And I bet you thought the worst.'

'Possibly.'

'You really ought to do something about that suspicious nature of yours.'

'Perhaps.'

'Have lots of people crawled out of the woodwork now that you're king?'

His face tightened. 'Some.'

'Well, I don't know what sort of people you usually hang out with but you should look at getting a new set of friends.'

'You're probably right.' Matt sighed and then snapped back from wherever he'd been. 'So how am I doing?'

'Not bad.'

'Not bad?'

'Well, you haven't actually apologised yet.'

'Good point.' He frowned and shifted in the seat. 'I'm sorry.'

Laura couldn't help grinning at his obvious discomfort. 'Not a fan of apologising?'

Matt grimaced. 'I haven't had a huge amount of practice.'

Lucky him. She'd had years of practice. Often apologising for things that hadn't been her fault. God, she'd been pathetic. 'I dare say you'll get better at it.'

He winced. 'I don't plan on having to.'

'No, well, I doubt kings generally have much to apologise for.'

Didn't they? Any more of those sexy little smiles, thought Matt, and he'd be apologising for a whole lot more than a misunderstanding and an overreaction.

Because despite the shapeless mass of beige cotton covering Laura from head to toe, the imprint of her lying there on the grass in just her bra burned in his head and she might as well be naked. Every time she tucked her hair behind her ears or reached for her glass and lifted it to her mouth the thick cotton rustled and reminded him of exactly what lay beneath.

His head swam for a second and his hands curled into fists. Oh, for God's sake. He really had to get a grip.

Right. Conversation. That had been the plan. Food might not be a bad idea, either, he thought, taking out a couple of plates, cutlery and a number of small plastic boxes. He pushed a plate across the table to Laura but she shook her head. He opened the boxes and piled a selection of things on his plate.

'So how's the accommodation?' he asked.

See. He could do conversation.

'Very comfortable, thank you. Who could complain about a four-poster bed and marble en-suite?'

The image of Laura hot and naked and wet in the shower slammed into his head and his mouth went dry as the heavy beat of desire began to pound through him. Perhaps best to steer clear of accommodation as a conversational avenue in the future.

'And the work?'

'Really great,' she said, giving him a dazzling smile that nearly blinded him.

'You're very dedicated.' Neither his culture minister nor his secretary could stop singing her praises. It had been driving him insane.

'I love my job.'

'So why the sabbatical?'

Her glass froze halfway to her mouth and she carefully set it back down on the table. 'What do you mean?' she said warily.

'Well, you're clearly good at your job, and you said yourself you love it. So why the sabbatical?'

'Oh, well, you know.' She shrugged and nibbled on her lip in that way that he was discovering meant that she was nervous. Excellent. When he'd thought that something didn't add up he'd been right.

'I needed some time out. Stress. Boredom. That sort of thing.'

Matt didn't believe that for a second. Her whole demeanour had changed and if pushed he'd have said she looked downright shifty. 'You don't seem the type to suffer from stress or boredom.'

'Then I guess it's working.'

Hmm. Never mind. He'd get to the bottom of her sabbatical soon enough. 'How long have you lived in Little Somerford?'

She visibly relaxed. 'A couple of months.'

'And before that?'

'London. Born and bred.'

'Do you miss it?'

'Bits.'

'Which bits?'

'The theatres. My friends.'

Matt tilted his head. 'You must be what…late twenties?'

'Early thirties,' she said cagily, her eyes narrowing.

'And you move from the bright lights of London and a good job to hole up in a remote village in the country. Why?'

Laura studied her feet. 'I fancied a change of scenery.'

'During your sabbatical?' he said dryly.

'Exactly.'

'Aren't you quite young to take a sabbatical?'

Her head shot up and her eyes flashed. 'What's with this obsession with my sabbatical?'

Matt lifted his shoulders and gave her a smile. 'I'm just interested.'

Laura frowned. 'You should meet my friend Kate.'

'Why?'

'You both have persistence in spades,' she said darkly. 'You'd get on like a house on fire.'

Matt grinned. 'Persistence is useful in my line of work.'

'I'd call it nosiness.'

'That's useful, too. Bit risky, though, I'd have thought, to take a sabbatical at such a relatively early stage in your career.'

Laura let out an exasperated sigh and then threw her hands up. 'Fine,' she said, glaring at him. 'I didn't exactly choose to take a sabbatical. I was made redundant.'

'Ah,' Matt said, his mouth curving into a triumphant smile.

'There were cutbacks in government spending. Projects were axed. Heads rolled. Mine was one of them.'

'Ouch.' Whoever had employed her had been idiots for letting her go. But their loss, his gain. Or rather *Sassania's* gain, he amended swiftly.

She stared at him for a second, then blinked. 'Well, yes,' she said. 'But actually, not as ouch now as it was at the time.' She gave him a quick smile. 'In fact with the benefit of hindsight I ought to have sent them a big bunch of flowers to say thank you.'

'Why?' Matt wished she wouldn't do that blinking thing. It made him lose his train of thought. The colour of her eyes was so deep, so intense that when the blue disappeared he thought it a shame, yet when it reappeared his head swam and he wished she'd kept her eyes shut.

'If I hadn't been made redundant, I wouldn't have been free to take on this.' She waved an arm in the direction of the palace. 'I have ex-colleagues who would give their eye teeth to be here.'

Matt dragged his attention back to the conversation and hmmed. He doubted any of them would have her dedication or enthusiasm. 'That explains the "sabbatical",' he said, 'but why leave London?'

The wince was tiny but he caught it and something stabbed him in the chest. 'London gets a trifle dull after a while, don't you find?'

'No.'

'Oh.' She frowned. And then shrugged. 'Well, each to their own.'

Barriers were springing up all around her telling him to back off. But as she'd pointed out, he was persistent.

'I don't buy it,' he said, deceptively mildly.

'Tough.'

Matt leaned forwards. 'Tell me.'

'No.'

But she was wavering.

'Maybe I can help.'

'You already did,' she said, and then went bright red.

'How?'

'Doesn't matter.'

'If it involves me it does matter.'

'Let's just say I met you at a time when my self-esteem wasn't exactly sky-high.'

'And I boosted it?'

'Something like that,' she muttered.

'You used me.' Matt sat back and wondered whether he was hurt or amused.

Her gaze flew to his. 'No. Of course not.'

Oh, she was terrible at lying. He didn't say anything,

just lifted an eyebrow and stared at her until her cheeks went even redder.

'Well, maybe just a little bit.' She screwed up her eyes as if not wanting to see his reaction.

She needn't have worried. He had no complaints. 'Charming,' he said mildly, folding his arms over his chest and grinning. 'I'm devastated.'

Her eyes flew open in shock and then she relaxed and returned his grin. 'I can tell.'

'Nevertheless, I think you owe me an explanation.'

'I don't see why. Can you honestly say you didn't use me?'

'This isn't about me.'

Laura nodded and took a deep breath. 'OK, fine. The day I was made redundant I got home early to find my boyfriend at the time with his secretary. In our bed.'

'Ah.'

'I know. Tacky, or what? They'd been having an affair for three months, would you believe, and I hadn't a clue. I'd rented my flat out when I moved in with him and, what with three being a bit of a crowd, I couldn't exactly stick around. So I trawled through the websites of a number of rental agencies and found the cottage in Little Somerford and I left.'

'What a jerk.' The hammering urge to hunt her ex-boyfriend down and pummel the living daylights out of him thumped Matt in the chest, taking him completely by surprise.

She blinked. 'Well, yes. But I guess he wasn't wholly to blame.'

'Seems to me that that kind of behaviour is inexcusable,' he muttered, wondering exactly where such a violent reaction had come from.

She bit her lip. 'True, but I was too easy-going, too

easy to please. Too afraid of confrontation. I let him get away with too much. I let him walk all over me.' She shrugged.

Easy-going? Afraid of confrontation? Matt nearly fell off his chair. That didn't sound like the Laura he knew. Since the moment he'd met her she'd been feisty, fearless and determined.

Snapshots flew around his head. Of Laura on the path, batting her eyelids and pouting. Arching her back on his sofa and staring up at him with that come-hither look. Sitting in his office, limbs crossed, chin up as she told him she wasn't leaving.

His stomach churned with a weird combination of lust, admiration and something that felt suspiciously like jealousy.

'Which has kind of been the story of my life,' she was saying. 'Much as it pains me to admit it, I have been a bit of a doormat.'

Matt dragged himself back to the conversation. 'You could have fooled me,' he muttered, his voice not betraying any hint of the confusion battering his brain.

Laura grinned. 'Ah, well, that's because after the double whammy of losing my job and my boyfriend I went on an assertiveness course.'

'That sounds dangerous.'

'It was. Very. Module One was entitled "How to Embrace Confrontation". Module Two covered learning how to say no. And Module Three focused on how to get what you want.'

'You must be a fast learner.'

Laura nodded. 'Like lightning.'

'For someone allegedly afraid of confrontation,' he said dryly, 'you're pretty good at it.'

She grinned and his stomach swooped. 'It's turned

out to be surprisingly liberating. As has going for what I want and saying no.'

Sometimes saying no wasn't all it was cracked up to be. Sometimes the only word a man wanted to hear was yes. In exactly the breathy pleading way she'd said all those little yeses that afternoon.

'Anyway. Change is good, don't you think?'

'Depends on the change,' Matt muttered, struggling to keep his focus on reconciling the Laura he knew to the one she described and not on the yeses. 'Where did the pushover tendencies come from?'

'My parents' divorce when I was thirteen, I suppose.'

'Tricky.'

'Very.'

'Amicable?'

She winced. 'Hideous.'

'I'm sorry.'

Laura shrugged. 'Things had been bad for years, even though at the time it all seemed so sudden. I think I probably compensated by trying not to put a foot wrong, in the childish hope that if I was good enough they'd stay together. Which was nuts, of course,' she said. 'I know it had nothing to do with me and they're far happier apart, but I guess old habits die hard.'

'If ever.'

Laura shook her head. 'Ah, you see, that's where you're wrong. My people-pleasing days are well and truly over.'

That was a shame.

The thought slammed into Matt's head before he could stop it and stayed there flashing in neon, reminding him just how well she'd pleased him.

'Anyway why the sudden interest?'

Matt shrugged and shoved the thought aside. 'I'm interested in all my members of staff.'

For a second there was an odd sort of stunned silence. Laura's face paled and Matt felt a chill suddenly run through him as if the sun had disappeared behind a cloud.

She blinked. Bit on her lip. Nodded slowly. 'Of course,' she said in a strangely soft voice, getting to her feet a little jerkily. 'Right.' She nodded again. Ran her hands over her hips, pulled her shoulders back and flashed him an overly bright smile. 'Well, as a member of staff, and a brand-new one at that, I ought to be getting back to work. Thank you for the wine.'

Before Matt could ask her what the matter was, Laura had spun on her heel and was stalking off in the direction of the hedge as if she couldn't get away fast enough.

He watched her disappear through the gate, bewilderment pummelling at his brain. What the hell was all that about? Matt rubbed his face. He'd thought their conversation had been going swimmingly. He'd got to the bottom of her sabbatical and was beginning to discover what made her tick. And even more surprisingly, he'd found himself enjoying her company.

So what had happened? Had he said something? Done something?

God. He swore softly under his breath. He was famed for being decisive, intuitive, shrewd and for having a certain ruthlessness that had made him a billionaire by the time he was thirty. He'd built up a multimillion-pound business from scratch. He'd negotiated impossible deals and turned the most desperate of companies around. Now he was running a country with every problem going.

Yet he'd never understand women. They were completely unfathomable.

Even Alicia, who'd been so transparent and straightforward, had eventually become incomprehensible. Matt's jaw tightened as the memory of his ex-fiancée filtered into his head. Her lack of guile had been one of the reasons he'd asked her to marry him. She hadn't tried to wrap him up in complex emotional games. Their relationship had been easy, light and fun.

Until he'd started to get more caught up with his business. As it had grown he'd had to devote more and more time to it and less to her.

At first she'd been remarkably stoical, supportive even, but even the most understanding fiancée would have got fed up eventually.

Matt had been torn, and while the relationship limped on for a while it hadn't survived. The end had been messy and painful. Hurtful accusations had flown all over the place. Guilt and blame had built and built, until things had finally erupted. The only thing that had kept him sane during and after their break-up had been his work.

Now he avoided relationships like the plague. They were perplexing, unpredictable and ultimately emotionally destructive, and he never wanted to go through all that again.

Matt set his jaw and put everything back into the hamper. Laura was perplexing, unpredictable and he had a horrible suspicion she could be pretty emotionally destructive.

So there'd be no more seeking her out, he thought, getting to his feet and heading back to the palace. No more lunches. No more conversation. And definitely no more wanting her in his bed.

When their paths crossed he'd be cool and distant. Because he was far better off alone. Always had been, always would be.

Staff, thought Laura for the billionth time that afternoon. Huh.

Disappointment and hurt scythed through her all over again and she threw down her chisel before she could do any permanent damage to the frieze she was working on.

God. How stupid could she be? If only she were wearing steel-capped boots she could have given herself the kicking she deserved. Because she was such an idiot.

She closed her eyes for a second and felt her cheeks burn as her mind hurtled back to the rose garden. There she'd been, going all soft and squidgy and mellowing with the wine and the sun and the heat of Matt's gaze. Bizarrely she'd found herself enjoying the conversation despite it dredging up things she'd rather not think about. It had actually been a relief to talk about the old her, and she'd discovered she rather liked the person she was beginning to become.

Unfortunately there hadn't been a hint of arrogance, nor a patronising glance in sight. And while Matt had been annoyingly persistent he hadn't interrupted her and he hadn't dismissed anything she'd said. In fact the way his body had tensed and his eyes had blazed when she'd told him about her ex had had her heart leaping with something she wasn't sure she wanted to identify and desire whipping through her so fiercely that she'd begun to wonder why exactly business and pleasure shouldn't mix.

And all the time he'd just been interrogating her as he would any employee.

Agh. Laura opened her eyes and scowled. The fact that she was still smarting over it two hours later was infuriating. And what was making things worse was the knowledge that she didn't have any real reason to smart. Which irritated her even further.

Because Matt was right. She was staff.

So what was she getting so het up about?

Laura plonked herself on the floor and chewed her lip. Was it really the fact that he'd wangled so much personal information out of her without divulging even his age, which was what she'd been telling herself for the past hour or so?

Or was it actually the fact that she'd spent the entire conversation on the point of combusting while Matt had sat there, ice cool and controlled and totally indifferent?

As the heat and desire that were never far away flared to life and started zooming around her body, Laura swallowed. Well, that cleared that up, she thought, hauling herself out of denial and sticking her chin in her hands.

She might as well admit it. For all the decisions she'd made, all the self-analysis she'd done, all the stern talking-tos she'd given herself, she was finding it increasingly difficult to remember exactly why she wasn't leaping into Matt's arms and tumbling him into bed.

Whereas he, on the other hand, appeared to have forgotten that that mad passionate afternoon in his house had ever taken place.

Huh. Talk about unflattering.

Laura frowned and her mind raced. She'd had enough of constantly flailing around for control while Matt remained the epitome of cool. Wasn't it about time she redressed the balance? Wouldn't it be interesting to see if she couldn't shake him up a bit and get him on the wrong foot for a change?

Her heart began to hammer and her stomach buzzed with adrenalin. Yes. Why the hell not? And tonight, at the party she'd heard Matt was hosting, would be the ideal occasion.

She hadn't been invited. He wouldn't be expecting her. She had a killer dress and shoes that made her feel a million dollars.

What could be more perfect?

CHAPTER EIGHT

MATT had had the event this evening arranged to evaluate the country's entrepreneurial spirit and ascertain the existing barriers to business. He'd had invitations sent out to five hundred of Sassania's most innovative and exciting entrepreneurs and the ballroom was now filled with a buzz that gave him more satisfaction than he'd have ever imagined.

So far the evening had been going splendidly. He'd had a number of extremely worthwhile conversations, and had gained a valuable insight into the way to kick-start the economy and stimulate growth.

After all the political problems he'd had to deal with recently, not to mention the unsettling effect Laura had on him, spending an evening within his comfort zone made a nice change.

As did the way he now felt, or rather didn't feel, about Laura. After she'd left him in the rose garden, he'd gone back to his office, summoned up some of that famed ruthlessness and had simply told himself to get a grip and not to feel anything.

So he didn't. When she crossed his mind, he felt absolutely nothing. Not a flicker of desire. Not a hammer of his pulse. Not a twitch of his body. The abrupt way in which she'd left him after lunch? Hah. Didn't bother him one jot.

Laura, metaphorically speaking, was history, and he hadn't been so relaxed in weeks.

Striding over to the podium and adjusting the microphone, Matt felt an exquisite sense of calm settle over him. Oh, yes. He was back on track and back in control. And nothing, but nothing, could upset it.

Laura hovered at the pair of giant doors that opened into the ballroom, her gaze zooming in on the man standing on the podium speaking to the assembled throng, and her breath caught.

Matt looked absolutely magnificent. Dark and dangerous and devastatingly gorgeous. His dinner suit fitted as if made for him and the snowy white of his shirt emphasised his tan. The aura he emanated and the magnetism he radiated were holding every one of his guests captivated.

God, she'd only just arrived and hadn't heard any of his speech, yet *she* was captivated. Her eyes slid helplessly back to him and her blood began to heat. Who knew what he was talking about? She was far too distracted by the hint of a smile curving his mouth and the sexy raise of an eyebrow he gave every now and then. Every inch of him seemed to reach out to her and she was moments away from discarding all her intentions of lofty hauteur, and swooning.

A woman to her right let out a little sigh and Laura felt like going over and patting her arm in sympathy. And then batting everyone out of the way, stalking over and staking her claim on him.

Her totally unfounded claim, she reminded herself, biting her tongue and forcing herself to focus.

'Small businesses are the backbone to any economy,' Matt was saying, his gaze sweeping over the assembled gathering, 'and I plan to see that measures are implemented to—'

His eyes collided with hers and for a second, time stood still. He paused. His face tightened. His eyes blazed and Laura's heart skidded to a halt. Her mouth went dry. Her entire body froze and then burned as awareness sizzled through her.

And then Matt continued his sweep of the room as if nothing had happened and time set off again.

'—to encourage their development. Thank you.'

Applause rumbled around her as Matt stepped down, but Laura barely registered it. She could hardly breathe with the nerves that were suddenly attacking her from all sides.

Oh, God, she thought, struggling not to sag against the door. This had been *such* a bad idea. Because for that brief moment Matt had not looked happy to see her. In fact he'd looked downright furious.

Her heart tumbled. How had she ever thought she could get the upper hand with a man like him? He was a king, for heaven's sake. A natural born leader. He was alpha through and through, whereas she had spent her whole life sitting squarely at the omega end of the scale. OK, so she might be inching up that particular alphabet but still she was in way over her head.

What the hell had she been thinking? What had given her the nerve to presume she could shake him up? Come to think of it, why on earth would she want to shake him up anyway? Shaking Matt up would be like rattling a lion's cage while leaving the gate open. Had she gone completely nuts?

Laura's heart began to race. She ought to leave.
Pretend she'd never come. Now.

But with Antonio Capelli striding towards her, smiling warmly in welcome and taking her elbow, it was far
too late to flee.

Oh, *hell,* thought Matt, plucking a glass of champagne
off the tray of a passing waiter and forcing himself not
to down it in one.

What was Laura doing here? He deliberately hadn't
invited her so he must have done something truly horrendous in a past life to deserve this kind of torment, he
thought grimly, gripping the glass and muttering some
sort of appropriate response to the question he was being
asked.

When his gaze had skated over the room and landed
on her, everything had seemed to judder to a halt. His
heart had thumped and for a split second his head had
gone blank. He'd forgotten where he was, what he was
doing and more worryingly what he was supposed to
be saying.

It had taken every ounce of strength he possessed to
drag his gaze from hers and continue his perusal of the
room. With every fibre of his being suddenly on fire
what he'd really wanted to do was leap off the podium,
shove everyone out of the way and drag her off somewhere private.

So much for his famed ruthlessness. He could only
hope to God that no one had noticed him falter.

Matt felt his eyes narrow as he watched Laura being
wheeled off by his secretary and suspicion began to
wind through him. If Antonio had had anything to do
with Laura's presence at the party he could well be finding a new job come the morning.

But never mind, he told himself as they disappeared into the melee. There were five hundred people in the room and there was absolutely no reason why he'd even need to go up to her, let alone have to speak to her.

All he had to do was forget she was there and everything would be fine.

Forgetting Laura was at the party was easier said than done, Matt thought, an agonising hour later.

He might not have had any need to approach her, but that didn't stop him being aware of every move she made. It didn't stop him subconsciously manoeuvring himself towards her, and it didn't stop him wanting to march over and throw out any man she spoke to, smiled at or laughed with. Of which there were far too many.

Running a finger around the inside of his collar, Matt felt uncomfortably hot and weirdly on edge. His muscles actually ached with the effort of keeping his body where it was and his brain hurt with the effort of concentrating on the conversations going on around him.

Unable to help himself, he glanced over to where she was chatting and smiling, her eyes sparkling and her cheeks pink. He caught her eye. She arched an eyebrow, as if she was well aware he was avoiding her, and something inside him snapped.

This was absurd. Trying to ignore her wasn't working. Why the hell shouldn't he just go over and say hello? That wouldn't kill him, would it?

Gritting his teeth, Matt excused himself and started to make his way over to her.

Which wasn't as easy as it sounded. She was standing only a few metres away, but she might as well have been in a different country. To his intense frustration people kept coming up to him like heat-seeking missiles. Interrupting his trajectory and wanting to have a word.

By the time he finally made it to her, he'd agreed to a dozen things he probably shouldn't have, and his already stretched-to-the-limit patience was dangerously close to snapping.

It wasn't helped by the lifted chin or the cool haughty smile she greeted him with. Or the long strapless blue dress she was wearing that matched her eyes and clung everywhere. Did she have *any* idea how little it left to the imagination?

Matt thrust his hands in his pockets. 'Good evening,' he said, his tone far sharper than he'd have liked.

'Your Majesty,' she said, dropping into a graceful curtsey.

What the hell? Matt ground his teeth. 'Don't do that.'

She rose and gave him a smile that had his heart pounding. 'Am I doing it wrong?'

'No.' She did it very well. Sank so low that he could see straight down the front of her dress. 'But don't do it again. Not you.'

She sighed dramatically and pouted. 'And I spent such a long time practising.'

Matt blinked and tried to keep his eyes out of her cleavage and some sort of grip on his control. 'What are you doing here?'

'I thought it might be a good idea to see how the ballroom works. From a restoration perspective.'

'Gatecrashing?'

'Not at all,' said Laura coolly. 'Once I explained my intentions to Signore Capelli, he added me to the guest list.'

Hah. As he'd thought. He'd definitely be having words with his secretary.

'Nice dress.' His voice sounded strangely hoarse and he cleared his throat.

'Thank you. Nice suit.'

'Thank you.'

She tilted her head back to take a sip of her champagne and Matt's gaze dropped to her throat. Soft and creamy skin. Completely exposed. He curled his hands into fists deep in his pockets to stop himself reaching out, pulling her against him and setting his mouth to the pulse thumping at the base of her neck.

Then she lowered her glass and shot him a languid look and a smouldering smile that set his body on fire. 'Are you all right, Matt?'

He pulled himself together. 'Fine. Why?'

'You look a little uncomfortable.'

'Just a trifle warm.'

'So why are you glowering? This is a party. You shouldn't be glowering.'

'It's my party. I can do whatever I like.'

Her smile deepened. Turned faintly knowing, and Matt's pulse hammered. Would anyone notice if he hauled her away somewhere private to continue the party alone?

'Well, you must be busy,' she said, her voice unusually husky. 'Don't let me keep you.'

'You aren't.'

'Great speech.'

Had it been? He couldn't remember. Her gaze shimmered at him with something he couldn't identify but made desire pound through him.

Matt's head swam. What on earth had got into her

tonight? Where had this sultry hauteur sprung from? And what was he going to do about it?

'This is a lovely room,' she said, looking up and giving him another view of her throat.

'I don't want to talk about the room,' he grated.

If she was surprised by his tone, she didn't show it. In fact her eyes began to sparkle with something that looked suspiciously like triumph. Which only wound him up further. 'Then what do you want to talk about?'

He didn't want to talk at all. 'Why did you dash off like that earlier?' he said, drawing on the first thing that sprang to mind.

Laura lifted her shoulders and Matt had to force himself not to glance down. 'Things to do.'

His eyes narrowed. 'Running away from me seems to be becoming a habit.'

'Not at all. You simply reminded me of my place, that's all.'

Matt frowned. What the hell did that mean? Her place was in his arms. Beneath him. On top of him. Whichever way, plastered against him was where she should be.

His jaw clenched as the desire pounding through him grew hotter, more insistent.

He'd had enough of this. Enough of the eyelash batting and the sultry little smiles. Enough of the hammering desire and tight tension keeping him awake all night and ruining his concentration all day. Enough of trying to resist her.

For whatever reason, Laura was in a dangerous mood tonight and, despite his best efforts to hang on to it, Matt's control was slipping away like sand through an hourglass. He'd never felt such a need clawing at his gut.

Never felt such desperation. Never had so little desire for conversation.

To hell with the entrepreneurs. He'd done plenty to ease their concerns. Now it was his turn.

Stepping forward, Matt took her elbow and pulled her against him.

'What are you doing?' Laura muttered, her breath catching.

'We're leaving,' he said as the scent of her spun into his head and obliterated all rational thought.

'We can't.'

'We can and we are.'

She glanced up at him, a tiny frown creasing her brow. 'Is something wrong?'

'Very.'

'What is it?'

Out of the corner of his eye Matt caught the flash of movement, a glimpse of someone heading over to talk to him. Oh, no. No way. 'Have you seen the Sala dell'Anticollegio yet?' he said loudly, wheeling her off in the opposite direction and not giving her time to answer. 'Incredible vaulted ceiling. Badly in need of some TLC.' As was he.

So much for lofty hauteur, thought Laura, tottering alongside Matt in her three inch stilettos.

It had all been going so well. She'd been cool and collected and she'd been enjoying the party hugely. Well, as much as anyone burning up with longing could.

She'd felt Matt's eyes on her the entire evening, making her heart thump with a weird kind of anticipation and her body tingle. How she'd managed to hold any kind of sensible conversation was a miracle. At one point she'd even let out a low groan and had had to quickly turn it into a cough, which had been mortifying.

But by and large she'd kept herself under control.

Until Matt had started to make his way over and her self-possession had begun to slip away like silk over skin.

The closer he'd got, the harder she'd found it to move. Her feet seemed to have taken root. She'd lost track of the conversation going on around her. All she'd been aware of was Matt heading towards her, his expression turning grimmer by the second as yet another person engaged him in conversation, until he'd finally stopped in front of her, vibrating with an electric kind of tension that had her entire body buzzing.

And all she'd been able to think was who exactly was meant to be shaking up whom?

He ushered her through the doors and across the hall. He opened the door opposite, practically pushed her in, followed her and then closed it behind him. At the sudden silence after the vibrant noise of the party the edginess winding through her tripled. Her heart hammered and a flutter of nerves clutched at her stomach.

'Did you really bring me here to look at the ceiling?' she said, her voice sounding thick and husky and totally unlike hers.

'What do you think?' Matt's eyes glittered as he moved past her and switched on the table lamp. Soft golden light bathed the room and Laura glanced up.

'I think it isn't vaulted and doesn't need any restoration.'

The glimmer of a smile played at his lips. 'So I lied.'

'Tut tut.'

Matt turned, shoved his hands in his pockets and

stared at her until her bones began to melt. 'You wanted to know what was wrong.'

Had she? When? Oh, yes. Just before the madness had taken over. 'I did,' she said, fervently hoping he wasn't going to launch into an attack on her work or something.

'You're what's wrong.'

Her heart lurched. 'Me?' That was almost as bad.

'You.'

'Why?'

'You drive me to distraction.'

Oh. Laura went dizzy for a second with the lust that shot through her. And then the knowledge that she'd been completely and utterly hoist by her own petard slammed into her. For a second the room spun. Shock ricocheted right through her. Swiftly followed by a deluge of relief and then everything suddenly fell into place.

She'd tried and tried to deny her attraction to Matt and she was sick of it. Sick of feeling constantly on edge and jumpy. She wanted Matt. So badly. And it seemed he wanted her, too.

The realisation was too much to resist and beneath the heat of his gaze the fragile barriers she'd tried to erect to protect herself came crashing down. What harm could just once more do? 'Well, that goes both ways.'

'Does it?' he murmured, his gaze dropping to her mouth.

'Oh, yes.'

Matt tilted his head. 'So what do you think we should do about it?'

She knew exactly what she wanted to do about it, but the whole bump-on-the-head/kiss misunderstanding that afternoon in his house suddenly flew into her head and made her pause. 'What do *you* think?'

'I think we should get it out of our systems.' He took a step towards her, his eyes gleaming, and her pulse thudded.

What an excellent idea. 'How?'

'You know perfectly well how.'

Her heart began to gallop. 'I thought you didn't mix business with pleasure.'

'I don't.'

'So what's this?'

'I don't employ you. The state does.'

Thank heavens for that. 'Good point. So when do you think we should set about getting it out of our systems?'

'What's wrong with now?'

Thrills scurried through her. 'There are hundreds of people on the other side of the corridor,' she said a little breathlessly.

'I locked the door,' he said, taking another step towards her.

'Won't you be missed?'

'I doubt it.' His eyes glittered as he stared down at her. 'I, on the other hand, have really missed this.'

Matt closed the short distance between them took her in his arms, bent his head and dropped a kiss on the skin where her neck met her shoulder. Her whole body jerked as if she'd been branded.

'Oh, God, so have I,' she said, feeling her knees begin to buckle as the last tiny remnant of her resistance crumbled.

As Matt slid his mouth up her neck Laura felt herself melt against him and clutched at his shoulders.

'You look amazing. You feel amazing,' he breathed against her jaw.

So did he. A tremble ran through her. 'This is insane,' she murmured.

'I know.'

Matt's mouth found hers and captured it in a slow scorching kiss that frazzled her brain. Laura moaned. Wound her fingers through his hair and pressed herself closer. She felt him slip his hands down her body and she began to burn.

And then went cold when Matt suddenly stopped and swore softly. 'What?' she said as disappointment thundered through her. Surely he couldn't be having second thoughts? Not now.

'You're not wearing any underwear.'

The disappointment vanished beneath a flood of relief. 'Clingy dress.'

And then she couldn't say anything more even if she'd wanted to because Matt had slammed his mouth down on hers and was backing her up against the nearest wall and pinning her against it with his hips, one hand in her hair, the other on her breast.

Feeling desperation begin to take hold, Laura delved beneath his jacket, tugged at his shirt and pulled it from the waistband of his trousers. She ran her fingers over the skin of his back and felt a shudder rip through him. Unable to help herself, she pressed harder against the steely length of his erection and rubbed against it.

And then he was pushing her dress up, sliding a hand round to where she was hot and wet and aching, and pressing the heel of his palm against her.

Laura shook with need as she fumbled with the button of his trousers. She yanked the zip down, ran her hand over him and urged him towards her. Matt let out a rough groan, then put a hand over hers and pulled back.

She blinked. What now?

'Don't,' he said, his voice tight with barely restrained need.

'Why not?'

'Because if this is going to go any further we need to go upstairs to my room and I won't be able to walk.'

'Why do we need to go upstairs?' said Laura, not caring that she sounded desperate. 'I don't need a bed. I'm perfectly happy with a wall.'

'And an unplanned pregnancy?' Matt said, his eyes blazing down at her as he stepped back.

'Oh.' Laura bit her lip and tugged her dress down. An unplanned pregnancy was the last thing she needed. But still... 'God, I wish I was irresponsible.'

'So do I,' he said, adjusting his clothing. 'But luckily we don't have to be, because upstairs I have condoms.' Taking her hand, Matt marched her across the room, unlocked the door and flung it open.

And came face to face with Signore Capelli, who was standing there, his hand raised as if about to knock.

Laura's heart banged in shock. And then lurched with something else when Matt dropped her hand as if it were a hot coal and sprang away from her. She glanced at him. Saw his face had turned to stone. Then she glanced at Signore Capelli who was decidedly not looking at her, and she felt herself grow beetroot at the thought of the damage Matt's hands must have done to her hair. What must he be thinking?

'Yes?' Matt growled.

'I apologise for disturbing you, sir,' said Signore Capelli, looking cool and unperturbed, as if he encountered this sort of situation all the time, 'but you're needed in the ballroom.'

Matt shoved his hands through his hair and bit out a sigh. Then he turned to Laura, his eyes blazing. 'Stay here,' he said. 'I'll be right back.'

But by the time Matt got back, Laura had gone.

CHAPTER NINE

LAURA was cursing Matt beneath her breath and punching the pillows on her bed when the hairs on the back of her neck sprang to attention and alerted her to the fact that she wasn't alone. Her heart suddenly thundering, she whirled around and nearly swooned.

Matt stood in the doorway, his big body tight with tension and his eyes glittering. His bow tie hung loose around his neck and a couple of his shirt buttons were undone. He looked dishevelled, exhausted and utterly gorgeous.

'I asked you to wait,' he said roughly.

What did he have to sound annoyed about? Laura thought, her stomach churning with pique, frustration and disappointment. She was the one who'd been left hanging there. Waiting. Listening to the heavy tick-tock of the grandfather clock and going slowly insane. 'Don't you ever knock?'

'No.'

'You should. It's rude.'

'I asked you to wait. You left. I don't think you should be lecturing me on rudeness.' His eyes glittered. 'What happened? Changed your mind?'

As if. She clutched a pillow to her stomach as if it might somehow provide some kind of defence against his potent magnetism. 'I did wait,' said Laura witheringly. 'For over an hour.'

There was a brief silence. Then Matt frowned. 'It wasn't as long as that.'

'Yes, it was.' Obviously he'd been so caught up in whatever it was he'd been doing that he'd completely forgotten about her. Exactly as she'd suspected.

'Oh,' he muttered, rubbing his face. 'I'm sorry, I got tied up.'

'Evidently,' she said waspishly, the hurt still stinging. 'So what do you want?'

His gaze dropped to her chest, where she was pretty sure he'd be able to see the curve of her breasts beneath the fine silk of her negligee and she tossed the pillow onto the bed to cross her arms over her chest.

'What do you think?' he said, stepping into the room, his eyes darkening. 'We have unfinished business.'

Her gaze dropped to below his belt and her mouth went dry at the impressive bulge behind the zip. Laura gave herself a quick shake, swallowed hard and lifted her chin. 'No, we don't.' She arched an eyebrow. Gave him a smile. 'At least *I* don't.' The minute she'd got to her suite, she'd stripped, marched into the bathroom and had had a hot, steamy, extremely satisfying shower. Steam and the scent of roses still billowed from room. Her cheeks were still pink. Her body still hummed.

For a second Matt just stared at her as the implication of her words sank in and his eyebrows crept up. 'Oh,' he said softly, giving her a slow smile that made her tingle all over again. 'I'm sorry I missed that.'

'So am I.'

'We'll just have to start again. Because look what I found.'

He strode across the marble floor, stopped a foot from

her and tossed a box onto the bed. Out spilled condoms. Lots of them. Laura stared down at them, back up at him and her pulse began to race.

'Oh.'

'Quite.' And then he frowned. '*Did* you change your mind?'

He sounded uncertain all of a sudden and pique evaporated. 'Of course not,' she said, giving him a smile that she hoped didn't reveal her relief too much. 'I just got bored of waiting.'

'Good.' Matt pulled her into his arms. 'Now where were we?' he said, staring down at her and a wicked smile curving his mouth. 'Oh, yes, I remember.'

He slid his hands down her body, bunched the silk in his fingers and lifted it. Laura raised her arms and let her bare breasts brush against his chest as he drew it up and over her head. She heard him take a sharp breath, then felt him give her shoulders a little push and she fell back on the bed.

Her breath shot from her lungs as she landed and then vanished all over again as Matt began to whip his clothes off. He pulled off his bow tie and tossed it on the floor. Seconds later his jacket and shirt joined it, followed by his trousers and shorts, and desire began to hammer through her.

Oh, God. His body was truly magnificent. The first time they'd had sex she'd been so desperate that there hadn't been time to savour and learn. And then up against the wall earlier this evening she'd barely had time to reacquaint herself with it.

But that was going to change, she vowed, her head swimming as she ran her gaze down him, over the broad chest, the flat stomach, lean hips, powerful thighs and finally lingering on the gloriously thick hard length of his erection.

Laura swallowed and shuddered as a bolt of longing gripped her. This time they'd take it slowly. Touch and taste and linger and eke out every drop of pleasure.

'Are you ogling me?' Matt murmured and Laura realised he'd been standing there watching her watching him for goodness knew how long.

'Certainly am,' she replied, biting on her lip to stop herself from whimpering.

He looked down at her, his eyes gleaming as they roamed over her.

'What are you doing?' she breathed, half wondering why he wasn't launching himself at her.

'Returning the compliment.'

Her body burned and she dragged in a shaky breath. 'Oh, OK.'

'Of course,' he mused, sinking onto the bed beside her and trailing his fingers over her cheek, down her neck, over her upper chest and then cupping her breast. 'It would be better if I had a pair of binoculars.'

Laura shivered and felt the muscles of her abdomen contract. 'Would it? Why?'

'Then I could ogle you from behind the curtains the way you were ogling me.'

'I was not ogling you,' she said weakly, swallowing and trying not to drown in the pleasure shooting through her.

'You were watching me for half an hour,' he murmured.

'Five minutes. At the most.'

'Fifteen. At the least.'

Laura sighed and closed her eyes and gave in. 'Well,

if you will insist on going around without your shirt on, what do you expect?'

'I was in my own garden,' he said against her ear. 'I have every right to go around without my shirt on. Or anything if I feel like it,' he added, dropping a trail of kisses along her jaw.

Lust began to pound through her. 'That's true.'

'I'd never have you pegged as a voyeur,' he muttered, his mouth moving lower, dropping a trail of kisses down her neck and over the top of her breasts. 'Who knew?'

'So arrest me.'

She gasped as his mouth closed over her nipple. Pleasure spun through her, arrowing down straight to the centre of her, and for a second she lost all track of the conversation.

He lifted his head. 'I would if I could remember where I put my handcuffs,' he said, switching his attention to her other breast.

Laura's entire body began to buzz and desire hammered at her with an insistence that demanded attention. Oh, forget slow and sensual. She just wanted him thrusting inside her. Right now.

Wrapping a leg around his calves, she urged him up, wound her arms around his neck and kissed him hard and deep. Tilted her hips and ground them against him, desperate for release. The shower had been good, but now she wanted the real thing.

Matt, however, clearly had other ideas. He lifted his head, breathing raggedly, his eyes blazing. 'What's the hurry?' he murmured.

What was the hurry? Laura bit her lip. She was on the point of exploding. That was the hurry. And then mortification swept down to mingle with the desire pummelling through her and she forced herself back under control.

'No hurry,' she managed thickly. 'I just thought, you know, you might be uncomfortable. In pain. Or something.'

'So altruistic.'

'That's me. Always thinking of others.'

'I hope not,' Matt said, lifting an eyebrow. 'I don't want you to be thinking about anyone but me.'

'Ah,' she said. 'Well, that's up to you.'

Matt's eyes flashed. 'Is that a challenge?'

'Maybe.'

'I like challenges.'

'Excellent,' she breathed and sighed with delight as he shifted down her body, spread her legs and settled himself between her thighs. At the touch of his mouth at her molten centre, she nearly leapt off the bed.

Oh, God. Forget thinking about anyone else. Forget thinking full stop. At the sheer force of the pleasure shooting through her, her brain shut down. Every drop of her conscious thought zoomed in on his mouth, his lips, his tongue and what they were doing to her.

Her heart thundered. Her hands clutched at the sheets and then tangled in his hair. She lifted her hips, couldn't stop her back arching as all the pleasure churning around inside her sharpened, shot to her core and then splintered.

Laura cried out as she broke apart. Felt a sob rise in her throat as Matt gripped her hips, tormenting her still further, sucking and licking at her, drawing out every tiny drop of pleasure as shudders continued to rack her body.

Matt moved up her, covering her still quivery body

entirely with his. 'Still thinking of others?' he muttered, his eyes blazing as they bore into hers.

Laura couldn't speak, just shook her head.

'Good.' And then a wicked gleam lit the depths of his eyes. 'Maybe I'd better make sure, just in case.'

Oh, God. Could she take any more? Surely it wasn't possible. Surely her body needed time to recover? But already she could feel herself softening and ripening and humming with renewed desire. 'That might be wise,' she said, finally regaining the power of speech, albeit a soft and breathy one.

'I'm delighted you agree.'

His mouth found hers and as he kissed her he stroked a hand down her body, over the damp triangle of curls at the juncture of her legs and slid a finger deep inside her.

Laura gasped into his kiss and felt herself clench around him.

'Unbelievable,' he muttered against her mouth.

'Incredible,' she panted.

'That, too.'

As he stroked her waves of pleasure began to roll over her. Unable to resist, she lifted her hips and pressed herself harder against him. Her breathing shallowed. Sped up. A ball of tension swelled and tightened inside her. Her heart thundered.

She felt Matt reach over, faintly heard the rustle of foil and then he was on top of her, pushing her knees even farther apart and driving into her.

Laura groaned in desperation. Her legs wrapped around his waist, pulling him farther inside her, and her hands tangled in his hair.

With every thrust of his body, every scorching kiss, he pushed her higher. Mindless with need, Laura tilted her hips to take him deeper. She could feel the tension in him too, the focus, as he pounded harder and faster into her.

And then just when she thought she couldn't bear the clawing desperation any longer, he pulled out of her and drove into her one last time, deeper than he had ever before.

Laura shattered. A tidal wave of pure pleasure crashed over her as her orgasm hit and rippled out along every single one of her nerve endings. A second later Matt let out a rough groan and collapsed on top of her.

As she floated back down to earth she became aware of his heart thundering against hers, his breath harsh and fast against her neck, and something inside her chest squeezed.

But before she could work out what it was Matt was propping himself up on his elbows to take his weight and lowering his head to give her a long slow devastating kiss that wiped her mind.

'Like I said,' he murmured, gazing down at her as he gave her a faint smile, 'unbelievable.'

Despite that thing in her chest squeezing even tighter, Laura couldn't help a satisfied smile creeping across her face. Matt gently withdrew from her and rolled onto his back to deal with the condom, then pulled her on top of him and tugged the sheet up over them.

'You know, I've never slept with a king before,' she said, her gaze roaming over the lines of his face.

'I should hope not,' said Matt dryly. 'Most of them are over sixty.'

He trailed his hands over her back and she could feel her skin tingle. She folded her arms on his chest and rested her chin on her wrists. 'How old are you?'

'Thirty-three.'

'Pretty young to become king.'

'I guess.'

'How did it all come about?'

He frowned and the fingers creating havoc on her back stilled. 'Do we have to discuss this now?'

'Why not?'

'Because there are lots of other things we could be doing.'

That was true, she thought, feeling him stirring against her abdomen and beginning to slide beneath the surface of the desire that was sweeping through her. It would be so easy to just give in. Especially with the way Matt's hands had moved lower and were now stroking her bottom and sending tingles all the way round to her core.

But she wanted to know about him. Had done for weeks, and to absolutely no avail. Matt was as chatty as a clam. Torquemada himself would have trouble getting Matt to open up, and God knew she was no Torquemada. But now, with him trapped beneath her, all relaxed and amenable and perhaps prepared to lower his guard a fraction, maybe she did have a chance. And who knew, it might be her only opportunity.

Ruthlessly quashing the desire whipping through her, Laura called into service a hitherto dormant will of steel and reached behind her to remove his hands from her bottom. 'Not right now,' she said, placing them either side of his head and keeping them there with hers. 'You know pretty much everything there is to know about me, yet I know virtually nothing about you.'

Matt frowned. That wasn't true, was it? She knew... Hmm. So maybe it was, but that was understandable. He was reserved. And why wouldn't he be, what with journalists constantly hounding him for his life story?

'So read the papers,' he said.

'But I have such a reliable source right here,' she said, looking up at him from beneath her eyelashes and giving him a seductive smile.

If he had any sense whatsoever he'd be levering himself up and heading back to his own room, because Matt didn't do post-coital conversation. Or any conversation of a personal nature, for that matter.

However his body wanted more of her. Much more. He wanted to watch her shatter in his arms again. Wanted to shatter in her arms.

Hmm. Maybe he could dispense with a few facts and then turn his talents to persuading her to find another use for her mouth.

'Fine,' he said. 'My favourite colour is blue.' Cornflower blue, he thought, looking into her eyes and momentarily losing his train of thought. 'My favourite food is chilli and I don't have time for hobbies. Anything else?'

Her eyebrows shot up. 'Are you kidding?' she said softly.

'What do you want to know? Ask me anything.' Whether he'd choose to answer was another matter entirely.

Laura tilted her head on his chest. 'OK,' she said slowly. 'Seeing as you're such a novice at this sort of thing, we'll start with my original question. How did you become king?'

Matt relaxed. That was an easy enough question to answer. 'Six months ago a Sassanian delegate showed up at my office and offered me the job.'

'Just like that?'

'Pretty much.' It hadn't been quite that simple. At first he'd almost summoned security to remove what he'd thought was a madman. But after the delegate had persuaded him to listen, Matt had wasted no time in accepting. His business was well established and so successful that it practically ran itself and, to be honest, he'd been getting a bit restless. The visit from the Sassanian delegate couldn't have come along at a better time.

'Did you know you were heir to the throne?'

'Of course, but my family had been in exile so long we'd more or less forgotten about it.'

'So what happened?'

'They had a coup.'

'Nasty.'

Matt twined his fingers through hers and felt her shiver. 'Actually, not too bad as coups go. It was bloodless. I think the country had come to the end of the road and everyone knew it. It had been in steady decline for years. It was socially, financially and morally bankrupt. Corruption was rife. It still is. Public services are virtually non-existent.'

'And it's down to you to sort it out?'

'Sorting out problems is what I do.'

'Handy.' A smile curved her lips and Matt's stomach tightened.

'Not really,' he said. 'I was told I was the main reason why they voted to restore the monarchy.'

Her eyes widened. 'That sounds pretty drastic. Couldn't they have just employed you as a consultant or something instead?'

'They wouldn't have been able to afford me. This way they get me for free.'

'So cynical.'

'I prefer realistic.' At the look of affront in her eyes on his behalf, something inside him thawed. 'But if it makes you feel better,' he said, faintly bewildered by the feeling, 'I believe they thought a figurehead would unite the country and restore confidence.'

'So no pressure, then.'

'Fortunately I thrive under pressure.'

'What's the plan?'

'I cut out the dead wood and restructure the finances.'

'Sounds simple.'

Matt thought of all the problems he'd already encountered in the short time he'd been here. 'It isn't.'

'How's it going?'

'Slowly.'

'How does it feel?'

'Feel?'

Laura nodded, watched a frown appear on his forehead and felt him tense. Matt clearly didn't do feelings, at least not of the emotional kind. Well, that was tough, because she was on a roll, and frankly rather stunned by how much he'd divulged, even if it had been all fact based. No way was she giving up now.

'How does what feel?' he muttered.

'The king thing.'

'It doesn't feel anything.'

Matt's expression shuttered but she carried on undeterred.

'It must feel something,' she said cajolingly. 'I don't know, exhilarating, nerve-racking, weighty… Maybe even a little bit scary?'

Matt regarded her thoughtfully, his eyes unfathomable as he appeared to analyse the emotions she'd listed. 'I guess it's challenging,' he said eventually.

Challenging? 'That's it?'

'That's it.'

'Oh.'

'Don't sound so disappointed,' he said, a smile tugging at his mouth. 'You know how much I like challenges.'

'Oh, I do,' said Laura, her eyes darkening and her breathing shallowing for a second before she remembered what she was supposed to be doing and giving herself a quick shake. 'So what have you done with your business?'

'What do you mean?'

'Well, presumably you can't run a business and run a country.'

'I still have it. I've simply taken a step back.'

'Until you decide what you want to do with it?'

'Quite,' he said non-committally.

'And what are you going to do about your house?'

'Which one?'

'How many do you have?'

'A few.'

Naturally. 'I mean the one in Little Somerford.'

'I'm not going to do anything about it.'

'Oh.' She frowned.

'What?'

'Well, I know it's your house and it's really none of my business, but it does seem a shame to leave such a lovely house empty and neglected.'

She felt his heart thump. 'It's not neglected. A gardener goes in twice a week and I employ a part-time caretaker.'

'OK,' said Laura, nibbling on her lip and ignoring the feeling she might be treading on eggshells. 'Maybe neglected isn't quite the right word. Unloved would be better.'

'Unloved?' He frowned. 'It's a house. It doesn't need to be loved.'

She gasped and gave him a quick smile. 'Wash your mouth out. All buildings deserve to be loved. How long have you had it?'

'Eight years.'

'And how much time have you spent there?'

'Not a lot.'

'That would explain the emotional neglect.'

His expression tightened. 'I'm busy.'

'That's no excuse.' Laura sniffed. 'I bet you wouldn't let one of your businesses slide into neglect.'

'True. But then I'm not looking to make a profit on the house.'

'Just as well. You know,' she mused, 'if I owned something like that I wouldn't be able to stay away.'

'Unfortunately I don't have that luxury,' he murmured, his gaze dropping to her mouth.

'It breaks my heart to see something like that drifting into decline. If you're not going to maintain it, and if you're hardly ever there, what's the point of having it?'

Matt lifted his gaze. 'I like having it.'

Her eyes widened. 'It's a status symbol?'

His eyes went bleak and Laura's heart squeezed. 'If you like,' he said.

'Oh, the poor thing,' she murmured. 'No wonder it was so lonely.'

'Lonely?' His tone suggested he thought she was nuts.

'Yes, lonely. A house like that should be alive. Filled with laughter and activity and a family. There should be hordes of children running all over the place.'

He tensed and she sensed barriers springing up all around him. 'Perhaps.'

'Do you have any family?'

'Not much. I'm an only child. My father died of cancer when I was sixteen. My mother lives in London.'

'Don't *you* get lonely?'

He froze beneath her. 'No,' he said gruffly. 'I'm better off alone.'

Her chest tightened at the bleak look that haunted his eyes. 'That's sad,' she said softly.

And then he rolled over, trapping her beneath him and Laura's heart began to thump and her breath began to quicken. 'So make it better,' he muttered, lowering his head and covering her mouth with his.

Matt watched Laura sleeping. Stared at the fingers of moonlight turning her blond hair to silver and listened as her breath whispered across his chest.

And with every rise of her breasts, every fall, every soft breath he felt another tiny strand of his carefully controlled life unravel.

Dammit, how could he have been so careless? What was it about Laura that had him lowering his guard and revealing so much about himself like that?

He didn't do feelings. Hadn't done for years. He didn't need her making him question decisions he'd made years ago. So why was he?

Why did she have him suddenly doubting his role on Sassania? His belief he was better off alone? And what was all that nonsense about his house needing to be loved?

Matt's heart hardened and he told himself not to be so absurd. His role on Sassania was clear. He liked being alone. And just because he hadn't ever got round to sorting out the house he'd bought intending to live in it with a wife and family, it didn't mean anything.

Laura and her pseudo-psychiatry could take a hike. He really didn't need it. He was fine the way he was.

So why did he find himself wanting to tell her *more*?

Matt's heart thudded and his blood ran cold. Feeling highly unsettled, he eased himself from beneath her arm, swung his legs over the bed and got up. He pulled on his clothes and ran his hands through his hair.

Staring down at her as her mouth twitched in her sleep, he fought the urge to throw his clothes off and get back into bed with her, and picked up his shoes.

That kind of thinking led to madness.

He needed time to regroup. Regain some sort of control and decide what the hell to do about everything.

Work was the solution, he thought, heading to the door and sanity. Work was *always* the solution. And as neither Laura nor the attraction he seemed to have to her showed any signs of going away, maybe it wouldn't be a bad idea to put some physical distance between them.

There was bound to be a conference going on about something somewhere in the world.

Laura felt sunshine prick her eyes, gingerly opened them and then grinned and stretched.

Wow. What a night. Every muscle in her body ached with a delicious kind of languor. In between acquainting herself with every inch of him and vice versa she'd lost count of the number of orgasms she'd had.

But the spectacular sex aside, what was giving her an even warmer glow this morning was the fact that Matt had opened up. Just a crack, but far more than she'd thought he would have done.

OK, so she'd asked the questions, and he hadn't volunteered much that she hadn't asked, but to be honest she hadn't expected him to venture anything at all. But he had and the balance in their relationship was definitely moving in her direction. Which was progress.

Laura froze mid-stretch and her heart lurched. Hang on a second? Progress? What was that all about? Since when had progress mattered? And since when did she and Matt have a relationship? The last thing she wanted was a relationship. She and Matt weren't about relationships and progress, were they? No. They were just about sex. With any luck lots of it.

In fact she might just remind him of that very thing right now.

Fizzing all over with desire, Laura rolled over, fully expecting to slam up against the hard warm naked body of Matt, but instead met nothing but cool air.

Oh. Desire vanished as she sat up and felt the pillow that still bore the indentation of his head. Cold. Hmm. So much for embarking on a raging affair right now. Matt's absence did not bode well for a long leisurely start to the day.

Nor did the note she suddenly spied on the bedside table. Clutching the sheet and wrapping it beneath her arms, she rolled over, picked it up and then fell back against the pillows.

Gone to Athens. Didn't want to wake you.

Laura read the note twice. Not that she needed to when the message was perfectly clear, but the first time she'd got a bit distracted admiring his handwriting and remembering the feel of his hands on her body.

But when she read it a second time the bottom fell out of her stomach and disappointment flooded through her.

Gone to Athens? Laura didn't know what to think.

Matt hadn't mentioned anything about a trip so what on earth was he doing in Athens? Especially when they'd scheduled a meeting for this afternoon to discuss the budget for the restoration work.

And why hadn't he wanted to wake her? She wouldn't have minded. Surely he hadn't had to leave so suddenly there hadn't been time for a quick goodbye. Surely she was worth more than eight words, one apostrophe and two full stops.

And after what they'd shared she deserved a kiss at the very least.

Laura's throat tightened as the note slipped from her fingers and fluttered to the bed. That wasn't fair. She wasn't forgettable. She wasn't dispensable. And she wasn't going to have another man walk all over her.

CHAPTER TEN

So MUCH for assuming that out of sight out of mind might actually work, thought Matt grimly, striding along the corridor to his suite and scowling. Attending the conference in Athens had been a complete waste of time in that respect.

From a professional point of view it couldn't have gone better. He'd networked, held discussions and drawn up agreements.

People had congratulated him on his new role and he'd been able to answer their questions about his plans for the country, for the first time feeling confident that he knew what he was talking about.

But while all that had been going on he hadn't been able to get Laura out of his head and it was driving him demented. Much more of this tension and this aching, this clawing kind of need, and he'd snap. He'd start making mistakes and the Sassanians would wonder what the hell they'd done in voting in favour of him to restore their battered country.

Maybe he should just give in and suggest a fling. A fling didn't mean a relationship, did it? A fling just meant lots of the mind-blowing sex he'd been missing and very little conversation.

Matt stalked into his dressing room, yanking his tie

off and undoing the top button of his shirt. He flung his jacket over the back of a chair and kicked off his shoes. A cold shower. That was what he needed. And then he'd seek her out, put his proposal to her and see what she had to say.

He undid the buttons of his shirt, tugged it from his trousers and marched through to his bedroom.

And stopped dead.

Laura was standing by the French doors that opened onto his private terrace, the sun streaming in behind her giving her a blazing kind of corona.

For a second Matt thought he was hallucinating. That somehow his feverish imagination was playing tricks on him.

But then she jumped, her gazed dipped to his bare chest and she let out a little gasp and from the heat that suddenly whipped through him Matt realised she was no hallucination.

Which, on reflection, was great. He was so hard it hurt. Whatever the reason she was in his bedroom, her timing couldn't be more perfect.

'Good trip?' she said, the ice in her voice slamming a brake on his thoughts.

Hmm. Matt went still. Perhaps suggesting a fling at right this moment might not be wise. With the hostility rolling off her in his direction, he'd probably get a slap in the face.

'Great,' he said, wondering why she was quite so frosty.

'I'm so glad.'

'What are you doing in my bedroom?'

'Waiting for you. I heard you were back.'

'I was just about to take a shower,' he said, taking his shirt off and seeing her little white teeth catch her lip.

'Why did you leave without saying goodbye?'

That was what the hostility was about? Matt rubbed his jaw. He'd left without saying goodbye because he hadn't been able to trust himself not to get all caught up again in the spell she'd woven over him. He'd done it for all the right reasons, but that didn't stop the trace of hurt in her voice making a stab of guilt dart through him.

'Didn't you get my note?'

'I did.'

Matt shoved the guilt aside. 'That explained everything.'

'Eight words, Matt. Eight words. After the night we shared do you really think they explained everything?'

Well, yes, he did. He couldn't have put it more simply. 'I didn't want to wake you.'

'I wouldn't have minded.'

But he would have.

'You want to know what I think?' she said, tilting her head and shooting him a shrewd glance.

Not really. He had no intention of discussing his motives for hurtling off to Athens. 'What?' he said, because she was probably going to tell him anyway.

'I think you were avoiding me.'

The air in the room thickened. Grew warmer. Tighter. Matt's eyes narrowed. How had she managed to work that out? 'Nonsense,' he said flatly.

'Is it?'

'Why would I be avoiding you?'

'That's what I haven't been able to work out.'

Matt shrugged. 'There's nothing to work out. The opportunity to attend the conference in Athens to discuss alternative sources of energy simply cropped up at the last minute, that's all.'

'That's what Antonio said. Very last minute apparently.'

'It was important.'

'More important than our meeting to discuss the cost of the work I'm doing?'

Ah. Matt went still. He was caught between a rock and a hard place. If he agreed, he'd upset her, and that wouldn't be conducive to persuading her to have a fling, but if he denied it then she'd really wonder why he'd gone.

'You're right,' he said, deciding that focusing on her earlier concerns was his only way out. It had the added benefit of appeasing his conscience. 'I should have said goodbye. I'm sorry I didn't.'

Laura frowned. 'Waking up alone didn't feel nice. It made everything we'd done seem a bit sordid.'

God. Sordid was the last thing it had been. 'I'm sorry,' he said again. 'Anything I can do to remedy the situation just let me know.'

Laura nodded and bit her lip. 'There is something you could do.'

'What?'

She tilted her head and gave him a slow smile that had relief spinning through him and his heart hammering. 'Give me my goodbye kiss now.'

Matt's body tightened with anticipation and lust. 'I could do that. But I should warn you that it probably wouldn't stop there.'

Her eyes took on a sparkle that he felt in the pit of his stomach. 'I was kind of counting on it.'

'What were you thinking of?' He knew what he was thinking of.

'Sex. Illicit sex. And lots of it. Without any strings attached whatsoever.'

Matt's pulse began to thunder. 'Are you sure?' She really didn't seem the type.

'I've never been surer of anything. With my relationship history I don't want strings and I don't want complications. A relationship is the last thing on the planet I need right now. I find them stifling and suffocating and I feel like I've just started to learn how to breathe. So all I want from you is multiple orgasms. What do you think?'

What did he think? His head was so fuzzy he could barely think at all. Because, God, she really was perfect. 'I think it's an excellent idea,' he said hoarsely.

'Good.' She gave him a sexy little smile that had lust pounding through him. 'So about that shower you mentioned...'

It was a good thing Laura hadn't been planning to finish that sentence because as Matt suddenly sprang forwards and scooped her up in his arms her breath whooshed from her lungs and lust robbed her of the power of speech.

She'd taken such a gamble. Offering herself to him for nothing more than a fling like that. It was so reckless. So uncharacteristic. But she was sick of being sensible. She'd been there, done that, and had still ended up dumped and jobless and miserable.

And what was so awful about a fling anyway? She'd spent the entire week that Matt had been away thinking about it. Weighing up the pros and cons and driving herself to distraction with her endless analysis.

In the end she'd thought what the hell? A fling was

temporary. A fling was hot. Best of all a fling was not a relationship.

And now, thank God, it looked as if her gamble was about to pay off. In spades.

Wrapping her arms around Matt's neck, she clung on for dear life as he carried her across the room to the bathroom. His heart hammered against her shoulder. She could feel his muscles taut and tense and rippling with the effort of carrying her. Gazed at all that bare brown skin in such close proximity and couldn't resist planting a hot wet kiss to the pulse pounding at the base of his neck.

Matt swore softly and his arms tightened around her. A shudder ripped through her. She felt an answering one run through him. So she did it again.

He shoved a shoulder against the bathroom door and lowered her to her feet. Clamped one arm around her waist to keep her against him, and reached out with the other to switch on the shower.

Bringing his mouth down on hers, he unzipped her dress, slid the straps down her arms and it fell in a pool at her feet. Laura kicked it aside and grappled with his trousers. Matt unclipped her bra and it fell to the floor. And then off came knickers and shorts and he was backing her into the shower.

Laura gasped as needles of water hammered down over her, making her already highly sensitised skin tingle and fizzle even more. And then his mouth was on hers again and his hands were sliding over her back, up and down her sides and over her breasts.

He reached for the soap but she took it from him and gave him a tiny smile.

'Let me. All that travelling must have been quite exhausting.'

'It wasn't the travelling.'

'You didn't really go all the way to Athens just to discuss alternative sources of energy, did you?'

'No.'

Hah. She'd been so right. He *had* been avoiding her.

A flicker of amusement flared in his eyes. 'I also discussed the possibility of raising finance via the issuance of government bonds.'

'Oh.'

'And if this is what I can expect on my return I must do it more often.'

If that was what he wanted to pretend, she was fine with that. Laura grinned. 'Turn around.'

The flicker of amusement faded. 'Only a fool would turn his back on such a dangerous smile.'

'I'm only armed with shower gel. I'm hardly dangerous.'

'You think?' he murmured.

A tiny crease appeared between his brows and she lifted a hand to smooth it away. 'I promise I'll be gentle. Turn around.'

Matt's eyes glittered but he did as she asked and planted his hands high on the wall.

Faced with the sexiest back view she'd ever seen, Laura swallowed. She squeezed a ball of gel into her palms and then pressed her hands to his shoulders. Rubbing and squeezing and pressing, she massaged her way over his shoulders, down his back. Touching and exploring every inch of him, every dip, every contour.

She felt his skin tighten, felt his muscles clench as her hands moved over his body. The water cascaded down him, sending the suds rippling to the floor. As inch after inch of glorious back was revealed, Laura put her hands on his arms and moved forwards so that her mouth could follow the same trail as her hands had just made.

Her breasts brushed against his back. She heard his sharp intake of breath, felt him brace himself. As desire began to whip through her Laura slid her hands down his sides, curved one round his waist and wrapped her fingers around the hard length of his erection.

His penis leapt beneath her touch, and as she started to move her hand along the length of him he let out a low groan. His great body shook as she explored him. She felt him shudder, heard his breathing roughen.

Removing her hand, she stood up on her tiptoes and whispered in his ear, 'Turn around.'

'If I do, I might not be responsible for the consequences.'

'I'll take full responsibility,' she said huskily, moving back a little, giving him room to turn.

And then she gave him no room at all. Pushing him up against the glass wall, she began to kiss her way down his body. His skin twitched beneath her lips and when she knelt and took him in her mouth, he groaned.

'God, Laura,' he said roughly as she ran her hands over his thighs.

His hands dug into her hair and she felt him shudder as she took him deeper. She heard him moan, curse softly, could sense the battle raging within him as he clung on to control.

She wanted him to lose it. She wanted him as desperate for her as she was for him. But then he was pulling her head back and hauling her to her feet and gathering her into his arms. 'Enough,' he muttered, his eyes blazing into hers and making the desire swirling around inside her grow and spread and burn.

'Not nearly,' Laura said, winding her arms around his

neck and kissing him fiercely as he switched the water off and lifted her into his arms.

But when *would* be enough?

The thought hammered in Matt's head as he strode to the bed with Laura curled in his arms. Because right now, with desire coursing through him, his head pounding and his entire body aching with need, he didn't think he'd ever get enough of her.

He lowered her onto the sheets and stared down at her for a second. Her lips were red and swollen from their kiss. Her eyes shone and the smile she was giving him made something in the region of his chest squeeze.

The blood rushing through his head, Matt sank onto the bed beside her. But as he rolled on top of her Laura wound her leg around his and rolled them over again so that she was on top of him.

'Forget the travelling,' she said, giving him a demure little smile that made his stomach clench. 'Carrying me all over the place must be utterly draining.'

'You don't weigh much.'

She shrugged. 'Indulge me. I've had plenty of opportunity to Embrace Confrontation and say no. But I think my "getting what I want" needs more work and right now I want you to just lie back and let me have my wicked way with you.'

Desire hammered through him. 'Oh. Well, in that case, it would be churlish of me to interfere with your journey to self-discovery.'

'Precisely.'

'In fact you can practise on me all you like.'

'You're too kind,' she said, lowering her head and brushing her lips against his. So tantalisingly brief Matt's heart practically stopped.

'Not kind,' he muttered. 'Totally selfish.'

Then she angled her head, set her lips to his and slipped her tongue into his mouth and his blood began to boil. Matt tangled his hand into her wet hair and swept the other down her back over her bottom to pull her tightly against him.

She went still for a second, moaned and then began to move. He felt himself growing harder against her. So hard he was hurting. Matt winced at the ferocity of the ache that gripped him.

'Are you all right?' Laura breathed against his mouth.

'I'm not entirely sure.'

'Where do you hurt?'

'Why?' What was she going to do? Torment him further?

'Maybe I can kiss you better.' Oh, yes, definitely torment him further.

'For God's sake, Laura,' he muttered. 'I'm not made of stone.'

'So I can tell.'

He gripped her head and kissed her so long, so thoroughly and so hard he couldn't think straight.

'Condoms,' she gasped.

Thank God someone was still faintly in possession of their faculties. 'In the drawer.'

She leaned away from him, fumbled for a second, then rolled one over him. Nearly passing out with the effort of not climaxing right then and there, Matt gritted his teeth and lifted her onto him.

Laura moaned and bit her lip and Matt's hands curled into fists with the strain of letting her take charge. She closed her eyes and rotated her hips and panted. Matt's head swam. His penis throbbed deep inside her. His heart thundered and as her pants became quicker, shorter, more and more ragged, her movements jerkier and more out of control, he couldn't stand it any longer.

Rearing up, he clasped her against him and flipped her over. Swallowing her gasp of shock he anchored her legs around his waist and mindlessly drove into her.

Shock flashed in her eyes and then vanished as they glazed over with passion. Laura's nails raked his back as he kissed her. She clutched at his shoulders. Threw her head back and groaned. He swallowed her whimpers and broke off the kiss to explore the soft skin of her neck with his mouth.

Clinging on to his control by his fingertips and on the point of losing his mind, Matt pulled out of her and then thrust again, utterly unable to stop himself from burying himself as deep inside her as he could.

And then he heard her cry out his name as shudders racked her body. She convulsed around him, drawing him in deeper and tighter. With that last remnant of control spiralling off, Matt drove into her once more and hurtled into oblivion.

It took several minutes for his heart to slow and his breathing to steady. When they did, it was as if the whole room had been tossed in the air and had settled differently. Almost the same but not quite.

A smugly satisfied smile curved her lips and his pulse began to speed up all over again. 'Oh, I *knew* this was a good idea.'

Matt wasn't so sure. Something suddenly made him think an affair with Laura was a very bad idea. However no-strings.

'You,' she said, fluttering her eyelashes up at him, 'are incredible.'

So was she. Pretty irresistible, too. And a dozen other things he really didn't want to think about.

'I really do have to go,' he said, leaning away from her, picking up his watch off the floor and frowning.

'Now?'

'Yes.'

'Oh. Well. Of course,' she said lightly, pulling the sheet up over her chest and tucking it beneath her arms. 'Maybe we could have lunch?'

Matt shook his head and got up. 'I have a meeting.' Lunch, or any kind of interaction that wasn't of the horizontal and naked sort for that matter, wasn't an option.

Her face fell and a flash of disappointment flickered in her eyes. 'Sure,' she said, with a smile that he thought looked a little forced. 'Fine. I guess I'll see you around, then.'

That wasn't what he'd meant, either. Feeling like a heel, Matt leaned down and gave her a long slow kiss. 'What are you doing tonight?' he said, pulling back before he could decide to cancel his meeting and spend the rest of the afternoon in bed with Laura.

'Nothing.' A relieved grin spread across her face and his heart suddenly thumped with something that felt weirdly like alarm.

'I'll see you later,' he muttered, telling himself not to be ridiculous. A casual affair with Laura was nothing to get alarmed about.

'Great.'

Except it wasn't all that great, thought Laura, sitting in the library and idly flipping through a book of old photographs and plans a fortnight later.

At first she'd been only too happy with the arrangement. It had been her idea after all, and as they'd seen each other every night since Matt had returned from

Athens she didn't really have anything to complain about. Her horizons had been broadened considerably and the sex had been getting better and better. And as a bonus, her body, having never been put to such energetic use, was more toned than ever before.

Her fling with Matt was exactly what she'd wanted. Hot hassle-free fun.

So why was it leaving her feeling increasingly dissatisfied?

Laura closed the book with a thump, sat back and frowned. Why did it hurt that he didn't ever seem to want to meet up for lunch? Or dinner, or on any of the other occasions she'd suggested? Why did it hurt that he never asked her to do anything other than spread herself across the nearest available flat surface?

When had hot casual sex become not enough?

Suddenly finding the library stifling, Laura got up and stepped out onto the terrace. The breeze caressed her skin as she wandered across the stone, leaned her elbows on the balustrade and gazed over the gardens.

Oh, God. Maybe, despite all her efforts to convince herself otherwise, she just wasn't cut out for an affair. Maybe Kate had been right, and she was more of a commitment fiend than she'd realised.

And if that *was* the case, she thought, following the path of a butterfly as it fluttered from one exotic flower to another, where did it leave her? Her mind whirred. Did that mean she *did* actually want a relationship? With Matt?

Her heart sank. God, she hoped not. Because what a disaster that would be. She could still recall the look on Matt's face when she'd suggested their fling. His relief when she'd told him she wanted nothing more from him than mind-blowing orgasms couldn't have been more transparent.

Wanting a relationship with Matt would bring nothing but pain and she'd be an idiot to hope for more than a fling.

But the more she thought about it, the more undeniable it became. And the more undeniable it became, the faster her heart plummeted.

Uh-oh.

Who'd she been trying to fool?

She *did* want more than just mind-blowing sex. She wanted to know what Matt was thinking. What he was feeling. All the time. She wanted to know what had made him the man he'd become and what his dreams were. She wanted to know how he felt about the death of his father and why he was so driven. She wanted to share her life, her dreams with him.

She wanted everything.

Which so hadn't been part of the deal.

Laura pinched the bridge of her nose and sighed. Matt would never agree to accommodate her on any of that. That night he'd spilled out all the stuff about himself had been a blip. One he clearly regretted making, judging by the way he'd vanished to the other side of Europe at first light.

Ever since then, he'd revealed absolutely nothing. And neither had she. The last thing he'd want would be her poking and prodding at his psyche.

Unless, of course, he'd been thinking the same…

No. Laura straightened and planted her hands on the balustrade. That was nuts. Nothing more than extremely wishful thinking on her part. Because she was pretty sure that Matt was *not* sitting at his desk right this second wanting to share his dreams with her and figuring out what she wanted.

That kind of thinking could only lead to heartache.

But it didn't stop her mind racing. Wondering if he *might*. Wondering what would happen if he did.

Her heart pounding, Laura set her jaw. Whatever Matt's frame of mind, whatever he might or might not be thinking, a casual fling was no longer what she wanted and she couldn't carry on pretending it was.

So she therefore had two possible courses of action. She could either take the cowardly way out and board the next plane home or she could pluck up her courage, risk everything, and ask him.

CHAPTER ELEVEN

'So how was your day?'

Matt lay back and felt a warm kind of satisfaction steal over him. His day had been tougher than most. He'd had to authorise the arrest of a number of government officials and there was a problem with the funding of the new hospital. The only thing that had kept him going had been the thought of losing himself in the soft warmth of Laura's body. And it had been every bit as amazing as he'd expected.

'Fine,' he said, rubbing his eyes and tucking her in closer.

'Surely it can't be fine every day.'

Matt sighed as a wave of fatigue washed over him. 'What do you want me to say, Laura?' he murmured against her hair. 'Do you really want to spend the time we have together discussing the intricacies of Sassanian politics?'

She wriggled away from him and propped herself up on her elbow. 'Well, why not?'

'Because, frankly, I have enough of that during the day.'

'Then maybe we could talk about something else.'

'Why do we have to talk at all?'

'Because we never talk,' she said calmly, 'and I don't think it's natural.'

We never talk. All you do is work.

Despite the lingering heat still flickering through his body, Matt's blood ran cold as echoes of Alicia's hurt-filled accusations reverberated around his head. And just like eight years ago, his brain switched into neutral and his body filled with the familiar hammering instinct to escape.

'I don't have time for this,' he muttered, throwing back the sheet, getting out of bed and reaching for his jeans.

But Laura got there first, yanked them from him and snatched them out of reach. 'Now who's running away?'

Matt froze. He wasn't running away. Was he? Still? Realisation slapped him in the face. God, he was. Look at the way he'd gone to Athens just because Laura had managed to wangle a few snippets of information out of him. And now look how desperate he was to dash back to his suite just because she wanted to talk.

And what was so dangerous about talking anyway? People did it all the time.

'Fine,' he said, pulling on what few clothes still remained within his grasp and lying back on the bed. 'What do you want to talk about?'

He heard her take a deep breath and all the hairs on his body quivered in alarm. 'Us.'

Matt frowned. 'What about us?' As far as he was concerned there wasn't an 'us'.

'Where do you see this going?'

'Why does it have to be going anywhere?'

There was a long silence. 'I'll take that as a "no-where", then, shall I?'

'What's wrong with carrying on the way we are?'

'Aren't you getting bored?'

'No.' And then a horrible thought struck him. Maybe *she'd* had enough. 'Are you?' As the possibility that she might say yes flashed into his head something in the region of his chest began to ache.

'Not exactly.'

The force of the relief that lurched through him nearly winded him. 'What does that mean?'

'Well, the sex is fine—'

'Fine?'

A tiny smile flashed across her face. 'OK, much better than fine.' The smile faded and his stomach clenched. 'But it's all we ever do.'

'What's wrong with that? I thought that was what we agreed. What you wanted?'

Laura let out a sigh. 'It was. I did.'

'But?' He turned his head to look at her, and then when her eyes met his and he saw what was in them wished he hadn't.

'I want more.'

In the silence that followed Matt's heart plummeted. He should have known a no-strings affair with Laura was too good to be true. For, despite all her protests to the contrary, hadn't he had the niggling suspicion that she was no more cut out for a casual fling than he was for a full-blown relationship? Yes, he had. She was a relationship kind of girl.

But had he listened? No. Because it had been easier not to. And now he was suffering the consequences of his one moment of weakness.

He had to put the record straight. In no uncertain terms, because the tiny flame of hope flickering in her eyes was making his stomach churn. He wasn't about to casually knock down eight years of carefully built up barriers of self-preservation. For anyone.

'I thought you weren't interested in more,' he said flatly.

'So did I.' Laura lifted her shoulders. 'I was wrong.'

'Well, I can't give you more.'

At the rigidity of his expression and the bleakness of his tone Laura's heart wrenched. Oh, God. She should have taken the first course of action and simply got on the first plane out of here. Because this conversation wasn't looking good. In fact she was pretty sure that continuing it would only end in pain. Her pain. Yet she wanted to know why he was unable to give her more. Badly. 'Can't or won't?'

Matt's jaw clenched. 'Either.'

'Why not?'

'It wouldn't be fair on the Sassanians.'

Laura blinked. 'What on earth do they have to do with anything?'

'If I got into a relationship there'd be talk of queens and heirs and I won't let them get all excited about that when I'm not planning to stay.'

What? *That* was his excuse for his emotional obstinacy? Gossip? She'd never heard anything so ridiculous in her life. And then the last few words sank in and Laura fought not to gape. 'You're not planning to stay?'

'No,' he muttered, suddenly scowling as if furious he'd let that slip. Well, that was tough. Curiosity spun through her, briefly nudging the need to find out why he was so reluctant to commit to one side.

'Why?' she asked.

'I have a global business. My general manager can't run it for ever. I need to get back to it at some point.'

'But what about Sassania? And the Sassanians?'

'It'll be fine. They'll be fine.' A muscle began to hammer in his jaw. 'I'll leave it in the best state possible. I'm very good at what I do.'

'I don't doubt it. But this is a country. Not a business.'

'Same principles. CEO... King... They're just titles.'

Laura frowned. 'Surely it's more than that.'

'Not really.'

'But what about the people? Don't you feel some sort of duty towards them? Some sort of loyalty?'

Matt stiffened. 'I'm here to do a job. Nothing more, nothing less.'

'It's just a job?'

Matt glowered at her. 'What else would it be? A hundred years ago, the Sassanians executed my great-great-grandfather and sent my family into exile. I've never been here. Why would I have any sense of loyalty?'

Laura blinked. 'Well, I suppose I don't really know. I just assumed you would. Why else would you put such a lot of effort into the role?'

'I'm a perfectionist. Sassania has a smaller population than the workforce of some of the companies I've worked with, and an infinitely smaller budget. It's no big deal. Once the country's back on its feet the people can decide how they want to continue and who they want to take over.'

'And they know this is your vision, do they?'

'I've made no secret of the fact that I intend to return to my company. I've spent years building it up. Years of hard work and sacrifice. I'm not just going to give it all up because of some ancestral thing I had no influence over.'

'Well, I think that's awful.'

Matt's jaw tightened. 'I don't care what you think and I don't need to have my decisions questioned.'

'Well, you should.'

Matt's eyebrows shot up. 'What?'

'You're good at the king thing. I've heard people talking about you. They have high hopes of you and like it or not if you leave you'll be letting them down and leaving them far worse off than any dictator. And you know, you say you don't care about duty and loyalty and the people of this country, but you do. Why else would you have spent so much time working for it over the past fortnight?'

'To avoid precisely this kind of conversation,' Matt snapped.

Laura felt as if someone had thumped her in the solar plexus. Her breath shot from her lungs and her head went fuzzy.

He'd immersed himself in his work specifically so he wouldn't have to spend time getting to know her? Something inside her began to shake. Did he *really* think all she was good for was evening entertainment?

Oh, God. How could she have got it so wrong? Hadn't she secretly been hoping that that wishful thinking wouldn't be quite so wishful? That he'd listen to her and give her that thoughtful little look he often gave her when he was tossing something around in his head, and agree? That he'd lean over, tell her she was right, give her a long slow kiss and suggest they give it a shot?

Laura's heart began to ache. She was such an idiot. Would she never learn? 'Oh,' she said eventually. 'I see.'

Matt frowned. 'Have I ever given you the impression I was interested in anything else?'

'No.' He hadn't. She'd got it wrong all on her own.

Complete and utter fool. Why had she ever embarked on this conversation? Why couldn't she have stayed happy to carry on until their fling ended? Why had she ever been on that assertiveness course?

'So why can't you give me anything more?'

And why was she such a masochist?

Matt rubbed a hand over his face and pinched the bridge of his nose. 'I just can't.'

He vibrated with tension and Laura suddenly felt as if she were skating on very thin ice miles from the safety of the shore. But she had to know.

'That is not an answer to the question, Matt. If you really think you're leaving,' she said, thinking about the excuse he'd given her, 'you're deluding yourself.'

'Frankly, I don't really care what you think.'

Oh, that hurt. The pain that scythed through her nearly made her pass out. 'You bastard,' she breathed.

Matt flinched as if she'd struck him. 'OK, fine,' he bit out, his eyes suddenly blazing. 'You want to know the real reason why I don't want a relationship? Because relationships are messy,' he snapped. 'They sap your energy, your time and they screw up your judgement.'

The bitterness in his voice cut right through her and her heart clenched at the bleakness of his face. 'What happened?'

'I don't want to talk about it.'

'I know you don't. But you're going to have to, because I'm channelling Module Three, and without your jeans you can't escape.'

The ghost of a smile flickered at his mouth and then vanished. Matt rubbed his hand over his face and let out a heavy sigh. 'The last relationship I had was with my then fiancée, and it didn't end well.'

In the silence that followed his words you could have heard a pin drop.

Matt had been engaged?

Laura's brain began to pound. To whom? When? How? And what had gone wrong? God, there was so much she didn't know about this man.

'You were engaged?' she said faintly.

'I was.'

'When?'

'Eight years ago.'

'What happened?'

Matt shrugged as if he couldn't care less, but his face was tight and a tiny flicker of turmoil flashed in the depths of his eyes. 'Nothing spectacular. We were young. We simply drifted apart and eventually split up.'

'If it was nothing spectacular then why haven't you had a relationship since?'

'I haven't had the time.'

She didn't believe that for a second. 'What was her name?'

'Alicia.'

'Did you love her?'

'I asked her to marry me.'

'Not quite what I asked.'

His eyes flashed. 'Yes, I did.'

Laura ignored the stab of jealousy that struck her chest. 'So what went wrong?'

'Do you ever give up?'

Laura gave him a tiny smile. 'Not any longer.'

'My work got in the way.' Ah. 'The business was at a fragile stage. On the point of taking off. I had to devote a lot of time to it.'

'And Alicia didn't appreciate that?'

'Not particularly. Apparently we stopped communicating. *I* stopped communicating.'

'Fancy that,' murmured Laura.

'The less we communicated, the more we argued. The end was inevitable.'

'Does it still hurt?'

His jaw tightened. 'No.'

'So why still be so against relationships? They don't all fail.'

'I'm well aware of that,' he said tightly.

Laura took a deep breath and put her life in Matt's hands. 'So why don't we do this properly?'

'Do what?'

'You and me.'

'No.'

'Why not?'

'I still don't have the time.'

'That's such a cop out.'

'*What?*'

'Well, it is. You could make time. You know what? I think that deep down you're scared.'

'Rubbish.'

'Is it? I think you're scared that if you allow yourself to try a real relationship it'll hurt.'

'If that's what you want to think, be my guest.'

Why was he being so stubborn about this? Would she ever get through to him? Would he ever give them a chance?

And why did it matter so much that he did?

The inescapable truth smacked her in the face and her heart stopped. And then began to thunder.

Her head went fuzzy and a cold sweat broke out over her entire body.

God. No. That was impossible. She couldn't be…

She thought about the way up until now he'd made her feel. The giddy anticipation with which she'd looked forward to their nights together. The admiration and respect she had for the work he was doing, for the man he was.

She thought about the idea of leaving, of never seeing Matt ever again, or never being able to touch him again, and agony unlike any she'd ever known cut through her.

She was...

She was in love with Matt. She was head over heels in love with a man who was only interested in a fling.

And there wasn't a thing she could do about it.

Laura began to shake as anguish gripped every cell of her body. 'I think I should leave.'

Matt frowned. 'You don't have to leave.'

'Oh, I do.' Even though she longed to stay.

'Why?'

'You don't have a monopoly on self-preservation, Matt,' she said, giving him a shaky smile. 'We want different things, and that's never going to change, is it?'

His face was blank and it broke her heart. 'No. Fine. Go.'

'I'll send over a list of people I'd recommend to continue the restoration work.'

'Fine.'

'Is that all you can say?'

Matt shoved his hands through his hair. 'What else is there?'

So it was over. It shouldn't hurt so much. But the pain... The excruciating pain... Laura got to her feet and her legs nearly gave way. Somehow she managed to stand. Somehow she pulled on her clothes, but her fingers felt too thick and were shaking too much to do up her buttons.

'I know you think you're better off alone, Matt,' she said, pulling her shirt tightly around her as if that could somehow stop the cold seeping through her, 'but you aren't. No one is. Work won't keep you warm at night. Work won't be there for you when you have a bad day or when you're old and grey. I would.'

Matt shrugged and she wanted to shake him. Thump him. Make him hurt as much as he was making her hurt. Because he must know how she felt about him.

'I never wanted it to end like this, Laura,' he said flatly.

Laura's heart cracked wide open and a wretchedness more devastating than she'd ever known spun through her. 'Neither did I.'

CHAPTER TWELVE

THAT things with Laura had ended was for the best, Matt told himself for the hundredth time in the week since she'd left.

He didn't miss her prodding at his psyche or her incessant questioning one little bit. Nor did he miss the way those eyes of hers looked at him and seemed to drill right into his soul. And he certainly didn't miss her. He missed the sex, that was all. Which was absolutely fine because he would get over that eventually.

No. He was glad she'd gone. Thrilled in fact. He couldn't be happier. The conversation they'd had the night before she'd left had cemented in his mind exactly why he didn't do relationships and he'd been right to let her leave.

So why was he feeling so out of sorts? Why did he feel as if he were wading through treacle simply to get through the days? Why couldn't he focus? And why wasn't this run that he was in the middle of doing anything to relieve the tension in his body?

Undoubtedly it was the abrupt way their fling had ended, Matt decided, his feet thumping along the path that circled the lake. She'd ended it before he'd been ready to let her go, and that irritated him beyond belief. He should have been more persuasive in making her stay. He should have knocked that conversation on the head and simply made love to her until she was too breathless to talk.

If he'd had any sense at all, he thought, his lungs pumping hard enough to burst, he would have avoided getting involved with her in the first place. That would have saved him a whole lot of trouble.

But never mind.

Sooner or later he'd regain the ability to sleep at night.

Sooner or later he'd fall back into the swing of getting Sassania back on its feet.

And sooner or later he'd find someone to take on the work of restoring the country's monuments. So what if none of the people she'd recommended had been quite right?

It was simply a question of time, that was all.

But what if he didn't?

The thought slammed into his head and Matt stumbled. What if he never stopped tossing and turning and dreaming of her? What if he never got his focus back? What if she was irreplaceable?

No. That was absurd. He would. He had to. And no one was irreplaceable. Especially not someone who'd been so wrong about everything.

Or had she?

Matt's head went so fuzzy he thought he might be about to pass out. He stopped. Bent over and planted his hands on this thighs, his heart pounding and breath ragged.

Oh, God. She hadn't been wrong. The realisation banged around his head, making his body feel far weaker than the run had.

He *did* want to stay on the island and he *was* sick of always being alone.

And if she'd been right about that then what else had she been right about? *Was* he scared? No, he wasn't scared of anything.

Except possibly the depth of his feelings for Laura.

Matt froze and he shot up, his knees nearly buckling. His head throbbed. Spun. The barriers he'd built up around his heart suddenly shattered and as they did every emotion he'd ever buried crashed through him and everything he'd ever thought he believed came tumbling down around him.

Oh, God. No wonder he was in such a state. No wonder he couldn't sleep at night and couldn't think straight. He wanted a lot more than a fling with Laura. He wanted everything. Because he was in love with her. Deeply and completely.

The knowledge slammed into his head and he began to shake. Hell. When had *that* happened? When had the idea of going back to his previous life become so unappealing?

And how did Laura feel about him? Could he dare hope that she loved him back? His mind shot back to the look in her eyes, the one that had put the fear of God into him, just before she'd left. God, she did. Matt's heart began to soar and then plummeted.

Or at least she had.

His stomach churned with dread. Laura was the best thing that had ever happened to him and he'd let her leave. How could he have done that? Because he was terrified of screwing up again? Of pouring everything he had into a relationship and watching it crumble to dust?

But that wouldn't happen with Laura, would it? What

he'd had with Alicia would never have lasted. They'd been too young and had wanted entirely different things out of life. Ultimately he'd called off the engagement because he'd discovered he actually preferred working to spending time with her. Ultimately he hadn't loved her enough.

But with Laura, he loved her so much. And he'd behaved appallingly.

Realisations pummelled through him, each one thudding into his brain hot on the heels of another, making him feel quite weak. What was the point of wanting to return to his previous life when it suddenly seemed empty and lonely? What was the point of clinging on to his business when he wanted to stay on Sassania? And what was the point of having that big old house in Little Somerford, sitting there empty and neglected?

In fact without her, what was the point of anything?

Matt harnessed all the emotions suddenly pounding through him, set his jaw and ran back in the direction of the palace. He'd acted like a prize idiot and it was high time he started putting things right. He could only hope he hadn't left it too late.

CHAPTER THIRTEEN

'PIZZA, Chinese or Indian?' said Kate, sitting next to Laura on the sofa and holding up a fan of menus.

Laura continued zapping mindlessly through the TV channels. 'I don't mind,' she said listlessly. 'You choose. I'm not that hungry.'

Kate gently took the remote control out of Laura's hand, got up from the sofa and planted herself cross-legged on the floor between her and the television. 'Laura, you have to eat.'

'I do eat.' A bit. When she remembered. But to be honest her appetite for food had vanished. As had her appetite for most things. Like getting up in the morning. Fresh air. Breathing even. In fact there didn't seem much point to anything any more.

'More than a couple of slices of toast a day,' Kate said shrewdly.

Laura sighed. 'I know. And I will. It's just that at the moment I feel so…so…' She couldn't finish the sentence. Couldn't voice all the stuff that was churning around inside her. The pain, the emptiness, the yearning and so much more besides. 'Hollow,' she said eventually, blinking away the tears that stung the backs of her eyes.

'Pizza it is, then,' said Kate, tossing the other menus

down and waving the remaining one at Laura. 'Pizza's filling, and always good at a time of crisis. As is wine.'

Laura gave her a wan smile. 'Thank you,' she said. 'And thank you for letting me stay.'

'No problem.'

'Sorry for being such lousy company.'

'Don't worry about it. It's completely understandable. Now what would you like?'

Laura hiccoughed as surprise momentarily lightened her heart. Kate was actually asking her instead of steamrollering ahead. Wow. Maybe more things had changed than just her. It was a shame Matt hadn't and wouldn't.

'The usual,' she said, too dazed and mixed up to bother with something new.

'OK,' said Kate, picking up the phone and hitting the speed dial. 'Hello? Yes. I'd like to place an order...'

Laura listened to Kate rattling off their selection and felt a deep gratitude to her friend. Ever since her plane had touched down a week ago, and what a miserable journey that had been, she'd been operating on automatic.

Unable to bear the thought of going back to the village where the manor house would keep reminding her of Matt—not that she needed reminding when he'd taken up pretty much permanent residence in her head—she'd gone straight to London and had turned up on Kate's doorstep, watery-eyed and shaking.

She'd spilled out the whole sorry story, at which point Kate had enveloped her in a huge hug and pulled her inside, and had been plying her with wine and sympathy ever since.

Kate hung up, poured two huge glasses of wine and

handed one to Laura. 'It'll be here in half an hour. Are you going to be all right?'

Laura took a gulp and felt the alcohol hit her stomach. What choice did she have? She had to be all right if she was going to live any kind of life. Matt would never change and she'd be a fool to hope otherwise. 'I expect so. Eventually.'

'Matt's an idiot. But then he's a man, so what can you expect?'

Kate's scathing tone managed to drag a smile to Laura's face but not for long. Because Matt wasn't an idiot, just a gorgeous, sexy, emotionally deluded, infuriatingly obstinate man.

'So what are you going to do?' Kate asked.

Laura stared at the fireplace, as bleak and empty as her heart. 'I'm not sure. Look for a new job, I suppose. And then find somewhere to live.'

'You can stay here as long as you need.'

'Thanks.' She put her wine glass down and gave Kate a shaky smile. It was so tempting to stay in the warm cocoon of Kate's flat for ever, but sooner or later she had to pull herself together.

She'd been back a week and had been wallowing in self-pity all that time. She'd let herself become a mess. The last time she'd looked in the mirror she'd been horrified by what she'd seen. Her hair was lifeless. Her skin was grey and her eyes were flat. But not horrified enough to do anything about it.

But now she was. Enough was enough. She was fed up with constantly feeling so negative. It was high time she started to focus on the positives.

'You know, maybe it's a good thing me and Matt didn't last,' she said.

Kate looked at her doubtfully. 'In what way?'

'Well, I was just beginning to work out who I was and what I wanted. I was actually getting somewhere. So really, the last thing I needed was to get involved with someone. Especially a member of royalty.' She tried a laugh but it came out as a strangled gasp and she cleared her throat. 'I mean, if going out with a normal man makes me feel suffocated, can you imagine what going out with a king would be like?'

'Hmm, I see your point.'

'In fact,' she said firmly, as the alcohol began to take effect on her poor emotionally battered self, 'I'm going to become more like you.'

'Me?' Kate's eyebrows shot up. 'Crikey, really? I wouldn't go that far. I'm a workaholic who's never managed to hold down a relationship.'

'Exactly. You don't take crap from anyone. You're single. And you're happy, aren't you?'

'Well, yes, but—'

'But nothing. I've made my decision. No more men. Ever. And this time I mean it.' She drained her glass. 'You know, I feel better already,' she said.

'I'm not surprised,' Kate replied, glancing at Laura's empty glass and raising her eyebrow.

Yes, that was the solution, thought Laura, jumping to her feet to fish her phone from the depths of her handbag where it was beeping. She couldn't go on like this, moping all over the place. She needed to take charge. A life of celibacy. Emotional austerity. That was what she'd try. It worked for nuns, didn't it?

She'd head home tomorrow and get on with it. She couldn't hole up at Kate's for ever. And if she tried hard, after a while she might be able to wake up in the morning without thinking about Matt. Maybe after a while she might be able to go to bed without thinking about

Matt. And maybe, just maybe, she might get to spend a whole five minutes without thinking about Matt.

And then her heart might start to repair itself.

'You'll see,' she said firmly, flipping open her phone and clicking on her email to read the one that had just popped into her inbox, 'I'll be—oh.'

'What?'

As she scrolled through the message Laura's heart began to lurch all over the place. 'There's an email from Matt.'

Kate leapt up and rushed to her side. 'What does it say?'

'He's given me the house.'

'He's done *what*?'

'He's given me the house,' she echoed. 'I think,' she added, unable to believe what she'd just read.

'What do you mean you think?'

'I'm not sure. I can't think straight. You read it.'

Laura handed her mobile to Kate and crumpled onto the sofa, her mind struggling to make sense of it all. Why would Matt have given her Somerford Manor? Was it some kind of sign? Was he telling her that he'd never change and that she ought to find what she wanted with someone else?

But how was it that they were over yet he could *still* turn her brain into knots?

'Property law isn't my field of expertise,' said Kate finally, 'but this seems pretty comprehensive. He's definitely given you the house.'

Laura swallowed back the lump in her throat. 'Is it legal?'

'It looks like it. He's also given you a six-figure lump sum to do it up.'

'Oh.'

'Whatever his failings, you can't say he's not generous.'

'Only with things that don't matter,' said Laura as her heart began to ache all over again.

'Why would he give you his house?'

'I don't know.'

'Maybe he's winding up his assets here.'

'I doubt it.' His declaration that he had no intention of staying on Sassania still rang in her ears. 'It's probably a tax move or something.'

'Or maybe he knows how much you love it and just wanted you to have it.'

Laura ached. God, how she'd love to believe that. Because hadn't she secretly been hoping that Matt might have realised that he'd made a whopping mistake in dismissing what they'd had so casually? But he'd never think he'd made a mistake so she could stop that tiny flicker of hope. 'That's even less likely.'

'Well, it certainly solves your problem of where to live.'

And be constantly battered by memories of him and everything she'd lost? No chance. 'I couldn't live there.'

'So what are you going to do? Sell it?'

For some reason that didn't appeal either. 'Tell him I don't want it, I suppose.'

'Don't you want it?'

'Not if it doesn't come with him. And it doesn't, does it?'

Kate shook her head. 'The transfer deed is in your name only so it doesn't look like it. I'm sorry.'

Laura shrugged as if disappointment weren't crashing through her. 'Doesn't matter.' She took out her phone and sent a quick reply and then deleted the email. 'There,' she said, her voice shaking a little. 'Done. Crisis over.'

In the meantime, she thought dolefully as the peal of the doorbell rang through the flat, there was always pizza.

CHAPTER FOURTEEN

LAURA had been back home for half an hour yet her cottage felt as unfamiliar as when she'd first moved in. Had it really only been a handful of weeks? she wondered, flicking on the kettle. So much had happened, so much had changed. *She'd* changed.

But one thing hadn't changed. She arrived here bruised and battered from a doomed relationship, and here she was again.

She could tell herself all she liked that she was ready to move on, but the truth was that she wasn't. How could she be when every corner of her heart wrenched and every cell in her body ached?

When would it ever stop? When *would* she be ready to move on?

The doorbell rang and Laura jumped. If that was one of her neighbours asking for a lift, she thought, heading to the front door, they could forget it.

But as she pulled the door back and stared at the figure standing on her doorstep, Laura froze. All her blood drained to her feet and her head went fuzzy. There was a roaring sound in her ears and her breathing shallowed and quickened. She wondered if she might be about to pass out. Thought it might not be such a bad idea.

Because although it was one of her neighbours, she was pretty sure he wasn't there to ask her for a lift.

Matt looked as if he hadn't slept in weeks. His face was haggard and the lines on his face seemed more sharply etched. Her heart tightened with hope and longing and she had to force it not to, because she wasn't going down that road ever again. Blinking away the nausea, she pulled her shoulders back and curled her hands into fists to stop herself from reaching out, running over to him, wrapping her arms around his neck and kissing the life out of him.

Because however much she might wish otherwise, she'd missed him. God, how she'd missed him.

'What are you doing here, Matt?'

'Looking for you.'

'How did you know I was here?'

'I've been waiting for you.'

'Not too long I hope.'

'A while.'

'I've been in London.'

'Ah.'

He leaned against the door frame, his expression inscrutable, and Laura felt herself start to flap. 'What do you want?'

'I'd like to come in.'

Laura's heart began to hammer. Letting him inside her house would be such a bad idea, but if she left him on the doorstep then he'd know how much he still affected her and once again she'd be the one on the back foot.

'Of course. Please,' she said, mustering up the semblance of a smile. 'Do come in. Coffee?'

He stepped over the threshold and Laura felt as if all the oxygen had been sucked out of the hall. 'No. Thank you.'

He walked into her sitting room and stood with his back to the fireplace looking big and dark and gorgeous.

'So,' she said, desperate to fill the crackling silence. 'How's work?'

'Horrendous.'

Good. Hah. There was some justice in the world, after all. 'I'm sorry to hear that,' she said, feeling anything but.

'You should be,' Matt said with the glimmer of a smile that flipped her stomach. 'It's your fault.'

What? 'How is it *my* fault?'

'I haven't been able to get you out of my mind. I haven't been able to concentrate. I haven't been able to do anything much.'

Laura's breath hitched and her heart thumped as that flicker of hope she'd tried so hard to extinguish flared into life. 'That's not my problem.'

'Isn't it?' He sighed and rubbed his face. 'You don't want my house.'

She bit her lip. 'I don't understand why you gave it to me.'

'Don't you?'

'No. I've been going over and over it in my head and I just can't work it out.'

'Can't you? I'd have thought it was simple.'

Simple? Nothing was simple when it came to her and Matt. 'Then think again.'

Matt shrugged. 'I gave it to you because you love it.'

Laura went very still. Felt a rush of pain shooting

through her and bit back a gasp. Oh, she was such a fool. Hadn't she secretly been hoping that he'd given it to her as a sign that he'd changed his mind? 'Well, I don't want it.'

Matt flinched then tilted his head. 'And what about me? Do you want me?'

Laura's heart skipped a beat. What kind of a question was that? She wanted him with every breath she took, with every cell of her body. And he knew that. So what was he trying to do? Torment her even further?

'Absolutely not,' she said, steeling herself against the way his face paled beneath his tan and made her heart clench. 'So I hope you haven't come to try and persuade me back to Sassania. Because nothing on the planet would tempt me to do that. You were right about us,' she said, her need to protect herself from him lending strength to her words and fire to her voice. 'You know it's a good thing you finished our fling when you did, because I've decided that I really don't need another relationship.'

Matt went very still and his whole body tensed. 'Is that really what you think?'

Laura nodded so violently her head nearly came off. 'Absolutely.' Not.

He frowned. Took a step back, hit the fireplace and stumbled. He looked shaken. Uncertain all of a sudden. 'Then it seems I've had a wasted journey. Forget about the house. It was stupid of me. I'm sorry to have interrupted your morning.'

Laura watched him frown, then nod to himself and shove his hands in his pockets. Her heart lurched as realisation dawned and then began to thunder. 'Oh, my God, you were going to persuade me back to Sassania, weren't you?'

Matt's gaze collided with hers, but his eyes were completely unreadable. 'Don't worry about it. I dare say I'll get over it.'

'No, wait.'

He stilled. 'What?'

Ignoring her churning stomach and all the hope and doubt and nerves tangling up inside her, Laura took a deep breath. 'Why did you come here, Matt?'

'To offer you all those things you've just said you don't want.'

At the bleakness in his voice her throat hurt. Her head began to spin. 'But I thought you didn't do relationships.'

'So did I,' he said with a short humourless laugh. 'But then there are a lot of things I thought I didn't do which I apparently now do do.'

'Like what?'

'I sold my business.'

Laura blinked. 'Oh.'

'And my flat.'

'Why?'

'I'm going to stay on Sassania.'

'That's good.'

'I think so.' He sighed and shoved his hands through his hair. 'You were right about that. It's not just a job. It is my duty and my legacy, but apart from that I like it there. The people are good and I want to make things better.'

'You will.'

'Maybe. Who knows?' He shrugged. 'Anyway I should probably be getting back.'

He was leaving? Now? Just when things were getting interesting? No way. 'When you said you were going to offer me all the things I'd just told you I didn't want, what exactly did you mean?'

Matt froze. 'Forget it,' he said flatly.

She bit her lip. 'No.' She'd get to the bottom of what he was trying to say if it was the last thing she did. And knowing his reluctance to talk, it could well be the last thing she did. 'I don't want to forget it. I want you to tell me what you meant.'

'Fine,' he said, his whole body shaking with something that had her heart pounding crazily. 'I love you. I want to marry you. I want to take you back to Sassania and make lots of little Sassanian babies with you. I want you to restore your house so we can spend our summers there. I won't stifle you. Or suffocate you. You can do what you want. Be what you want. You'd never fade into the background. It would be impossible.' He paused, shoved his hands through his hair. 'My life is empty and soulless without you, Laura. I'm sorry I let you leave like that. I'm sorry I was such an idiot. And I'm sorry it's taken me so long to figure it out. But I love you. More than I ever thought possible.'

Laura reeled as the words tumbled out. 'Oh.'

There was a pause. Matt frowned. 'Oh?' he echoed. 'Is that all you have to say?'

'No, no,' she said faintly. 'It's just quite a lot to take in. I wasn't expecting you to be quite so, um, communicative.'

'I've been practising. You should have heard me the first time. You know how much I like talking about feelings.'

'I do.'

'Well, now I'm done.' He frowned and a vulnerability flashed across his face that made her heart ache. 'So what do you think?'

What did she think? She thought that if the happiness bubbling around inside her grew any bigger she'd burst. 'I think that practice makes completely perfect.'

Matt let out a breath. 'Then in that case do you think you can put me out of my misery and tell me how you feel about me?'

Laura smiled. 'I love you. But you already knew that, didn't you?'

He crossed the room, gathered her in his arms and crushed her against him. 'I had hoped. God, I'd hoped. But then when I got that email saying you didn't want the house…' His mouth twisted.

She laid her hand against his cheek and traced his mouth with her thumb until the twist became a smile. 'I didn't know what it meant. I thought it might be a tax break.'

Matt's eyebrows shot up. 'A tax break? I'm not that complicated.'

Not that complicated? Who was he kidding? 'Or a sign that I should find what I've been looking for with someone else, or something.'

'Don't even think about it. If you marry me, I'll make it my life's mission to give you everything you want.'

'Oh, well, when you put it like that, how could I refuse?'

His mouth came down on hers and Laura sank into his kiss. Her arms wound round his neck and their mouths fused together so fiercely, so completely, their hearts hammering so closely that she didn't know where she stopped and he started. By the time Matt lifted his head desire was thumping around her and her whole body felt weak.

'So a relationship, huh?' said Laura, leaning back and looking up at him once she'd got her breath back.

'I know,' Matt murmured, his eyes dark and warm and filled with love. 'And not just a relationship. Marriage. Who'd have thought?'

'Not scared any more?'

'Terrified, actually.'

Laura smiled. 'Me, too. Neither of us is exactly an expert at the things.'

'I guess we'll just have to muddle through together.'

Laura smiled and tugged at his T-shirt. 'Sounds good to me.'

EPILOGUE

One year later...

'So IT's finally finished,' said Matt, wrapping his arms around Laura's waist and drawing her back against him.

Laura let her head drop back and rest on his shoulder as she snuggled into his arms. She felt the last rays of the evening sun warm on her face, and thought she'd never been so happy.

All in all, over the course of the past year, she and Matt had muddled through remarkably well. Matt had got over his reluctance of talking about feelings with surprising enthusiasm and Laura had begun to understand him. Most of the time.

Their wedding six months ago had done wonders for the morale of the country, which was well on the way to recovery. Of course, she hadn't been able to continue working on the palace, but any disappointment she might have felt had been more than compensated by having the manor house to devote her energies to. 'It is,' she said, gazing up at the house she adored. 'What do you think?'

'I think you're amazing,' he said, breath caressing her ear and making her shiver.

Laura grinned. 'Of the house.'

'It's beautiful. You've done a fantastic job.'

'Thank you.'

'You know,' he said, sliding his hands up her body to cup her breasts, 'all that remains now is to work on the hordes of children you think should fill it.'

Laura put her hands over his and lowered them back to her abdomen, then twisted slightly in his arms to smile up at him. 'Funny you should mention that…'

* * * * *

CRAVING HER
ENEMY'S TOUCH

RACHAEL THOMAS

For Ruth and Sarah Jane and our
enjoyable writing retreat weekends
in our little Welsh cottage.

CHAPTER ONE

THE PURR OF a sports car broke the quietness of the afternoon, taking Charlie's mind hurtling back to the past. To events she'd been hiding from for the last year.

She had grown up in the glamour of the racing world, but her brother's death had sent her retreating to the country and the sanctuary of her cottage garden. It was a place that was safe, but instinct warned her that this safety was now under threat.

Unable to help herself, she listened to the unmistakable sound of the V8 engine as it slowed in the lane beyond her garden, appreciative of its throaty restraint. All thoughts of planting bulbs for next spring disappeared as memories were unleashed. Images of happier times filled her mind, colliding with those of the moment her world had fallen apart.

Kneeling on the grass in the corner of her garden, she couldn't see the car on the other side of the hedge, but she knew it was powerful and expensive—and that it had stopped in the lane outside her cottage.

The engine fell silent and only birdsong disturbed the peace of the English countryside. She closed her eyes against the dread which rushed over her. She didn't need visits from the past, however well meaning. This unexpected visitor had to be her father's doing; he'd been pushing her to move on for weeks now.

The heavy clunk of the car door shutting was followed by purposeful footsteps on the road. A few seconds later they crunched on the gravel of her pathway and she knew that whoever it was would see her at any second.

'Scusi.' The deep male voice startled her more than the Italian he spoke and she jumped up as though she were a child with her hand caught in the sweet jar.

The six foot plus of dark Italian male which stood in her garden robbed her of the ability to think, let alone speak, and all she could do was look at him. Dressed in casual but very much designer jeans which hugged his thighs to perfection, he appeared totally out of place and yet vaguely familiar. Over a dark shirt he wore a leather jacket and was everything she'd expect an Italian man to be. Self-assured and confident, oozing undeniable sex appeal.

His dark collar-length hair was thick and gleamed in the sunshine, his tanned face showed a light growth of stubble, which only enhanced his handsome features. But it was the intense blackness of his eyes as they pierced into her which made breathing almost impossible.

'I am looking for Charlotte Warrington.' His accent was heavy and incredibly sexy, as was the way he said her name, caressing it until it sounded like a melody. She fought hard against the urge to allow it to wrap itself around her. She had to. She was out of practice in dealing with such men.

Slowly pulling off her gardening gloves, she became acutely aware she was wearing her oldest jeans and T-shirt and that her hair was scraped back in something which almost resembled a ponytail. Could she get away with not admitting who she was? But the arrogance in those dark eyes as they watched her made her want to shock him.

He was undoubtedly her brother's business partner, the man who had whisked him deeper into the world of performance cars, so far that he'd almost forgotten his family's existence. Indignation surfaced rapidly.

'What can I do for you, Mr...?' The question of his name hung in the warm air around them, testing and challenging him. She stood tall as his astonished gaze travelled down her body, taking in her dishevelled appearance. Her skin tingled as those eyes all but caressed every part of her, making her breath catch as if he'd actually touched her.

'You are Sebastian's sister?' Accusation and disbelief laced through every word, but it was lost on her as the grief she'd thought she'd finally begun to get over hit her once more as he said her brother's name.

The urge to defend herself rose up, but she had no idea where it came from. 'Yes,' she said curtly, hearing the irritation in her own voice. 'And you are?'

She asked the question although she knew the answer and it was not one she wanted to hear. She curled her fingers into her palms, knowing that the one man she'd never wanted to meet, the man she held responsible, first for taking Seb away from her, then for his death, stood impudently in her garden. Looking for her.

If that wasn't bad enough, there had been a spark of attraction in that first second she'd seen him. Already she hated herself for it. How could she feel anything other than contempt for the man who'd deprived her of her brother?

'Roselli,' he said and stepped off the path and onto her newly cut lawn, confirming her worst suspicions.

He smiled at her as he walked closer, but it didn't reach his eyes. 'Alessandro Roselli.'

She glared at him and he stopped a few paces away from her. Had he felt the heat of her anger? She certainly hoped so. He deserved every bit of it and so much more.

'I have nothing to say to you, Mr Roselli.' She stood firm, looked him in the eye and tried not to be affected by the way his met and held hers, shamelessly, without any trace of guilt. 'Now, please leave.'

She walked across the lawn, past him and towards her cottage, sure that he would go, that her cold dismissal would be enough. As she neared him the breeze carried his scent. Pure, unadulterated male. Her head became light, her breath hard to catch. In disgust at the way he distracted her thoughts, she marched off.

'No.' That one word, deep and accented, froze her to the spot as if a winter frost had descended, coating everything in white crystals.

A tremor of fear slipped down her spine. Not just fear of the man standing so close to her, but fear of all he represented. Slowly she turned her face to look directly at him. 'We have nothing to say. I made that clear in my response to your letter after Sebastian's death.'

Sebastian's death.

It was hard to say those words aloud. Hard to admit her brother was gone, that she'd never see him again. But, worse, the man responsible had the nerve to ignore her early grief-laden requests and then invade the cottage, her one place of sanctuary.

'You may not, but I do.' He stepped closer to her, too close. She held his gaze, noticing the bronze sparks in his eyes and the firm set of his mouth. This was a man who did exactly what he wanted, without regard for anyone else. Even without knowing his reputation she'd be left in no doubt of that as he all but towered over her.

'I don't want to hear what you've got to say.' She didn't even want to talk to him. He had as good as killed her brother. She didn't want to look at him, to acknowledge him, but something, some undeniable primal instinct, made her and she fought hard to keep the heady mix of anger and grief under control. An emotional meltdown was not something she wanted to display, especially in front of the man she'd steadfastly refused to meet.

'I'm going to say it anyway.' His voice lowered, resembling a growl, and she wondered which of them was fighting the hardest to hold onto their composure.

She lifted a brow in haughty question at him and watched his lips press firmly together as he clenched his jaw. Good, she was getting to him. With that satisfaction racing through her, she walked away, desperate for the safety of her cottage. She didn't want to hear anything he had to say.

'I am here because Sebastian asked me to come.' His words, staccato and deeply accented, made another step impossible.

'How dare you?' She whirled round to face him, all thought of restraint abandoned. 'You are here because of your guilt.'

'My guilt?' He stepped towards her, quickly closing that final bit of space between them, his eyes glittering and hard.

Her heart thumped frantically in her chest and her knees weakened, but she couldn't let him know that. 'It's your fault. You are the one responsible for Sebastian's death.'

Her words hung accusingly between them, and the sun

slipped behind a cloud as if sensing trouble. She watched his handsome face turn to stone and even thought she saw the veil of guilt shadow it, but it was brief, swiftly followed by cold anger, making his eyes sharper than flint.

He was so close, so tall, and she wished she was wearing the heels she used to favour before her life had been shaken up into total turmoil. She kept her gaze focused on him, determined to match his aggressive stance.

'If, as you say, it was my fault I would not have waited a year to come here.' His voice was cool and level, his eyes, changing to gleaming bronze, fixed her accusingly to the spot.

He took one final step towards her, so close now he could have kissed her. That thought shocked her and she resisted the need to step back away from him, as far as she could. She hadn't done anything wrong. He was the guilty one. He was the one who'd intruded on her life.

'It was your car that crashed, Mr Roselli.' She forced each word out, his proximity making it almost impossible.

'Your brother *and* I designed that car. We built it together.' His voice, deep and accented, hinted at pain. Or was she just imagining it, reflecting her grief onto him?

'But it was Sebastian who test drove it.' She fought the memories he was dragging up. Demons she'd thought she'd finally shut the door on.

He didn't say anything and she held her ground, looking up into his eyes as they searched her face. Her heart pounded wildly and deep down she knew it wasn't just the memories of Sebastian. It was as much to do with this man. Instinctively she knew his potent maleness had disturbed the slumbering woman hidden within her—and she hated him for that.

'It couldn't have done your company's reputation any good when an up-and-coming racing driver was killed at the wheel of your prototype.' She injected a jaunty edge to her words, issuing a challenge. At the same time she wished she could run and hide—from the memories he stirred as much as from the way her body reacted to each glance from his devilishly dark eyes.

He didn't move. He didn't flinch at all. He was in complete control as his eyes glittered, sharp sparks like diamonds spiking her soul.

'It wasn't good for anyone.' His voice was icy cold and, despite the warmth of the September sun, she shivered, but still he remained, watching as if he could read every thought that raced through her mind.

She drew in a ragged tear-laden breath and swallowed hard. She couldn't cry, not now. Not again. She was done with crying. It was time to move on, time to forge a new path through life. She couldn't go back to what she'd been doing before. Her time in front of the cameras, representing Seb's team, was over. The memories would be too much, yet this man seemed hell-bent on bringing the past into the present.

'I think you should leave, Mr Roselli.' She stepped away from him, out of his shadow and into the sun as it crept out from behind the clouds. 'Neither is it doing me any good.'

With eyes narrowed by suspicion, he watched her as she took another step back and away from him. 'I am here because Sebastian asked me to come.'

She shook her head, the emotional meltdown she'd wanted to keep at bay threatening to erupt. 'I still want you to leave.'

She didn't care if he remained standing in her precious garden; she just wanted to escape him, escape the aura of a man obviously used to getting all he wanted, no matter what the cost to anyone else.

Alessandro closed his eyes and sighed as Charlie fled across the garden, heading for the open door of the cottage. Hysteria had not been on his agenda. He didn't need this now. For a moment he thought about turning and walking away, getting in his car and driving as fast and as far away as he could. He'd kept part of his promise to Sebastian, after all. But had he even achieved that?

'Maledizione!' he cursed aloud and strode after her, his legs brushing against the lavender which tumbled from the borders, raising the scent. Just being in the garden, with its proud display of flowers, made him remember the time he'd looked after his sister while she'd recovered from a car accident. It was a memory that wouldn't help at all right now.

As he neared the open back door he heard Charlie's frustrated growl. He didn't knock, didn't pause. He just walked straight in. He wasn't going to be dismissed so easily.

This woman had stubbornly refused her brother's requests to go to Italy and see the car they'd been working on and it had angered him. Then, after the accident, he'd offered his support, but he'd never expected her rejection or her cold and furious denial of his existence.

With her arms locked rigidly tight, she leant on the kitchen table, her head lowered in despair. She spun round to face him. 'How dare you?' Hot angry words hurtled across the small space to him, but he stood tall, despite the low beams of the old cottage, and took her anger.

'I dare because I promised Sebastian that I would.' He moved nearer to the small table, nearer to her, until only a pulled-out chair, left as if recently vacated, separated them.

'I'm sure Seb would not have made anyone promise to come and hassle me like this.' He watched as her full lips clamped shut on further words and he felt the strangest desire to kiss those lips, to taste her rage and frustration, to draw it from her and replace it with hot desire.

'Hassle?' He frowned at her and saw her green eyes widen, liking the swirling brown within their depths, reminding him of autumn.

'Yes, hassle. Hound. Harass. Call it what you like, but he wouldn't have wanted that.' Her words were short and sharp. Irritation made her breathing shallow and fast. Her breasts rose and fell rapidly beneath her T-shirt, snagging his attention as lustful hormones raced to places he just didn't need them going right now.

'He made me promise to bring you to Italy and involve you in the launch.' His words were sharper than he'd intended, but then he'd never expected to meet a woman who unleashed such a cocktail of fury and fire within him. She was not at all the sweet and happy girl Sebastian had told him about; she was sexy and passionately angry.

'He what?' She pushed the chair under the old pine table and moved closer to him.

Not a good idea, not when his body was reacting so wildly to her sexy curves. He wanted to drag the damn chair back out, keep the barrier between them. Maybe then he'd be able to think about the reason he'd come here instead of this long neglected need for a woman's body.

'The car is due to be launched. I want you there.' The words rushed out and he had the strangest sensation that she was depleting his control, weaving some kind of spell around him.

'You want me there?' Her voice raised an octave and he blinked hard, then realised how it had sounded to her. A little pang of conscience surged forwards but he pushed it back. Clearly she held him responsible for that night and he couldn't sully her memories with the truth. Not after the promise he'd made.

'Sebastian wanted you there.' What was the matter with him? This woman wasn't at all what he'd expected. She didn't look glamorous and the idea that she had, until recently, been living a luxury lifestyle didn't seem remotely possible.

Why did this ordinary and plain version of Charlotte Warrington, tousled and unkempt from the garden, arouse him so instantly? He couldn't process thought coherently, his body flooding with lust, demanding satisfaction.

She shook her head. 'No, he wouldn't have asked that. But then he wouldn't have been killed if it wasn't for you and your stupid car.'

'You know he lived for cars, for the thrill of speed. It was what he did, what he was good at.' Sandro pushed back the image of the accident, shelving the terror of all that had unfolded minutes after the crash, which had proved, within hours, to be fatal. He could relate to her pain, sympathise with her grief, but he couldn't and wouldn't allow her to apportion the blame to him.

He'd kept the truth from the world and the gossip-hungry media, out of respect for the young driver who'd quickly become his friend. Now it was time to carry out Seb's final request. He'd wanted his sister at the launch, wanted her stamp of approval on the car, and that was what Seb would have—whatever it took.

'It is also how he died.' Sadness deflated her voice and he saw her shoulders drop. Was she going to cry? Panic sluiced over him.

As she composed herself, his gaze scanned the small country kitchen, typically English and not at all the sort of thing he'd imagined her living in. Herbs hung drying from a beam and various fresh versions adorned the windowsill. Nestled among them, in a small frame, was a photo of Sebastian and Charlie.

He reached for it and saw her gaze dart from him to the photo, but she said nothing as he picked it up and looked at the picture. Instead of being drawn to his friend, he looked at the image of the woman who now stood close to him. A woman he knew through the media but had never met. The same woman who was now having a strange effect on him—or was that just his conscience?

From the photo her eyes shone with happiness, her deliciously full lips spread into a smile. She was leaning against a sports car, her brother, his arms wrapped protectively around her, pulled her close, equally happy.

'Rome. Two years ago,' she said, her voice almost a whisper, and he sensed her move closer to him, felt the heat radiating from her body. 'Before he became embroiled in your project and forgot about us.'

He took a deep breath in, inhaling her scent, something light and floral, like jasmine, mixed with an earthy scent from her time just spent in the garden. Carefully he replaced the photo on the windowsill, ignoring the barb of accusation in her last words. That was not a discussion for now. 'You are alike.'

'Were.'

That one word ratcheted up his guilt, the same guilt he'd told himself again and again he shouldn't carry and, finally, he'd thought he'd convinced himself. He should have known that coming here, facing this woman wouldn't be easy. That it would only increase the self-apportioned guilt instead of lessen it. The fact that he still kept Seb's darkest secret from everyone didn't help.

He looked down at her as she stood at his side and when she looked up, her mossy green eyes so sad, so vulnerable, his chest tightened, almost crushing him with a need to chase away that sadness, to put that happy smile back on her sexy lips once again.

'It's what he wanted, Charlotte,' he said softly, unable to break the eye contact.

'Charlie. Nobody calls me Charlotte. Except my mother,' she whispered. The kind of sexy whisper he was used to hearing from a woman after passionate sex. Inside his body, heady desire erupted as he imagined her lying in his bed, whispering with contentment.

'Charlie,' he repeated as wild need pumped through his veins. He really should stop his mind wandering to the subject of sex. He was in danger of complicating this mission beyond all proportions. She was the one woman he shouldn't want, couldn't desire. 'Seb did want you there.'

'I can't.' Her voice, still a throaty whisper, tugged at his male desires as they rampaged ever wilder.

'You can,' he said and, without thinking, he reached out and stroked the back of his fingers down her face. Her skin was soft and warm. Her breath hitched audibly and her eyes darkened in a message as old as time itself.

Slowly she shook her head in denial, moving her cheek against his fingers, and he clenched his jaw against the sensation, reminding himself he didn't mix business with pleasure and this had always been about business—and concealing his friend's downfall.

He thought again of the recent conversation with her father, of the assurances he'd made to him, binding him deeper into the promise Seb had extracted from him as his life had ebbed away.

'Your father thinks you should.'

It was as if an explosion had happened. As if a firework had gone off between them. She jumped back from him, the chair scratching the tiled floor noisily, her eyes flashing accusation at him.

'My father?' Her voice, laden with shock, crashed into his thoughts, bringing his mind well and truly back into focus. 'You've spoken to my father?'

Charlie was numb with shock. How dare he speak to her father? And why had her father not mentioned it? Why hadn't he warned her Alessandro Roselli, owner of one of Italy's biggest car manufacturers, was looking for her, wanting her to do something he knew she couldn't face yet? She'd only seen her father yesterday. He should have told her.

'What exactly have you spoken about with my father?' She kept her words firm, her fingers curled around the back of the chair as if the pine would anchor her, keep her thoughts focused and in control. Just moments ago she'd wondered what his kiss would be like, had revelled in the soft caress of his fingers like a star-struck teenager. What had she been thinking? 'You had no right.'

'I contacted him to ask if I could visit, to invite you to be at the launch. Your father knows it is what Seb wanted.' He folded his arms across his broad chest and leant against a kitchen unit, his eyes never breaking contact with hers.

For the second time that morning her shoulders sagged in defeat. She pressed her fingertips to her temples and closed her eyes briefly. Hopefully, when she opened them he wouldn't be watching so intently, so knowingly.

But it didn't make any difference. Those bronze-flecked eyes, which strangely felt so familiar, now bored into her. Right into the very heart of her, as if probing for every secret she'd ever hidden.

She dropped her hands and gripped onto the back of the chair again. 'You had no right to speak to my father. He doesn't need to be reminded of what we've lost and I'm more than capable of deciding for myself if I want to see you or not or if I want to be involved in the launch.'

'And do you?' He raised his brows and a smile twitched at the corners of his lips. The same lips she'd just imagined kissing her.

Did she what? Focus, Charlie. Her mind scrabbled to regain rational thought. She didn't know what she wanted except not to allow this man, this prime specimen of raw maleness, to know how unsure and undecided she was.

'I certainly didn't want to see you.' She raised her chin and injected calm control into her voice. 'If you recall, I asked you to leave. I don't want any part of the motor racing world any more.'

'Is that why you've hidden yourself away in the depths of the English countryside?'

The curiosity in his voice was barely disguised and the question came rapidly on the heels of the confusion he'd caused just by being here. She found it difficult to think about such things, but this man's presence was making it harder still.

'I withdrew from the frenzy of the media out of respect for my brother. I'm not hiding,' she said, aware of the curt tone of her voice. 'I couldn't continue to be on camera, promoting the team, not after Seb died.'

'Do you think he'd want you to stay that way?'

As he leant against the kitchen unit, unable to help herself, her gaze flickered to his hips and strong thighs. A sizzle of sexual awareness shimmied over her. Why did she have to find this man, of all men, so undeniably attractive?

'Meaning?'

'The cottage is very nice, but a woman like you shouldn't be ensconced here for ever.'

She looked back into his face, taking in the slant of his nose and the sensual curve of his lips. He looked directly into her eyes, almost knocking the breath from her body with the intensity.

Was he right? Would Seb want her to be involved? Then his last words finally registered in her mind. 'What do you mean—a woman like me?'

He walked around the table, appearing confined within the small kitchen. A room she'd never thought of as so compact, not until Alessandro Roselli had walked into it. He stopped at the opposite side of the table and she was thankful to have something more substantial between them.

'You live life in the fast lane—or did.' His accent had turned into a sexy drawl and his eyes raked over her. Again she was conscious of her casual and slightly grubby clothes.

'Well, now I don't and I have no intention of going back to it. Nothing you—or my father—can say will change my mind.'

'"Look after my little Charlie. She'd like you."' He

spoke firmly and she knew exactly who he was quoting. Only Seb called her 'little Charlie'.

He pulled out another chair and sat down. He was taking root, making it very clear he wasn't leaving any time soon, but his words unsettled her. She could almost hear Seb saying them.

'I don't believe you.' She folded her arms across her chest, trying to deflect his scrutiny, but she remembered the phone calls from Seb. He'd always tried to get her to date again, insisting that not all men were as heartless as her former fiancé. 'He would never say that.'

Absently, he reached out and pulled last night's local paper towards him. He looked as if he belonged in her home, in her kitchen. He looked comfortable.

'It is true, *cara*.'

'Charlotte to you.' Her previous thoughts linked in too easily with his term of endearment and it unnerved her. She wished she'd never invited him to use 'Charlie'.

'Charlotte…' he said, so slowly, so sexily he caressed each syllable. Heat speared through her body. She stood rigid, trying to ignore the heavy pulse of desire scorching through her. What the heck was the matter with her?

Maybe she'd been out of the *fast lane*, as he'd called it, for too long. Should she believe him, that Seb had wanted her involved? Not that she'd ever admit it to him, but those words could well have been spoken by her brother.

'What exactly did my father say?' She had to divert his attention. She couldn't stand here any longer whilst his gaze ravished her. It was too unnerving.

He looked up at her, the paper forgotten, and the heat level within her rose higher still. She swallowed hard. Her brother had been right. She did like him, but purely on a primal level. It was just lust, nothing more. Something she would get over and she could do without that particular complication at the moment.

'He said,' he taunted her, his brows lifting a little too suggestively, 'that it was time you got back in the driving seat.'

His words hung heavy in the air. Words which were true. Hadn't her father said exactly that to her only a few weeks ago?

'I wasn't aware there was more to you than the glamorous façade you've always displayed on camera—that you'd been taught to drive high-powered cars.' He watched her intently and she had the distinct impression he was trying to irritate her, push her into accepting that her brother had wanted her to be involved.

She thought of her job promoting Seb's team, following them to every racetrack in the world and being interviewed by the press. It was a jet set lifestyle, one she'd enjoyed and had been good at. She'd got there by working her way up from the very bottom and had learnt all there was to know about cars and driving. Despite the glamorous image she portrayed to the world whilst on camera, she'd always felt safer, less exposed when she was doing what she really loved. Working on the cars and driving them—something her mother had been set against.

Was it time to stop hiding away and be part of that life again? She pondered the question, aware of his gaze on her, watching and taking in every move.

'You'd be surprised,' she flirted, shocking herself by doing so. What was she doing? She never flirted. It only ever caused trouble. She knew that better than most and had seen it many times in her line of work. Light-hearted flirting always led to more. Her mother had fallen victim to it, leaving her and Seb as teenagers whilst she pursued her latest love interest.

He raised a brow, his eyes sparking with sexy mischief, doing untold things to her pulse rate. It had to stop. She couldn't stand here any longer beneath his scrutiny. She'd melt.

'I hope I get to find out.' His voice was almost a drawl, making her stomach clench.

'Coffee?' Diversion tactics were certainly required and coffee was the first thing to come to her mind.

'*Sì, grazie.*' The effect she was having made him slip automatically into Italian. Coffee was the last thing he wanted. Even a good cup of espresso wouldn't distract him from the fire in his body.

She looked at him, her tongue sliding unconsciously over her lips, and he almost groaned with the effort of staying seated at the table when all he could do was watch her. Desiring a woman dressed in elegant evening wear was normal, but the way he wanted this casual and rumpled version of Charlie was totally new and unexpected. It was also extremely inconvenient.

He watched as she moved around the kitchen, taking in her curves as she turned her back to him to prepare the coffee. He liked the way her jeans clung to her thighs, accentuating the shape of her bottom. Her scruffy T-shirt couldn't quite hide the indent of her waist, just as it hadn't hidden the swell of her breasts from his hungry eyes moments ago.

She turned and passed over a mug of instant coffee, then sat at the table. Inwardly he grimaced. Not what he was used to, but if it meant he had time to convince her

to at least be present at the launch then he would have
to put up with it.

He took a sip, watching as she blew gently on hers,
almost mesmerised by her lips. He had to rein in his li-
bido. She was an attractive woman and in any other circumstances he would have wanted more—much more,
at least long enough for the fire of lust to burn lower. But
he had to remember she was Sebastian's sister and, out
of respect for his friend's memory, she was off limits. He
shouldn't have allowed his attraction to show, shouldn't
have lit the fuse of attraction.

'Back to business,' he said tersely and put down his
mug.

'I wasn't aware it was business,' she said lightly. A
little too lightly, giving away that she was battling with
emotions, that she was stalling him. 'I thought this was
all about salving your conscience, freeing you of guilt.'

He did feel guilt over Seb's death—who wouldn't
in the circumstances?—but it wasn't what drove him,
what had made him come here. He'd come because of
the promise he'd made. 'It is business, Charlotte. I want
you to be at the launch of the car. Seb always wanted
you there. He knew how good you were with the media.'

'He never said anything to me about being at the
launch.' She put her mug down, pushing it away slightly,
as if she too had no intention of drinking it.

He was about to say how much Seb had missed her.
How he'd looked forward to her going to Italy. Anything
to persuade her, when her next words jolted him with the
raw pain entwined in them.

'But I suppose he didn't know he was going to die.'

He nodded, fighting his conscience and sensing she

was coming to the right decision by herself. He just needed to give her a little more time. 'Sadly, that is true.'

'When is the launch?'

Her eyes, slightly misted with held-back tears, met his. Despite his earlier thoughts, he did feel guilt. Guilt for her sadness, and worse. He felt compelled to make it right, to bring happiness back to her life. After all, she wouldn't be hiding away from the world, the racing world in particular, if she wasn't unhappy.

'Friday.'

'But that's only two days away! Thanks for the advance warning.' Her tone was sharp and he saw a spark of determination in her eyes that he recognised and related to.

'*Bene*, you will be there?'

'Yes, I will,' she said as she pushed back her chair and stood up. Dismissing him, he realised. 'But on my terms.'

CHAPTER TWO

'WHAT TERMS?' ALESSANDRO asked suspiciously, looking up at her from where he'd remained sitting at the table.

Charlie watched his jaw clench and his eyes narrow slightly. He hadn't expected that. It annoyed her that he'd thought he could just turn up at the last moment and ask her to go to the launch of the car, as if she was merely an afterthought. Until now she hadn't wanted anything to do with the car, but she'd started to realise that by being involved she might be able to find answers to the questions she still had about the accident.

She mulled the idea over, trying to ignore his scrutiny. If—and that was a big if at the moment—she did go, she'd want much more than just being a last-minute guest. One invited only because Alessandro's conscience had been nudged. She'd want to know all there was to know about the car.

She regretted deeply that she hadn't seen Seb in the months before the accident. If she had gone to Italy to see the car as it had turned from dream into reality, would she have been able to prevent the fateful night of the accident?

The launch could be the exact catalyst she needed to regain control of her life. It was time to put the past to rest, but she could only do that if she had answers. This could be the only opportunity she'd get to find out what had really happened to her brother. He had been, after all, a professional driver, trained to the highest standard, and for Charlie his accident was shrouded in questions.

'Before we discuss my terms, I need to know what happened that night.' She folded her arms in a subconscious gesture of self-protection and leant against the kitchen cupboards, watching intently for his reaction.

She'd expected guilt to cloud his face, to darken the handsome features, but his steady gaze met hers and a flicker of doubt entered her mind. She'd always held him responsible, blamed him, but right now that notion was as unstable as a newborn foal.

'What do you want to know?' His calm voice conflicted with her pounding heart. The questions she'd wanted answers to since the night of the accident clamoured in her mind. The answers now tantalisingly close after having eluded her for so long.

'Why was he even in the car? It wasn't fit to be driven—at least that's what I heard.' She straightened her shoulders and took a deep breath, desperately trying to appear in control. She was far from that, and deep down she knew it wasn't just because she had to face the man she blamed. It was the man himself.

Alessandro Roselli's powerful aura of domination and control filled the kitchen, but she couldn't allow herself to be intimidated. She met it head-on, with determination and courage. She would find out the truth, one way or another. She was convinced it hadn't yet been revealed and she wanted to put that right.

He sat back in his seat, studying her, and she had the distinct impression he was stalling her in an attempt to divert her attention. It was almost working. She'd never been under such a hot spotlight before. *Think of Seb*, she reminded herself, not wanting to waste this opportunity.

'Do you always believe gossip?' He folded his arms, looking more relaxed than he had a right to. Far too self-assured.

She frowned, irritation at his attitude growing. 'No, of course I don't.'

'So if I tell you there was nothing wrong with the car, would you believe me?' He unfolded his arms and turned in his seat, stretching his long legs out, one arm leaning casually on the table. But he was far from casual. His body might be relaxed but, looking into those dark eyes, she knew he was all alertness. Like a hunting cat, lulling its quarry into a false sense of security. But not this mouse. No, she was on her guard.

Forcefully, she shook her head. 'The only thing that will convince me of that is to see the report of the accident.'

He stood up slowly, his height almost intimidating, walked towards the window and looked out across her garden and the countryside beyond. 'Would that really help? Every last detail is in it.'

'Yes,' she said and moved towards him, drawn by an inexplicable need to see his face, see the emotion in it. 'I want every last detail.'

'Why do you think your father hasn't shown you the report?' His broad shoulders became a barrier, as if he was hiding something, concealing something he didn't want her to know, like his guilt. 'What are you hoping to find?'

'The truth.' Anger surged through her again as she imagined him talking to her father, conspiring to hide all the details. She still couldn't understand why her father wouldn't tell her everything. She'd always suspected he was covering something up. Did he have loyalties to this man which exceeded those to his daughter—or even his son's memory?

He turned to face her, his expression hard, making the angles of his face more pronounced. 'Sometimes not knowing the truth is best.'

'What?' She pressed her fingertips to her temples, hardly able to believe what he was saying. Her father and this man were keeping things from her. He might as well have told her exactly that. 'What are you talking about?'

Alessandro heard the exasperation in her voice and gritted his teeth against the urge to tell her what she wanted to know. A truth that would tarnish all the happiness she'd ever shared with her brother and a truth her father had expressly asked him to conceal from her. That had been the one and only condition her father had made when he'd contacted him. He intended to honour that—and the promise he'd made to Seb.

She stood before him, not able to look at him as she pressed long fingers against her temples, her head shaking in denial. The rise and fall of her shoulders as her breath came hard and fast gave away the struggle she was having. Instinctively, he took hold of her arms and she looked back up at him, the beauty of her green eyes almost swaying him from his purpose. 'Your brother was in a high speed accident. You do know that, don't you?'

'I know,' she whispered, thankfully a little more calmly, and looked up into his face, her eyes searching his, looking for answers he couldn't give. 'But I need to know what happened and why.'

'It is better to remember him well and happy, believe

me, Charlotte. It is for the best.' Her ragged sigh deflated all the anger from her body and he felt the resignation slip through her, defusing the fight which had raged moments ago.

'I know, but so many questions need answering.' She closed her eyes and he watched the thick dark lashes splay out over her pale skin. The urge to kiss her rushed at him, almost knocking the breath from his body.

When he'd arrived he'd never expected to find a woman he desired so fiercely. Only once before had such a need raged in him and he'd acted impulsively on it, marrying quickly, only to discover his wife had had ulterior motives all along. Under no circumstances would he put himself in such a position again.

The attraction which had sprung between him and Charlie the second their eyes had met complicated things, made his promise even harder to keep. He let her go and stepped back away from her, away from the temptation, curling his fingers into tight fists. The whole situation was testing far more than his ability to keep his promise.

She looked up at him, her chin lifting in determination. 'I will find out, Mr Roselli. Your and my father's insistence to keep things from me only makes it more important to do so.'

'Some things are best left alone. For Seb's sake, accept what you know and do as your father wants.' He moved away from her, back to the chair he'd sat in earlier—anything to put distance between them—but still the heady need which rushed through him persisted.

'For Seb's sake?' Her question jolted him and he realised how close he'd come to pointing her in the direction of the cause of the accident.

'Seb asked for you to be at the launch. It was one of the

last things he said to me.' There was no way he was going to tell her Seb's actual last words and he guarded himself against letting the truth inadvertently slip. He held her partly accountable for Seb's problems. She'd never been to see him in Italy, had never shown any interest, but that wasn't something he was prepared to discuss now. All he wanted was for her to agree to be at the launch.

'He really said that?' Her voice was so soft it was hardly audible, but it did untold things to the pulse of desire he was fighting hard to suppress.

'He wanted you there.' He watched the indecision slide over her face and waited. She was coming to the right decision slowly. All he had to do was wait.

Charlie couldn't shake the feeling of unease. Yes, she knew Seb's accident would have caused horrible injuries, but she couldn't rid herself of the notion there was something else. Something her father wanted to keep from her as much as Alessandro did. Did that mean he was to blame?

She changed tactics and adopted an attitude of acceptance, realising it was possibly the only way to find out. Slowly, she walked back to the table and stood looking down at him where he calmly sat, watching her.

'If I come to the launch I want to know all about the car first. I want to see everything you and Seb worked on. I want to live it, to breathe it.' A hint of the passion she'd always felt for her job and the world of racing started to fizz in her veins after being unmoved for many months, infusing her with excitement that she hadn't felt for a long time.

'There isn't much time for that.' He sat back in the

chair and looked up at her, observing every move she made until she wondered if he could read all her thoughts.

'If I'm going to be at the launch I want to be able to talk about the car, to bring it to life for everyone else. I need to know all there is to know.'

It was more than that, she admitted to herself. It was much more than just promoting the car. It was seeing what Seb had seen, feeling the excitement he'd felt as he'd driven it for the first time. Her thoughts halted as if they'd slammed into a brick wall.

Was she ready to know all the facts? She looked at the man she'd blamed for her brother's death. As far as she was concerned, he'd allowed Seb to drive a faulty car, despite the fact that her father had told her all the reports stated driver error. She'd blamed Alessandro and now he was here, offering her the opportunity to find out the truth for herself. Would he really do that if he had something to hide?

'I want to see all the files and every drawing Seb made.' She kept her voice firm, trying to hide the waver of confidence growing within her.

Alessandro got up and made his way around the table, coming closer to her, his face stern with contemplation. 'I can't allow it. There isn't enough time.'

Not allow it. Who did he think he was?

'If you knew anything about me, Mr Roselli, you'd know that I need to be involved—if I'm to do my job right, that is. You do want me to promote this car, put my seal of approval on it, do you not?'

She held his gaze, looked directly into his eyes. She would not be intimidated by him. He might be used to getting his way in business, but so was she. He pressed his lips together in thought, the movement drawing her attention briefly, but quickly she regained her focus, re-fusing to allow the pull of attraction to him to cloud her mind. Confirming her suspicions of his blame for the ac-cident would surely curb any misguided attraction she was experiencing.

'It's more than that, isn't it, Charlotte?' The firmness of his tone dissipated as he said each word until he ca-ressed her name, sending a hot fizzing sensation racing over her. It was worse than when he'd called her Charlie.

It was soft yet insanely hot, but she couldn't pay heed to that now. 'I need to know something about the car if I am to promote and endorse it. You understand that, surely.'

He took a deep breath in and she watched his broad chest expand, waiting expectantly, holding her own breath.

'I do but, given the circumstances, is it really wise?' He looked up at her and she tasted defeat as his dark eyes hardened in determination. But defeat wasn't on her agenda. She'd do this her way or not at all. How could he expect anything less when he'd been the one who'd let Seb get in the car, allowed him to drive it that night?

This was the only option. Her only chance to find out what had truly happened. At least then she might be able to move on from it. 'Don't worry—I won't dissolve into a heap of female hysteria again.'

'Maybe you should,' he said and stepped closer to her—too close—but she wouldn't move away. He must never know of the heat he fired within her, just from one look. Thankfully, he'd stopped his flirting of moments ago and had become more professional and she had to ensure it would stay that way.

'No, it is past time for that. I intend to do what my father advised last week.'

'And that is?'

'To get back in the driving seat.' She wouldn't tell him just yet that was quite literally what she intended to do.

He raised his hand to his chin, his thumb and finger rasping over the hint of dark stubble, the sound tying her stomach in knots. She couldn't listen to her body now, to the way it reacted just to being close to him, not that she really understood what it was asking of her. Heightened desire and intense awareness of a man was something she'd never experienced before.

Her previous relationships had been short-lived and unsuccessful. Back then, the breakdown of her parents' marriage had still been too fresh in her mind. Those relationships had also been a long time ago. The mess her parents had made of their marriage had ensured that life-long commitment wasn't something she considered possible. There was no way she was going to expose herself to more hurt and humiliation.

'I'm not convinced it is for the best, but if you are sure then so be it.' He spoke slowly, his accent heavy, as he continued to watch her closely.

'I am,' she said quickly before he had a chance to change his mind. Before she too changed her mind.

'Then we have a deal.' He reached out his hand, the same one that had been thoughtfully touching his face, and she took it quickly, anxious to seal the deal.

'We have a deal.' Her words came out in a rush as a jolt shot up her arm, setting off sparks all over her body as if she'd become a firework. Her breathing almost stopped as his eyes locked with hers, his fingers clasped tightly around her hand, the warmth of his scorching hers.

'Bene,' he said firmly, so firmly it was obvious he didn't feel any of the drama from touching her and she'd do well to remember that the next time he smiled at her as if she was the most beautiful woman in the world. He was flirting, just like all the men she'd known, including her father. And it was flirting which had destroyed her parents' marriage, driving her mother into another man's arms, tearing the family apart.

She closed the door on those thoughts. Now was not the time to become embroiled in them, not when she had the perfect opportunity to find out the truth of Seb's last hours.

Alessandro held onto her hand and looked into her eyes. Did she feel it too? Was the same sizzle of passion creating havoc in her body? She regarded him with a steady gaze, her full lips pressed into a firm line. Evidently not. Her beautiful face was a mask of stone; not a trace of emotion there.

He should be pleased, grateful that the deal they'd just made wasn't going to be overcomplicated by sex. His friendship with Seb and the promise he'd made when he was in hospital, hooked up to all sorts of machines, dictated this arrangement should be business only. At least with her cool demeanour it would be exactly that.

'If it becomes too painful, too much, you must tell me.' She frowned at him and pulled her hand free of his, ceasing the torment just that innocent touch had created within him.

'It won't.' Those two words were so full of strength he didn't doubt it for one moment.

'You are very sure of that, considering you told me to

leave only a short while ago.' Was he trying to reassure himself or her?

'You caught me off guard.' She reached past him and gathered up their discarded coffee mugs and as she turned to wash them he couldn't help but take another look at her curves, admire the womanly softness of them.

Enough.

Business. That was all it was—business. He also sensed that this was a woman who wouldn't accept a no-strings-attached affair. He had, after all, become adept at avoiding such women since extricating himself from a marriage which should never have happened.

He shrugged his shoulders, trying to shake off the pulse of passion. 'Then we shall travel to Milan today.'

'We?' Her eyes flew wide with shock.

'I have much to do ahead of the launch and if you seriously want to learn more about the car it would be a good idea, no?' He wondered at the wisdom of travelling with her when he found it hard to focus on much other than her glorious body.

'I'm not packed or anything. I'll travel out later. You'd better get back to your family.'

'That will not be necessary.' His voice was firm, perhaps a little too firm if the surprise on her face was anything to go by. 'There isn't anyone awaiting my arrival.' Those days were over and if he had any sense it would stay that way.

He didn't miss her raised brows, or the look of suppressed curiosity which crept into her eyes, and wanted to deflect any questions. 'There are also plans for the weekend, with customers going to the test track to drive the demonstration car. Seb had been really excited about that, told me you'd be in your element there.'

'But still,' she said, her soft voice torturing his un-expected need for her, 'I can make my own way there.'

Was she deliberately being difficult, provoking him to the point of frustration? 'I have a plane waiting. We can be there before nightfall.'

She looked at him, doubt clouding her eyes, and a vice-like grip clutched at his chest. Seb had always spo-ken very protectively of his sister—and now he knew why. She was woman enough to bring out the protective streak in any man. For years he'd avoided any such sen-timents, having had them destroyed by divorce. He was far from the right man to protect her and he wished he'd never made Seb any promises.

He couldn't do this, couldn't risk it. She was sweet temptation even though he knew she was off limits. He couldn't do anything against Seb's memory. This was Seb's sister, the woman his friend had always wanted to protect. If he allowed this carnal need to take over, he would be failing in his promise to Seb. He wouldn't be protecting her at all.

'So what are you going to do while I pack?' Charlie asked tersely, annoyed that she hadn't even left her home yet and he was already making decisions for her. She tried for flippancy. 'Drink more coffee?'

'No,' he said, sounding very Italian, even with just that one word. 'I will wait here.'

He was infuriating and she recalled what Seb had said about him once when they'd talked on the phone about his new venture. *A man who knows what he wants and allows nothing to get in his way.*

Alessandro did want her at the launch. That much was clear. But why? Was she disrupting his plans by dictating her own terms? She certainly hoped so. It was probably about time he learnt he couldn't have it all.

'Very well. I will be as quick as I can.' She made to move past him and he stepped back away from her, giving her room. So much room that anyone would think he didn't want her near him, but the heavy hint of desire in his eyes gave an entirely different message.

'I'm not going anywhere, *cara*.' The silky softness of his voice stirred the throb of desire which still lingered inside her body. She clutched the door frame of the kitchen as if it was the only thing that would keep her upright.

'I wouldn't expect anything less from a man like you.' Before he even had time to respond, she fled, dashing up the stairs to her room, enjoying the rush of anticipation that ran through her. She paused briefly. She'd always been excited by the prospect of jetting off when she'd worked for Seb's team, but never had such a handsome man been part of the reason.

He's not, she scolded herself and quickly changed, before applying light make-up. Then, with practised speed and efficiency, she packed a small bag, just enough for a few days in Italy. She'd shop for anything else she needed once there.

His expression of shock made her smile as she returned to the kitchen. He hadn't expected that. At least it proved he didn't know as much about her as he claimed.

'Have you your passport?' His accent was heavy as he moved towards her to take her bag.

His fingers grazed hers as she gave him the bag and heat scorched her skin. She looked up at him and a flush crept over her face. In his eyes she thought she saw de-

sire, the same desire she was sure must be shining from
hers. Would he see it? Recognise it?

She hoped not. From the first second her eyes had
met his, the pull of attraction had been strong. With each
passing minute it had strengthened, but she could not and
would not act on it. To do so would be disloyal to Seb.
Whatever had happened the night of the accident, this
was Seb's business partner.

She hesitated. Could she do this? Should she be considering going anywhere with this man? The desire he
lit within her contrasted starkly with the anger she felt
at her brother's death. As far as she was concerned, he
was the reason her brother had crashed.

She'd do well to remember that.

This was going to be harder than he'd imagined. Sandro took the case from Charlie, taking in her change
of clothes. Heels, tight jeans of soft beige with a white
blouse and dark brown jacket. Chic. Elegant. Not at all
like the dishevelled gardener he'd met on arrival. She
was now very much the woman he'd seen on television
promoting Seb's team. The woman he'd admired more
and more as Seb had enthused about her.

Don't go there. He pushed thoughts of her to the back
of his mind, focusing instead on maintaining a businesslike manner. One that would keep her where she needed
to be in his mind.

He watched as she opened a drawer and pulled out
her passport.

'I should really let my neighbour know I'm going
away.'

He frowned, unsure where that comment was going.
'Why is this?'

'She'll keep an eye on the place, water the garden.' Absently she picked up her phone and began tapping quickly onto the screen. 'At least for a few days.'

Garden, he pondered. That didn't fit with the glamorous image she'd built up as she'd promoted the team. Had this cottage, this garden been her escape from the media frenzy that had followed? He knew well about the need to escape. It had been something he'd had to do twice in his life now.

'You gave up your career to become a gardener?'

She turned to face him, putting her phone in her handbag at the same time. 'Why is that so shocking?'

'Seb never mentioned you were a gardener.'

'It is something I've always enjoyed, but I didn't feel the need to change my life before Seb's accident.' She looked up at him, her expression serious and focused. 'Seb's death changed all that. That's why I want to know all he did that day. I have to understand why it happened.'

Each word echoed with her accusation, leaving him in no doubt she blamed him. The only other person who knew the truth was her father—and he'd insisted that she must never know all the details of Seb's accident.

Thoughts of Seb grounded him and the urge to tell her everything, just to clear his name of blame in her eyes, was overwhelming. But he wasn't doing this for himself; he was doing it for Seb. He would do well to remember that when he next thought of succumbing to the temptation of Charlie. She was out of his reach. Put there by his sense of honour and his promise to Seb and subsequently her father. Out of his reach was where she had to stay.

CHAPTER THREE

AS DARKNESS BEGAN to descend the car pulled to a halt outside Alessandro's offices and Charlie got her first view of the place she'd heard so much about from her brother. His calls had always been full of excitement and pride as he'd enthused about the Roselli factory, workshops and test track.

Sadness crept over her too. This was where Seb had spent his final weeks and she could have been part of that if she'd accepted his offer to come out and visit instead of being so tied up in her career. The same career she'd dropped after Seb's death.

She got out of the car and stood looking up at the buildings, wishing she had come to see what he was doing. 'I should have come when he asked me to,' she said softly and was startled when Alessandro responded.

'Seb always hoped you'd come here one day.' His voice was gentle and not at all judgemental as he placed his hand in the small of her back. She drew in a ragged breath, her emotions all over the place. Memories of Seb mixed with the undeniable attraction she felt for Alessandro. Guilt added to the mix and washed over her. How could she even be thinking such thoughts? Quickly she blocked them out.

'I wish I had.' Her voice was a croaky whisper of raw emotion. She stood next to him in the warm evening air, her emotions exposed and vulnerable, as if she stood before him totally naked. She was certain that not only was he able to see every bit of her skin, but into her heart and soul.

He stopped outside a glass door and keyed in his pass code, his other hand sliding away from her back, the heat of his touch cooling, giving her space to think. Judging by the shiver which had run up her spine, she needed that space. Badly.

'Why didn't you?' he asked, pushing open the door, stepping inside and holding the door open for her, but she didn't miss the lightly veiled accusation in his voice.

'It was busy. You know how the end of the racing season gets.' She saw his jaw tighten, saw the sceptical look on his face and shame heated her cheeks. She'd also been worried about Seb's blatant attempts at matchmaking. He'd often teased her on the phone about finding the perfect man for her.

She could have come. She'd wanted to come, but she had been a tiny bit threatened by this new life Seb had found. They'd always been so close and when he'd met Alessandro all that had changed overnight. She was pleased he'd found something he was so passionate about; she'd just never expected it to take him so far away from her, physically or emotionally.

He shrugged nonchalantly but she knew what he was thinking. She could almost hear his words, heavy and accented, telling her she was selfish, and she retaliated as if he'd actually spoken. 'I didn't know time was against me.'

He let the door go and she stood in the semi-darkness of the large reception. His face was a mask of hardened fury as the accusation in her words hit him. Did he feel any guilt? Did he have regrets? Did he want to go back and change things?

He stepped forward, coming closer, and she wished there was more light, something to lessen the presence of a man who excited and angered her so intensely. She veered wildly between those two emotions as he looked directly at her.

'Whatever guilt you carry, Charlotte, I do not need it added to what I feel.' His voice had deepened, become growly, anger lingering dangerously beneath the surface like a serpent waiting to strike. He loomed over her in the dim light, every bit the predator, but she wasn't going to be his next victim.

'Just by saying that you are admitting guilt.' She rounded on him. The hours spent on the plane and in his car, when she'd thought everything through silently, had allowed her temper to brew and now it flared to life.

For a moment his gaze held hers, his eyes hard and glittering. Tension stretched almost to breaking point between them as silence settled after her angry words. In her head she could hear her heartbeat, the fast thump of blood rushing around her body. It should have been ignited by her anger, but the flutter in her stomach as he stepped closer made it something else entirely.

It was raw attraction. Something she didn't want to feel. Not now and not for this man.

He stepped even closer, his height towering over her in the darkness, and she looked up into his eyes, wanting to appear fearless but afraid he'd see just what an effect he could have on her. Could he hear her heart pounding? Had he noticed her breath, ragged and unsteady?

'Dangerous words, *cara*.' Each word was low and soft

like a cat purring, but she sensed the coil of tension in him, the cool detachment from the emotions that careered inside her. He was more like a tiger preparing to strike.

'I came here to see what Seb had been working on,' she said, trying hard to beat down the flutter of emotions, and walked away from him towards the stairs. 'So, can we just do that? Then I'd like to check into a nearby hotel.'

She didn't wait for his answer, didn't look at his face, but every nerve in her body told her he was watching her—intently. She was about to go up the stairs when light flooded the reception area and she blinked against it and turned to face him. The sleek clean lines of the interior of the building were exactly as she would have imagined and, unable to help herself, she looked around her, trying hard to ignore the man who stood in the centre of the marble floor and the superiority which radiated from him.

'This way,' he said and passed her as she waited at the foot of the stairs, his scent of musk and male trailing in his wake. 'We'll take the lift.'

She bit her bottom lip, anxiety rushing at her. Was she really ready to see what Seb had been working on? She wasn't, but this was what she had to do, what she needed to do before she could put the last year behind her.

She became aware that Alessandro was watching her, waiting for her to enter the lift. 'We don't have to do this tonight.'

Was that genuine concern in his voice? Her gaze locked with his and everything around them spun. Everything blurred as the dark depths of his eyes met and held hers. Time seemed to be suspended, as if everything was standing still. She lowered her lashes. Now was not

the time to get fanciful. She'd never been that way in-
clined, had never hankered after notions of instant attraction. So why now? And why this man?

'I want to.' The words rushed from her as she stepped
quickly into the lift. 'I just hadn't anticipated it. Today
started just like any other, then you arrived...' Her voice
trailed off and she looked down at her hands, feigning
interest in her unpainted nails.

'I should have contacted you first but I didn't think
you'd see me.' His tone was calm and so matter-of-fact
she glanced up at him. He appeared totally unaffected
by the whole situation.

'I wouldn't have.' She flashed him a smile and, from
the expression on his face, he hadn't missed the sarcasm.
'I wouldn't have seen you and I would never have come
here.'

The lift doors opened onto a vast office but she paid
little attention to the hard masculine lines and marched
out of the lift, drawn inexplicably to the wall of windows,
offering an unrivalled view of Milan's twinkling skyline.

She should feel too irritated by his assured presence
to notice even one thing about his office, but that was so
far from the truth it was scary. She should be thinking
of Seb, should be focusing on what he'd done here, not
the man he'd worked with.

'*Grazie.*' The deep tone of his voice unsettled her and,
as she stopped to look out over the city, she saw his reflection behind her, saw him move closer.

'What for?' Her gaze met his reflected in the glass
and a coil of tension pressed down inside her. She knew
at any minute it could snap.

'Your honesty. Saying you wouldn't want to see me.'
His reflection shrugged nonchalantly, his gaze so intense

it obliterated the view. All she could see was him. Then her heart plummeted in disappointment. None of this really mattered to him. It was all about the Roselli image and launching a new car.

'I have no reason to conceal my dislike of you, Mr Roselli.'

Liar! a voice called in her head. She didn't dislike him. She should. The fizz of attraction was at war with the blame she still laid at his door, despite his earlier assurances that the accident had been nothing more than a tragedy.

'Dislike. Is that not a bit strong?' He moved unbearably close, his eyes holding hers in the reflection in the window.

She had to stop this now, whatever *this* was. Something she couldn't control was happening between them and she didn't like it. Or did she?

'Oh, I dislike you intensely, Alessandro.' She turned, her words a hurried whisper. Who was she trying to convince? 'And right at this moment I have no idea what I'm doing here.'

His eyes turned blacker than the night sky, their swirling depths mesmerising. She couldn't break eye contact. The power he'd had as he'd looked at her reflection had been intense, but this all-consuming fire which had leapt to life in her was too much.

'You are here, *cara*, because you couldn't help yourself.' His voice was deep and gentle, caressing every heightened nerve in her body into submission. 'Because this is what you need to do—for Seb.'

At the mention of her brother's name the spell slipped away like morning mist as the sun came up. She could see everything sharply and in focus again. She was here for Seb—a fact she had to keep in the forefront of her mind—or lose it to the seductive charms of the worst man she could possibly fall for.

'Exactly.' Her eyes maintained contact with his and she saw the moment they turned to glittering blackness. 'So I'd like to see where he worked, what he did.'

Alessandro couldn't move, mesmerised by the intensity of what had just passed between them. For the last few weeks he'd been irritated at the thought of contacting Seb's sister, had put the moment off for as long as possible. But, whatever he had been expecting when they'd finally met, it wasn't the raw desire that coursed wildly through him.

If she'd been any other woman he'd have acted upon that need; he would have kissed her and explored the passion that lingered expectantly, just waiting for the touch-paper to be lit so it could explode into life.

'*Si, così,*' he instructed her to follow, unable to gather his thoughts quickly enough to use English, a situation he'd never known before.

'Thank you.' Those two words were so soft, so seductive he almost couldn't move. He fought the urge to press his lips to hers. Thankfully, she stepped back, enough to remind him what he should and definitely shouldn't be doing.

With intent, he made his way across the vast expanse of his office, resisting the urge to look in the windows and see her reflection following. He didn't need to. His body told him she was; even if he hadn't heard her footsteps on the marble behind him he would have known she was there.

'This is where Seb worked.' He went through a door

at the end of his office into the room Seb had claimed as his own, the emptiness of it almost too harsh. On the far wall was the first drawing that Seb had done of the car. But still the office looked stark.

Something akin to guilt touched him. He should have brought Charlie here sooner and not left it until the last days before the launch. He should have done this a long time ago, but he'd been anxious to conceal the truth— for Seb's sake as much as his sister's.

As Charlie walked past him he caught a hint of her perfume; instantly he was transported back to her garden and the sweet smells of an English summer. Her deep ragged breath, inhaled quickly, drew his attention back to the present.

'Is this what he did?' She stood next to the desk, her fingertips tracing the outline of the car drawing. He noticed her hand shook slightly and, when she looked back at him, hesitation weaved with panic sprang from her eyes. He had the strange sensation his heart was being crushed.

'Sì.' His voice was so raw he couldn't say anything else, painfully aware he was intruding on her moment of grief.

'What else?' She looked at him and he saw the gleam of tears collect in her eyes and the pressure on his chest intensified.

Thankful for the diversion, he walked over to the desk and opened the laptop, turned it on and looked across the desk at her. Her pretty face was pale, her eyes wide, reminding him of a startled doe. 'There are lots of photos on here, as well as all he created in the design programme.'

She hesitated for a moment and he wondered if it was

all too much. She stood and watched him as he opened the photos up on the screen and turned the laptop to face her. He felt her scrutiny and questions press down on him.

Slowly she reached out, one fingertip touching the screen. He watched her eyes, the green becoming much more intense as she looked at the photo of Seb sitting in the driving seat of the test car, and he inwardly cursed. Couldn't he have selected a more appropriate photo for her to see first?

'When was this taken?' Her voice was fragile as she continued to look at the screen. She swallowed hard, trying to keep the tears at bay, and for the first time ever he wished a woman would cry. She needed to let out her grief.

He hated the answer he was going to have to give. 'The day before the accident.' It took huge effort to keep his voice calm, to keep it steady, but even to his ears each word he'd just said sounded cold. He'd studied the photo since then, shocked to see a hint of trouble in Seb's eyes. Would she notice too?

She looked up at him and tears filled her eyes, making them shine like gemstones. Before he'd thought about the consequences, he moved around the desk and took her in his arms. Without hesitation, she sought the comfort he offered and pressed her face in her hands, her forehead on his chest as sobs racked her body.

'*Dio mio*. This is too much for you.' He wanted to clench his fists in anger but instead spread them over her back as the sobs continued, smoothing them over her and pulling her closer against him.

'No, it's not.' The strangled words came out in a rush, muffled by her hands and his body.

'It is, *cara*, it is,' he soothed, just as he'd done for his sister many times as they'd grown up, but this wasn't his sister. This was a woman he desired with every nerve in his body.

'I should, I should.' Sobs prevented her words from coming out and, without thinking, he lowered his head, pressing his lips into her hair. She stilled in his arms momentarily and he closed his eyes against the memories of when he'd thought his life was complete. He pushed back the knowledge that he'd failed to be the man his wife had wanted, lifted his chin and took in a deep breath.

It seemed like for ever that he held Charlie as she cried, each sob transferring her pain to him, increasing his guilt for not having been there the night Seb had decided to take the car out again. He would have seen the drink- and drugs-induced euphoria and could have stopped him. The discovery still shocked him now. How had they worked so closely together for all those months without him noticing Seb had such a problem?

He lowered his head, once more pressing his lips against her hair, his aim to soothe both of them. But, as he held her tighter, uttering words of comfort in Italian, he knew he had to stop, had to let her go. It shocked him to admit he wanted to be more than just a shoulder to cry on.

Thankfully the tears subsided and a huge sob shuddered through her. She looked up at him and they were so close they could have been lovers. Without any effort at all he would be able to press his lips to hers, but her tear-stained cheeks reminded him they were not lovers and exactly why they were here.

'I should have done this a long time ago.' Finally she spoke a little more calmly, her words slightly wobbly after crying.

'This is the first time you have cried?' Incredulity made him pull back slightly as he watched her expression change, become softer, less pained.

She smiled up at him, nodding. 'Thank you.' Her voice was barely above a whisper and she blinked as tears escaped her eyes. She rubbed one cheek roughly with her fingers but, before she could reach the other cheek and before he could think about what he was doing, he gently wiped the tears away.

Everything changed in that second. They became cocooned in a bubble of sizzling tension. Unable to stop himself, he held her face in his hands, her skin warm and damp from crying. Her green eyes locked with his, sadness and grief swirling with something quite different and completely inappropriate.

'Prego.' His natural response sprang to his lips but his voice was husky and deep. He couldn't take his gaze from hers, couldn't break that tenuous contact which held them together.

She closed her eyes and leant her cheek against his hand. Instinct took over and he caressed her face then pushed his fingers into her hair, the silky softness of it almost irresistible. He wanted to kiss her, to lower his head and taste the fullness of her lips.

He moved towards her and she opened her eyes. For what seemed like an eternity she looked up at him, her breathing fast and shallow. His heartbeat sounded so loud in his ears as he watched the green of her eyes change until they swirled with browns, like trees as autumn approached.

He wanted her. That was all he could think of at that moment. Nothing else was important. Nothing else mattered.

She moved nearer, her eyes closing, spreading her long damp lashes on her cheeks, and then her lips met his. It was a gentle kiss, full of hesitancy at first, but, as he pulled her close, one hand buried in her long hair, it deepened, became something much more. He shouldn't be doing this, not now, not ever.

Charlie's head spun and she knew she shouldn't be kissing him like this, knew it would only mean complications, but the need to feel his lips against hers was overwhelming. Her senses were on overdrive, every nerve in her body responding to him. Heat exploded deep inside her and she pressed herself against him. His arm tightened around her back, pulling her closer, and his fingers scrunched in her hair, holding her head at just the right angle as his tongue moved between her lips, entwining with hers.

Her arms slipped up around his neck, pulling him closer, deepening the kiss until she could hardly stand, her knees were so weak. Never had a kiss felt like this, so electrifying, so right.

With a force and suddenness that nearly knocked her backwards he released his hold on her and pushed his hands against her shoulders, forcing her back and away from him. She was so shocked she didn't know what to say, even if her laboured breathing had allowed her to speak. After a few seconds he let go of her, stepping backwards, a wary look in his eyes and a furious rush of Italian sprang from his lips.

Her grasp on the language was slight and she had no idea what he'd said, but his body language left her in no doubt. He had not enjoyed or wanted that kiss. So why had he encouraged her? Was this some kind of game?

'That shouldn't have happened.' She forced herself to stand as tall as possible, even though her knees were so weak they might crumple beneath her and a fire of heady need still raged inside her.

'Damn right it shouldn't have.' He flung his hand up in agitation, turned and marched across the office to the doorway. 'That can never happen between us, ever.'

Hurt scolded her but she kept her eyes firmly fixed on him, refusing to be intimidated. He didn't want her kisses—so what? 'I didn't think…' she stammered the words out '…I didn't know what I was doing.'

His eyes narrowed but he remained at the far side of the office. 'Apparently not. It's time we left here.'

'No—' she panicked, her embarrassment at his obvious dislike of her evaporating '—I haven't seen nearly enough.'

'Enough for tonight.' His voice was deep and hard, the complete opposite to the husky tones that had soothed her just moments before. 'You will stay with me tonight.'

'You?' The question shot from her lips before she could think.

'You are upset, acting irrationally. I cannot leave you in a hotel alone, not tonight.'

The firm words brooked no argument and if she was honest she had little fight left in her. The last twelve hours had been nothing short of shock after shock. From the moment he'd arrived in her garden she'd been on a roller coaster ride of emotions.

'Just call me a taxi to take me to a hotel in the city.' With bravado she was far from feeling, she walked towards him but he didn't move aside for her to leave the office. Instead, he looked at her, his brown eyes cold and remote.

'Seb was right.' The firmness of his voice caught her attention and she looked up at him, her gaze locking with his.

Angered at the mention of her brother, she glared at him. 'And what is that supposed to mean?'

A hint of a smile lingered at the edges of his mouth then he pressed them into a tight line of exasperation. 'I know more about you than you might think, Charlotte Warrington.'

'You've got a nerve,' she said as her own expression mirrored his.

'*Sì.*' He shrugged casually and turned away from her, leaving her wide-eyed with shock.

If she was sensible she'd just walk out of here, get a taxi to the airport and go home. But right now she wasn't sensible and she wanted this chance to get answers to questions that would otherwise niggle at her for the rest of her life.

The only problem was these answers were tied up with the man she blamed for Seb's death, the very same man she'd just thrown herself at, kissing him with a passion she'd never known before.

'I'm not going anywhere with you, especially after what just happened.'

He turned round so swiftly she almost walked straight into him, leaving her perilously close to him again. 'Do I need to remind you, *cara*, you kissed me?'

Her cheeks burned as the sexy depth of his voice practically caressed her body, reigniting the heat that had flared between them earlier. 'That,' she hissed at him, 'was a big mistake. One that won't be happening again.'

'*Va bene!*' His gaze searched her face, resting briefly

on her lips. 'In that case, there is no danger in you staying at my apartment tonight.'

'Danger? You make me sound like some sort of predatory female.' She was becoming more and more infuriated by him. Maybe a hotel would be the best option, but as that thought settled in her mind she knew she didn't want to be alone right now. Not after all she'd been through in the short space of time since he'd forged into her life, but her only choice of company was Alessandro Roselli.

He just quirked his brows at her, the humiliating spark in his eyes clear. She held his gaze, refusing to back down.

'Why do you want to do this? Why is it so important I'm at the launch?' She gestured around the room, glancing back at the drawing on the wall.

'As I explained, I made a promise to your brother. One I intend to keep.' He walked through to the large office they'd entered earlier and across to the lift. 'This way, *cara*.'

Charlie couldn't shake off the feeling that he'd won. What he'd won she didn't quite know, but he had. One night in his apartment wouldn't be that hard, would it? First thing, she'd arrange a hotel in Milan and as soon as the launch was over she could go back to her cottage and get on with her life. The quiet life she'd led since Seb's accident; the one that kept her safe.

Alessandro shut the door of his apartment and watched Charlie as she walked into the open-plan living area. She hadn't said a word since they'd left his office but, despite that, the tension between them had increased. So much that he now questioned his sanity in bringing her here.

'The guest suite is ready for you,' he said sternly, eager to create some boundaries because if there was one woman who needed to be behind them it was this one.

'Thank you,' she said so softly it was almost a whisper.

He watched her as she walked around the apartment, judging the artwork he'd collected over recent years, taking in just about every detail with a hint of suspicion on her face. There was nothing modern about the apartment, from the grand façade of the old building to the ornate interior. It was a complete contrast to the office they'd just left—exactly what he'd wanted it to be. It was a showcase for the real Alessandro.

She wandered over to the balcony doors and looked down onto the busy streets of Milan. He used that time to rein in the hot lust which pumped around his body after the journey back from his office. Since the moment her lips had touched his something had changed and he feared it might be irreversible.

'Would you like anything to eat or drink?' The polite question gave him just that bit more time to regain control and bring normality to the evening.

She turned and looked back at him. 'No, thank you. I'm tired. It's been an unexpectedly busy day and I need to be fresh tomorrow.'

'Fresh?' The word sprang from him, a frown furrowing his brow, but she kept her gaze on him.

'Yes, there is a lot to do before the launch, lots I need to know.' She looked completely focused but the gritty determination in her voice rang alarm bells in his head.

'You're right,' he said and turned from her, picking up her small overnight bag before heading towards the guest suite. A good night's sleep would be beneficial to him too, but somehow he doubted he'd get it. His body still craved hers, still yearned for her touch, her kiss.

He crunched his hand tightly around the handle of the bag. He'd made a promise to Seb and he would keep that promise, no matter what. The thought of his friend, who had also been a partner in the business venture, reminded him that Seb had been the last person to stay in the guest suite.

He pushed aside the guilt. Seb had been staying with him. He should have seen the signs, spotted the problem. He couldn't change that now, but he could keep the painful truth from Seb's beloved sister.

He paused outside the door and turned to look at her. 'Your brother stayed here too. Did you know that?'

'No.' A startled whisper formed the word and she looked at him, confusion marring the beauty of her face. 'I don't understand. He was looking for somewhere to rent.'

'That is true.' He opened the door to the suite and walked in and she followed him, looking around her. There wasn't any evidence that anyone had ever stayed here. 'It was a sensible option. We were both working on the same project.'

'Did he find somewhere to move to, or was this the last place he stayed?'

The very question he'd dreaded had just been delivered with clear words. 'This was the last place.'

'But his things?'

'I sent them on to your father.'

She looked around the room, from the large bed to the dark wardrobe and drawers, as if she didn't quite believe him. 'I see.'

Silence floated down around them, a silence so heavy

he wanted to break it, to say something. But what else could he say? Everything so far had caused hurt and pain. 'There is another room. Much smaller, but if you would prefer it...'

She shook her head, the light above them catching the darkness of her hair, making the brown tones glow and come alive. 'I'd like to stay here, please.'

Now he really did question his sanity. Not only had he kissed her, responded to the invitation her lips had made, but now he'd put her in the very same room Seb had last stayed in. The promise he'd made to his friend to look after Charlie, to involve her in the project was becoming more difficult to keep by the minute. As was concealing the truth.

CHAPTER FOUR

'DID YOU SLEEP WELL?' Alessandro's polite enquiry pulled Charlie from her thoughts as they sat having breakfast together in the tranquillity of his apartment. The jeans and shirt he wore hugged his body to perfection and she fought hard to keep her mind where it should be—on her brother and the car she was here to help promote. Thinking about the handsome Italian she'd kissed last night wasn't going to help her at all and she forced herself to be as rational and in control as he appeared.

'Yes, thanks,' she replied, taking a sip of freshly squeezed orange juice. Sleeping in the room Seb had used should have helped her, but it hadn't. It had had the opposite effect. She'd wept silent tears for her brother, finally finding release from the grief she'd kept locked away, but little comfort. It hadn't banished the idea that Alessandro was to blame for the accident or that he was hiding something from her.

He looked at her, his keen gaze lingering on her face just a little too long. She was aware the dark circles beneath her eyes would tell him she hadn't slept well at all. Thankfully, he had the good grace to let it go.

'There are a few things I need to do this afternoon in

preparation for the launch, but we can either go to the office or to the test track this morning.'

Test track. Those words careered into her, dragging her back to a time when she'd always been at the test track, her father and brother at her side. It was where she'd learnt to drive, really drive, much to her mother's disgust.

'I'd like to see the car,' she said thoughtfully. 'It feels as if I haven't been at a track for a long time.' She'd missed the thrill and excitement of the place. Her garden, whilst a safe sanctuary she'd been happy in, suddenly seemed tame.

'*Si,*' he said as he sat forward, placing his now empty cup back on the table. 'Seb told me it was a big part of your childhood too.'

She looked into her juice, not able to meet the intensity in his eyes. They made her feel vulnerable and she didn't do vulnerable. 'I spent a lot of my time there. I loved it.'

'What did your mother think of that?' His question nudged at issues which had erupted often when she was a teenager.

'She didn't have any objection to Seb being there.' Charlie hesitated and looked up into his handsome face and instantly wished she hadn't.

He appeared relaxed as he sat back in his seat again, but something wasn't quite right. He reminded her of a big cat, lulling its quarry into a false sense of security. Any moment he would pounce, strike out and get exactly what he wanted with unnerving accuracy.

'I sense a *but*.' He spoke softly, then waited, the silence hanging expectantly between them.

Before she could think, his question had thrown open things she'd do better to keep to herself—because it was a very big *but*. How much had Seb told him? Did he know of her mother's disapproval of her involvement in the racing world? Did he know she'd hated the lifestyle, hated the way her husband had flirted with all the women. Her mother had resented being second best so much she'd left the family home, deserting her teenage children.

'My mother didn't like me being there. She didn't think I should be driving those cars and certainly not working on them. She thought I should behave more like a lady instead of a tomboy and it became a constant battleground as I grew up.' She wasn't bitter any more. In fact she could now see why her mother had been so against the racing world, why she'd wanted her daughter as far away from it as possible. But she wasn't about to go into all that now, especially not with Alessandro.

He smiled, a gorgeous smile that made his eyes sparkle, full of mischief. 'Now I understand. Your insistence on being called Charlie was to remain a tomboy.'

'Something like that.' She finished her juice, wondering how she had become the topic of conversation.

'But you are a beautiful woman, Charlotte, why hide it?' The intensity in his eyes scared her, made her heart pound, and she bit down on her lower lip, suddenly very much out of her depth.

'I was a rebellious teenager,' she explained, giving in to the need to offer some sort of explanation. Heat infused her cheeks and she looked out over Milan to hide her embarrassment. It was time to change the subject; she'd said more than enough to him. This wasn't about her—it was about Seb. 'Can we go now? I'd like to see the car.'

'Of course,' he said as he stood up, preparing to leave. 'If you are sure this is what you want to do.'

She'd never been more certain about anything, which

was strange, given that just twenty-four hours ago she'd thought she never wanted to see this man. His timing had been impeccable, arriving so soon after the conversation she'd had with her father about getting her life back again.

'Before we go,' she asked, unable to keep the hint of suspicion from her voice, 'what did my father say to you when you told him about the launch?'

He looked directly at her, his stance bold and intimidating. 'It appears he wants only your happiness.'

'I need to contact him, tell him I will be at the launch.'

'He knows.' She looked at him. There was not a hint of conceit on his handsome face, but she sensed he was keeping something from her. She decided to let it go—for now. At the moment, seeing the car which had become Seb's world was at the top of her list and talking like this wouldn't help at all. She tried to deflect his interest with light-hearted words.

'And will he be there too?'

'He hopes to be.'

'That sounds like Dad.'

'This way,' he said as he picked up his keys and slipped on a leather jacket. The understated style only emphasised the latent strength of his body and she had to pull her gaze away, force herself to think of other things. This was not the time or the place to become attracted to a man—especially not this man.

Alessandro wasn't able to negotiate the morning traffic of Milan with his usual ease. He could hardly concentrate on driving. His main focus was instead on the woman beside him. She didn't say anything, merely looked around her, taking in the vibrancy of the city he loved.

'Have you always lived in Milan?' Her voice was soft

and should have soothed his restless mind, but it didn't. The slight husky tone to it only intensified the way his body seemed on high alert just being next to her.

'For most of my adult life, yes.' He knew it was only small talk, but discussing his family with outsiders wasn't what he usually did. But Seb had become like a brother to him, even in such a short time, so didn't that make Charlie anything but an outsider?

'Seb mentioned your family lives in Tuscany and produce wines.' Her voice was light in an attempt to make conversation, but such questions made him uneasy. When a woman asked about family, there was usually intent behind it. But what motivation could Charlie possibly have?

He shrugged and turned onto the open road, leaving the city behind as they headed for the test track. The sun shone with the promise of another hot day. 'That is true, but my love was for cars, not wine. So I moved to Milan, finished my education and began working for my uncle, turning the company around and making it the success it is today. The rest, I believe you would say, is history.'

'And this car? Was that also part of your love for cars?' She almost caressed the words, setting his pulse racing at an alarming rate.

He glanced across at her, watching as she looked around the interior with genuine interest, proving all that Seb had told him about her was true. She wasn't much older than his sister but, at twenty-four, had made her way to the top of her career, promoting first her father's racing team, then Seb's. She was a successful woman in her own right, and that success had been born out of her passion for cars and racing, which was why Seb had wanted her at the launch of the car.

She ran the tips of her fingers across the dashboard in

front of her, leaving him in no doubt of her love of cars—
and that she was a woman of passion. She'd shown him
that much last night with her kiss. He pressed down on
the accelerator in a bid to focus his attention on anything
else but her, and the car responding willingly. Thinking
of last night's kiss wouldn't help to quell the lingering
desire she'd awakened.

'Impressive,' she said quickly, laughter filling her
voice.

Inwardly he groaned. She thought he was putting the
car through its paces for her, when all he'd been doing
was giving his mind something other than her to focus
on. Again he glanced at her, shocked to see a smile on
her lips, and instantly he wished he wasn't driving, that
he didn't have to concentrate on the car so that he could
enjoy her smile—the first real smile he'd seen on those
sweet lips.

'It is not far now.' *Grazie a Dio!* He didn't think he
could take much more of this enforced proximity, the way
her light perfume weaved its scent throughout the car.
His body was excruciatingly aware of each tiny movement she made.

The streamlined car willingly ate up the miles as they
drove in a silence laced with tension—not angry tension but that of restrained desire. Her kiss last night had
more than hinted at her attraction for him. He couldn't
deny that he was tempted by her but it was something
he wouldn't act on. To do so would be to dishonour his
friend's memory and the promise he'd made.

A sigh of relief left him as they turned off the road and
down a smaller road which led to the Roselli test track.
Never before had a drive here been so long and so tense.
Thankfully, he parked the car behind the large building

which housed the prototypes for all his cars currently being tested.

Charlie got out of the car, her full attention now on the building before her, and he knew she was anxious. The tight set of her shoulders betrayed her nerves. 'You don't have to do this. We can just go back to the office.'

She turned to look at him, her hand reaching up to keep her hair from her face as the wind toyed with it. Instantly he remembered how he'd pushed his hands through it just hours ago, how he'd clutched it hard to enable him to kiss her deeper, and the way she'd responded.

Maledizione! Did he have to keep going back to something that should never have happened?

'Mr Roselli, I want to do this and I will, no matter how many times you try to dissuade me.' The fire of her spirit sounded in every word and, as she looked at him, her pretty face set in fierce determination, he fought the urge to smile.

'I think we can dispense with formalities now, don't you, Charlie?' He saw her green eyes glitter as he used her preferred name.

'As you wish, Alessandro.' The sweetness of her voice didn't mask her irritation.

'Sandro,' he said as he locked the car and came round to her. 'I'd much prefer it if you'd call me Sandro.'

Her gaze locked with his, challenging him with unsaid words. They held the same fire and courage Seb's always had, although the green of hers was more like emerald. Hard and glittering.

'As you wish, Sandro.' She shrugged casually and turned to look up at the building. 'Now, can I see the car?'

'It is only the test car. The actual car will be revealed at the launch.'

She glanced briefly at him before returning her attention to the modern building, its streamlined design which curved around them. 'Even better. I'd like to know what changes have been made since Seb drove it.'

There it was again. Accusation.

'It is an exact copy of the prototype Seb drove. There weren't any improvements to be made.'

She turned and looked at him, her brows raised in surprise. 'None at all?'

He watched her intently for a moment as she did anything other than look at him. 'No. This way.' He moved purposefully towards the door, keyed in his code and stood back for her to enter, hoping she wouldn't pursue the conversation further. He didn't want to lie to her, but at the same time he didn't think she would be able to handle the truth.

His team of mechanics were working on another project and glanced up as they entered. He noticed she ignored their speculative gazes and instead walked towards the grey test car parked in the centre of the white workshop floor, ready for them.

He followed but held back as she approached the vehicle, wanting to give her time with something that had been as much a part of Seb's life as it was his.

She paced slowly along the car, her long jeans-clad legs doing untold things to him, and he gritted his teeth against the sizzle of attraction. This was one woman he couldn't have but, as she slid her hand over the front wing of the car, following the sleek angles of the bodywork, he couldn't help but wish he was the car.

'Can I?' She gestured towards the door and he nodded, not able to string even a few words together in any language after those thoughts.

As she slid into the driving seat he moved towards the car and leant on the open door. He looked down at her, trying hard not to notice how the seat curved around her thighs. Instead, he kept his eyes on her face, watching as she openly devoured everything with hungry eyes. Slowly she wrapped her fingers around the steering wheel, clutching it tight until the leather creaked. She looked as if she belonged behind the wheel of a car and as if this particular car had been made for her.

'It's amazing.' Those words were so light and husky. He gritted his teeth hard, trying to subdue the lust which now throbbed in his veins, demanding satisfaction.

With a sudden movement which caught her attention, he pushed his body off the car door. 'We'll take it out now,' he said as he gave the signal to his team to raise the doors. Sunlight poured in as they silently opened.

'I'd like to drive.' Her words were firm as he walked back to the car, reminding him of the stubborn little girl he'd grown up with. His sister had nearly always got her way with such a tone, especially with him.

'Maybe it would be better if I drove first.' He didn't want her thinking too much about her brother whilst behind the wheel. It was obvious she blamed him for Seb's accident and grief could manifest itself in various forms. 'You can sit back and enjoy the ride, just as Seb would have wanted you to.'

'You didn't know Seb that well if you think that.' She raised her delicate brows suggestively at him and smiled. He knew he was beaten. 'Seb would want me to drive so he could sit there and listen. He'd want to feel the car and be at one with it.'

He leant on the car, one hand on the roof, one hand on the open door, and lowered his head, bringing him very close to her. The enticing scent of her perfume met him and he resisted the urge to inhale it. Her passionate little speech just now had already done enough.

'*Va bene*, you may drive, but carefully and I will, of course, be with you.'

She smiled up at him, a genuine heartfelt smile that made her eyes light up. Right there and then he decided he wanted her to smile more and assigned himself the mission of making that happen.

'I am able to drive.' Her lips formed a sexy little pout as she put on a show of pretend petulance and it was all he could do not to lean down and kiss her. The first woman who'd stirred his dormant body since he'd extricated himself from the mistake of his marriage and she was out of bounds. So far off limits she might as well be on the moon.

'I don't doubt that you can, but having dealt with one female who drove too fast I'm reluctant to do it again.'

'Oh.' The word was full of disappointment and he couldn't hide his smile.

'My sister. A while ago now. She took a corner too fast, despite my warnings, and ended up a bit the worse for wear.' He made light of it when really he wished he could go back and change things, make her listen. Just as he now wished he could with Seb.

'Well, you don't need to worry about me,' she said and started the engine, the throaty growl forcing her to raise her voice slightly. 'Sebastian Warrington was my brother, after all.'

She was wrong, so wrong. He did have to worry. His promise to Seb meant that not only would he involve her in the launch but he'd look after her, be a brother figure to her, and he couldn't do that when hot lust shot around his body like off-course fireworks.

He walked around the front of the car, watching her through the windscreen. Her face was full of concentration as she studied the array of information on the driver's screen. As if she sensed his scrutiny, she looked up and smiled, this time a more hesitant smile. Should he be letting her do this? He knew only too well what could happen if someone drove beyond their capabilities.

Her gaze followed him as he moved to the other side of the car and opened the passenger door. 'Ready?' He kept the word light as he slipped down into the seat and shut the door. It was a lightness he didn't feel, not when they were suddenly very close, much more so than in his car.

She nodded her head and looked forward, focusing on the task, but he couldn't concentrate. The engine growled in anticipation and the car moved slowly out into the morning sunshine. He breathed a sigh of relief that she wasn't as hot-headed as her brother had been the first time he'd taken it out.

Carefully she manoeuvred out onto the track and with a steady speed began the first circuit. He looked over at her, taking the opportunity to study her as she focused on driving. Her thick hair was scrunched up in a haphazard sort of style, looking as if she'd just left her lover's bed. Her lips were pressed together in concentration, the same gesture Seb had used when he really focused on driving, but on Charlie it was cute, sexy even.

The engine grew louder as she pushed the speed up, bringing his mind back from the dangerous territory it had just wandered to.

'Relax.' The laughter in her voice didn't match the

intense concentration on her face and, probably for the first time ever, he didn't know what to say. With shock, he realised she was making him nervous. He sensed she was holding back, that, just like her brother, she wanted to take the car to its upper limits, but was she capable? Could she really drive a car like this to its full potential?

'You're not nervous, are you?' The teasing question finally focused his mind. 'I have been taught to do this properly.'

'No,' he lied as he tried to sit back and relax. With each passing second it was obvious she could drive and if she'd had the same tutor as Seb, what more guarantee did he need? 'I make a bad co-pilot. I like to be in control at all times.'

She glanced quickly at him, the green of her eyes flashing with amusement. 'Are we just talking about driving?'

He couldn't help the laugh that rumbled from him. 'I was only referring to driving, but now you come to mention it…'

'Let's see what she's made of then.' The laughter in her voice gave way to a serious tone full of purpose.

Before he could utter one word of protest, the car lurched forward like an angry stallion, pressing him back in the seat. The trees around the track blurred as the engine roared. His heart pounded and he had images of arriving at the scene of his sister Francesca's accident and comforting her while he waited for help to arrive.

'Slow down!' he demanded, hating the sense of being totally unable to avert a crisis.

'Don't spoil it now. I know what I'm doing.' Her raised voice did little to assuage the doubt he had in himself to trust her driving ability.

'Charlotte!' He snapped her name loudly, keeping his eyes firmly fixed on the corner they were hurtling towards.

Charlie could barely hear Alessandro. Her heart was thudding with the excitement of being behind the wheel of a powerful car again. It had been too long and she had no intention of stopping now. This was exactly what she needed to chase the demons away.

She pressed harder on the accelerator, elated to find the powerful engine still had more to give. As the countryside blurred to a sway of green she knew this was the right thing to do. Seb had driven this car, felt its power and had been at one with it. Driving it now brought her closer to him; it was as if he was here with her.

'Slow down, Charlotte. Now.' Alessandro's curt tone was full of authority but she couldn't stop now, couldn't deny herself this moment.

'This is amazing,' she enthused, pushing the car to its limits around a corner. Tyres squealed but held the track like nothing she'd known before.

'Do you ever do as you are told?' The rich timbre of his voice was edged with steely control. She sensed him sitting there, rigid with anger at her disobedience. The thought made her laugh.

'Didn't Seb tell you that I'm exasperating?' Another corner took her concentration and beside her he cursed fluidly in Italian. Was she really worrying him or was it just that she wouldn't do what he wanted? There wasn't any doubt in her mind that he was the type of man who liked to be in total control of every situation.

'That, *cara*, is something we didn't discuss. Slow

down.' His voice was firm, full of discipline, making her smile and itch to push the car harder.

'Do you always spoil everyone's fun?' She slowed the car enough to be able to talk with him, but the engine protested, tempting her with its power once more.

'Only when my life is on the line.' The acerbic tone of his voice didn't go unnoticed as he raised it to be heard over the engine. They headed down a long straight and she had to resist the urge to push the car harder.

'Your life is not on the line, Sandro—don't be so dramatic. I've been trained to the highest level to drive cars just as powerful as this.' She drove into the next bend, restraining herself from showing him just how capable she was of handling the car.

'By whom?' Those two words were curt and heavily accented and she wondered again if he genuinely was afraid.

'My father. He taught Seb and me everything he'd learnt, so relax and enjoy your car, feel it, be at one with it.'

She pushed the car into another bend, her body infused with adrenaline, something she'd missed when she'd taken up the more genteel pursuit of gardening. It just hadn't given her the same buzz.

A long straight stretch spread out before her again as she came out of another bend and, forgetting everything, including the hurt and pain of losing Seb, she pushed the car to its limits one last time.

It felt so good. Nothing like it on earth had ever come close. It was exhilarating. The car ate up the tarmac as they sped along the straight stretch.

'*Dio mio*, stop!' The harsh command penetrated the bubble of excitement she'd slipped into and she let her foot off the accelerator, the car slowing.

'We're halfway around the track; I can't just stop!' she protested, but moderated the speed to a more sensible level.

'Stop. Right now.'

'Right now?' Anger sizzled inside her. Anger because she had to do as he told her. Anger because she'd lost control in front of him but, most of all, anger at him. If things had been different, it might have been Seb at her side.

'Now, Charlotte.' His hard tone brooked no argument.

'Okay, have it your way.' As the words snapped from her she pressed hard on the brake pedal.

Tyres squealed in protest as the front of the car lowered dramatically to the tarmac, but it was nothing compared to the anger which still hurtled around her. This was all his fault.

'Are you insane?' The car jolted to a stop and those words rushed at her.

She couldn't look at him yet. Her heart thumped so wildly in her chest she was sure he could hear its wild beat. She was mad, yes, she'd lost control. In her bid to forget the real reason she was here she'd been reckless, but it was still his fault.

'Yes—' she turned her head sharply to look at him, her breathing coming hard and fast '—I was mad to come here with you.'

Before she could think in any kind of rational way, she threw open the door, unclipped the seat belt and bolted—from him and the car. She ran from everything she'd tried to hide from these last twelve months.

'Charlotte!' She heard the deep tone of his voice, now edged with exasperation, but she didn't turn, didn't stop. She marched off the tarmac and onto the grass without any idea of which way to go. All she wanted was to get away from him, away from the car and away from all the pain which now surged through her.

Pain he'd induced.

As she began to break into a run he reached her, grabbed her arm and pulled her so quickly to a stop that she was turned and jolted against the hardness of his chest. For an instant all the breath seemed to leave her body and she couldn't speak. All she could do was stand looking into his eyes, glittering with anger as he held her captive with his firm grip. Her breathing was now so rapid she was panting as if she'd just run a hundred-metre sprint.

'Let me go.' Her furious demand only made his hand tighten on her arm.

'Not until you calm down.' He said the words slowly, but she didn't miss the glinting edge of steel within them.

'It shouldn't have been you.' A cocktail of emotions rushed to find expression. 'I should have been here with Seb. Not you.'

'I should never have brought you here, not after what your father told me.' Each word was delivered in a cool and calm tone, but there was still that underlying steel.

'My father?' She gasped in shock, trying unsuccessfully to release her arm from his grip. 'What has he said?'

'That you've been hiding from this since the funeral.' He released her arm but remained excruciatingly close. It was all becoming too much. Memories of Seb entwined with whatever it was between her and this man. She couldn't deal with either of them at the moment.

'I have not been hiding from anything—except the cruelty of the media.' She looked up into his face, so close she could smell his aftershave, but fury kept her expression hard.

He blinked, his head drawing back from her just a fraction. 'The media?'

She pulled free from him, turned and stalked away, tossing her next words over her shoulder. 'Yes, the media. You know the ones. They like to dig all the dirt on you and your family when you're down.'

'Charlotte, don't walk away from me.' His tone was harsh but she carried on walking—or was she running yet again?

'Just leave me, Alessandro. Take the car back and leave me.' She stopped and turned to look at him; his strides were so long that he was almost directly behind her and again she found herself against a wall of pure maleness.

'No, *cara.*' He spoke more softly, looking down at her.

Infuriated, a well of exasperation opened deep within her. 'Worried what everyone will think when you go back alone?' She couldn't prevent the tart edge creeping into her words.

'I don't give a damn about anyone else. The only thing that matters right now is you.'

She looked up into his eyes; the angry glitter was gone from them now. She resisted the urge to close hers, to give in to the invitation of his words and let him care for her, soothe her. But that hadn't been what he'd meant.

'Why? Because of your promise to Seb?' she retorted, fighting back once more.

His brow furrowed and he shook his head in denial. Guilt niggled at her. She was deliberately provoking him. *It's his fault Seb isn't here*, she reminded herself sharply.

'Not completely.' He stepped closer, so close she could just reach up and kiss him if she wanted to. Just as she'd done last night.

Mesmerised by his nearness, the heady scent of his aftershave doing strange things to her senses, she remained exactly where she was. Their eyes locked and she was sure he was thinking the same thing, feeling the same hot sizzle arcing between them.

Slowly, maintaining eye contact, she raised her chin up and saw his eyes darken to the blackness of a starless sky. She paused, an unspoken question emanating from her. His answer was to claim her lips with his.

CHAPTER FIVE

CHARLIE CLOSED HER eyes as every limb in her body weakened beneath the power of his hungry kiss. Just when she thought she wouldn't be able to stand any longer his arms wrapped around her, pulling her so tight against him that she was in no doubt he wanted her.

What was she doing? Kissing this man—and, worse again, wanting so much more?

Although she knew she shouldn't, she couldn't help herself and, just as she had done the previous night, she wound her arms about his neck, sliding her fingers into the curls he had tried to disguise.

Adrenaline from the drive still pumped around her, fuelling this new heady passion to heights she'd never before experienced. Every part of her was on fire, burning with desire for the man she supposedly hated above all others.

'This is…' she began as his lips left hers, scorching a trail down her throat until she couldn't utter another word.

'Amazing, no?' His husky voice sent a thrill of shivers through her.

No, not amazing. It's wrong. It shouldn't be happening.

Inside her head the words formed, but that was where they stayed as he claimed her lips once more, so deeply and passionately she gasped in pleasure against him. She couldn't think any more. The only thing that mattered was satisfying the hot need which blazed inside her.

'And this...' He almost groaned the words out as he lowered his head to kiss down her throat. She arched her back, leaning against the strength of his arm, knowing exactly what he wanted.

A sigh of total contentment slipped from her and she let her head drop back as his kisses moved down her throat until he reached the soft swell of her breasts, visible at the opening of her blouse.

Then passion exploded as he kissed her nipple, dampening the silk of her blouse. Her bra offered little defence against the persuasion of his seduction and she buried her fingers into the thickness of his hair, a soft sigh escaping her lips as she surrendered to the pleasure of his mastery.

'This is good too, no?' His accent became heavier with each word as desire engulfed them, wrapping them up together. He nipped at the hard peak of her nipple, sending a spark of urgent need straight to the very core of her.

'It's so good, but so wrong.' Her voice was a throaty whisper as she pushed her fingers deeper into the curls, pressing him against her, even though she knew it was reckless. Each breath she took intensified the sensation until she couldn't do anything but close her eyes to the pure pleasure of the moment. Wrong or right, she gave herself up to it.

'Oh, *cara*, it's wrong, so, so wrong, but so right.' He moved his attention to her other breast and she almost sank to the grass beneath her feet as his tongue worked its magic, her breathing ragged and fast.

'We shouldn't.' Barely a whisper now, her voice sounded hoarse as each breath rushed from her.

It was so good she thought she could hear horns—car horns blasting around them, their fast rhythm matching the pulse of desire inside her. The sound became louder and suddenly he straightened, pulling her upright with a jolt.

'*Maledizione.* I should have known we'd be seen.'

The sound of horns was very clear now and she realised it wasn't just horns, but emergency sirens. She jumped back from him as if scalded by his very touch, wanting to put as much distance between them as possible while she fought to regain control over her body, extinguish the heady need he'd ignited. Thankfully, he seemed to want the same and walked abruptly away.

What had she been thinking? Nothing. Absolutely nothing. That was the problem. She hadn't been thinking at all. She'd allowed her seesawing emotions to get the better of her and when she next spoke to her father she'd find out just what he and Alessandro had discussed. Had her father tried to continue the matchmaking Seb had started?

Alessandro took in deep breaths, trying to cool the heat in his body as he strode back to the track. The approaching ambulance was almost upon them as he reached the car. He didn't look back at her, but knew she'd started to follow him. Every nerve in his body responded to each step those lovely long legs took.

After a few quick words with the ambulance crew he sent them back to the workshop, by which time Charlie was at his side. What would have happened if they hadn't been interrupted? The thought of what he could at this minute be doing sent his pulse sky-high.

'Get in.' The command was gruff, but that was the

only way to deal with this. Denial wasn't usually his style, but right now it suited perfectly. He got into the driving seat and waited, his gaze firmly fixed ahead as she got in beside him.

'Sorry.' That one word from her was so soft, so quiet he wondered if he'd imagined it.

What was she sorry for? Driving like a maniac or setting light to the fire between them? Either way, he didn't want her apology. He just wanted to get as far away from her as possible so that he could reassemble the barrier he always kept around him.

He didn't ever want to be so emotionally exposed with a woman, but Charlie had slipped under his radar, almost destroying the defence he'd erected after his marriage. It had taken just one kiss.

'I can't believe you'd drive like that. What would Seb say?' He clutched at the first thing that came to mind to use as a weapon against the hum of desire threatening to rise once more, just from being close to her. He could still smell her scent, still taste her and his body craved more, wanting absolute satisfaction.

'Seb would be pleased. He taught me to drive like that but, judging by your reaction, I guess he didn't tell you that I am a test driver for the team. I can drive as fast and as safely as any racing driver.'

'That may be so, but he wouldn't have wanted you to risk your life.' Angrily, he rebuffed her explanation.

A heavy silence filled the car and he wished the words unsaid. When she didn't say anything else he started the car and gently moved off, keeping the speed to a sensible level.

'Did I scare you?' The question flew out and he

gripped the steering wheel, the muscles of his forearms flexing.

She had scared him, but he wasn't about to admit that to anyone. As the speed had increased all he'd been able to think of was Seb, lying in the hospital bed in pain, and the way he'd forced him into a promise he now had serious doubts he could keep. How could he look after Charlie as if she were his sister when all he could think of was taking her to his bed?

'Yes, damn it, you scared me. You knew I had to deal with my sister after she'd had an accident.' He wasn't about to confide in her the real cause of his fear. That would mean looking deeper at what had just happened between them. Accepting that there even was something there, some undeniable attraction that was so powerful it took over, given the slightest opportunity.

'I don't see how me driving on a test track has any connection with your sister having a bump on the road.' He could hear the irritation in every word and was relieved to see the workshop coming into view.

'That *bump*, as you put it, caused her to defer her last year at university and all because she couldn't slow down, as I'd asked her to do.' His mind began to tie in knots, talking on one subject, trying to rationalise another and fighting the need to pull over and finish what he'd started back there.

He'd never been this off-kilter before. Shock and the unrelenting need to regain control had unbalanced his emotions, but he couldn't let her know that.

'What happened?' Curiosity filled her voice and it was all he could do not to look at her. The heat of her gaze burned into him.

He drove back into the workshop, switching the engine off. Silence settled around them and he looked about the workshop, thankful the mechanics had had the presence of mind to make themselves scarce. He'd have some smart talking to do with them later; of that he was sure.

He threw his hands up in frustration. 'She drove too fast. That's it. Just as you did out there.'

He didn't need this conversation right now. It wasn't what they should be discussing, even though it went part way towards his reasons for demanding she stop.

He could feel her watching him and turned to look at her, instilling as much control as he possibly could into his voice. 'She took a bend too fast, hit the wall and ended up in hospital. All because she couldn't slow down.'

'But I'm a skilled driver; I test drive for Seb's team.' Her expression served only to exasperate him further. Couldn't she see the similarities between her and Seb? He was a skilled driver too and now he was dead.

'Skill isn't everything, *cara*. Seb was incredibly skilled.' Her eyes widened and he had the strangest sensation that he'd walked into a trap. One of his own making.

'Seb went out in a car that should never have been on the test track. Is that what you are saying?' The accusation was hurled at him, but he knew it was the driver that shouldn't have been out on the track that night. If he hadn't been meeting with potential customers, maybe he would have seen the state Seb was in. Stopped him from taking the car out to the test track.

'Nobody knew he was here, Charlotte. He took it upon himself to take the car out.' He desperately tried to instil patience into each word. She was hurting and this was the moment he'd been dreading, the moment she'd accuse him of negligence and he wouldn't be able to deny it. Not if he kept the horrible truth from her.

'I thought he was staying with you. Surely you knew he'd gone to the test track?' Her eyes narrowed and he knew for certain she blamed him.

'He was staying with me, but he also did his own thing. I thought he was on a date that night.'

'And you just happened to be at the track within minutes of the accident.'

'Am I on trial here?'

'By me, yes.'

'Va bene. For the record, I was on my way back from a meeting and called in to collect paperwork. I wanted to go over the problem we had with the first prototype. The second had just come out of the workshop so I wanted to talk to Seb about it.'

Her face watched his expectantly and he wondered if she'd already heard this from her father, or read about it in the press. It had been a tough few months after the accident and he'd had to deal with the guilt he felt, even though no blame had been apportioned to him or his company.

'But Seb was out in the car?' she asked, pre-empting him.

'I'd seen Seb's car outside when I parked, but thought he'd gone out with one of the mechanics. When I noticed the test car gone, I knew he was out in it and jumped into the pickup. That's how I was able to be there just minutes after it happened.'

He could still hear the sickening thud and scrunch of metal, then the protest of the engine before the ominous silence. He'd known instantly it wasn't going to be good and was on his phone, calling for the emergency services as he'd pulled up alongside the twisted wreck.

'Thank you,' she whispered, her gaze lowering so that

her thick long lashes brushed against her cheeks and he had to fight hard not to reach out to hold her or offer her comfort. He just didn't trust himself, he wanted her so fiercely.

'Come, that is enough for today. I'll take you back to the apartment.'

A little sigh escaped her as she got out of the car and, without a backward glance at it, walked towards the door. Quickly he caught up with her and as soon as they were outside the workshop he put his arm around her shoulders in an attempt to console her.

'Don't.' She pulled away from him and stood by the passenger door of his car, looking anywhere else but at him and very much like she was hurting.

Damn it. He should never have responded to her kiss last night and certainly shouldn't have done what he had today. Now he couldn't offer her comfort, couldn't keep his promise to Seb and look after her—like a brother. How could he go back from that intensely heated moment they'd shared at the trackside?

The drive back to the apartment had seemed to last for ever, but Charlie kept up the act of hurt and betrayal. It was hard, but more preferable to the role of wanton seductress that she'd just played out with him at the trackside. She was completely shocked by her behaviour. She'd never thrown herself with such abandon at a man and couldn't understand what had possessed her to do that today—other than hot lust. All she wanted now was to lie on her bed and be alone, to calm her body and her heart.

'I have work at the office this afternoon.' His words were firm but she knew he was looking for a way out, trying to avoid a discussion about what had happened between them. Well, that suited her just fine. She didn't want to acknowledge it either, much less discuss it.

'I may go shopping,' she said, trying to sound light and carefree. 'I need something to wear at the launch tomorrow evening.'

'I will send a car for you in a few hours. Rest first.' He stood tall and proud in the middle of his living room, the opulence of it still not quite fitting with the picture of the man Seb had painted in her mind.

Rest. She wasn't sure she could, but she was glad that at least she'd be alone. His gesture of comfort had been hard to shrug off earlier. She wanted nothing more than to be held by him, to be safe in his arms, but she didn't trust herself. Whatever it was between them, she could only ignore it if she physically kept her distance.

'Alessandro?'

'Yes.' He looked at her, his dark eyes no longer full of the passion she'd seen in them at the test track. Now they were cold, full of dismissal.

'Your sister? Is she all right now?'

'Yes, thankfully, she made a quick recovery and even graduated with full honours.'

She nodded, unable to say anything, the pain of losing Seb more raw than it had ever been. She wished she could allow Alessandro to hold her. She'd never felt so alone. 'But Seb didn't.'

Without another thought, she went to him, needing his strong embrace and the warmth of his body. He didn't say a word as he took her in his arms, infusing her with his strength, but it felt different. Every muscle in his body was tense.

She pulled away. She shouldn't have done that, not after this morning.

'I won't be back tonight,' he said curtly, picking up his car keys.

She blinked in shock. Was she driving him out of his own home? 'Because of me?' Her voice was hardly a whisper and she bit her bottom lip with her teeth.

'Not you—me.' The sternness in his voice didn't go unnoticed. 'I think it's for the best. Boundaries have been crossed, but it won't happen again.'

She stepped back further from him. 'Good, but you don't have to stay away on my account.'

'I do, Charlie, I do need to—for Seb and the promise I made him to look after you.'

'You are looking after me.' She really should let him go, simply because she didn't trust herself not to want him. His offer to leave her alone became more tempting by the second as her heart hammered harder while he stood before her.

'My staff will see to your every need and a car will be available to take you wherever you need to go. I will see you at the launch.'

'Not before?' Stunned, she couldn't believe it. The launch was the next evening. Was he going to keep as far from her as possible for the next twenty-four hours? Did the boundaries they'd crossed mean that much?

Alessandro stood and looked at her, wanting nothing more than to take her back into his arms, hold her and inhale her sweet scent. But he couldn't. It would be disastrous if he did. He'd already proved she was the one woman who made him lose his mind and he knew if he stayed there would be no stopping him.

'No, it will be better if I don't.' He kept his voice level and stood rigidly straight, but didn't miss the look of disappointment slide across her face.

'But this is your home.' Her delicate brows furrowed in confusion and concern.

'Tonight it is yours. I will go elsewhere.' He had to. He already knew beyond doubt that he had very little self-control where she was concerned. He didn't want to be involved with any woman, but especially this one.

'To a friend?' She dropped her gaze and he knew exactly what she thought. That he was going to warm the bed of another woman. Well, so much the better if it stamped out the electricity that raged between them and the heady lust he felt for her. One thing was for certain; it couldn't go on, not if he wanted to honour his promise to Seb and keep his sanity.

'Something like that, *sì*.' He moved towards the door, needing to go before he relented and told her he was intending to spend the night in his office, something he did on occasion. His office was all geared up for such nights, but this would be the first time he'd been driven there by a woman.

It certainly wouldn't be as hard as staying here with Charlie when all he wanted was to make her completely his. But she could never be that to him, not now.

'*Buonanotte, cara.* Sleep well.'

CHAPTER SIX

IT WAS ALMOST twenty-four hours since Alessandro had left her at his apartment. Charlie had enjoyed the indulgence of being alone to begin with. She'd spent the first hours in her room, the same room Seb had stayed in, looking for anything left behind that connected with him. Any clues as to what he'd been doing in the days before the accident, but that had proved futile. She realised it was foolish to think there would be any evidence left in the room a year after he'd last been here. So she'd turned her attention to the rest of the apartment to learn about the man who owned it.

Old and new blended tastefully with the ornate interior of the grand building and she still couldn't help but be shocked that he didn't live in a new and modern apartment with the same masculine lines as his office. She wondered which was the real man—the one who worked in the modern minimalist office or the contented man who surrounded himself with fine art.

Now, she stood looking out over Milan as she waited for the car to take her to the launch party, unable to comprehend how much she was looking forward to seeing Alessandro again. A brief call from him, which had sent a sizzle of anticipation down her spine, had informed her he would send his car at six. As an ornate clock struck the hour she began to have second thoughts about the long red dress she'd bought that morning.

Second thoughts were too late. The car pulled up and her breath hitched as Alessandro got out. From her vantage point at the window above him she could see that he now wore a tuxedo and looked more sexy and stunning than any man had a right to. She drank him in. He looked like every woman's dream, the strength of his body still evident despite the high-class tailoring.

She watched as he shut the car door, grateful she had time to get her wayward thoughts reined in. She saw the black fabric stretch across his broad shoulders as he leant down and spoke to the driver. Unable to tear her eyes away, she stood watching, enjoying her unobserved vantage point.

As if he sensed her presence, he looked up at her. Despite the three floors that separated them, his gaze met hers, sending her pulse rate into freefall. If he could do this from that distance, what was it going to be like when she was actually with him?

She didn't have to wait long to find out as the key turned in the lock of the front door and he walked into the apartment, overpowering the splendour of the living room completely.

He stood and looked at her very slowly, his gaze moving down from her head to her toes, peeping out of the red sandals that gave her a few inches more height. Defiantly she looked at him, desperate not to let him know that inside she was melting from the heat of his gaze.

'Sei bellissimo.' He moved towards her, each step making her heart pound harder. His Italian was more sexy

than his accented English. Her heart soared. He thought she was beautiful.

Shyness swept over her and she lowered her gaze. The vibrant red dress she had bought in a moment of defiance was having more of an effect than she'd imagined possible. She'd been drawn to the red sequins which sparkled on the bodice, and the jaunty single shoulder which had slashed red across her pale skin. But now she wondered and looked down at the silk of the floor-length dress. 'It is not too much, is it?'

'Too much,' he said in a husky tone as he stepped closer and lifted her chin with his fingers, forcing her to look into his handsome face. 'You look beautiful.'

'Thank you.' She shyly accepted his compliment and stepped back, away from temptation. All she could think of was kissing him again, feeling his arms pressing her against his hard body. But she couldn't; she had to remain aloof, keep him at a distance. He'd already proved what he was capable of doing to her. 'I'm glad you approve.'

He didn't say anything. He didn't have to; the intensity in his dark eyes told her he more than approved. His gaze was so hot she could hardly breathe and she caught her bottom lip between her teeth.

'We had better go.' A ripple of awareness cascaded through her as his deep, sensual voice left her in no doubt that he wanted to kiss her, that he too was fighting an attraction so strong the outcome now seemed inevitable.

'Yes.' Aware how husky her voice had become, she moved quickly towards the door, the silk of her dress moulding to her legs as she moved. He followed her, his shoes beating a purposeful rhythm on the marble floor.

Whatever it was that had simmered between them that

first afternoon in her garden had ignited spectacularly, threatening to engulf them at any second. She drew in a deep breath as she realised she wanted the increasing desire to burn freely between them. After several years of pushing men away, using her off-camera tomboy image to discourage male attention, this was what she now wanted. Was it just lust or was she ready to risk her heart again?

He shut the door of his apartment with a resounding bang which echoed in the coolness of the marble hallway, startling her and knocking all those tempting thoughts out of her mind. She turned to face him. 'Is something wrong?'

Purposefully, he walked towards her, stopping so close she could smell the heady scent of his aftershave, feel his breath on her face. She looked up at him and swallowed hard against the urge to kiss him.

'This is wrong.' The deep tones of his voice were heavy with accent and raw with unquenched desire. The sheer potency of his sexual magnetism made any kind of reply impossible. All she could do was look into his increasingly black eyes.

He lowered his head and brushed his lips over hers, the kiss so light her lips tingled. She sighed in pleasure, swaying towards him. She wanted him and whatever she said, however much she denied it, her body would call to his. Could something so potent be so wrong? Did she have to give her heart to taste the desire between them?

'So, so wrong, *mia cara*.' His lips left hers fractionally as he spoke, his voice husky with the same passion which flowed around her body. Her stomach churned nervously as her body heated in response to his desire-laden words.

'How can it be wrong?' She drew in a deep breath, trying to calm the erratic beating of her heart. She looked deep into his eyes, searching the bronze-flecked brown as they became inky black.

'It's wrong because I promised Sebastian I would look after you.' He stepped back away from her, breaking the powerful spell and leaving her so weak she thought she might crumple on the floor. 'I did not promise to seduce his sister and right now that is all I can think of doing.'

Her breathing was becoming ever harder to control, the sequin-encrusted bodice of the dress tightening with each attempt to breathe normally. He'd admitted he wanted her and her body hummed with a need she'd never known before, one that demanded satisfaction.

'We will be late.' She said the first thing that came to her mind to avoid confronting what sparked between them.

He laughed, a sound so sexy and throaty she blushed. Why had she said that?

'Is that an invitation, *cara*?' He pulled the cuff of his jacket back with long tanned fingers and looked at his watch. 'When I make love to a woman I take my time, give pleasure and enjoy it. You're right, if I take you back in there now we will be late. Very late.'

The smile on his lips, the invitation in his eyes were all too much, shocking her and giving her a much-needed reminder why she was even here with him. 'That can't happen, Alessandro. I'm not here to be your latest conquest.' Desperately, she tried to hide her desire, her confusion behind the words.

'Are you sure about that, *cara*?' He folded his arms across his broad chest and leant back against the wall, looking so handsome and sure of himself.

'You're impossible,' she fumed and turned towards the stairs, rushing down them so quickly her dress billowed out behind her and her heels tapped out an angry rhythm. His gentle laughter followed her, teasing and so sexy. She let out an exasperated groan.

Once at the bottom of the stairs, she pulled open the door of the building, drawing the warm early evening air deep into her lungs, wanting to banish the lustful throb that still hummed inside her. Seconds later, he was at her side, his hand in the small of her back, guiding her towards the door of the car as the driver opened it and stood back.

Swiftly, she got in, thankful of the roomy interior. At least she didn't have to sit close to him. But that roomy interior vanished as soon as he got in and, despite the expanse of leather seats between them, he felt too close. Her pulse, still unbalanced from that fleeting kiss, raced, making her light-headed.

She looked out of the window as the car pulled away, leaving the historic centre of Milan and the impressive Duomo behind. She feigned an interest in the passing streets she was far from feeling after their *encounter* outside his apartment. She couldn't trust herself to look at him, didn't want to see the hot desire in his eyes. Not now, on the night of the launch—a moment that was for her brother.

Relief surged through Alessandro as they reached the exclusive hotel where the launch party was being held. At least with other people around him he could distract himself. From the second he'd seen her, the red silk of her dress clinging to her narrow waist, enhanced further by all the red sequins, he'd been lost. Her one bare shoulder distracted him so completely that all thoughts of keeping her at a distance after the test track kiss had vanished.

He wanted her. More than he'd ever wanted any woman.

The driver opened his door and he got out amidst flashes from the waiting press and made his way around to Charlie's door. He held her hand as she stepped out, fighting the sizzle that shot through him from that contact. He didn't miss her hesitation as the photographers went crazy, flashes lighting up the ever darkening sky, their calls resounding around them.

'I hadn't expected so many,' he said sternly as she came to stand at his side. He should have warned her. Escaping the intrusion of the press had been her reason for retreating from the racing world and now she was in the thick of it again. 'Sorry, I didn't think to tell you they'd be here.'

'I expected it.' She smiled up at him, then faced the cameras as photographers shouted at them. 'Just not so many.'

He put his arm around her, pulling her close, feeling only a slight resistance as she continued to pose for the media. Seb had told him she was the best, knew just how to work the press to the team's advantage and, despite his doubts, he saw immediately this was true. But she was smiling and posing under duress and a tinge of guilt slipped over him.

The tension in her body increased and he turned her away from the press, heading into the hotel. All around, people chatted, sipping the champagne being circulated, but as they entered a hush fell on the room. Beside him, Charlie drew in a deep breath, straightened and as he looked across at her he saw a smile light up her face.

'I had not anticipated such a turnout.' He spoke softly, for her ears only. 'It seems you have many people wishing to meet you.'

'My presence here is a way of absolving you of any wrongdoing…in the eyes of the media and public, that is.' She whispered the words with her smile still in place and he suddenly saw how she must be feeling, how this whole evening must be for her.

'That was not my intention.' He placed his hand against her back, felt the heat and tried to ignore it.

'No, I don't think it was.' She looked up at him and, despite the smile on her lips, he knew that inside she was hurting. He could see it in her eyes and wanted to protect her from it.

She turned her attention to those around them, her smile easing the tension in the room, and a hum of conversation gradually started again. He took two flutes of champagne, handed her one and moved into the room, aware that every man there was looking at her with admiration.

A stab of jealousy spiked him, but instantly he dismissed it. She wasn't his and never could be. His urge to protect her and keep her at his side was thwarted as they were engaged in conversation before being separated.

Even though she was on the other side of the room, deep in conversation with several Italian racing drivers, he was aware of her. Each time she laughed, the gentle sound rippled through the air and he had to defuse the heady pulse of passion or he'd be in danger of dragging her away and doing just what his body demanded.

He made his welcome speech, repeating it in English for her benefit, but he couldn't look at her because if he did he wouldn't be able to stay here in front of everyone and remain calm. His prepared lines became jumbled and he improvised. Something he'd never had to do before.

'Now, to the moment everyone is waiting for,' he said as the doors of the hotel courtyard were folded back to reveal the shape of his car beneath a black cloth. Appreciative sounds came from those around him but, instead of giving the signal to pull off the cloth, he turned back to the audience.

Charlie looked up at him as he stood on the presentation stage, questions in her eyes, but he continued with his original plan.

'I'd like to introduce, for those who don't know her, Charlotte Warrington, sister of the late and very much missed Sebastian Warrington, who played a big part in developing this car.'

He turned, ignoring the need to look at her again, and gave the signal to reveal the car. Delighted sounds and applause came from everyone as the brilliant red of the car sparkled beneath the lights.

Finally he looked towards Charlie. She was slowly making her way towards the car, the red of her dress a perfect match for its gleaming paintwork, but the expression on her face sent alarm bells ringing. The smile she'd hidden behind from the moment she'd arrived in front of the cameras was gone. In its place was an expression of sadness that stilled the applause.

He stepped down and briskly made his way over to her, the audience parting ahead of him. He didn't know what to say, didn't know how to offer her support, and he cursed the fact that she'd only seen the plain grey test car until now.

'Charlotte?'

Slowly she turned to look at him. 'It's beautiful, San-

dro.' The fact that she'd shortened his name didn't go unnoticed. All her barriers were down; she was exposed,
vulnerable, and it was because of his carelessness.

'You were meant to see it yesterday afternoon.' She
looked up at him, her eyes greener than he'd ever seen
them. He didn't need to add that their test track kiss had
thrown all his plans into disarray. Her expression and
hint of a blush told him she knew why.

'Seb would be proud.' Her soft voice was firm and she
turned to those around her, the smile she'd been using all
night firmly back in place. The shutters had rolled back.

Charlie looked at Alessandro, blinking back the tears that
momentarily threatened. 'Thank you.' Her voice was almost a whisper and, despite the throng of people around
them, eager to get a good look at the car, it seemed as if
it was only them there.

He moved closer, his eyes holding hers, and her heartbeat sped to an alarming rate. His height and broad shoulders made her feel small and defenceless but the intensity
in his eyes cancelled that and she basked in his bold desire for her.

'Seb would also be proud of you.' His gentle words focused her attention back on the task at hand, giving her
a chance to quell the almost primal need racing through
her, need that only he could satisfy. 'You outshine the
car.'

She laughed gently. 'That's not what I intended.' She
hadn't. If she'd known the car was red she would have
chosen a different colour dress, but red had been Seb's
favourite. 'I should have known Seb would have wanted
the car to be red.'

He didn't say anything and worry flitted through her.

His mouth was set in a firm line and she used the offer of more champagne to dilute the tension between them. He followed her lead and took a flute, clinking it against hers as he raised it to her. 'To Seb.'

The tribute, spoken sternly, poured cooling water over the fire which was still raging inside her since the kiss a few hours ago outside his apartment. How did he manage to awaken her so completely yet still leave her yearning for more?

'To Seb.' She took a sip, her gaze remaining locked with his. Those flecks of bronze became more diluted as his eyes darkened again. Whatever was between them wasn't going away; it was intensifying. Each glance, each touch and definitely each kiss increased the sizzle of attraction.

She couldn't deny it any longer.

She didn't want to deny it.

She wanted to be with him, wanted to feel his lips on hers and keep kissing him. She craved his touch and caresses, needed to feel his body against hers. But men like Alessandro Roselli, who had looks and wealth on their side, never wanted more than a brief affair. She'd learnt that the hard way, rebounding from a broken relationship with her childhood boyfriend into the arms of an up-and-coming racing driver, only to find he was using her to further his career.

Despite that, she still wanted to explore what was between them, but only if he didn't want any kind of commitment from her. She didn't want her heart exposed to pain. But would one night be enough to quench the thirst of desire?

'It's been a successful evening, *grazie*.' His words dragged her attention back, his gaze a soft caress and his words so tender and warm, making her yearn to hear it as he kissed her again and again.

'It's not over yet.' She couldn't believe she'd said the words aloud, offering something she'd only just realised she wanted. Judging by the look of surprise on his face, neither could he. But it was what she wanted, she realised as she watched his expression change, riveted to the spot by her bluntness. She wanted to forget all reason and abandon herself to the pleasure of his kisses, his caresses.

He raised his glass fractionally, not breaking eye contact, and her stomach twisted into knots of excitement and apprehension. 'Then I will drink to its continued success.' His rich voice was vibrant and warmth surged through her faster than lightning.

Shyness took over, banishing the boldness that had made her promise something she wanted but knew she shouldn't. She lowered her gaze and looked into her champagne as if the bubbles could give her the answers. 'Sorry, I shouldn't...'

Her words of apology, withdrawing her bold statement, were cut off by a familiar voice and she whirled around to see her father. He shook Alessandro's hand warmly and she marvelled at the ease with which they greeted one another.

'My flight was late.' Her father smiled at her, seemingly unaware of the tension between her and Alessandro. 'But I see you have done yourself—and Seb—proud.'

'I didn't know you were coming.' She sent up a silent prayer of thanks. Her father's arrival had stopped her from throwing herself at Alessandro and making a fool of herself into the bargain.

'I'm not staying. I will be leaving for Rome in a few hours, but I had to come and see you emerge like a butterfly back into the real world, and what a very beautiful butterfly you are.' He looked at her, his smile gentle, and she knew he really was proud and very pleased she'd stepped back into the limelight.

'So, the car—has it gone down well?' Her father turned to Alessandro and within minutes they were immersed in conversation. One she would normally relish hearing, but she needed to put space between her and Alessandro, cool things down. Maybe now it was time to mingle with potential buyers, do what she'd come here for.

Alessandro watched as Charlie talked animatedly with other people about the car, about its performance, and he recalled how well she'd driven it. She was more than qualified to sing its praises but it wasn't the drive, however fast, he was remembering. It was the kiss. Holding her in his arms and feeling her body against his.

Just a few guests lingered now, along with the racing drivers she'd been talking to earlier. Had she given them the same hints she'd given him? The way they hung on her every word certainly suggested as much.

An unknown need to be territorial made him stand as close to her as possible, but just doing so infused him once more with sizzling need. 'Thank you, gentlemen,' he said firmly, ignoring the way she shot him a startled glance. 'Any more questions you may have can be directed to my office.'

The remaining guests left, animated discussion of speed and performance trailing in their wake, but Alessandro watched Charlie as she leant back against the wing of the car, her red dress so perfect a match she almost became one with the slumbering beast.

Heat scorched through him as he remembered her earlier words and he undid his tie, letting it hang down, and pulled loose his top buttons. He'd never been so suffocated by desire before, had never experienced this continuous aching need.

He wanted her with a ferocious need, his promise to Seb becoming lost in the mists of heady desire. He should turn and walk away. To have kissed her at the test track had been so wrong. It had unlocked a thirst that needed quenching. Did she feel the same?

He looked at her and her eyes met his, darkening by the second. She smiled, a shy seductive smile that made his pulse leap. Instantly, he closed the distance between them, taking her in his arms and claiming her lips. She tasted better than ever; the anticipation of the last few hours had been worth the wait.

He caressed her cheek as he deepened the kiss, her response setting fire to his senses so instantly there was only one way to put out the flames now. Her skin was so soft and as his fingers caressed her bare throat he felt the wild pump of her pulse.

She wrapped her arms around his neck, her breasts pressing against his chest, and he moved her back against the car, pressing into her as heady lust robbed him of all thought.

'Sandro,' she murmured against his lips, pushing him almost too far.

It was all he could do to stop himself ripping the red dress from her, wanting to reveal her glorious body to his hungry gaze. Somewhere on the periphery sense prevailed.

This couldn't happen here and if he didn't stop kissing her there was a very real probability that it would. He pulled back from her, seeing her thick dark lashes flutter open to reveal eyes swirling with passion. 'My car is outside.'

Would she remember her covert promise to him that the night was still young? Her kiss certainly suggested as much, but did she want him enough to put all their differences aside for one night?

Shyly she looked up at him, a small sexy smile lifting her lips. Then, without further words, he took her hand and led her away from the car, through the brightly lit room where the hotel staff had started to clear up.

Movement caught his eye and he glanced over to see a photographer at a table, packing away his camera. Alessandro scrunched his eyes in suspicion, then, as her hand touched his arm, bringing her so close again, he dismissed the idea. He had far more important things to worry about than a rogue photographer.

He looked down into her upturned face as they stepped out into the warmth of the night, her smile reaching her eyes. 'It has been a very successful night,' she said as the car stopped outside the door.

'One I hope will continue in the same way.'

Demurely she looked down as he opened the car door. Once inside the car, he pulled her close against him, her head resting on his shoulder as if they'd known each other for ever. He didn't want to kiss her now. He didn't trust himself to be able to stop if things got heated. No, this was going to be played out in the comfort of his bedroom, where nothing and nobody could disturb them.

CHAPTER SEVEN

CHARLIE LIFTED THE front of her dress with one hand, the other still firmly in Alessandro's as they made their way up the marble staircase to his apartment. It was late and she should be tired. Last night she'd hardly slept and this evening she'd enjoyed the champagne just a little too much, but every sense in her body was on high alert.

Alessandro turned the key in the door and then looked at her, a seductive gentleness in his eyes. 'I want to kiss you again.' His voice was hardly above a whisper and his eyes searched her face.

He was so strikingly handsome, his tie hanging loosely and his white shirt open at the top button—exactly the romantic image that turned a girl's head. She smiled up at him, suddenly so sure that this was what she wanted. He wasn't the kind of man to want commitment and, for once in her life, neither did she. She wasn't looking or thinking beyond this moment.

'I shouldn't, but I do.' He moved closer, his height almost as overpowering as the tension that fizzed between them.

'Why shouldn't you?' Her voice was husky and she looked up at him, unsure what he meant.

'I promised Seb to look after you, not seduce you.'

The resolute growl in his voice made her heart race faster than any car she'd driven.

'Seb wouldn't be cross.' She couldn't keep the light teasing note from her voice. He was fighting this attraction as much as she was, which made her want him even more. She wanted his kisses, his touch and to be totally his—tonight, at least

She wanted him more than she had wanted any other man and it scared her, but at least with Alessandro there wasn't any danger of anything more than a brief affair. The idea of getting involved in another relationship didn't appeal. She'd been hurt once before and that was enough. 'I want you to kiss me again, Sandro.'

'But if I do—' he lowered his voice and his eyes softened as he looked down at her '—I'm not going to be able to stop. Not this time.'

She walked away from him and into the apartment, feeling empowered by his desire for her. Slowly she turned as he shut the apartment door, its click ominous, warning her she'd passed the point of no return. But she didn't care. She didn't want to stop. Not now. This passion, which had ebbed and flowed between them since the moment they'd met, needed to reach its conclusion. There wasn't any other option now.

He might be the man she still saw as responsible for Seb's accident, even though her father didn't, but he was also the man who'd ignited a fire of hot need within her. From the second she'd seen him standing in her garden she'd fallen for him. This attraction was something she couldn't turn her back on. Not yet. It was a totally new experience for her.

'I don't want you to stop, Sandro.' The husky whisper that came from her sounded so unreal and she watched as he stepped towards her, his tie hanging loose, his shirt unbuttoned and the hint of golden skin of his chest creating an evocative image. One which seared into her mind and would, she knew, remain there for ever.

He took her hand once more and, with a seductive look which whispered a thousand words, he drew her towards him, pulling her close. '*Mia cara*, I have wanted you since the moment I first saw you.'

A tremor of panic slipped over her, his words too serious. Did he want more than just this moment, this night which held the promise of so much pleasure? It wasn't what she wanted. She couldn't give him more. She pushed her hands against his chest, the firmness of it making her breath catch, but she refused to let it sway her from what she had to say, what she had to make clear.

'I don't do for ever, Sandro.' She'd been sure all along he just wanted a fling, a brief affair. The image of her and Alessandro, together and happy in the future, didn't fill her mind. It was more than just risking her heart. It was about letting go of pain and grief and she wasn't ready to do that yet. But one night meant only putting it aside and not engaging her heart. 'It's all I can give you.'

'So serious, *cara*,' he said and pressed a light kiss to her forehead. 'Isn't my divorce proof that I'm not able to commit to a relationship? Tonight belongs to us, *cara*.'

Before he could say anything else she looked up, bringing his lips tantalisingly close to hers, the shock of discovering he was divorced dulled by the passion which sizzled inside her. It proved he didn't do forever either and all she wanted now was to lose herself in the moment, forget the world existed. 'Kiss me, Sandro.'

In answer he kissed her so gently she thought she might actually cry. His previous kisses had been hard and demanding, but this was so tender, so loving. He held her as if she were a delicate flower he was afraid he might crush. She swayed towards him, desire making her light-headed as he continued the kiss.

Just when she thought she couldn't stand the torment any longer he stopped kissing her and, with blatant intent, led her through to his bedroom. As with the rest of the apartment, old blended stylishly with new and the corner of the room comprised of windows offering unrivalled views of the Duomo, lit up and sparkling like a thousand jewels against the night sky. But all that was lost on her. All she could see was him.

'Un momento.' He released her hand and closed the cream curtains before flicking on the bedside lamps, creating a room for romance. Then he walked back towards her, slipping off his jacket as he did so and tossing it carelessly onto the armchair that filled another corner of the room.

'Wait,' she said and walked towards him, smiling coyly, her gaze meeting his from beneath her lowered lashes. With unashamed enticement she reached up, flattened her hands against his chest, revelling in the strength and his ragged intake of breath. Slowly she pulled one end of his tie until it fell from his neck. Holding it up, she dangled it in front of him like a trophy, her brows raised suggestively.

'Tease.' He reached out, took hold of her waist and pulled her against him, his hold keeping her there, leaving her in no doubt he wanted her.

Still believing she was in charge, she undid first one button of his shirt and, meeting no resistance, continued with each button until she was forced to gently pull the shirt from his trousers. As she unfastened the final buttons she slid her hands inside and over his chest. Hair covered his muscles, but couldn't hide them from her exploring hands. The heat of his body emboldened her further.

She looked at his face, his eyes so dark and heavy with desire that shivers of delight rushed over her. Very slowly she pushed open the shirt and kissed his chest, little kisses as light as a feather all over him, his musky scent invading her senses. She heard him groan with pleasure, his hold on her waist tightening, and she smiled.

She pulled back from him and pushed the shirt from his shoulders. 'This has to go.' Her voice was husky and she almost didn't recognise it, but then she'd never done anything so bold before.

One-night stands had never been for her, not after the devastation caused to her parents' marriage, when her mother had succumbed to temptation. But this was different. Deep down, she acknowledged that if it had happened at a different time, in a different place it could have been so much more than one night.

She pushed that thought aside, refusing to allow it to defuse the sexual tension which filled the room.

He lifted his arms behind her as he unfastened the cuffs of his shirt, pressing her unbearably close. Before he released her, his lips pressed hard to hers, his breathing deep as his tongue slid into her mouth, teasing and tasting. She kissed him back, demanding more. For a moment his kiss matched hers, then abruptly he pulled back. 'The shirt?'

She smiled, feeling more brazen by the second. 'Yes, the shirt,' she whispered. 'It has to go.' She slid her hands up his chest, making him groan and close his eyes as she lingered there before pushing the white material from his shoulders. He moved first one arm from her, then the other and the shirt fell to the floor.

Again he pulled her close, but this time his fingers caught the zip at the back of her dress, slowly pulling it lower and lower; all the while his eyes held hers. Shyness swept over her and she resisted the urge to look away as his hand slid over her shoulder, pushing the one sleeve away and revealing her skin to his kisses.

The dress slipped down her body and slithered into a heap of silk and sequins at her feet. She stood against him, conscious of the fact that she now only wore the red underwear she'd bought to go with the dress and the strappy sandals she'd fallen in love with instantly.

Before she had time to think, he'd swept her off her feet and carried her to the bed. She lay where he'd placed her and looked up at him. He kicked off his shoes and was reaching for the fastener on his trousers when she knelt up on the bed and pushed his hands away. 'My turn.'

Who was this bold woman, this seductress? And why did it have to be this man who'd revealed her? This was a side of her she'd never known existed. Never before had passion taken over, making her want things with scant regard for the consequences.

A string of Italian that she was unable to understand flew from his lips as she opened his trousers, letting them slip down, leaving him in only a snug pair of black hipsters. As she looked up at him he caught her face between his hands and bent to kiss her. The spark was well and truly lit. Electricity shot between them. There would be no stopping now.

Before she had a chance to catch her breath he tumbled her onto the bed, his body pressing her into the softness of the covers. His kiss became urgent and demanding and she surrendered willingly to his domination.

His hands cupped her breast and inside her something exploded as she arched herself up to him, wanting his touch and so much more. Kisses trailed down her throat and she sighed in pleasure as her fingers slipped into the silky thickness of his hair. His tongue teased her nipple through the red lace of her strapless bra and her fingers tightened in his hair.

As if reading her urgent need, his hand slipped under her arched back, his fingers expertly flicking open her bra, releasing her breasts to his erotic kisses. Possessively he took a nipple in his mouth, swirling his tongue around it, making her cry out with pleasure. Moments later he moved his attention to the other nipple as his hand slid down her side and over her thigh, pulling her closer to the hardness of his erection.

'So beautiful,' he said huskily in between kisses and he moved back up her throat; the warmth of his body scorched hers until she felt as if flames licked around her.

She moved her hands down his back, savouring the latent strength beneath her fingertips. Lower she moved until she slipped her fingers in the back of his hipsters but, before she could make any attempt to remove them, he moved quickly onto his back, taking her with him until she sat astride him.

'That was…' she blushed beneath his open admiration, once again empowered by his need '…very masterful.'

His hands held her hips, keeping her exactly where he wanted her, and a hot stab of desire rushed over her. Following his need, she moved against him. With eyes as black as ebony he held her gaze until, drawn by something inexplicable, she lowered her body over him, bringing her lips against his.

'I am,' he said hotly between fast passionate kisses. 'Now, all night you will be mine.'

Charlie liked the sound of that; she wanted all night with him, wanted to enjoy this wonderful feeling again and again. 'Make me yours,' she whispered against his lips. 'Now.'

With the same suddenness of moments ago, she was once more lying on the bed, Sandro at her side. His fingers hooked into the lace of her panties and slowly pulled them lower, his eyes holding hers all the while.

She quivered as his fingers moved back to touch her, closed her eyes as a wave of pleasure rushed over her like the tide washing over the sand, taking her higher, almost to the point of no return. He took her lips in a hard and bruising kiss, his tongue as demanding as his touch, and her breath came hard and fast. It was too much and not enough both at the same time, leaving her wanting more.

Just when she'd almost slipped over the edge he pulled away from her. She opened her eyes, looking up at him and blinking against the pounding and unsatisfied passion of her body. He reached across her and roughly pulled open the drawer of the cabinet beside the bed.

Of course. Protection. How had she not thought of that? His eyes met hers, a knowing light in their depths, as if he knew she'd almost lost control. She watched as he dispensed with his underwear and rolled on the condom. Anticipation zinged through her and a pulse of heady need throbbed heavily between her legs.

He moved over her and she opened to him, wanting him deep inside her, but he paused. Propped up on his hands, his muscles straining with the effort, he looked down at her, his breathing deep and fast.

'Sandro?' She couldn't keep the question from her voice. Was he having doubts? What had she done?

Then his mouth claimed hers in a hungry and possessive kiss as he pushed into her, taking himself in deeply. She gasped against his lips, his kiss smothering the sound as he moved inside her, sending firecrackers of explosion all around her.

She moved with him, taking him deeper still. He dropped down against her, his warm skin pressing against her body as he kissed her neck, his hands grasping her hair tightly. A flurry of hoarse Italian erupted from him as he thrust harder, sending her over the edge and beyond. Further than she'd ever been before.

She dug her nails into his back, moving with him as the ecstasy crashed into her. His grip on her hair tightened as he gasped out his release and kissed her hard. Then, as the heady lust ebbed slowly away, their bodies tangled, she wrapped her arms around him, keeping him against her, and softly kissed the dampness of his face.

She'd just experienced something she'd never before known and wanted to hold onto the moment just a little longer.

Alessandro could hardly think, the beat of his pulse was so loud. He couldn't move; every muscle in his body had been weakened by the power of hers. She kissed his face and he closed his eyes against the tenderness of that kiss. It was too intimate, too loving and he didn't deserve it.

He didn't deserve any of this and had almost stopped, but his name on her lips, husky and seductive, had made that impossible. Quickly he pushed aside the guilt. She'd wanted this as much as he had, leading the seduction like a temptress.

In a bid to hide the turbulent emotions racing through him, he propped himself up over her and looked down into her flushed face. 'You make love as wildly as you drive.'

She trailed her fingertips over his chest and looked up at him, coyness and temptation filling those emerald-green eyes. 'Are you going to insist I stop again?'

He should do—this wasn't what he'd imagined when he'd promised Seb he'd look out for his little sister, but then he hadn't expected to be so attracted to her and certainly he'd never have guessed at the passion hidden within her.

Gently he kissed her, tenderness that he hadn't felt for such a long time filling him. She responded, her kiss telling him that the fire of passion still burned within her, as it did inside him. He needed to cool things down, needed to calm the riot of emotions which raged within him. Emotions that were so intense and completely unwelcome.

'*Sì*. For now.' He pushed his protesting body away from hers, trying to ignore the wounded look on her beautiful face. Before he had a chance to question his motives, he left the bed and made his way to the bathroom.

Moments later, his face stinging from the cold water he'd splashed over it, he returned to the bedroom, but the bed was empty, the rumpled covers the only hint of the passion that had just played out there.

A rustle caught his attention and he looked towards the door where, clutching the red silk dress against her nakedness, Charlie stood. She was running away again. Was this what she always did? He should let her walk away— every rational sense inside him shouted the advice—but the hot-blooded man she'd resurrected wasn't about to let her slip away from him now.

He strode over to her, heedless of his nakedness and empowered by the shock and need that filled her eyes. She still desired him, just as he desired her. This passion wasn't spent yet.

'Come back to bed, Charlotte.' His voice was deep and raw, leaving him with the distinct impression that his emotions were as naked as he was.

'But...'

He silenced the hoarse whisper by tilting her chin up and kissing her lips, still swollen from his earlier kisses. She sighed and kissed him, dropping the dress carelessly to the floor. He pulled back but still held her chin and looked deep into her eyes, saw the green darken to resemble the heart of the forest, hidden from the sun.

'Tornare a letto, cara.' He brushed his lips on hers as a frown of confusion slipped over her face. Desire rushed through him and all he could think about was making love to her again and again. This might not be for ever, but it was certainly for now and, as far as he was concerned, *now* would last all night. 'Come back to bed, *cara.*'

Charlie all but melted at his feet, almost as crumpled as the sea of red silk on the floor between them. The raw and potent desire in his eyes couldn't be ignored. Neither could the kiss that promised so much more. She couldn't deny she wanted him. She knew she shouldn't and briefly wondered if this was how it had been for her mother. Had her mother been drawn inexorably towards the flame of desire, a flame that had then extinguished all the love she'd had for her husband, Charlie's father?

'Don't look so worried, *cara*.' His soft words broke her thoughts. Now was not the time to worry about the past. Unlike her mother, she wasn't married or committed in any way. She was free to enjoy this for what it was, a short and passionate affair.

But what of Seb? What would he have said? Hurriedly, she pushed that thought to the back of her mind, remembering what she and Sandro had enjoyed earlier. Seb had always wanted her to be happy and right now her whole body was alive with happiness.

She smiled at Sandro as he took her hand and led her back to the bed, the passion that had raged between them earlier beginning to heat again. Desperate to drown her misgivings, she wrapped her arms about his neck, pressing herself against his nakedness, and kissed him as if her life depended on it.

Suddenly he tumbled her back on the bed, his body over hers as his hot kisses stoked the fire of passion ever higher and she was lost once more.

CHAPTER EIGHT

'BUONGIORNO.' THE SOFT Italian greeting stirred her senses and Charlie opened her eyes. Sunlight poured in around the closed curtains, but all she could focus on was the man beside her. Every limb in her body was replete with Alessandro's lovemaking and she stretched, smiling up at him, enjoying the way his eyes clouded with passion. 'Breakfast awaits.'

'Breakfast? How long have I slept?' She sat up, pulling the soft sheet modestly against her. He stood by the bed, dressed in jeans which hugged his strong thighs and a black T-shirt which highlighted the contours of his chest to perfection.

His gentle laugh knotted her insides and she dragged her gaze from him, to look at the clock which ticked beside the bed. 'Long enough, *cara*, but then we didn't sleep much last night.'

She turned quickly to look at him, heat infusing her cheeks as his words confirmed her memory was correct. Was it all over now—the one night of passion she'd willingly entered into? Was this now time to go back to her room, to return to the professional relationship they'd had initially? There was still more promotion scheduled for the car over the weekend and into the following week.

How was she going to get through the weekend after what they'd shared last night?

'Thank you.' She was confused by the way she felt and the need to distance herself from him. Wanting to return to the businesslike dealings they'd had with one another until last night. 'I'll get dressed, then we can discuss what's next on the promotion agenda.'

'Oh, no, *cara*. There is only one thing on the agenda right now.' A teasing smile lingered on his lips and the suggestive tone of his voice made her stomach flutter wildly. He still wanted her.

Her heart thumped as he strode back to stand beside the bed. Her mouth was as dry as a desert and she tried to moisten her lips but, from the smouldering look in his eyes, that was a mistake. 'There is?' The strangled whisper only just managed to squeeze out.

He leant on the bed, so close that her lips parted without her consent, waiting for his kiss. When it came it was soft and teasing and loaded with promise. She closed her eyes, slipping under his masterful spell far too easily. 'I'm taking you somewhere we can be alone, somewhere we can explore what is between us.'

She pulled sharply back from him. 'But the launch… the promotion? You're supposed to be hosting a promotional afternoon at the test track.' She'd already expressed a wish to be there and was torn between the idea of spending time alone with him and being with the car her brother had designed.

'Someone else can handle that.' He moved towards her again, stretching his body across the bed, making her want to reach out and touch him, feel his strength. 'We have far more important things to do.'

'But…' She raised her hand, pressing it against his

shoulder, stopping him coming any closer. The sheet she'd pulled against her slipped down, exposing her breasts, but she held her ground, keeping a firm expression on her face.

His eyes looked down at her, his appreciative gaze sending heat to the centre of her again, and her breath hitched audibly as if he'd caressed her. '*Per Dio*, but you are so hard to resist.' His accent became heavy and she released his shoulder and clutched the sheet quickly against her once more, shyness rushing over her now that daylight flooded the room.

'It was only meant to be one night, Sandro.' Her voice was barely above a whisper and she felt emotionally exposed and vulnerable.

'You need to stop running, Charlie, and face what scares you.' His body, tall and overpowering, dominated the room but his expression was gentle. Did he understand her fears? Empathise with her?

She looked up at him, willing the carefree attitude she'd had last night to infuse her again. With alarming clarity she realised she was using not just Seb's accident but her disastrous love life as a shield. Retreating behind it and potentially denying herself more pleasure than she could imagine.

'I want to be at the test track.' She injected a firmness she was far from feeling into her voice and, from the look on his face, he knew she was already running.

'It is not necessary, not after last night.' He stood back up, his height dominating the room. 'We will spend the weekend at my villa. I intend to explore what you started last night, enjoy it. Do you not feel the same, *cara*?'

Should she lie? Tell him she didn't want to be with him any more when the heat of her body and the pounding of her heartbeat told her she did? She slipped from the bed, dragging the sheet she clutched with her. 'What about the car?'

'The car will still be there on Monday.' His voice was deep and the darkness of his eyes told her he wasn't thinking about the car at all.

He was right. The car would still be there after the weekend, but the passion which still burned fiercely between them wouldn't be. She didn't want it to be anything more than a brief affair. This way, it would burn itself out, enabling her to concentrate on what she'd come to Italy for. The truth about Seb's accident.

'Just the weekend.' She smiled at him, enjoying the power she seemed to have over him. 'But no more.'

'Bene.' He moved to the door of the bedroom, filling it with his oh-so-sexy body, and she could hardly think. 'We leave in an hour.'

Alessandro revved the car along the open road, the bustle of Milan far behind them, but tension still filled him. He'd seen the panic in her eyes as she'd sat in the bed, but he'd also seen the desire. Whatever was holding her back hadn't been quite strong enough and he sensed it was more than just her brother. That was only a smokescreen.

His body longed for the moment he could make her his again, but he questioned if he was right to do so. If he was a betting man he'd stake everything on the fact that Seb had never intended this to happen when he'd made Alessandro promise what now turned out to be impossible. How could he possibly look after Charlie when all he wanted to do was make love to her again and again?

Inwardly he cursed. The idea behind bringing her to

his villa was to be somewhere the ghost of her brother's memory couldn't reach. Whatever had happened last night wasn't about Seb—or the car. It was about them and the hot lust which zipped between them from just one look. After last night the temperature of that lust had risen instead of cooling, as he'd thought it would have done.

'*Benvenuti* Villa Dell Angelo.' Pushing his doubts and thoughts of Seb aside, he pulled off the road and into the driveway of his villa, perched on the hillside. Beyond it, Lake Garda glittered like a thousand jewels in the midday sun. This was his new place of sanctuary and Charlie was the first woman he'd ever brought here.

'It's beautiful.' Her soft gasp of pleasure did untold things to his body and he tried to keep his mind on the here and now instead of roaming back to last night or fast forwarding to the pleasures that would await him as darkness fell once more.

'*Sì, grazie.*' He stopped the car, turned off the engine and looked across at her. 'But not as beautiful as you.'

She blushed and dropped her gaze, amazing him that a woman who had been so bold in the bedroom just hours ago could be so shy from his compliment. That boldness did, however, salve his conscience and ease the guilt he felt at breaking his promise. Whilst it was true he had needed little invitation last night, she had instigated it, even warning him she didn't do for ever. She'd wanted last night as much as he had, despite the innocent blushes which now coloured her cheeks.

He got out of the car before he gave in to the temptation to kiss her again. 'I have arranged for lunch on the terrace, then we will drive down to the local town of Desenzano for the afternoon, maybe take a ferry across the lake.' If he didn't take her out he knew they would spend the whole afternoon in bed and, whilst the sex was amazing, he wanted to know her better. That thought shocked him and he frowned as he watched her taking in the view. She was beginning to get to him, tear down his wall of protection.

'Sounds lovely.' Her heels tapped out a gentle beat as she walked towards the terrace, the warm wind pressing her white sundress against her body, making him draw in a sharp breath as he fought for control. He'd never been this affected by a woman before, not even the woman he'd married, foolishly believing he loved her.

'I'm glad you approve,' he said with a smile as he watched her walk and pushed the memories from the past to the back of his mind where they belonged.

Charlie couldn't help but stop as they rounded the corner of the ornate villa. A large infinity pool stretched away, blending with the views of the lake far below, becoming one with it. Under the shade of trees, a table was laid out for lunch, looking so luxurious she felt as if she'd stepped into another world. This was on another level to the glamour her career had showed her so far. It was pure indulgence.

'If we take a ferry maybe we should do a little exploring before returning to dine in Desenzano.' He gestured her to sit and then took his seat opposite her. Beyond him the view seduced her almost as much as the man himself and she tried hard to keep her mind focused on the here and now, instead of allowing it to drift towards thoughts of what their time together would bring.

'And then?' What was the matter with her? Why did she need to act the seductress still? *Because that's what you were last night and that's what he's expecting.* The reprimand shot swiftly through her mind. She had been brazen, but they'd both agreed this was just an affair, a short dalliance. Right now she might be someone she'd never been before, but that didn't mean she couldn't enjoy it. Once it was over and the launch complete she would return to her life in England and try to move on.

He raised his brows, leant back in his chair and smiled—a slow lazy smile that was so sexy she almost couldn't breathe—but his next words made that breath catch in her throat. 'Then we spend the night making love.'

His bluntness shocked her, but she smiled teasingly back at him, enjoying the freedom to be different from normal. It was as if he'd unlocked a new and completely unexpected version of herself, one that lived a carefree and happy existence. 'Promises, promises.'

'All night, *cara*, you will be mine, that I do promise, but first we eat.' He watched her with a steadfast gaze that dissolved the few remaining doubts which lingered in her mind. He wanted her, she wanted him. Was it so wrong to put aside everything else and enjoy the mutual attraction until it fizzled out?

It *was* wrong. It went against everything she believed in. She didn't do affairs and certainly didn't want a relationship with anyone and definitely not with Alessandro, but the connection between them was impossible to ignore. For the first time in her life she was throwing caution to the wind, almost seeing it being snatched away to float above the blue waters of the lake.

She picked up her glass of wine and lifted it to him. 'To tonight,' she toasted, enjoying the smile that tugged at his lips and the hum of anticipation that warmed her body.

'Salute!' He raised his glass to her and she watched his eyes become as black as midnight, the desire-laden and smouldering look on his face making her heart constrict and her body heat.

The ferry from Desenzano to Sirmione offered a cool breeze which was a welcome relief from the heat of the afternoon. Charlie, feeling like a child, wanted to sit at the front of the paddle steamer to gain a prime view of the lake and surrounding countryside and Alessandro seemed happy to indulge her. He made her feel special and cherished with his attention.

Passengers chatted and laughed all around them but still she felt as if she were in a bubble, just the two of them, wrapped up in the attraction which sizzled stronger than ever between them. He put his arm around her as they sat, pulling her close, and the moment took on a magical quality, as if they were in love and not just lovers.

In love.

The words rang in her mind. It couldn't be possible to be in love so soon. She was just being seduced by the sunshine, the luxury of this life she'd stepped into, but most of all by the man himself. Love didn't just happen. It grew and flourished within a happy relationship and this wasn't a relationship. It was an affair.

'I suppose this is a regular trip for you.' She tried to quell the unease of her emotions and distract her thoughts. She was probably just one of many. A man like Alessandro would never be short of female company.

'I bought the villa a year ago but have been too busy with the car to use it.' He looked ahead of them, the wind playing in his hair, his eyes hidden by dark glasses, then suddenly he turned to look at her. She saw herself reflected in his sunglasses and hated that she couldn't see the expression in his eyes.

'Did Seb ever come here?' The light question made his mouth set in a firm line and she wondered what she'd said wrong.

'No. It's why I brought you here. I wanted it to be just the two of us. No memories. There will be enough of those when we return to Milan.' His voice was hard and the clipped edge to it warned her off further questions.

He had at least confirmed one thing. This was still nothing more than a weekend affair. Once they were back in Milan it would be over and just a few days after she would leave for England and the life she needed to get back together. A brief affair was all she'd wanted, so why did it hurt to know she could so easily be dispensed with?

'I'm glad you brought me here. It has been a hard year and right now I feel I have a reprieve from thinking about Seb and the accident,' she said honestly. Certain aspects of her time in Italy had been painful. 'It's time to put the past behind me.'

The sound of the ferry's motor as it manoeuvred towards the shore halted further conversation, something she was grateful for. She didn't want to admit to him he'd been right, that being at the launch was not just what Seb had wanted but what she'd wanted.

She looked ahead of her as the ferry docked with a bump. The medieval castle dominating the town of Sirmione as it rose up from the blue waters of the lake unleashed a childlike need to explore. She pushed aside all other thoughts, determined to enjoy the day and Alessandro's company. 'I can't believe you've never been here or done this,' she said as she stood up, trying to lighten the mood.

'No, but now I will share the experience with you.'
The smile on his lips almost melted her heart; it was far
hotter than the sun. As the holiday-makers scurried off
the ferry he pulled her into his arms and kissed her. The
passion in that kiss must have been obvious to anyone
who saw them, but she didn't care. All she wanted was
to lose herself in his desire, to enjoy the short time they
would have together before reality intervened.

'Sandro,' she murmured against his lips as her eyes
fluttered open.

'We need to go now.' His voice was gravelly. He lifted
his sunglasses onto his head and looked into her eyes,
leaving her in no doubt as to why they had to go.

He took her hand and led her off the ferry. A knowing smile from a crew member was cast their way, making her blush again. Could everyone tell how much they
wanted one another?

'The castle is the place to see,' he said as they walked
alongside the walled moat of the impressive building.
Swans moved gracefully over the rippling water and she
wished she could be as free as them. Free to let go and
love, to pair for life. But she couldn't, and certainly not
with Sandro. She'd set the boundaries and he'd set the
time limit. They would be lovers—for the weekend only.

Swept along with the tourists, they walked over the
long bridge towards the impressive arched entrance and
into the courtyard of the castle, its thick and high walls
offering respite from the sun. He pulled her close, his
arm around her waist, and she shivered, but not from
being in the shade.

She feigned an interest in the history which oozed
from the walls, desperate not to look at him or show just
how much she wanted him. With his arm around her,

they walked slowly over the cobbled courtyard and to-wards the steps up to the wall. As they reached the top, applause and cheers caught her attention and she turned to look back down into the courtyard, where a radiant bride posed with her new husband for photographs.

'Wouldn't it be fantastic to be married here?' She said the words aloud, without thinking how they would sound to him.

'If you find the right partner, yes.' His brittle words snagged her attention but she didn't look at him; instead she kept her attention on the happy scene playing out below them—a scene she'd always secretly hankered after. That was until her mother had destroyed all faith in fairy tales and happy ever afters.

'Sorry.' She was. A moment ago they'd been happy—smiling, laughing and kissing like lovers without a care in the world—and now she'd said the wrong thing.

'You have nothing to be sorry about, *cara*. Mine was a marriage that should never have happened. We were too young and wanted such different things.' She glanced at him to see that he too was watching the happy couple, his face set in hard lines of repressed anger.

'Love can deceive all of us,' she said and leant against the railings, preferring to look at him instead of the bride and groom.

'It wasn't love.' He snapped the words out and looked down at her. 'It was deception.'

'Deception?'

'We had known each other since childhood,' he began, keeping his attention focused on the events unfolding in the castle courtyard. 'It stood the test of time when I moved to Milan. Marriage seemed the normal progres-sion and very much expected by our families.'

'So what went wrong?' She asked the question quietly, sensing his simmering anger.

'It wasn't me she really wanted, but the lifestyle she thought I could give her. What she hadn't accounted for in her scheming was that I would be putting every last cent back into my uncle's business. She soon tired of my frugal ways and found a man who could give her what she wanted.'

Charlie touched his arm, compelled to reach out, and he turned quickly to look at her, his eyes hard and glacial. She understood his feelings of betrayal. They almost mirrored hers.

For a moment he was silent, looking at her with unguarded curiosity. She held his gaze, trapped by the intensity of it.

'Seb told me you were once engaged.' Her heart plummeted but she smiled up at him, keeping her expression emotionless.

'Yes and, like you, we were too young. I was also far too naïve.' The sudden need to talk about something she'd hidden away surprised her. Was it his honesty that had triggered it? Whatever was happening between them, she was conscious of the earlier buoyant mood deflating as vulnerabilities were exposed. 'Let's not talk about it now; let's just enjoy our time together.'

'That is why you don't do for ever? Your heart has been broken?' He ignored her attempt to change the subject and lifted her chin with his fingers, brushing a kiss on her lips, sending her already distracted body into overdrive.

'I'd much prefer a wildly passionate affair,' she lied and moved closer to him, pressing her lips against his. A broken heart was only part of it and for the first time she realised what was really holding her back. What if she had the same capability to leave as her mother had?

'My sentiments exactly.' He deepened the kiss and she was vaguely aware of people passing them on the walkway and the wedding celebrations below moving away.

'Come on, let's explore.' Finally she pulled away from him, a teasing note in her voice. A little bit of distance between them was needed. Her heart was pounding and imagining all sorts of happy-ever-after scenarios with him.

'We shall go back a much faster way,' he said as they emerged from the castle, his voice full of laughter but the intent in his words clear. 'I've arranged for a private trip back; that way I can kiss you without feeling the world is watching.'

Excitement fizzed inside her at the thought of being alone with him but, as they stepped into the small speedboat waiting within the moat of the castle, the reality was very different. It was compact, forcing them close together, but it also meant they were very near to the driver.

Heat from Sandro seeped into her as she sat next to him. The boat made its way under the small castle bridges which reminded her of Venice, out of the medieval port and onto the lake. Soon they were speeding across the water and quickly she knotted her hair into a ponytail as they rushed back towards the small town of Desenzano. Alessandro pulled her tight against him and she closed her eyes, relishing the rush of air past her as the boat sped along and the feel of his strength. This was like a dream, so romantic and loving it would be easy to get carried away.

'I have a table booked at the best lakeside restaurant,'

Alessandro said as the powerboat slowed and pulled alongside the quay. Flags flapped erratically in the wind and she grabbed her hair again with one hand to stop it from blowing all over her face as he took the other and helped her from the boat.

Time was passing too quickly. It hardly seemed possible they'd been together all day, but already the sun was slipping lower in the sky. Once dinner was over they would go back to his villa, a thought which sent shivers of anticipation zipping rapidly through her.

All through dinner Alessandro had fought the urge to take her back to his villa. The tension had mounted rapidly, almost to boiling point. She felt it too, of that he was sure, and, as she'd sipped her coffee, her eyes became as dark as moss, suggestion in their depths as to what the night would bring.

They were kindred spirits, both healing from failed relationships, both wanting only the here and now. But, as they made their way back to his car, he imagined what it would be like to be with Charlie every day, to spend weekend after weekend like this.

Such thoughts had to be stamped out. She didn't do for ever, she'd made that perfectly clear, and the promise he'd made Seb to look after her as if she were his sister loomed over him, mocking him as his desire for the one woman he couldn't have raged ever stronger.

Now he powered the car along the road, the setting sun casting an orange glow all around them. He'd enjoyed his day with her but he knew he would enjoy the night much more. Here in his villa he was free to let go and love her. No promises hung over him, taunting him with guilt at what he was doing. Hurt from the past couldn't reach him any more and for just one more night she was his.

He sensed her watching him and glanced over at her. Did she guess at his eagerness to get her home?

'We have all night, Sandro.' She smiled lightly but the passion in her eyes told a very different story, as did the sexy purr when she said his name.

Would it be enough? he asked himself as he turned into the driveway of the villa, the last glimmer of the sun slipping beneath the horizon before them. Sunrise would mean their last day. They could only be lovers for the weekend. A weekend that was drawing rapidly to a close.

'Ma per amare una donna...' He tried hard to bring English to the fore as images of them together made his pulse race. Finally he managed to. 'But to love a woman like you I need more than one night.'

She reached up and touched his face, her fingertips snagging over his light growth of stubble. 'We only have tonight, Sandro. This can never be anything more. We don't belong together.'

Reminded of her earlier warning, he caught her hand and kissed her palm. 'Tonight only, but it will be one you will remember for ever.'

CHAPTER NINE

IF THAT FIRST morning waking in Alessandro's bed had been amazing, this morning was delicious. Charlie luxuriated against the warmth of his body like a kitten, content and sleepy. She lingered on the edge of sleep a moment longer, her back against his chest and his arms possessively keeping her close.

It was bliss and she didn't want to wake and face the day. Their last day together, and after their night of hot passionate sex she wasn't sure she wanted to begin the day. Birdsong drifted in through the open balcony doors and finally she opened her eyes to see the soft linen curtains stirring gently in the breeze.

It was like a dream, her body still singing from the hours of lovemaking, and now she felt safe. Loved. It was something she could get used to, but she mustn't. Thoughts of love drifted perilously close to the surface and she pushed them aside, aware something had changed. Deep down she wanted to be loved, but her disastrous engagement made that almost impossible. *This is just a weekend affair*, she reminded herself sternly as his arms pulled her tighter against him.

'Would you care to join me for a morning swim?' His lips brushed against the back of her neck and a flutter of butterflies took flight in her stomach. She closed her eyes against the heady sensation, ignoring her doubts of moments ago. It was still the weekend and still time to enjoy this affair.

'I don't have anything to wear.' She wished she did. The pool had looked inviting in the morning sun yesterday, but the thought of Sandro in it too made it infinitely better.

'Not a problem.' He kissed her ear and whispered to her, 'We are totally alone; nobody can see us.'

She turned in his arms, her pulse rate leaping wildly at the thought of swimming naked with him. 'Are you sure? No staff.'

'No staff. Nobody except you and me.' His words were heavy with accent and much more, making her body sing with desire she thought had long since been quenched.

He pulled her against him but she pushed at his chest with her hands, delighting in the chance to tease him again. 'I thought you wanted to swim.'

'I've changed my mind.'

In one swift move she leapt from the bed, the shock on his face making her laugh. Suggestively, she raised her brows. 'Well, I'm going for a swim.' Not wanting to pass up on the opportunity of such a luxurious pool, she rushed through the open balcony doors and down the stone steps that led to the pool. She glanced around briefly, checking they were as alone as he'd said, acutely aware she was still totally naked.

Without waiting to see if he followed, she dived into the cool blue water, glided forward then broke the surface. The sense of freedom was immense and she struggled to comprehend how just a bikini could hinder the feel of water against the skin. Only a short time ago she had been asleep but now her whole body was alive, invigorated by the cool water and the prospect of Alessandro joining her.

It was already warm. She swam to the end of the pool and, with her arms over the edge, looked out over Lake Garda as it stretched out below her. The sun's morning rays cast a golden glow over the tree-covered hills and mountains and already she could see the ferries, like tiny white shapes on the water, as they started their daily cruises.

Behind her she heard a small splash and moments later felt the water ripple against her neck as Alessandro dived in. She smiled but continued to survey the view, waiting with anticipation for him to join her. Her body trembled and her heart rate soared as she heard his strong strokes through the water. Then he was beside her, his arms on the edge, looking at the view too.

Embarrassment filled her. Swimming naked was not something she had ever done before and yet here she was, naked in Alessandro's pool. With breathing becoming difficult and her heart thumping hard, she needed to divert her attention, cool things down. She didn't even dare look at him.

'Stunning, isn't it?' She really couldn't believe she was here, enjoying a weekend of total luxury with the sexiest man she'd ever met.

'Semplicemente bellissimo.' Whenever he spoke Italian she got shivers of excitement down her spine, but this time she was certain he wasn't referring to the view and she turned to face him.

Shyness rushed over her at her nakedness and the hungry look in his eyes. She tried to mask it with bravado. 'Race you.' Without waiting to see if he'd taken up her challenge, she pushed away from the side of the pool, propelling herself through the water before beginning to swim back towards the villa.

Just as moments ago, she sensed him coming closer. Splashes of water landed around her as his strong arms carried him past her and to the end of the pool. His hand on the edge, his bronzed shoulders glistening in the morning sun, he waited for her to draw closer.

'I should have known you'd win.' She breathed out the words after the exertion of a brisk swim. Of course he'd win. She doubted he ever lost—at anything.

'You shouldn't challenge me, *cara*.' His voice was mocking and, without thinking, she splashed water at him, laughing in a way she hadn't laughed for a long time. 'And you shouldn't splash me either.'

Before she could do anything more, he hauled himself out of the water and effortlessly sprang to his feet to stand on the side of the pool looking down at her. She couldn't help but look at him and as her eyes travelled downwards shock set it.

'You cheat!' The words rushed from her as she took in the trunks clinging to him, water dripping from them. 'You tricked me. You let me believe we would both be naked.'

She hung on to the side of the pool, embarrassment colouring her cheeks. The smile on his face was too much. 'I never mentioned that I would be naked. Now, are you coming out or not?'

'Not.' She pouted up at him then swam slowly away, knowing he would be looking at her body.

She looked over at him as she swam, saw him grab a towel from a lounger and ruffle his hair dry, then stretch out on the lounger, watching every move she made. Her pulse rate went into overdrive.

'Do you make a habit of this, Miss Warrington?' His teasing question irritated her, yet made her smile too. He was playing games with her, toying with her like a cat did a mouse.

'Swimming naked or passionate weekend affairs?' She tossed the question at him as she reached the end of the pool, this time turning her back on the view of Lake Garda. There was a much more interesting view to take in now.

'Both.'

'I've never swum naked before.' She pushed away from the side, this time on her back, revelling in the chance to tease him just a bit, making her feel that little bit more in control. She had never had an affair, no matter how long, but she wasn't going to tell him that. She was tiring as she reached the end of the pool again but didn't want to come out of the water, not whilst he watched her so intently.

'I've never had a naked woman in my pool before.' His look was playful and the smile that moved his lips incredibly sexy.

She looked over at him, liking the way the sun gleamed in his damp hair. His long legs were as tanned as the rest of him and she feasted on the image he created, adding it to the one from their first night together, storing it away. This would be a scene never to be repeated.

'Well, that does surprise me. A man like you.' She kept her voice light and flirty, trying to echo his mood, but her heart was racing as heady need spread through her.

'A man like me?' He leant forward on the lounger, placing one foot on the floor. 'Just what is a man like me?'

She wished the words unsaid but continued with her carefree tone as she slowly swam to the side of the pool, holding the edge in front of him and trying to hide her nakedness. 'Don't try to deny you don't have women dropping at your feet.'

'Only those who are looking for something I can't give.' The brusque words, in complete contrast to his sexy and carefree stance, made her smile.

'Oh, and what's that?' she said, laughing teasingly at him.

'Marriage and security.' The air stilled around them and his mouth hardened just enough to warn her she'd strayed into dangerous territory. He sat back in the lounger again, as if to get as far away from the conversation as possible. Yesterday he'd talked of the end of his marriage to his childhood sweetheart. Was that the reason he'd never settled down again? She could certainly relate to that.

'And you don't want that?' She rested her arms on the side of the pool and looked at him, seeing an array of emotions flash across his face.

'No.'

The word was so final a chill slipped over her despite the warm sun on her back. She moved in the water, rippling sounds filling the heavy silence, but she couldn't look away, couldn't break the eye contact.

'I totally understand.' She did, but wished she'd kept that to herself as his eyes narrowed suspiciously.

'You do?'

'Oh, you know, once bitten, twice shy, as we say in England.' She turned her back and swam away from him, not wanting this discussion she had inadvertently started.

They should be enjoying their last hours together, not mulling over the past.

'You shouldn't hide from it, Charlie.' She stopped swimming as he said the very same words her father often said. Treading water, she turned to face him and swam back to the side of the pool, wishing she was wearing something so she could get out—of the pool and the conversation.

'Hide from what, Sandro?'

'Love.'

She blinked in shock, not quite able to believe a man who freely admitted to not wanting commitment would even use that word. 'I'm not hiding from it. I just haven't found it yet.'

'And when you do?'

She couldn't understand where the questions were coming from. She'd made it clear she didn't do for ever, so why channel the conversation this way? 'My mother left us as teenagers, Sandro. She left my father, turning her back on us. I haven't believed in happy ever after since.'

'And the man you were engaged to? Did you love him and dream of living happily ever after?' His scrutiny was intense and she hated the feeling of being trapped in the pool, forced to answer his questions.

'Maybe I wasn't ready to love after that.' That statement stunned her and she blinked against the admission, realising the truth of it.

'And if you were to fall in love?' His dark eyes fixed hers and she clutched harder to the side of the pool.

'If I was sure I'd found a man to love, one who would love me, then I might just think about for ever.'

'So you'd get married?' His voice rose in question and disbelief.

'Marriage isn't the only way to have love, Sandro.' He furrowed his brows speculatively at her and she turned the heat on him, deflecting it from herself. 'What about you—would you marry again?'

Alessandro looked down at Charlie, her wet hair slicked back from her face, highlighting the beauty of her eyes. She was stunning, but she was also talking of things he'd begun to question as he'd held her sleeping body against him this morning.

He'd been adamant he was done with love, done with marriage, but such thoughts had begun to filter from the back of his mind. Images of him and Charlie, sharing love and happiness, lingered on the edge, hazy images that hadn't yet become sharp and focused. Images that shouldn't even be there.

Just as he had done as she'd curled against him and slept, he wondered what it would be like to wake every morning, take her in his arms and kiss her awake. In just a few days she'd weaved a spell so potent he didn't want to let her go. Because she still blamed him for Seb's accident, he couldn't ask for more—not until he cleared himself of blame in her eyes. And he couldn't do that without telling her everything. And that would break his promise to Seb.

'Your silence says it all.' Charlie's voice hurtled him back to the present.

'With the right woman,' he said truthfully. He had thought the right woman didn't exist for him. His first marriage had been testament to that. Now the woman he wished could be *the right woman* had made it perfectly clear she didn't want anything more than this weekend.

'I hope you meet her then.'

He watched as she pushed away from the side of the pool, once again swimming on her back, exposing her pert breasts to him. The water sparkled under the sun but it couldn't detract from the beauty of her naked body as she swam. He was beginning to think he had.

'Are you ever going to come out of that pool?' Desperate to change the subject, he stood and picked up a towel. 'You'll be a mermaid before long.'

She laughed and swam to the steps at the far end of the pool, her slim figure clearly visible in the water, unleashing coils of lust within him. Lust. That was all this was—all it could be. He had to keep that at the forefront of his mind when dreams he'd long since hidden away threatened to reappear.

'I'm not mermaid material.' Slowly, as if aware of his eyes on her, aware of the hot lust she evoked within him, she climbed up the steps. Water rushed off her skin as she stood at the edge of the pool, pulling her hands down her hair, scrunching it into a ponytail to wring the water from it.

He couldn't move, couldn't take his eyes off her. Rivulets of water rushed over her breasts, down her stomach, and he fought hard against the urge to carry her back to his bed. She was so beautiful as she stood like a nymph with the morning sun glistening on her wet skin. It was like watching a film play out in slow motion as she walked towards him. Her angelic beauty stunned him into silence.

Unaware of what he was doing, he walked towards her and wrapped the towel around her, pulling her close against his now dry skin, relishing the wetness of hers. His gaze met hers, her green eyes heavy with unguarded passion that made his heart thud.

She reached up and brushed her lips over his and he closed his eyes as an intensity pressed down on his heart. Would he ever get enough of her? He knew the answer to that as her arms reached around his back, locking them together. No, he never would. She deepened the kiss, sending heat and need rushing through him again.

'We should take this inside,' he ground out as she pulled back and looked up at him. Her smile told him she knew exactly what she did to him and fully intended to continue the teasing she'd started as soon as she'd woken this morning.

'Yes,' she whispered. 'One last time.'

'One last time.' He repeated her words and kissed her, drinking her in, wanting more than one last time, but she hadn't set the boundaries for their weekend—he had and now he couldn't take this any further. He was already guilty enough of abusing the trust Seb had placed in him. As soon as they returned to Milan he had to put their relationship back where it belonged. On a professional level.

She pulled back from him and clutched the towel around her shoulders, although it didn't hide her luscious body completely from his view. With a coquettish little smile she took his hand and led him back up the stone steps and into the bedroom.

The sun now poured into the room, its rays falling onto the bed he'd hastily left after he'd heard her splash into the pool. The cream covers strewn aside, evidence of the hot hours they'd spent there last night.

She dropped the towel as she walked towards him, the makeshift ponytail hanging over one breast sending a rivulet of water down her sexy body. He took in a deep breath, savouring every last detail about her. Her impatience was clear as she closed the distance between them.

Before he knew what had happened she was in his arms, her body pressed hard against his, the torment of her nakedness too much. With an urgency he'd never experienced he lifted her from the wooden floor, her legs wrapping around him, only his trunks between them.

He carried her towards the bed, the heat of her against his arousal almost too much. Gently he lowered her onto the bed, watching as she slithered up towards the pillows. He crawled up the bed after her, his heart pounding in his chest so hard she must hear it. He wanted her so very much and intended to make the most of these last moments as lovers.

With frantic moves he tugged his trunks down, kicking them away as his gaze held hers, then took one slender ankle in his grasp and pulled her slowly back towards him. Her eyes flew wide but her heavy breaths, which made her breasts rise and fall provocatively, drove him on.

He moved over her, wanting to be deep inside her, to make her his one last time. He should be taking it slow but he couldn't hold back any longer.

'Sandro, stop.' She pushed against his chest, the urgency in her voice breaking the mind-numbing lust which robbed him of all coherent thought. 'We need protection.'

'*Maledizione.*' He shook with the effort of regaining control and looked at her face. With her eyes so wide and so green, all he could do was lower his head and kiss her. 'Forgive me.'

He didn't recognise the hoarse voice that had said those words. Never had he lost control quite so spectacularly and somewhere deep inside he was thankful that at least one of them had retained some sense.

He reached across to the bedside table and grabbed the box of condoms, tipping the last one out. Her words of moments ago floated back to him. *One last time.* He pushed the thought roughly aside as he rolled the protection on.

'Sorry,' she said shyly. 'But we don't want any consequences from this weekend.'

He looked at her, realisation hitting him. There were already consequences from this weekend, though not in the form of pregnancy. The consequences for him were that he'd unwittingly given his heart away, fallen for a woman he shouldn't even have had an affair with, let alone love.

'You're right, *mia cara.* There cannot be any consequences.'

She kissed him gently, her lips so light and teasing, sending him almost over the edge. 'None at all.' Her words whispered against his lips and he pushed all other thoughts from his mind until he couldn't hold back any longer.

'No,' he ground out as she pulled him towards her, wrapping her legs about him, taking him deep inside her. For the last time he made her his, the passion all-consuming.

His release was swift and she clung to him as he buried his head in her damp hair. '*Il mio amore,*' he murmured softly in Italian as he kissed her neck, not knowing what he was saying, his thoughts translating to words involuntarily as passion took over.

Was it his way of saying goodbye? He didn't know, but was grateful the words of love he'd voiced in his language hadn't appeared to have been understood, or even heard.

* * *

Charlie smoothed down the white dress she'd arrived in yesterday and glanced around the room one last time, not sure if she was checking for forgotten items or committing it to memory. Both, she told herself, because there wouldn't be any coming back. It was over. In just two more days she'd be back in England, back to her life. The moments of passion they'd shared would be locked away for good.

She walked around the room, her sandals tapping slowly on the wooden floor. She could still hear the soft words of Italian Sandro had spoken as they'd made love that one last time. She hadn't understood much of it, but one phrase now replayed over and over in her head.

Il mio *amore.*

My love.

She shook her head in denial. It must have been in the heat of the moment, something he said to every woman he made love to and nothing more. She clung to this idea, knowing she didn't want it to be anything more. Especially not from Alessandro.

They might have put aside their differences for a weekend of passion, enabling them to explore the explosive attraction that had been present from the very beginning, but as soon as they returned to Milan those differences would return. They would engulf them and mock her for her weakness at giving in to lust, because lust was all it was, all it ever could be.

As she thought of returning to Milan, she knew that, deep down, she could never forgive him for failing to ensure that the prototype that Seb had crashed that night was fit to drive. Their differences encroached like a menacing shadow. What had she done? Not only had she slept with the man responsible for Seb's death, but had enjoyed a whirlwind affair. One that had jumbled her emotions and tied her in knots.

Quickly she grabbed her bag and left the room, not daring to look again at the bed which had been the focal point of so much pleasure, so much passion. She should be ashamed of herself. And, deep down, she was, but at least she'd got it out of her system, cleansed away the irrational desire she'd felt for him the instant her eyes had met his. There wouldn't be any *what ifs* when she returned home. But there would be recriminations.

Her heels clipped down the marble stairs, echoing around the vast hallway, and she paused as she saw Alessandro stood by the door, keys in hand, looking as desperate to get back to normal as she was.

Despite her bravado and knowing this was how it should be, her heart sank. If things had been different, if she didn't hold him responsible for Seb's accident, would they have been leaving as lovers too? She swallowed down the thought, straightened her shoulders and met his gaze head-on.

'It is time to go, no?' Her step faltered briefly at his heavily accented question, or was it a statement? Whatever it was, it was right. It was time to go, time to leave their passion within the luxury of this villa.

'It is,' she said and continued down the stairs, her chin held high. 'Time to get back to reality.'

CHAPTER TEN

CHARLIE HAD NEVER been so tense. The drive back to Milan had been almost silent, with the exception of a few attempts at polite conversation which had withered like flowers in parched earth.

She followed Alessandro into the apartment, trying not to notice the masculine scent of his aftershave, which trailed tantalisingly in his wake. She might have decided to distance herself from him but her body was having a hard time accepting it.

'I will book into a hotel, if you can recommend one close by.' She forced the words out, knowing it would be for the best. What they'd shared over the weekend had no place in the present and certainly not the future. She'd made it very clear to him she wasn't looking for more than a passing distraction and he'd made it easy, setting the time limit and taking her away.

But now they were back in Milan. Back with their problems. All she wanted was to get through the next two days and leave—but not until she'd found what she'd come to Italy for. Answers.

He turned to face her, his expression set in a hard mask, his eyes unreadable. 'That will not be necessary. The room you occupied on the first night is ready for you.'

Her room was ready for her. Didn't that tell her enough? He'd obviously instructed his housekeeper to put the few things she'd left behind back in the room Seb had once used, effectively removing her presence as a lover from his apartment. It was what she wanted, what she needed, so why did it hurt so much?

'Under the circumstances, it would be best if I stayed in a hotel.' She forced herself to believe her words. After all, she had little hope of him doing so if she didn't.

'No.' The word snapped from him as he tossed his car keys onto the marble worktop of the kitchen in an irritated fashion. 'The circumstances, as you so nicely put it, are that we are back after a weekend away. Our weekend of fun is over. It was not a for ever arrangement and nothing more than an affair.'

'All the more reason I stay in a hotel, don't you think?'

He looked at her sternly and the hard businessman he was showed through. 'You said it wasn't for ever, so why do you need to leave? The weekend affair we agreed on is over, now it is back to business.'

'Very well,' she relented, but knew she had to go back to England sooner than originally planned. Once their meeting at the test track was over tomorrow she would be on the next plane home. She'd walk out right now, if only she had the answers she needed.

Resigned to staying in his apartment one more night, she walked over to the windows, looking out at the Duomo. When she'd first arrived its magnificence had captured her imagination, now she just looked blankly at it. So much had changed in just two days, but each mile they'd driven on their way back to Milan had wiped out their weekend, kiss by kiss. They were back where they had started, but the simmer of sexual tension was now tinged with regret. At least for her it was; for Alessandro it had been replaced by indifference.

With a small sigh she turned and absently looked at the newspaper neatly placed on the ornate desk which occupied the corner of the living area. Already a photograph of her and Alessandro arriving at the launch party had a front-page position. The few words written beneath were incomprehensible and she turned the page. Maybe more of the launch would be on another page.

She froze.

The image which leapt to life from the page scorched her with hot memories. She and Alessandro were there, in the paper. Not the happy smiles of their arrival, but the passionate kiss against the car. The kiss that had happened after everyone had left.

She looked down at the picture, which sparked with passion, showing lovers locked in their own world, oblivious to everything, even the intrusion of the photographer. When and how had this been taken? Then her body chilled. Had Alessandro known of this? She recalled his intent as he'd taken her in his arms, the way he'd rendered all thought impossible as his lips had claimed hers.

He hadn't kissed her because he'd wanted to, because he'd been unable to resist, but to set up the perfect photo opportunity. One that would show to the world he wasn't in any way to blame for Seb's accident, that she and her family had more than given their stamp of approval to a car which had taken the life of a young driver.

'Did you know about this?' She closed the paper, unable to look at the sizzling photograph a moment longer. He approached the table, a frown on his face, and she looked up at him, hostility masking her shock.

'*Sì*. It is what I requested.' His calm words did little to soothe her jangled nerves. So he had set her up, used her like a pawn in his game. Not only did her presence at the launch suggest she didn't blame him or the Roselli company, it showed an intimate moment she had no wish for the world to see.

She blinked in surprise. 'What you requested?'

'Come, Charlotte—' his accent lavished her full name as he looked down at her, having glanced briefly at the paper '—a front-page photograph of us together is exactly the sort of advertisement I'd hoped for. You brought glamour and style to the occasion and, of course, your family's blessing.'

'What about this?' Furiously she dashed back the front page and watched as he looked down at the photo of their passionately hot kiss. 'Did you request this?'

He scanned the words beneath the photo, words she didn't understand. His silence was almost too much as he placed one palm on the desk, leaning down to read. The suspense of what it all meant was wrapping up with her initial anger until she thought she might explode. 'Did you?'

'No.' He shook his head, continuing to study the piece. 'Not this.'

'What does it say?' Anger overtook the suspense, filling her mind and her body. He'd set her up. He'd used her. Had that been his intention even as he'd entered her home and tried to convince her to go to Milan? She swallowed down the sour taste of deceit, determined not to let her feelings out. She had to remain calm.

He turned to look at her, his eyes locking with hers, but the brown of his were devoid of any emotion and her stomach lurched sickeningly. What had she done—to herself and to Seb? She'd sullied Seb's memory and her reputation into the bargain, falling into the worst trap imaginable.

Alessandro looked into the confusion of her eyes and tried to push back all the guilt he'd so far managed to keep at bay. She was angry, there wasn't any denying that, but she also looked scared and he didn't blame her.

'It says your passion shows your approval of the car which claimed the life of your brother.' He didn't translate word for word what had been written beneath that blisteringly hot photograph. He didn't think her anger would allow him enough time, so quickly he'd summed it up, leaving her to draw her own conclusions.

'What's next, Sandro? A photo of me, naked in your pool?' The accusation in her voice cut hard and deep. Did she really think he was that callous?

What could he say? This photograph alone went against everything he'd said to her that day in her cottage. He'd persuaded her to come to the launch in Milan, telling her Seb had wanted it. Now, thanks to a rogue photographer, something he would swiftly sort out, she thought he'd set her up.

'That will not be possible. You would not have been seen by anyone.' He pushed the image of her swimming naked aside. Now was not the time for such heated recollections.

'Damn you, Alessandro. You tricked me into swimming with nothing on, even had the nerve to come out in your trunks. What will the next headline say?' Her eyes were sharp, her expression strained as she pressed her lips tightly together, expectantly waiting for his answer.

He clenched his fists against the urge to hold her, pull her towards him and calm her. Instinctively he knew that would be the worst possible thing to do. She was pushing him further away, something he was certain she would have done even without the help of the newspaper report.

He glowered at her, his pulse racing erratically. 'I did not trick you at all. Your swim this morning will remain between us.'

'I don't believe you.' The words fired from her like bullets and she stepped closer to him, chin lifted and standing so tall with indignation he would hardly have had to lower his head to kiss her lips. The temptation was great, but he resisted.

'Have I lied to you, *cara*?'

Of course he'd lied to her. From the night of the accident and the moment he'd discovered the truth, the real reason Seb had crashed, he'd been lying to her. But they were lies to protect her and Seb, to keep the Warrington name out of the papers. They were lies he had to continue with. He'd made a promise, first to Seb, then to her father and he would keep both of those promises. He was a man of honour, whatever the cost.

'If you can set up publicity like this—' she flicked the paper, not taking her eyes from him '—then you are capable of anything, any lie, just to get what you want.'

He shook his head slowly, admiring the fire of anger emanating from her, not wanting to dampen the passion. But her passion was something he could no longer have; there were too many secrets, too many lies between them.

She made a sound that was like a growl and put her hands to her face, fingers splayed over her eyes. Then she dropped her hands, letting them fall with a slap against her as exasperation got the better of her. 'I was stupid ever to have believed you—or trusted you.'

He shook his head and reached for her, desperate to offer some comfort at least. She flinched, stepping back out of his reach.

Her eyes, angry and glittering, searched his face, finally narrowing in suspicion. 'You've done nothing but lie to me, Sandro; since the moment you arrived at my cottage it's been nothing but lies.'

'*Dio mio!* How can you say that?' Exasperation coursed through him and he pushed his fingers through his hair, unable to comprehend the circles she was spinning around him. Circles that made the temptation to tell the truth almost too much.

'Because of this.' She snatched the paper from the desk, shaking it in front of him. 'You used me. This has nothing at all to do with Seb. You're just trying to ease your conscience, ease your guilt over the accident.'

'My conscience is clear, Charlie.' It was—he was doing this for Seb.

'Charlotte.' Her voice cracked like a whip as she corrected his use of her name, glaring up at him. 'And once again you are lying. I don't believe Seb really asked for me to be at the launch. It was you who wanted me there all along; you were just preying on my emotions.'

'Seb did ask for you to be there; that much is true.' Her anger lacerated him but he stood firm against it, holding the truth inside.

'That much? So you are lying about something?' Her voice lowered in suspicion and she looked at him through narrowing eyes.

He had to think fast, keep ahead of her suspicions. 'I

have not lied, but certain things need to remain out of the limelight.'

'Like this?' She stabbed at the photo of them kissing and inwardly he breathed a sigh of relief. He'd almost blown it, almost revealed there were things he was holding back on. Her anger fizzed around him, preventing her from thinking in any rational kind of way.

Charlie couldn't take any more and tossed the offending newspaper back onto the desk, glaring angrily at the man she'd been stupid enough to fall in love with.

Fall in love?

Panic rushed through her faster than any car she'd ever driven. She couldn't love him. Not Alessandro Roselli. Not the man she blamed for Seb's accident and the man who had cruelly tricked her and used her emotional weakness for his own ends.

'You can't run and hide from this, Charlotte.' Alessandro's words filtered through the hazy fog of anger and shock that obscured just about everything. Hadn't he used that phrase earlier? Then he'd been referring to love. Now it was truth. She sensed he was keeping something from her—and she was sure it wasn't love, despite his murmured words of endearment just hours ago.

'I don't run.' She stood in the doorway of the room she'd used the first night at his apartment, swallowing down the bitter taste of reality, refusing to admit any such thing to him.

'Then what are you doing now, *cara*?' His words were softer, coaxing and cajoling. She was running, she was hiding; they both knew it, but she'd never admit it to him. Especially as it was love she was running from. She had no choice. This man didn't love her and never would.

He'd agreed to the weekend affair for exactly the same reasons as she had. He didn't do love.

'I'm not the only one running or hiding, Alessandro.' She spoke calmly even though her heart was thudding painfully in her chest and her knees were suddenly weak.

His eyes narrowed in suspicion. 'What is it you want to say, Charlotte?'

She ignored the way he used her name, the way his accent caressed it, keeping herself focused on what she really wanted. 'You are hiding the truth of Seb's accident.'

'I've told you all there is to tell,' he said, his eyes searching her face.

'We both know that's not exactly true.' She lifted her chin in a show of defiance, looked him in the eye and continued. 'You told me what you want me to know.'

'It wasn't the car, Charlotte.'

'So it was the driver. It was Seb.' She wasn't about to let this go now. Whatever the truth was, she had to know.

'It was. I'm sorry.' He reached out to her but she flinched.

'Don't.' The word was spat out as she battled with the idea that the accident had possibly been Seb's fault and that Alessandro, for whatever reason, wasn't going to tell her.

'You should talk to your father,' he said quietly, seemingly indifferent to her anger.

'I intend to. Right now.' She turned and moved into her room, purposefully keeping the door open. She wanted him to see her ring her father, watch whilst she asked for the full facts.

Angrily grabbing her phone from her bag, she dialled the number. It rang out before going to answerphone. But she wasn't beaten yet. 'If you will excuse me,' she said tartly as she began to shut the door, 'I have packing to do.'

With that she turned her back on him, resolutely shutting the door behind her. She dropped to sit on the bed, all the fight deflating from her. Outside, a nearby bell tower chimed the hour and she fought against threatening tears.

It was time to go home. Time to go back to her life and pick up the pieces that had been discarded the day she'd heard that her beloved brother had died. Just as her father had been trying to persuade her to do for many months. But she was sure he wouldn't have wanted her to fall in love with Alessandro Roselli and that was just what she'd done.

She thought of her mother, but she dismissed the idea of confiding in her. She was always too willing to blame the racing world for bringing her family down and tearing it apart. It would only give more weight to her argument against the whole lifestyle.

Resigned to the pain that Alessandro's betrayal had brought, she pulled out her tablet and searched for London-bound flights, booking on one the next evening. At least that would give her time to go back to the test track in the morning. She had one last thing to do before she went.

Then it would be goodbye and this time she meant it to be for ever.

Alessandro had watched her walk away, desperate to call her name, to make her turn and look at him. But it wouldn't do any good. They should never have become lovers and they could never be together. The hours they'd shared at his villa must be forgotten and he hoped they hadn't been tailed by any more photographers. It was bad enough her father might see the one of them kissing, but what if he saw her, cares cast aside, enjoying time with him? Not that they'd be shots of her at his pool—security was good at the villa—but they'd spent a lot of time out and about, doing tourist things.

She had paused in the doorway and turned to look at him, her green eyes large and full of sadness, and as they met his he'd felt the disappointment crash over him like a stormy sea.

'Goodnight, Alessandro.' Her voice had lost the anger and hard edge of earlier but he remained where he was, rooted to the marble floor, unable to decide what course of action was best.

'*Buonanotte*, Charlotte.' He couldn't stand and watch her any more, not if he wanted to keep his distance, so he turned and marched off to his study, a place he could lose himself in work. Behind him, he heard the bedroom door click softly shut but it sounded loud and piercing in his head, like a gunshot.

He didn't sit at his desk, didn't open his laptop and work. He couldn't. His mind was going over every single detail of the last few days. From the moment he'd seen her working in her garden to the hot passionate nights they'd shared.

What was the matter with him? He couldn't want her, couldn't have her, but he did. He wanted to wake up with her each and every day. He paced the room, stopping to look out across the rooftops of Milan as the sun slipped lower in the sky, casting its orange glow onto the old buildings.

When he'd promised Seb he'd look after her as if she was his own sister he had never imagined it would be so difficult. What would he do if the situation was reversed, if it was his sister involved with a man who would break her heart?

He clenched his hands into tight fists, the thought of anyone hurting or taking advantage of his sister filling him with rage like an aggressive and territorial lion. Yet that was what he'd done. He'd gone back on his promise to Seb, just by kissing Charlie and by taking her away to explore the passion that had sparked to life the instant they'd met—he hadn't looked after her, as he'd promised her father he would.

The only thing he had been able to do right was keep the truth from her and even the success of that seemed in doubt as she probed into every drawing and detail Seb had made, and asked the manufacturing team pointed questions about whether certain design developments had been made before or after the accident.

He closed his eyes and memories of the day Seb had told him the truth descended. He could still hear Seb, his voice weak as he lay in the hospital bed, begging him to keep the drink and drug problem from his sister.

Please, Sandro, don't tell her. It will break her heart. Whatever else you do, don't tell her.

Seb's words came back to him, as clear as if he was at his side again. Alessandro rubbed his hands together, the light pressure of Seb's grasp once again on his hands, and in his mind he could see Seb's face, so like Charlie's, begging him to keep his secret.

Had he known then he wasn't going to make it?

With a furious curse, Alessandro strode back out of his office. He couldn't let Charlie sit there alone, worrying about everything. Outside her door, he paused. Was he doing the right thing? He was normally so decisive, so sure of what needed to be done, but where this woman was concerned he was the opposite.

He knocked on the door and almost instantly it was opened. 'You can't stay in there all night.' He attempted light-hearted chatter, something she'd proved to be very good at over the weekend. The frosty glare she sent him told him that he hadn't yet mastered that art.

'We could go out for dinner.' He didn't like her silence, as cold as her eyes, and he had the feeling he was in ever-deepening quicksand.

She raised a haughty brow at him. 'So you can set me up again, get yet another photo of us together?'

'Charlotte…' He stepped closer but she moved back, using the door as a shield.

'No, Sandro. I'm not prepared to take the risk. We should never have spent the weekend together.' She moved further behind the door. Hiding from him, from what they'd shared.

She was right and he moved away, not missing the relief on her face. 'I knew nothing about that photograph and I'm sorry it has upset you.'

'Please, I don't want to talk about it now.' Her green eyes looked moist and guilt tugged at him. He wasn't doing a very good job of looking after her at all.

He nodded his acceptance of her reason, knowing he was only making the whole situation worse. 'I will find whoever it was who took the photo and personally deal with him.'

'It won't take away the fact that you used me and Seb to promote the car, to clear its reputation and your name.'

'I have no need to clear my name, Charlotte.'

'You do to me.' Those words stung him as they hit

home and finally his business sense returned. He needed
to step back, assess the situation and plan his next move.

'Very well, I will.' He walked away, not stopping to
see how his words had been received. If she wanted proof
he'd find it, but how could he do so without giving away
Seb's secret—or his true feelings for her?

CHAPTER ELEVEN

CHARLIE HAD SECRETLY hoped Alessandro would have gone to wherever it was he went that first night, but as she'd emerged from her room earlier that morning he'd been preparing coffee, looking so handsome she'd actually stopped to take in every detail, from his expensive charcoal suit to the shiny black shoes.

Now, enclosed in his car, painfully aware of every move he made as he drove, she wished she'd taken the early morning flight to London. Instead, she'd been lured by the opportunity to be at the test track again, hoping she would find out what Alessandro was keeping from her about Seb's accident. Because something was, of that she was certain.

'I have a meeting at lunchtime.' His accented voice jolted her from her thoughts as they drove. She wanted to look at him, savour his handsome profile, but couldn't allow herself to. She'd imprinted more than enough images into her mind during their weekend. It was time to stop, to let go of something that could never be and should never have happened.

'I need to be at the airport this evening, so I will arrange a taxi.' Her words, though flowing and easy, didn't feel it. She was sure it sounded as if she was stumbling over each one and she ran her fingers through her hair nervously.

He turned to look at her just at the moment she gave in to temptation to look at him and for a split second their gazes met, then he focused back on the road as they turned into the test track.

'You said you weren't running.' His voice was deep and stern, but she fixed her attention on the workshops as he pulled up and parked. The engine fell silent and her heartbeat thumped so loudly she was sure he would hear it.

'I'm not running.' The angry words flew from her before she had time to think. 'I'm going back to my life, to the things I did before Seb's accident. It's what he would have wanted. The only good thing that has come out of this visit.'

She got out of the car, anxious to put some distance between herself and Alessandro. It didn't matter how much her body craved his, she had to remember what he'd done, how he'd manipulated her to get what he wanted in an attempt to assuage his guilt and clear his name.

She all but marched off towards the workshops, hearing the driver's door shut behind her then feeling his presence closing the distance as he caught up with her. Her pulse leapt as she reached the door but, before she could do anything, he pressed his palm against it, preventing her from opening it, stopping her from escaping him.

'That is all? There must be something else you want to accuse me of?' His voice deepened and she raised her eyes to meet his, determined not to let him know how much he affected her.

'"Something else" being the fact that you virtually sold me to the press for your own gain?' She hurled the words at him, indignation spiking her into action. 'Or is it the fact that you seduced me? You let me believe I was doing all this for Seb, when it wasn't. It was for you.'

His brows lifted suggestively, his expression of smug satisfaction almost too much to tolerate. 'As I recall, *cara*, it was you who seduced me.'

She clenched her hands into tight fists, digging her nails into her palms. Pain made her gasp, emotional and physical pain. It was just what she needed to remind her of what was at stake. Not only her brother's good name and her reputation, but her heart.

'Don't flatter yourself. What I did, I did for Seb.' She flung the first words that came to mind at him, then bit down on any more. She didn't want to let him know how much she was hurting, how hard she had fallen for him. He must never know. It would give him the trump card.

'Not because you wanted to, because you couldn't resist the fire that leapt to life between us the moment we met?' He loomed over her, trapping her and forcing her to confront this.

'Okay. So I couldn't resist the *fire*, as you put it. But that fire is well and truly out now.' She pushed his hand aside and opened the door, thankful to see mechanics and drivers busy at work. He'd never pursue her now, not so publicly.

Behind her, she heard him talking rapidly in Italian, heard his footsteps as he marched across the spotless floor of the workshop. She had no idea what he was saying, but it seemed that everyone was ready to do as he asked, waiting for their instruction.

At a loss as to just what she should do now they were here again and with so many curious glances her way, she went over to a car she hadn't seen here last time. Obviously it was a new prototype for yet another road sports car. The black paintwork shone beneath the bright lights of the workshop and the elegant curves of the wing of the car caught her eye. It was very different from the flashy red one her brother had played a part in. That had been exactly what she would have expected from Seb.

This had more style, as if designed for speed and comfort. The grille at the front was far more sedate, more classical and looked much less aggressive than Seb's. It was still low and sporty, its power subtly evident, but with a sophistication that made her immediately think of Alessandro. Was this car all his work?

As he spoke to his team, Alessandro watched Charlie walking towards the car. He saw her head tilt to one side in contemplation as she stood by the front wing, looking along the line of the car. He could almost hear her mind working, assessing the car's capabilities.

With a few final instructions, he left his team and walked over to where Charlie was now looking inside the latest prototype. This was his design; everything he'd ever wanted in a car was going into it.

'This looks like it has the potential to be a car in a league of its own.' Her voice oozed enthusiasm that no amount of animosity between them could disguise. 'Who designed it?'

He wasn't about to tell her it was his work, not so soon after the launch of Seb's car. He'd never intended for her to see it, worried she'd think he'd moved onto a new project before Seb's car had even been launched. 'A team effort.'

'A good one,' she said, running her fingers along it, just as she had done with the first car. 'A really good one. Black suits it.'

He couldn't listen to her praise for his work, even if she didn't know it as such. This was the woman he'd done nothing but try to protect, the woman who heated his blood, making him want her more than any other. Now she hated him and was about to walk out of his life. But he couldn't stop her.

'I have arranged for Giovanni to take you back to the apartment to collect your belongings and then on to the airport.' He had to keep the conversation on neutral territory. If she continued to talk about the car, he knew his passion for it would show, just as his passion for her could so easily come out.

'Yes, of course, thank you.' Her curt tone reminded him of her earlier anger and he knew he was doing the right thing. If he stayed any longer he would tell her anything to disperse that anger which hovered around them and relight the passion they'd shared at the weekend.

The best thing he could do was go. Walk away and never look back.

'*Arrivederci*, Charlotte.'

Before he lost control of his emotions he stalked from the workshop, his footsteps echoing loudly across the floor. He could feel her eyes on him, feel the intensity of her gaze, and he reminded himself of her warning that first night they'd spent together.

I don't do for ever.

Audaciously, he'd echoed her warning, using his first marriage to back up the claim, but had he really meant it? At that moment he had, but now, as he strode out of her life for ever, he knew that it was no longer true. He wanted for ever and he was turning his back on the one woman he wanted. Truly wanted.

As the sunlight dazzled him and the door shut behind

him he knew it was over. Whatever it was between them, it was gone. All that was left was his one-sided desire for a woman who thought he'd set her up and who held him responsible for her brother's accident.

This really was goodbye.

He got into his car and reversed hastily backwards, tyres squealing in protest, then he sped off, wanting only to get as far away from her as possible. The sooner she returned to England, the better.

Embarrassment washed over Charlie as she suddenly became aware of someone standing at her side. She was still looking at the closed door, could still hear the screech of tyres that suggested Alessandro couldn't get away fast enough.

'Scuzi,' the man at her side said; thankfully, he seemed unaware of her emotional turmoil. 'We will leave for Milan in one hour, but you may wait in Signor Roselli's office.'

She smiled at his heavily accented English, as appealing as Sandro's, but it didn't have the same effect on her. It didn't melt her from the inside, making her want to close her eyes as he spoke. 'Thank you; I will be ready.'

She turned and walked to the office, nerves cascading over her. This was the one place she hadn't been able to look for evidence of Alessandro's guilt. Was this where she could find out the secret he was keeping?

She opened the door and immediately felt Alessandro's presence. How could he affect her so, even when he wasn't anywhere near her? She took a gulp of air into her lungs, focusing on what she'd come to Italy for in the first place. Proof of who was to blame for her brother's death.

She sat in the chair at his desk, unable to shake the

feeling of unease, and glanced out at the workshop to see the team working on other cars. Her presence at Alessandro's desk didn't seem to worry them and she relaxed a bit.

At first she flicked through some design drawings, spread out and pushed to one side, then turned her attention to the files on the shelf above the desk. One stood out, as if calling for her attention, and she reached for it, feeling more and more like a spy.

The first few sections held nothing but engine reports but, as she flicked through the file, one unmarked section at the back caught her attention. She opened the page and looked at the photo of the car, a grey prototype the same as she'd driven, its specification listed below. With trembling fingers she turned the page.

Accident Report.

The words rushed at her and her stomach lurched sickeningly. She blinked, as if doing so would erase the truth that was set out in black and white before her.

'Oh, Seb,' she whispered and closed her eyes, but the words were imprinted there already. 'Why didn't you tell me?'

The question bounced around the office and she glanced at the team beyond the window, sure they would have heard it. Satisfied they hadn't, she looked back at the page, the words still a shock.

'Driver error.' She whispered the words, then paused before continuing. 'The driver was found to have significant levels of alcohol and drugs in his system.'

She leant her elbows on the desk and pressed her hands against her face. Could this be true? Could she believe it? She read the rest of the report, each point stating the car was in good working order.

With a heavy heart she closed the file and pushed it away from her, not wanting to read another word of it and wishing Alessandro was here to explain why he was using her brother as a scapegoat.

Alessandro had already shown how calculating he could be with the photo of the launch. Had this accident report been fabricated too?

The man she'd spoken to earlier knocked on the office door, dragging her from her thoughts. 'Now we shall leave.' He'd discarded his overalls and was every inch the Italian in his jeans and leather jacket, but he was far from the Italian she really wanted. The one she hated and loved.

Did that mean it wasn't hate? Or did it mean it wasn't love? Two powerfully strong emotions and they were tearing her apart. So what did she want it to be? Hate would mean staying in the past, never moving on, and she couldn't do that any longer. Love would mean forgiveness.

She stood and smiled, pushing her jumbled thoughts about all she'd just read to the back of her mind. 'Yes, I have a plane to catch.'

'*Sì, sì,*' he said as he walked towards the same door Sandro had left from an hour earlier. Where was he now? In his meeting, not giving her a second thought? Or was he relieved she would now be about to leave Italy and his life?

She pondered those questions as the car left the test track and within a few minutes they were on the busy roads and heading back to Milan. Charlie sat in silence, watching the countryside flash past, so caught up in her emotions she didn't even give the car they were in any thought. Her mind was with the man she loved. A man she should never have fallen in love with.

'Goodbye is hard, no?' The driver spoke, dragging her from her despondent thoughts.

'Yes,' she said before she'd realised it, adding quickly, 'but only because it is also saying goodbye to my brother.'

She hadn't expected this personal conversation and was glad to see they had reached Milan. Very soon she would be on her own, which was what she craved more than anything right now.

Thankfully, the traffic congestion took the driver's attention away from the conversation and she smiled at his exasperated sighs as they negotiated the streets towards Alessandro's apartment.

'I will get a taxi from here,' she said as she got out of the car outside the old building that she still couldn't believe was home to such a modern and powerful man.

'No, my instruction was to bring you here,' he said as he pressed the required numbers into the keypad, obviously used to letting himself in. Was this Sandro's right-hand man? Could he tell her the truth about the accident report? 'Then we go to the airport.'

She sensed he wanted to deliver her to the airport as soon as possible. Maybe that would be for the best. Alessandro had obviously asked that she be escorted all the way, to ensure she had actually left. 'Thank you. I will only be a few minutes.'

The driver handed her a key and she rushed up the stairs, into the apartment, trying not to think of all that had happened there in such a short time. Not wanting to linger, she grabbed her already packed case and left. As she shut the door, she closed her eyes briefly, pushing memories of being with Sandro to the back of her mind. But it wasn't easy. Even though she knew she shouldn't, she loved him. How did you switch that off? Finally, she went back down to where the driver was waiting.

Moments later they were once again in the traffic, heading towards the airport. She kept her eyes firmly fixed ahead of her as she thought of all that had happened. Would Seb have approved of her and Sandro—would he have been happy they were together?

'Did you know my brother?' She asked the question casually. This would be the last chance she got to talk to anyone from the test track and she wasn't going to waste this opening, no matter how small.

'*Sì*, he was a good driver, a very good driver, but things got too much for him. We tried to help.' His attention was kept on the busy road, his words had been said in such a distracted way, he obviously hadn't thought about them.

So it *was* true. She tried hard to keep her voice normal when all she wanted to do was scream and shout, but she couldn't. It was obvious this man thought she knew all about it.

'I didn't realise you'd helped him too,' she said as calmly as possible, luring him into divulging more of the truth. Each word he said confirmed all she'd seen in the report.

'Alessandro helped most, but I was also there that night and it became my secret too.'

What kind of sister had she been, not to have noticed Seb's problems? Guilt spiked cruelly at her. Not a hint of what she'd read had reached the press. Part of her clung desperately to the hope that this was because it was all part of an elaborate fabrication by Alessandro. She didn't want to believe it of Seb; it was too painful.

'Sorry, I didn't mean to upset you,' he said and she

opened her eyes to see him looking at her whilst they'd stopped at a red light.

'I do still find it upsetting, sorry.' She dabbed the corner of her eye with her fingertips, glad when the lights changed and they moved off, taking his gaze from her. Did he know he'd walked into her trap?

'The airport,' Giovanni said as the terminal buildings came into view and the relief in his voice would have been comical if she hadn't been so strung out by his conversation.

He pulled into a space and got out, but she wasn't done yet. Whatever he knew, she had to find out. Good or bad, she just had to hear it. Could it be any worse than all she had just read?

'Please—' she put her hand on his arm, using all her feminine charm, bombarding him with questions. 'You said you were there too. How bad were Seb's problems? Did they really cause the accident?'

He looked at his watch. 'You will be late for your flight.'

'Please.'

He sighed and then put his hand over hers as it clutched at his arm. 'He'd been drinking heavily that day—and the drugs…' He shrugged, his face apologetic. 'They made him wild, irrational. We couldn't stop him.'

'We?' she whispered, scared to let go of his arm in case she fell to the floor with shock.

'*Sì*, Signor Roselli and myself. Of course, we said nothing after the accident that would blacken your brother's name.' He took her hand and held it between both of his and looked at her, genuine concern in his face. 'I thought you knew.'

'I did,' she bluffed, not wanting to tell him she'd only

just discovered what now appeared to be the truth. 'It hurts to hear it again. I'm sorry.'

'Now you must go; you will be late for your plane.' The relief on his face only cemented the bad images of her brother, under the influence of drink and drugs, driving the car. How had she not known he had problems? How had he managed to hide it so well from her?

'Yes, my plane.' She forced the words out slowly. They sounded hollow to her ears, but she picked up her small case and walked away from this man and the truth that had shattered everything she'd held dear.

Once inside the building she ran to the Ladies, her insides churning alarmingly. She splashed cold water over her face, not caring about her make-up, just wanting to stave off the nausea. She looked at her reflection in the mirror, as if for reassurance.

Could it be true?

She didn't want it to be, but certain things were slotting into place, suddenly becoming much clearer. Seb had dropped out of the final races of last year's season, claiming injury, but had dismissed it as they'd spoken on the phone, telling her to stop mothering him. Had he had a problem even then?

'No, it can't be true... Sandro would have said something.' She spoke aloud to her shocked reflection.

Then it hit her like a brick being hurled through the air. Alessandro Roselli had been covering for her brother, not to keep Seb's good name but to save his own damn reputation. To do that he'd dragged hers through the mire too. That photograph of them kissing backed it all up.

She pressed her palms to her face and took in a deep breath. There was only one person other than Alessandro who could confirm this.

Her father. He'd flown out to Italy as soon as news of the accident had reached them. Seb had died just hours after he'd arrived, but her father would know if drugs and alcohol had been the cause.

She frowned at herself in the mirror. Why hadn't he told her? Why had he kept it a secret and then still supported Alessandro? There was only one answer. It wasn't true and he knew nothing of the cover-up story that was being used. The report must be a cover-up. It had even been left in easy view, just waiting for her to find it.

Frantically she searched in her bag for her phone and with shaking fingers pressed call on her father's number.

'Hello, Charlie.' Her father sounded cautious and not his usual self.

'Is it true, Dad?' She didn't waste any time on pleasantries.

On the other end of the phone her father sighed, then horrifyingly she knew it was. She clutched the washbasin with her free hand, watching the colour drain from the shocked face with hollowed eyes which looked back at her from the mirror.

'Oh, Dad, why didn't you tell me?' She shook her head in disbelief, feeling ever more disconnected from the woman staring back at her in the mirror.

'You didn't need to know. Where are you, Charlie?' She could hear the restrained panic in her father's voice and her heart clenched.

'On my way home. We'll talk soon. I have to check in or I'll miss the flight.'

'Charlie?'

'Yes, Dad.'

'See you soon.'

Her heart constricted as if a snake were torturing her,

squashing every last beat from her, and she couldn't say anything else. Instead she cut the connection before she cried, before she lost complete control. That was something she had to save until later. Much later. Right now she had a plane to catch.

CHAPTER TWELVE

ALESSANDRO STALKED AROUND the check-in desks, scanning the throng of passengers, but with each passing minute his impatience increased. Where was she? He still didn't want to accept what had drawn him to the airport instead of his meeting, but when the call from Giovanni had come through he'd been glad he was only minutes away. He couldn't let her leave without talking to her, checking she was all right.

The queue for the London flight was diminishing fast and his agitation increased. Giovanni had told him she'd acted as if she'd known everything. But how? He stalked over to the desk again, the operator who'd denied him passenger information earlier giving him a suspicious look.

Maledizione! Where was she? It was as if she'd just vanished. That or she'd got through security so quickly because she hated him. He didn't blame her. He hated himself right now. He should have found a way to tell her, found a way around the promise he'd made to Seb and her father. Hadn't he done just that so he could have a weekend affair with her? So why hadn't he been able to do the same with the truth of the accident?

Angrily he stabbed his fingers through his hair and

marched away from the check-in desk. Even his charm had deserted him as he'd tried to find out if Charlie had checked in or even what flight she had booked. Now what? Book on the next flight to England?

Suddenly his attention was caught as he saw a woman hurriedly leaving the terminal building and quickly he raced after her. His heart beat like a drum with the hope that it was Charlie, that she'd changed her mind, but once outside in the evening sunlight he couldn't see her. Taxis pulled away in rapid succession. He had no idea if she was in one—or if it had been her.

More deflated than he'd ever been in his adult life, he stood as everyone bustled past him, hurrying to or from the airport, all seemingly happy. The roar of jet engines as they soared into the sky sounded like a death knell. Each time he heard one, his heart died a bit more. She could be on board.

But what if she wasn't?

What if the woman he'd seen, the one he'd wanted to be Charlie, was her? Where would she go?

Realisation hit him. There was only one place she'd go to be alone with memories of her brother. One place she'd be sure he or his staff wouldn't be. But should he go there and disturb her?

The answer was simple. He had to. He had to find her and tell her everything, explain why he'd kept the secret. She already hated him. He didn't have anything to lose. He'd rather she hurled accusations at him than disappear with a revelation like that on her mind. Purposefully, he strode back to the car park and set about the tedious task of negotiating Milan's traffic.

The drive to the hotel proved almost impossible as a minor bump had closed the most direct route, forcing

him down narrow side streets and testing his patience
to the full. All the while he imagined her there, with the
car that had been at the launch, alone and hurting. Hurt
he'd caused.

With a big sigh of relief he pulled up at the hotel,
jumped from the car, tossed the keys at the doorman for
parking and went through the revolving doors. Slowly he
made his way towards the room that had become a temporary showroom for the sleek red beast that had consumed
Seb so utterly. Benign and innocuously it sat there, its
secrets hidden within its beauty. The silence of the room
hit him. Quickly he looked around, but couldn't see her.

Then a small movement caught his attention at the far
end of the room. She was there, sitting at a table with
her back to him. Relief rushed through him at top speed.
Cautiously he moved towards her.

Charlie sat, totally lost in thought, the feeling of betrayal
stinging more than a swarm of bees could. The two men
she loved had betrayed her. She looked down at the cup
of coffee, now very cold, as if it could answer her problems, tell her what to do.

Why had she come here? Why hadn't she just got on
the plane and left? Because she needed answers and she
couldn't go anywhere until she got them. The only problem was that Alessandro held those answers—and he'd
just driven away from her at top speed.

With a sigh she looked at the sleek red car. The secrets locked within it had only just started to slip from
its powerful clutches.

'Why, Seb?' She whispered the question aloud but silence came back at her, a painful echo.

Suddenly a sizzling sensation hurtled down her spine

and she knew she wasn't alone. There was only one person who had that effect on her. The man she hated and loved with equal passion. Alessandro Roselli.

'Haven't you done enough damage already?' The venomous tone of her words surprised her as much as him, but she kept her back to him, looking resolutely at the car.

'I did what I had to.' He came to stand beside her but still she didn't look at him.

'Of course you did.' The crispness of each word was colder than a frosty morning. 'You did exactly what you needed to do to keep your name from being dragged through the dirt.'

'You've got it all wrong, Charlie.'

'Charlotte,' she snapped and looked up at him, confused by the anger and the raw betrayal which filled her. 'And I haven't got it wrong at all.'

'It isn't what you think.' He moved to stand in front of her, obscuring her view of the car, her link to her brother.

She stood up and moved past him, towards the car, anything other than stay beneath his intense gaze. 'So you deny you brought me here under the pretence it was what Seb wanted, seduced me so that you could get the ultimate photograph for the press and then keep the truth of Seb's problems from me.'

'I never meant to hurt you, Charlie.'

'Charlotte!' She whirled round and stood to face him, catching her breath at the hard look in his eyes. Where had the loving man she'd spent the weekend with gone— or was that also part of his game plan?

'I can see you aren't prepared to listen to anything I have to say.' He sat down in the chair she'd just vacated but couldn't disguise the tension and irritation in his body.

'Too right I'm not. Everything else you've said has been lies.' Memories of the last time they'd made love, the tender words of Italian he'd whispered to her, slipped into her mind and she realised they too must have been lies.

She turned from him and closed her eyes against the pain. She'd opened her heart to him, given herself and her love, only to find he'd used her as a scapegoat. Behind her, his silence confirmed everything she thought and, despite the pain, she had to hear it all. Maybe then she'd stop loving him.

Purposefully, she returned to the table, pulled out another chair and sat down. She was going to get to the bottom of this if it was the last thing she did. Part of her didn't want to hear it, didn't want to accept that her brother had become embroiled in such a world. But she had to know—everything.

'I saw the report, Sandro.' He didn't say anything but his firm gaze held hers.

'Giovanni told me, or rather confirmed, about the drink…' her breath hitched in her throat and she could hardly form the words as she sat at the table with him '…and drugs. Why didn't you?'

He leant forward in the chair, his elbows resting on his knees and his hands clasped together. His expression was one of concern as he looked up at her and his eyes met hers. 'It was what your father wanted.'

She shook her head. 'Don't use my father. He would never keep such a thing from me.' Even as she said the words she recalled the brief call she'd made to him at the airport. The silence as she'd challenged him. He hadn't admitted anything, but his silence had been deafening.

'Have you spoken to him?'

'At the airport, yes.' She looked into his eyes and the

fight began to slip from her, receding like the tide going out. 'I don't understand why he'd do that.'

'He didn't want you to know. He wanted to keep your memories of Seb untainted.' The gentleness of his voice was almost too much and she shook her head rapidly, wanting to deny everything she was hearing. Her father might have wanted to protect her, but what about Sandro? What were his motives?

'And what about you? Why did you lie to me?' Fierceness exploded from deep within her, a need to shield herself from the fallout of his deceit.

'What do you think would have happened if the press had found out?' His firm question almost knocked the breath from her as she realised the implications of what he said. Shock sank in, washing away the strength she'd just found, and he reached out and took her hand.

Her gaze darted to his tanned hand covering hers, the dusting of dark hair which disappeared under the cuff of his shirt. She could feel the heat from his touch infusing her, awakening all she wished to suppress.

She pulled her hand from under his at the same time as jumping up from her chair, making it scrape noisily on the marble floor. 'What would the press do?' She gulped the words out, hardly daring to form an answer to that question.

'What would they do with a story like that, Charlie?' He sat back in his chair, all cool, calm sophistication, but the glittering hardness of his eyes told her he knew exactly what they would do.

'That's easy,' she retaliated harshly. 'They'd ruin your reputation.'

He stood up, his body full of restraint and composure, but ice had filled his eyes, chilling her to the core.

'Whatever you may think, Charlotte, I have done nothing wrong.'

'You lied—to me and the world.'

'Damn you, don't you see?' He strode towards her, his face full of anger, the angles sharp. 'I wasn't protecting myself. I was protecting Seb—and you.'

In exasperation he flung his hands up and marched towards the gleaming car and, before she could say anything more, he turned to look at her across the room, but it might as well have been across a continent.

The first bubbles of anger rose up like a shaken bottle of champagne and her breathing deepened, but still she couldn't find her voice. How could he stand there and use Seb again, after all that had happened?

Just like she'd seen happen on the podium, the champagne burst out, showering her with fizzy drops of anger. 'How dare you hide behind my brother's reputation after engineering that photo of us kissing? Right here.' She pointed at the car as she crossed the floor to him, her footsteps hard and forceful. 'That photo alone was enough to clear your name. That kiss absolved you of any blame and now it's splurged all over the papers and probably the Internet too.'

He looked taken aback by her outburst but he didn't move. He stood tall and strong as she moved closer and closer, stoking the fiery anger higher and higher.

'I didn't force you to kiss me.' His cool words poured cold water over the flames and for a moment she just looked at him. She couldn't answer that, couldn't offer any defence, because he was right. He hadn't forced her. She had wanted that kiss so badly.

'You manipulated the situation.'

'By "the situation" I assume you mean the heated passion that raged between us from the moment we met?' Suddenly the frozen depths of his eyes heated, so intense they almost scorched her skin.

'That was just a convenient smokescreen.' Despite the bravado, her voice trembled—and she hated herself for it.

She should never have given in to the heady desire that had filled her body and starved her heart. Somewhere deep down she was sure she'd known that, but at the time she'd known she would regret not tasting the desire which had been between them from the beginning. She hadn't wanted to spend the rest of her life wondering *what if?* Now she was going to have to live with the fact that not only had she been used so callously, she'd fallen in love with the man who'd lied and cheated his way into her heart.

Alessandro saw the emotions play out across her face like a movie. Shock, denial, hatred. They were all there. Even passion and longing, but not once did he see anything which resembled what he felt for her.

'So you don't deny it existed.' It was like walking a tightrope. At any moment he could lose his balance and fall. He held his nerve, calling on every bit of control he had. 'You don't deny you wanted me when we kissed right here.'

She looked at him, her eyes saying things he hoped were true but her lips stony silent. He moved forward but she stayed rooted to the spot.

'Don't run from the passion which exists between us, *cara.*'

'I don't need to run from that. I can handle the passion.' Finally words tumbled from her with a force so fierce he drew in a sharp breath. 'But it wasn't passion, Sandro. It was lust.'

He remained still and silent, sensing there was more, but right now she was visibly shaking with emotions so powerful. He watched her beautiful face as she closed her eyes against them, her long lashes spreading across the paleness of her skin. His heart twisted and it was all he could do not to reach for her and hold her against him.

'Lust I can deal with.' She spoke again, her voice firm and resolute. 'What I want to run from is your deceit.'

'My deceit?' He knew what she was referring to and regret piled on top of the guilt because he hadn't had the strength to find a way to tell her everything. This guilt was intensified because he'd pushed aside the promises he'd made to spend the weekend with her, to indulge the lust, as she called it.

'You lied to me, kept the truth from me, then used the spark of lust which was there, even at my cottage, to lure me to the launch night. To this very spot, and engineer the photograph that would prove to the world my family had forgiven you.'

Slowly he shook his head. How was he ever going to prove he had nothing to do with the photo, that it was just a lucky shot for the photographer? 'I know how it must look,' he began, but she cut his words off.

'What would Seb say if he knew what you have done, how you tricked me so cruelly? What would he say about us?'

A glimmer of hope trickled through him at her mention of 'us' and he gave voice to the conclusion he'd reached just a few hours ago. 'Maybe it was what he wanted all along.'

'How can you know that? Much less say it.' She turned

from him and for a moment he thought she was going to walk away. He knew he couldn't go after her again. As she stood, lost in thought, he moved towards her cautiously.

'Seb made me promise to look after you,' he said softly and saw her shoulders rise and fall with each breath she took. 'Not just that night after the accident, but several times before. He played on my loyalty to my sister.'

'That doesn't mean anything.' She turned her head slightly and he saw her profile as she looked distractedly at the floor. Pain and hurt lingered on her face.

Her voice trembled and finally she turned to look at him and, like the moment he'd unveiled the car, he saw her with all her vulnerabilities exposed, all her barriers down. 'You should still have told me about the drink and the drugs. I had a right to know. I don't care about anything else, not even that stupid photo, but that was the one thing you shouldn't have kept from me. Not even because of a promise.'

He fought really hard against the urge to hold her, to soothe all the pain, but right now he didn't dare. If she ran again it would be for ever; he knew that much.

'Seb was beside himself, desperate that you should never know, and I made the promise to keep him calm. By the time your father arrived I was firmly fixed into it. I'm sorry, Charlotte. I had no choice at all.'

As he spoke he thought of why he was here, what had made him race to the airport in the first place. All he'd been able to think about was taking her in his arms and holding her, comforting her as he had that night in his office. He should have told her the truth then but she'd been too fragile, so he'd kept the secret.

How did you tell the woman who had just kissed you

with such passion news like that? Selfishly, he'd kept silent, enjoying the spark that had been lit between them. Now he knew that spark wasn't just lust, not for him at least. It was love.

He loved her. He didn't just desire her—he loved her, so much it hurt.

He needed Charlie, or Charlotte, as he thought of her, when passion blazed in her eyes. She was Charlie behind the wheel of a car and Charlotte in his arms, and he loved her—completely and unconditionally.

Charlie thought of what Alessandro had just said, the situation he'd been forced into. He had kept that promise to Seb. He hadn't been the one who had told her the truth, so did that make the whole situation any more honourable?

She closed her eyes against the pain of finally knowing the truth and the knowledge that it was time to move on, time to leave her garden of sanctuary and live life as Seb would have wanted her to do. As the realisation dawned, Alessandro put his arms around her and pulled her close. This was where she wanted to be, in the arms of the man she loved, but that still didn't mean he loved her. He'd agreed to her terms of 'not for ever' as they'd stood in his apartment on that first night, had even taken her away to his villa to enable him to distance the affair from everything else.

'Why are you here, Sandro?' She looked up at him, hardly daring to hope. But he *was* here, holding her so tenderly—didn't that mean something?

'I couldn't let you go, not without explaining.' His face was full of concern, but she searched for more, desperate to find even a trace of something else.

'So, *cara*. Why are *you* here?' The term of endearment, said in the most gently seductive tone, gave her just enough hope. 'You know the truth yet you are still in my arms.'

She looked up at him, wondering if he'd see the reason shining from her eyes. He'd been protecting her from the truth all along. She didn't hate him. She loved him. He had honoured Seb's promise at great cost to himself and that just made her love him even more, but could she say those words aloud?

'I couldn't go, not yet.' She lowered her lashes, not wanting to see what was in his eyes, not daring to hope. 'I needed the truth.'

Was it her imagination or had his arms loosened slightly around her? She swallowed hard and took a deep breath.

'And now that you have it?' He let go of her, walked towards the car, pressing his palm against the fiery red paintwork. 'Now that you know the truth, will you return to your life, move on?'

It was as if he was letting her go, allowing her to walk away and find her destiny. Did he not know *he* was her destiny? That if he didn't want her she didn't have a life to return to? She couldn't stop her limbs from trembling and couldn't find the words to tell him what he needed to know.

'Sandro, I...' Her shaky voice deserted her; she began to feel suffocated, as if she couldn't get enough breath into her lungs.

He looked over at her, his brow furrowed into a frown, but it was his eyes that finally showed her what she needed to see. His gaze darted to her as her words died as she saw it. In the dark depths she saw the same hopelessness which filled her heart and she knew she had to say those words. With a jolt she also realised why he wouldn't say them first.

I don't do for ever.

Her words on that first night they'd made love drifted through her mind like a haunting spirit. 'Sandro, I have to say this. I can't go without telling you.'

Slowly she walked towards him, her heart pounding so hard in her chest she almost couldn't think. He looked away from her and jabbed his fingers through his hair, turning his body away, deflecting anything she might try to say. Had she misread the hope in his eyes?

'Just go, Charlotte. If that's what you want to do, there is nothing more to say.' She saw his jaw tense as he gritted his teeth, felt the raw pain and knew she hadn't misread anything.

'I love you, Sandro.' The silence that suddenly shrouded them was so heavy she almost couldn't stand and for a moment he didn't move, frozen in time.

When he did, it was such a small movement, disbelief all over his face as he stepped towards her. In slow motion he reached for her hands, taking them in his and drawing her towards him. She was desperate for him to speak, to say something, but he just looked at her, his hands firmly wrapped around hers.

'Ti amo, ti amo...' His seductive accent caressed each word and his lips, which had moments ago been pressed into a hard line, smiled. Wonder and happiness sparked from his eyes and she fell into his embrace, feeling as if she had come home. She'd found where she needed to be to move on in life.

Right here in the arms of the man she loved.

* * * * *

A LONE STAR
LOVE AFFAIR

SARA ORWIG

One

Tony Ryder couldn't suppress his jubilation.

It had taken years for him to acquire Morris Enterprises. Years—plus being in the right place at the right time.

Late at night, he had stepped off the elevator on the nineteenth floor of the twenty-story glass Morris building in downtown Dallas. Wall lights shed a softened glow in the empty corridor as he passed open doors. His father had made offers over the years for this company and never succeeded in acquiring it. Now one giant coup would make his controlling father back off. That made all the hours of work more than worth his efforts. Tony was growing as wealthy as his father and finally gaining the man's respect.

Tony had grown more pleased with the offices from the lobby to the top floor. Strolling the empty hallway, he paused to look at framed awards mounted on the beige walls. Farther along was a glass-enclosed case of trophies for graphic arts achievements. He noticed the same director's name on several awards and trophies. Moving on, he passed through open doors into a darkened office and switched on the light. He was in the graphic arts sector—a part of the company that he would change drastically. He intended to retain a few of the graphic arts people and offer the others generous severance packages, absorbing the remaining employees into his own public relations department.

He shut the light and continued along the silent, dimly lit hall, turning at the next open door into an anteroom. Light spilled inside from a doorway. Crossing the anteroom, Tony entered another spacious, elegant office. He stopped abruptly as a blonde looked up.

"Sorry, I didn't mean to startle you," he said, surprised and curious to find someone working after ten. His first thought was that he was looking at his most gorgeous employee. As she stood, his gaze drifted swiftly over her. In an all-business navy suit and matching silk blouse, she looked as if she had just arrived at work instead of putting in extra hours. Her blond hair was secured in a roll on the back of her head. He had the strange feeling of meeting her before, but he knew he would have remembered her. A sizzling current startled him. He was caught in wide blue eyes that darkened and mesmerized. Silence stretched until he realized they were entrapped in each other's gaze. When she touched a paper on her desk, the spell broke.

"You're working late," he remarked.

"I believe you, too, are working late," she replied.

He stepped forward to extend his hand across her desk. "Sorry, I'm Tony Ryder."

"Isabelle Smith," she said. "I know who you are." Her hand was slender, warm, and should have been like other feminine handshakes. Instead, the electric current he had first experienced just at the sight of her, magnified. Startled by his intense reaction, he focused intently on her, momentarily immobilized by his reactions.

"I'm here because I had something to finish. You're visiting rather late," she said. "Looking over your new acquisition?"

While her voice was neutral, her eyes were cool and assessing. He sensed she did not approve of him.

"You're right. And you're the Morris graphic arts department director."

"You've either done some homework about the business you just bought, or read the sign on my door." She walked around the desk and motioned to a chair. "Please have a seat," she said, taking a leather chair that was turned to face him. As she moved closer, he caught a whiff of exotic perfume. "I don't know whether you actually get involved or have staff who do that for you."

"I have staff, but I also want to be knowledgeable about my investments," he said as he sat near her. She crossed her legs and he couldn't resist one swift glance that made him want to look back for a thorough assessment. She had long, shapely legs. "I'm involved in whatever I own. What's so urgent to keep you working this late when you know your department will be split up?"

"So the rumors are true," she remarked, the frostiness in her tone increasing. "I intend to finish a few projects because we've already signed contracts. That won't change with the new management. I feel I need to wind things up before you actually take charge."

"You say that as if doomsday approaches."

She shrugged a slender shoulder. "That seems to be your approach to your acquisitions. I've done my homework and you have a reputation."

"Do I now?" he asked, amused. "Tell me what this reputation is."

"Ambitious. Driven. What I might label 'smash and grab.'"

He tried to bite back a smile. "I never thought of my actions in such a manner."

"I'm sure I'm not winning kudos with my new employer, but

I suspect it really doesn't matter what I say. I imagine you've already made decisions about the direction you will go."

"How would you describe yourself? You work far into the night. You're a director. Ambitious? Driven?"

She smiled faintly. "Touché."

"So we are both workaholics—there are rewards. Regarding the future of the company, I change only what I feel needs changing. As a director, you'll retain a position if that relieves your mind."

"'A position'—but not necessarily a director? I know changes are coming. I have a feeling you've looked into my background."

"So is your family patiently waiting at home?" he asked, having already noticed the absence of a wedding band. Her manicured nails were long. Everything about her looked precise, immaculate, professional. Keeping a barrier around herself, she was reserved with him. She made no effort to hide her resentment of his purchase of the company.

"I'm single. You make the news enough for me to know that you are, too."

"The single life lends itself to becoming a workaholic. There are far less distractions."

"You view a family as a distraction." Even though she spoke in the same tone, her disapproval had obviously escalated.

"At this point in life, family is not for me, because I'm wound up in business. Evidently, not for you, either."

She gave him a frosty smile.

They were lightly sparring, yet he experienced a scalding attraction that she seemed to also feel—an odd combination he had never encountered. Challenges were always interesting and she was definitely one.

"Do you often work this late?" he asked, enjoying talking to her. She was a beautiful woman, yet she wore the suit as if it were armor, hiding her figure. He rarely received such a cool reception from a gorgeous, single woman, much less one who was his employee. He couldn't resist the urge to try to break through the puzzling wall she maintained. Was it all men? Or just him, because he had bought out her employer?

"Occasionally," she replied, tilting her head. "Do you usually work this late?"

"If necessary. I haven't seen the building and this is a good time to wander freely. It surprised me to find you working."

"You bought this company sight unseen?"

"The building, offices and layout weren't significant factors. It's the people, the departments and what Morris Enterprises is involved in. I'm sure you know that."

"Yet you'll change the people and the departments." Her voice held a touch of frost. Otherwise she sat still, poised, looking as if she discussed an ad campaign.

"Some things will change. I've just acquired three highly successful hotel chains, plus a restaurant chain and a trucking business. This will grow my business. Even as we absorb this company, I think we can enlarge Morris Enterprises. You've built this department significantly—Morris has grown since you came on board. You have an impressive record," he said, recalling being briefed on Morris executives' performance reports. He'd decided then that she held potential, but he would move her down the corporate ladder because she would be going into a larger company. In spite of the compliment, he could not get a smile from her.

"Thank you. No one seems to know when you'll actually take over and begin changes."

"Soon. When I do, I'll interview the executives first," he said, unable to resist another swift glance at her legs.

"This encounter can almost count as my interview. You've asked some direct questions and I'm certain you've formed an opinion."

She was direct, straight-forward and not the least intimidated to be talking to the new owner of her company. She continued, coolly composed, yet along with their matter-of-fact conversation, he felt an undercurrent of awareness.

Amused again, he shook his head. "No, you'll have your formal interview. This is just a late-night chat, nothing more."

"Why do I think you've already made your decisions?" Big blue eyes stabbed into him.

"I can have an open mind. On the other hand—can you? Morris sold the company to me. I didn't do any arm-twisting." He couldn't resist another brief glance at her long legs. What would she be like when she let down all the barriers?

"You came to him with an offer he couldn't refuse and you knew he has been on the verge of retirement for the past three years." This time she didn't hide the frost. Her voice conveyed a cold anger.

"Can you blame me? This is a first-rate company."

She looked away and he studied her profile, long thick eyelashes, flawless peaches-and-cream skin, a straight nose—looks that would be unforgettable. Again it crossed his mind that they had met before, yet how could he forget her? If he had met her, the recollection would come.

"If you'll excuse me, it's late. I think I'll close for tonight," she said, standing.

Amused that he was being dismissed by her, as he stood, he asked, "Can I give you a ride home?"

She shook her head. "Thanks, no. I have my car."

"I'll see you out. I've been all through the building." He was unaccustomed to being brushed off by a woman where there was an obvious chemistry between them.

She smiled. "You don't have to see me to my car. This wasn't a date."

"I know I don't, Ms. Smith."

"It's Isabelle."

"And I'm Tony to my employees," he said. "I'll walk out with you. Then I'll know where to park when I come in Monday."

"I think you can find the parking spot that will have Reserved on a placard in front of the best space in the lot," she said.

He watched while she shut down her laptop and placed it in a bag that she shouldered. She pulled keys from the bag, switched off a desk light and turned toward the door. When he blocked her path, she looked up, wide-eyed.

"I wish now we'd met under other circumstances. You're definitely annoyed with me," he said.

"It won't matter. You have many interests and a sprawling enterprise that has absorbed this one. We'll rarely see each other. I hated to see Morris sold. You can't blame me for that."

"I think it's more than the sale," he said quietly, standing close enough to smell the perfume she wore. Her blue eyes were incredible, crystal clear, deep blue, thickly lashed. Glacial at the moment. When his gaze lowered to her mouth, he inhaled as he viewed full, heart-shaped lips, a rosy mouth that looked soft.

As he looked, her lips parted and he glanced into her eyes again. For an instant her guard had fallen and the look he caught was warm, receptive. It was gone in a flash as she gave a tiny shake while she passed him.

"It's very late, Tony…"

Against all human resources training, he reached out and touched her arm. "I don't have a policy against employees seeing each other off the job, dating, getting engaged or marrying."

Again that surge of electricity sizzled to his toes as she looked up sharply with a flash of fire in her eyes. But just as suddenly, the fire died and whatever she had been about to say was gone.

"Where I'm concerned, it won't matter."

"No deference to your employer?" he asked quietly, fighting an urge to ask her for a drink.

"Tony, it's getting late," she whispered, and broke away. He had seen the pink rise in her cheeks. Why was she fighting him and so angry with him? He hadn't moved her out of her job yet.

Puzzled over the degree of her animosity, he walked with her to the elevators. He pushed a button before she could reach it and they rode down in silence.

He could feel the barriers back in place, the chill in the air between them.

"I saw your ad campaign for the Royal Garden chain. It was well thought out and successful. Bookings jumped after the television ads started," he said.

"Thank you from my staff and me. They did an excellent job."

"Do you ever take full credit for anything?" he asked, looking at silky strands of blond hair wound in a roll and wondering how she would look with her hair unpinned.

"If I'm the only one to work on it. Otherwise, I don't deserve to take all of the credit."

"Will there ever be a time you can see me in any way other than your employer?"

"Of course. If I leave Morris, or if you do," she answered sweetly, and he smiled.

When the elevator doors opened, he stepped back to let her exit. He fell into step beside her and they both greeted the night security guard before going outside. Tony crossed the parking lot with her to her car.

"I hope you give my company a chance," he said. "I have the feeling you've already formed an opinion and have one foot out the door."

"Not yet," she said, as she clicked her key to unlock her car. While he held her door, she slid behind the wheel.

"I'll see you next at the reception we're having for the executives Thursday evening. You will attend, won't you?"

"Certainly. I believe it's mandatory unless one is in the hospital."

"We all need to meet one another."

She gave him a doubting look as if she didn't believe a word he said.

"Good night, Isabelle," he said, wishing he could prolong the time with her.

"Good night," she replied.

When she started the engine, he walked to his car. As she drove past, her profile was to him and she never glanced around.

"Isabelle Smith," he said, mulling over her name and the past hour. The only things he knew for certain were that she didn't like him and she resented his buying out Morris.

He remembered another Smith he had known. She had been a freshman or sophomore in college and he had met her at a party when he had been on campus for a seminar. Her name hadn't been Isabelle and she had been a carefree, fun-loving, sexy woman. It had been an instant hot attraction that ended in a passionate night together even though she had been a virgin. A blue-eyed blonde with a resemblance to Isabelle Smith, but only a slight similarity and one he dismissed as swiftly as it came to mind. Partying with him, Jessie Smith had been wild, friendly and filled with fun. She had constantly smiled until passion replaced her smiles. He hadn't forgotten her and he didn't think he ever would. He couldn't recall her major or where she was from. Even though he had wanted to, he had never tried to contact her because she would have been too big a distraction in his life at the time. His focus had been on building his fortune. She had faded from his life, but never from his memory. That had been an unforgettable night. There was enough of a resemblance in coloring and name to give him the feeling he had met Isabelle Smith before tonight, but she definitely was no Jessie Smith.

His cell phone beeped, indicating a text from his sister.

As he climbed into his sports car, he paused to read her message. In minutes he headed home. When he entered his neighborhood, he slowed, driving beneath tall trees with thick trunks in one of the oldest areas in Dallas. Bare limbs interlocked overhead, bordering sweeping lawns of two- and three-story mansions. A high, wrought-iron fence surrounded Tony's property and with a code he opened iron gates. As he wound along the wide driveway, he saw a familiar sports car parked at the front.

He pulled into his garage and entered his house, going straight through to open the front door. A woman with a mass of curly black hair and thickly lashed dark brown eyes matching his stepped out of the parked car and dashed toward his door. She crossed the illuminated wide porch.

He closed the door behind his younger sister. "Sydney, what brings you on the run at this hour?" he asked, smiling at her. He loved his sister.

"Dad. He wanted to see me tonight. I need to talk to you, Tony."

"Sure. Let's go to the family room. Want something to drink?"

"Cranberry juice if you have it."

Several small lights came on automatically as they entered a large room that held comfortable leather furniture, a bar and a large fireplace. Tony crossed to the bar to get a cold beer for himself and juice for his sister.

As soon as he had a fire blazing, he picked up his beer and sat on a chair facing his sister, who sipped her juice. "Okay, let's hear it. What's Dad done now?" Tony asked.

"Tony, he's pressuring me to dump Dylan," she said, focusing worried brown eyes on her brother.

"So? Sydney, it's your life. Do what you want," Tony answered.

"It's not that easy." She looked away as if lost in thought. Her gaze returned to Tony. "Dad's threatened me. If I marry Dylan, he'll disinherit me."

"Dammit. That's drastic. He must have talked to my friend Jake's dad who held such a threat over Jake's head. Our dads are old friends and both control freaks. That's where Dad got this idea of threatening you. It worked with Jake because he married."

"That's not all. Dad will stop all support and I'm on my own to finish medical school. I may have to make a choice between med school and Dylan. If I have to choose, Dylan wins. Worst of all, Dad will cut me out of the family completely. 'Don't come home' and all that."

"Mom won't go along with any such ultimatum," Tony said, losing his temper with his interfering father.

"She already has. For once, Mom sat in with us when he talked to me."

"That's serious," Tony remarked, giving his sister his full attention. "I don't think I've ever had Mom step in to back up Dad. I'm shocked."

"Mom doesn't like Dylan. She thinks he's a nobody and will embarrass the family. Even worse, he's an artist who had to put himself through college by relying on scholarships. It doesn't matter to them that his grades are excellent or what it took to accomplish sending himself."

"Graphic art is a respectable career," Tony answered, thinking about Isabelle, although it had been years since he'd had any worries about his family having to accept a woman in his life. "This is partially why I work like crazy. He's beginning to back off with me—especially since I acquired Morris Enterprises— because I'm going to make more money than he has and he can see it. Syd, I'm finally getting respect out of him."

"I doubt if I can ever say that. I thought if I made it through medical school, I would, but I don't think that any longer. If you're sympathetic to me at all, it will only increase the tension between you and Mom and Dad. As for Dylan, he just isn't from our circle of friends and his family is low income with blue-collar jobs. I'm afraid Dad will try every way he can to give Dylan difficulty. He'll try to sabotage Dylan getting work, or staying with a company. He will try to keep him out of any family gatherings."

"I don't think so, Syd. He wouldn't do that to you."

"Tony, really," she snapped, glaring at her brother.

"You'll know in time. As for the other, I'm one-quarter of this family and I'm not cutting you out, so you can see me on holidays."

"If you're even in the country. Thank you for offering, though."

"And don't worry about med school. I can support you right now. I have the money and can easily and gladly do it. Just tell me how much and I'll write the first check tonight," Tony said, feeling as protective of his sister as ever. Seven years older than Sydney, he had spent his life looking out for her and being a buffer between his parents and her. They had always been close.

"I don't want you to do that. I didn't call you to get you to finance me."

"I can afford it. I want to. End of argument."

"Oh, Tony," she said, her eyes filling with tears as she jumped to her feet to run and hug him. "You are the best brother in the whole world."

"I can support you without missing the money." He set down his beer. "I'll get a check."

"You don't need to now. Dad hasn't done anything yet."

"Don't wait until he does something. Let me give you a check and you put this money away. Open a new bank account Dad knows nothing about with a bank where no one knows him. This is a big enough city that you can get away from Dad's scrutiny. The minute he cuts you off, you let me know and I'll take up supporting you. In the meantime, you'll have this to fall back on if you need it. I'll be right back."

She wiped her eyes. "You really are the best brother ever."

He left to get a check, filling it out and returning to take it to her. She was back in the chair, her long legs tucked beneath her. When Tony handed her the check, she looked up with wide eyes. "Tony, this is enormous. I don't need money like this yet."

"Take it and do what I told you. This way you can open that new account and you'll have money any time you need it."

"I can't take this much."

"Syd," he said sternly, giving her a look, and suddenly she smiled, folding the check.

"Thank you, best brother in the whole world."

"You're welcome," he remarked dryly. "I'd talk to Dad, but we both know it will do no good. He's stubborn and he's a control freak. The only thing that Dylan can ever do to wring respect from Dad is what I'm doing—make as much money as Dad. I had a running start with influential connections, a top-notch education and family money. Dylan has none of that."

"I know. He can never make the money Dad did, but I don't care."

"Have you told Dylan?"

"Not yet, but I will. I'll miss my family, but at least you're not cutting me out. It's getting bad between Mom, Dad and me."

"Sorry, Syd. Dad has really focused on you. For now, it's you and not me."

"He won't bother you. I think you've thrown him for a loop with this latest acquisition. He wanted that chain for years." She was quiet for a moment.

Then Tony said, "Since he found out about Morris, he hasn't interfered in my life. I don't think he ever expected me to make as much money as he does."

"I wish I could and get him to stop meddling," she said. "But my calling is in the medical field, not business. I can't make the money I'd need to gain his respect and stop his interference."

Tony squeezed her shoulder. "Do you really love Dylan?"

She turned wide brown eyes on her brother. "Yes. You've asked me before. Each time I tell you yes, I'm more certain and my love has grown stronger. I don't care about the inheritance.

We'll get along. I have faith in Dylan. His grades were tops. He has an excellent job with a big company and hopes someday to go into business for himself. Dad says Dylan is a nobody. Mom and Dad both want me to marry one of those boys I've grown up with, Paul, Jason, Will. I'm not in love with any of them. I don't want to marry them and they bore me." She waved her fingers at Tony. "Mom and Dad would like you to marry Emma or Darcy."

"The day the sun rises in the west," he remarked. "The folks haven't said anything about that to me for several years. This past year Dad's gotten quiet on all fronts."

"You're surpassing him in business and he never, ever expected that to happen. You can thank me, too, for taking their attention."

"I definitely thank you."

"I know Mom and Dad mean what they say. They both want us to have 'society marriages.' But I love Dylan and I'm going to marry him."

"Let Dylan know what Dad has threatened. Fill him in so he knows exactly what it means. If Dylan still wants to marry you, then he's been warned. Dylan seems to truly love you from all you've told me. I trust your judgment with him. The more he knows the more he'll be prepared to deal with whatever our father does."

"Tony, why do we have parents like this?"

"Look at my friends and their interfering dads—Jake and Gabe Benton, Nick Rafford. Dad's no worse than theirs. When we were growing up, their interference was effective. Now, it's not."

"Thank heavens! I don't want him running my life," she said. "I'm meeting Dylan in thirty minutes, so I need to go, but I just had to talk to you."

"Call whenever you want. You know I'm always here for you."

"Thank goodness," she said. "You always stand by me in a crisis and you've been there when I'm hurt."

Tony smiled at her. When he could, he protected her from their parents' interference, but it was impossible to always deflect their attention.

She finished her juice and jumped to her feet. "I better run. Thanks for listening. I feel so much better with your encouragement and support."

"Sure. I'll need yours sometime."

She gave him a smile. "That will be the day. Whatever they throw at you, you manage to overcome. Tony, thank you so, so much."

"Forget it. You're there for me. You come talk whenever you want," he said, draping his arm around her shoulders and giving her a light hug.

She smiled up at him, then her expression changed. "Tony, they'll try to get you to sever ties with me."

"Doesn't matter. You know I'll never do that."

"Thank you," she said quietly.

"Syd, I would think Dylan knows the graphic artists in the city. He probably knows the top one with Morris. Her name is Isabelle Smith."

"I've met her at parties Dylan and I have attended. I don't really know her except to say hi. We've talked a little. From what Dylan has said, she's very good and he admires her work. They're friends because of their mutual interest in art. Now she works for you. She's gorgeous," Sydney said, her eyes dancing. "Thinking of dating an employee?"

"I'm allowed. I'm just curious because they are both in the same field."

Sydney laughed. "I'll ask Dylan about her. Maybe sometime the four of us can go to dinner."

"Syd—" he said in a threatening voice, and they both laughed.

"Watch out. You'll get Dad on your case if you start seeing an artist. Actually, you won't. I think you've stopped him cold as long as you don't lose the fortune you've made."

"It's a damn big relief. You stop worrying so much. You and Dylan can weather Dad's interference. If you're really in love, it won't matter what Dad does."

"I hope not. He has a lot of influence."

At her car Jake held the door. "Don't pay too much attention to our parents. When Christmas comes, it may be a whole different story."

"If it's not, I can live with it. I can't live with losing you."

He smiled. "You'll get along. And I'm always here for you. Take care, Syd."

"Sure. Thanks for the check, but mostly thank you for being the brother you are."

As he entered the mansion, his thoughts returned to earlier and Isabelle Smith. He wanted to see her again. He definitely would have an interview with her. Since he'd acquired Morris, three executives had resigned. He guessed from her frosty manner that she was going to resign, too. It was a plus-minus prospect. He wanted her to stay. On the other hand, if she didn't, it might be less complicated to see her socially.

Now he was looking forward to Thursday evening's reception more than before.

Two

Isabelle gripped the steering wheel tightly. Her insides knotted. Tony Ryder was a page out of her past. He obviously had not remembered her, and nothing about her had jogged his memory. A night she wished she could forget. The most passionate night of her life, and one that she had never been able to understand.

A singular time in which she had acted in a totally uncustomary fashion. Had it been Tony who had triggered her responses? The spring night? The looming end of the semester? She could never account for her actions to herself.

One thing remained the same—the white-hot, sizzling attraction experienced by both of them. Even though she had tried to keep from responding in even the slightest manner to his magnetism tonight, she'd failed. He had felt the same witchery, revealing his responses in small ways.

His riveting looks and commanding presence made him larger-than-life to her. It was impossible to see him in any ordinary manner. When they were together, she could feel the rising heat they generated. The man probably went through life getting everything he wanted. Between his money, his looks, his background, his sharp mind—how could he fail in any under-taking?

She wanted him out of her life and she definitely wanted away from him. She hoped she'd have a new job and be gone from Morris without Tony having a clue who she was. No way did she want to work for Tony Ryder. Tony was clearly not into commitment and she was. She had read about him on business pages. He was a workaholic and obviously avoided long-term relationships. As she approached each birthday now, her yearning for a family and a love she could trust increased. She wanted a lifelong relationship while Tony did not have even long-term relationships.

She had told Tony she would attend the company party, but now she had second thoughts.

Finally at home, Isabelle turned on Beethoven, showered and changed into pajamas, and poured a tall glass of cold milk. She couldn't shake thoughts of Tony and their encounter tonight. Tony Ryder was even more handsome and appealing than he had been the night she had met him when she had been in college.

How could he forget someone he had slept with? It had been such a passionate night. She grew warmer just thinking about it before making an effort to put those memories firmly out of mind.

Of all people to buy out Morris Enterprises.

Mr. Morris had planned to work four more years and then sell the company when Tony had come along with a dream offer. How she wished Tony had found other interests. Four more years with Morris would have been great. Now her future was uncertain. She had to start fresh with a new company. She would lose clients and accounts she knew well.

When she had started at Morris, she had thought the company would never change hands. The original shipping business had started with the trucking company in the 1920s. In 1946, Morris opened the first hotel. Within two years it had become a Texas chain, and in a few more years, a national chain. As the company had continued to grow, the word with employees was that the Morrises would never sell. Until the current Morris, whose only son was immersed in the Beltway political scene. After Morris's daughter married a jet-setting Frenchman, she no longer had interest in the family business.

Change happened, especially nowadays when companies changed hands with the right offer. Probably due to her awards, the recognition she had received for achievements in her field, plus the large number of companies she had dealt with because of her job with Morris, she had three excellent job offers to consider.

Thursday night she would put in an appearance, speak to Mr. Morris, as well as those she was close to at Morris, and then leave. She didn't care to schmooze with Tony.

She sat down at the kitchen table with her milk and the file of papers from businesses that had made her offers. She had them in order of preference with first choice Tralear Hotels, Incorporated, the hotel chain where Vernon Irwin, the former president of Morris, was going. Vernon wanted her, as well as five other Morris employees, to move with him and he had made her a highly tempting offer.

She had to get away from Morris before Tony realized who she was.

When she went to bed, she had dreams about Tony Ryder. One of her first thoughts on waking in the faintly gray dawn— *would* Tony remember who she was? Even more unsettling— how would she say no to him when she remembered what it was like to be with him?

On Thursday, Tony entered the luxurious reception room on the top floor of the Morris building. A piano player provided background music and a buffet of hors d'oeuvres were on tables scattered along three walls. A crowd had already gathered. As his eyes swept the room, disappointment ruled, because he did not see Isabelle.

He spotted the table with Seymour Morris and Vernon Irwin, who had already taken another job as president of Tralear Hotels, Incorporated, a fast-growing hotel chain. Three vice presidents who were still on the Morris payroll were also at the table. Casually looking for Isabelle, Tony crossed the room to greet the former CEO and each executive.

"Join us, Tony. You can humor an old man and sit for a spell."

"I'd be glad to," Tony said, smiling at the white-headed CEO. "I've looked forward to getting to meet more Morris people."

"Excellent. We'll introduce you and your executive staff in an informal manner shortly. I'll officially turn everything over to you and go. Vernon will introduce the Morris executives."

"No need for you to rush away. I look forward to meeting them to put faces with names." Tony wanted to ask about one director in particular, but he refrained. Instead, as he conversed with those around him, he idly watched the crowd.

"Why don't we do the introductions and let me officially move on. I can turn it over to you and get these old bones home to bed."

"Yes, sir," Tony replied, biting back a smile at the references to old and tired because he had already discovered that Seymour Morris worked out daily and had for years. Seymour was into polo, swimming, racquetball and golf.

As he moved to the microphone with Seymour, a blonde caught his attention.

In a plain black knee-length dress, Isabelle stood out. How had he missed her? Or had she just arrived? His insides clenched and flames heated him. Looking gorgeous, she stood talking to a cluster of Morris people. The short dress revealed her long, shapely legs and he could take a slow look now when she was unaware of his gaze on her. Her hair was looped and piled on her head, but this time a few strands escaped to frame her face.

She laughed at something someone said and his heart jumped. Instantly a vivid memory of Jessie Smith struck him.

His gaze narrowed while he focused intently on Isabelle, looking slowly, trying to compare her to a memory.

"Mr. Morris. I see your graphic arts department director, Isabelle Smith. Is that her full name?"

"As far as I know," Seymour answered, turning to the man at his side with a questioning look.

Tony's gaze remained riveted on Isabelle. He wanted to excuse himself and go talk to her, but that was impossible.

"It's *Jessica* Isabelle Smith," the vice president answered.

"Jessica Smith," Tony whispered, repeating the name. Jessie Smith. It *was* her. Jessie Smith was back in his life.

He couldn't keep from smiling. His new acquisition had a surprising, incredible perk. Now he could think of two reasons for her coolness when they had met Tuesday night. She could resent that he had not contacted her after their night together. Or she didn't want to recall that night or rekindle the friendship. He watched her, remembering the college girl he had met, taunted by a visual picture of a laughing blonde, stunning in tight, faded jeans that molded to her slim legs. The same riveting blue eyes and flawless skin. A mouth to elicit erotic fantasies. And a cascade of long, almost waist length, silky, pale blond hair that, instead of being tightly pinned and conservative, tumbled freely over her shoulders. A party girl. Fun-loving, flirty with him, burning him to cinders in bed.

Why had she switched to her middle name, Isabelle? Nearly everything about her had changed, with the exception of her gorgeous looks, her captivating blue eyes, silky blond hair and that blazing attraction. Tony recalled her in his arms that night, warm, naked, eager. She had been all the things then that she had not been when he encountered her Tuesday night—the night they had met, there had never been a barrier around her.

She must have remembered him from the start. Was she angry he hadn't pursued her after that night of passion?

Barely aware of his surroundings or the looming task, Tony's attention kept returning to her while he attempted to chat politely with Seymour.

Finally, one of Seymour's vice presidents quieted the room, introduced Seymour Morris and turned the microphone over to him.

Smiling his way through the opening, Tony heard none of it. His gaze kept resting on Isabelle, who was now facing the speaker, keeping her gaze firmly on the vice president or on Seymour. During the time Tony had watched her, not once had she looked at him.

He heard Seymour announce his name, introducing him as the new CEO and head of Ryder Enterprises, and he smiled during the applause. As he stepped to the microphone, shook Seymour's hand and looked around the audience, his gaze rested on Isabelle. This time he made eye contact.

The instant they looked into each other's eyes, the air electrified. Erotic images from the past taunted him as he pulled his attention back to the moment.

"I want to thank all of you for the warm welcome I've received. Seymour Morris and the Morris family have built a premier company with the help of outstanding employees. This is a blue-ribbon company with a blue-ribbon record." He waited a few seconds while there was polite applause.

"In the coming weeks I'll be talking to each of you more in depth. I think I already have appointments with most of you. If you need to see me sooner than your appointment, just let my secretary know. I'm looking forward to a banner year for Morris. I'll turn this over to my executive president, Jason Hoyt, who has a few words to say and some introductions."

He stepped aside and once again barely heard introductions

until they went back to the Morris people and one by one, the vice presidents and then the directors were introduced.

They were scattered throughout the room and each person waved while they received brief applause. As each name was called, he looked carefully at the person, recalling the information he had received regarding them. Finally, he heard, "Isabelle Smith, director of the graphic arts department."

Smiling, she stepped forward to wave, her gaze never meeting his. It didn't matter. His heart jumped while he studied her intently again, remembering Jessie, comparing, feeling faint doubts that were fading each time he looked at her. Off and on he had thought about her, wondering where she was and what she was doing. At the time he had been working almost every waking minute and he hadn't wanted to get involved with a woman because business would have suffered. She was back in his life. Now he could better understand her anger over his not contacting her after their night of partying and making love. Also, he could get through that barrier she had thrown up. As they made the next announcement, she glanced at him.

Certain she was Jessie Smith, he was jubilant.

The minute they finished the introductions and speeches, Tony turned to Seymour to offer his hand. "Thank you, sir. I have high hopes for Morris."

"I think you'll do well. This has been a great company. I have to tell you, there are moments this retirement gets to me, but I have no Morris heirs to pass this on to, so this is the end of the line. Life is filled with changes. I hope you pass this company through as many generations of Ryders as we have had Morrises."

"Thank you. You've built a great company and I'm looking forward to my involvement in it."

Seymour grinned. "Your father wanted this company in the worst way. I've fought him off for years. Lucky for you that you happened along when I wanted to retire and it didn't hurt that you had a better offer than your dad," Seymour added, chuckling. "Even though he didn't make the sale, I know he's probably still celebrating since you have a family business the same as I do. He may be out of it, but it was his and it's still Ryder."

"That he is. Best wishes on your retirement," Tony said, anxious to get through the formalities.

When he had the chance, he turned to look for Isabelle. Once again, he couldn't spot her. While his pulse drummed, he began to move around the room and then he saw her near the door, talking to three people. With her coat in hand, he suspected that she had been on her way out when someone had stopped her.

He tried to avoid rushing, but he crossed the room, putting off conversations with people who approached him.

And then she turned and walked out the door.

He lengthened his stride to catch up with her in the hall. "Jessie," he said.

Isabelle stopped, her heart lurching. *He remembers* was the first thought that went through her mind. Her palms became damp as she turned to watch him approach. Looking like an ad for expensive men's clothing in his charcoal suit, Tony had a commanding presence that was different from the party guy she had met in college. The thick mat of unruly curls were the only hint of a less serious side to him, something beyond the driven, ambitious mogul whose entire focus seemed to be on acquiring an even larger fortune.

As he halted only inches in front of her, there was a warmth in his gaze that hadn't been present on Tuesday night. He gripped her arm lightly, his fingers barely holding her, yet it was a heated touch. "Let's go where we can talk and not be interrupted."

"I'm not sure we need to talk," she said. "You're my new employer. I'll see you sometimes at the office," she said, starting to put on her coat. He took it and held it out for her. As she slipped her arms into the sleeves, his hands brushed her shoulders. The faint touch should have been impersonal but was scalding.

"Oh, no. You're not getting off that easily. Why didn't you tell me?"

She looked up at him as he walked beside her. "I didn't think you remembered," she said, her pulse racing.

"I've never forgotten. Tuesday night, I thought about you— the Jessie Smith I knew, but dismissed the idea because of your name, Isabelle, your appearance, which is far different. And your whole manner."

As they left the building, he held the door. "Let's go have a drink somewhere and we can talk."

She shook her head. "We're not taking up where we left off. Different time, different world. You're my new employer. End of discussion. I have other job offers, so soon I'll be leaving Morris."

"Don't act in haste," he said, his dark brown eyes unreadable. His handsome looks held her attention, more so now than when she was younger.

"I won't do anything rash. I've been interviewing, studying my options."

"Perhaps, but you haven't heard what we'll offer," he said.

"Frankly, I doubt it will top the offers I've received. And you'll have no difficulty replacing me, if you even want to with your ad department all in place. We both know that."

"Why not hear what we'll do? What do you have to lose?"

She smiled at him. "Nothing to lose. I'll listen at the office. There's no need for us to discuss work tonight."

"How about dinner tomorrow night?" he asked, and her heartbeat skipped. Acceptance was on the tip of her tongue. But she had had one foolish night with him. She didn't want another. Her aim was to meet someone with marriage potential— definitely not Tony Ryder's MO, he was not the settling-down type. She wanted marriage and family. Tony wanted success. Focusing on his workaholic drive, she could say no far more easily.

"Thank you. I have never thought it wise to mix business with my personal life. That's the path to all kinds of complications."

"I think you cut off your options too hastily," he said, smiling at her. "I'm still glad to find you again. I suppose it's Isabelle now and not Jessie."

"Definitely. Jessie was a nickname from childhood. My grandmother was named Isabelle and I loved her and always wished Isabelle had been my first name. When I graduated from college, I saw an opportunity to move into a different world with different friends and change to the name I like best. I prefer Isabelle and most of my coworkers don't even know Jessica, much less Jessie."

His gaze roamed over her features, his scrutiny making her breathless. "I hope you come to work sometime with your hair down. I remember your long hair," he said in a husky voice.

And I remember your broad shoulders and rock-hard body, she thought. "I don't wear my hair down to work," she answered in what she hoped was a remote voice. "It doesn't seem as professional."

"So when you knew I was coming, you began looking for another job?"

"Actually, the companies contacted me. I intended to look other places, and now I've had promising offers."

"You've said you'd wait and give us a chance."

"I will, but I'm pretty sure I'll be leaving and even more certain you'll never miss me." It was tempting for her to add, *You didn't before.* "I need to go. I told Mr. Morris goodbye. I'll miss him, but he seems happy with the prospect of retiring."

"I'll walk you to your car," Tony said, falling into step beside her. "Catch me up. Did you go from college to Morris?"

"No. I worked for an ad agency for two years and then came to work here."

At her car she stopped and smiled. "Good night," she said, pulling her coat close around her.

"Night, Isabelle. I'll see you at the office."

She slid behind the wheel. He closed the door and stepped back.

As she drove away across the parking lot, she glanced in the rearview mirror. He stood staring at her car.

She had turned down dinner and told him she was quitting. Exactly what she should have done, but there was part of her that wanted to accept his dinner offer and stay in his employ.

This had to be for the best. She didn't want any more nights of mindless liaisons, a brief casual relationship with her employer that meant nothing to him. She wanted out of this company and away from Tony Ryder with her heart and her self-respect intact. And she didn't want the office gossiping about her relationship with the new owner. Tony Ryder was not the person to get involved with and she regretted that he had recognized her. She intended to keep reminding herself that he was not the kind of man she wanted to spend her time with.

Even so, there was part of her that wanted to stay at Morris. A part of her that knew she would see more of Tony if he was her boss.

As she studied an ad layout at the office Friday morning, Isabelle received a call from Tony's secretary, who wanted to set up a meeting. Within minutes Isabelle had an eleven-o'clock appointment Monday with Tony, his president of operations and the president of promotion and information. She was still tempted to turn in a resignation and skip the interview, but she was curious how badly he wanted her to stay. What offer would he make?

She had already decided which company she would prefer

to join. She had had the third interview, which had culminated in a job offer that included more money than she was making. She would oversee a larger graphic arts department in an office with a more convenient location. She did not expect Tony to top their proposal, giving her the opportunity to tell him she had a better offer. Going with that thought firmly in mind, she spent the weekend getting ready for her business move, hoping to take off a few days in between employers. Saturday morning she went to a midmorning meeting of Dallas Regional Graphic Artists. She had belonged to the group since she had started her career.

As she expected, a close friend greeted her upon her arrival. Dylan Kinnaly—who was seriously involved with Tony's sister, Sydney—broke away from a cluster of people and hurried toward her. The tall, slender man had a worried frown that indicated something bad had happened.

"Have you met him yet?" Dylan asked. "You said Tony Ryder takes over now."

"Hello, to you," she answered with amusement. "Yes, I've met him. He wants me to stay with Morris."

"Sydney's parents had a long talk with her about me. I was hoping to talk with you when we get a chance. Can you stay after the meeting?"

"Sure, the room will be empty," she said, her curiosity rising. Dylan had become a good friend over the years and she had been surprised when she had learned he was seeing Tony's sister.

She had first met Sydney Ryder at an annual film festival held by one of the local art museums. Later, she had seen her a few times at professional events when Dylan had brought her along. She couldn't keep from liking Sydney and couldn't blame her for anything her brother did. But Sydney was a reminder of Tony, and for that reason Isabelle had refused the few invitations from Dylan to go to dinner with them. When she had told Dylan about meeting Tony in college, swearing him to secrecy about telling

Sydney, Dylan understood her refusal to get to know Sydney better.

"The meeting's beginning so we'll talk later."

They took seats and listened as a speaker took the podium. The meeting was short, lasting only an hour.

It wasn't until they were alone that Dylan turned to her. Since his blue eyes were clouded with worry, she braced for bad news. "Sydney called me last Tuesday night. Her parents gave her an ultimatum. If she doesn't drop me, they will disinherit her, stop paying for medical school for her and cut her out of family holidays."

"Dylan, I can't believe that. Why?" Isabelle asked, aghast and wondering about the tensions in Tony's family. "How can they interfere in your lives that way? Why would they?"

"I'm not *society*. They want her to marry one of the men she's known all her life. Also, they think I'm after her money."

"That's dreadful," Isabelle answered. "Sounds like something out of the eighteenth century."

"I don't want any of Sydney's money," he said, his long fingers turning his pen in his hand. "I don't want to hurt her, either. We've talked it over. As far as I'm concerned, I see only one solution—I ended our relationship. For her sake."

"That's even worse. Does she go along with your decision?"

"No. She wants us back together, but they're threatening too big a disaster for her. I don't want her going through anything so stressful over me. She's always loved her family and they've been close. She's very close with her brother."

"What's does Tony think of all this?"

"He said he would send her to medical school, not to worry about that one."

"Good for him," Isabelle said, relieved and aware of a grudging respect blossoming for Tony. "He can afford to do that. I was afraid he would side with his folks."

"Not at all. He gave her a generous check. He told her he

would never cut her out on holidays—or ever. He urged her to tell me their threats. Tony is damn supportive, but from what Sydney has told me, Tony has had bitter battles with his dad."

"I'm glad Tony took that stand," she said, her respect growing stronger. "I think more of him for not siding with them, and for urging her to tell you their threats."

"They may treat him the same way when he gets engaged if it isn't someone they approve of."

"Tony Ryder is a complete workaholic," Isabelle said. "I can't imagine him getting married. He won't have the same problem with his parents. I'm sorry, Dylan. If she truly loves you and you love her, maybe you should give it more thought before you break off with her."

"I just don't want to cause her to lose her inheritance—or her parents."

"She's in love with you. I understand your feelings, but think about it."

She gazed into eyes that were darker blue than her own. Dylan was a good graphic artist and they had helped each other in years past on projects. She hated to see him hurt and she thought the Ryders were being ghastly about him.

"What about you and Tony Ryder?" Dylan asked. "Have you seen him yet? Does he remember you?"

"Yes and yes. He remembers me and he wants me to stay with Ryder Enterprises."

"You're damn good at what you do. You've built that department. Will you?"

She shook her head. "The department will never be the same. I don't want to stay. There's no future with Tony."

"I don't blame you. If I could do it over—" He paused to think and shook his head. "I'd still want to know Sydney. I love her and you can't turn that off. Not the last-forever kind of love."

"Dylan, I'm so sorry. They should be delighted with you."

He smiled. "Thanks. I naively thought they would at least be friendly to me. They aren't even that. I'm not supposed to set foot in their house."

"This goes from bad to worse," she remarked. "What a family. Maybe you don't want to marry into it. Do you know Sydney really, really well?"

"I love her with all my heart. Enough to get out of her life and avoid causing her heartache."

"I'm sorry. I don't have a solution for you, except to urge you to rethink walking away from the woman you love and who loves you. Think about what's important. Think about what Sydney wants."

Dylan smiled briefly at her, and they got up to head out. As they walked toward the door, he said, "No one has a good solution, but thanks for listening. Be careful with Tony if he wants you to go out with him. You could end up in a dilemma with his family. Sydney said they have women picked out for him."

Isabelle laughed. "Don't worry. There's no danger. Tony Ryder is in love with his work. He's married to his job. I don't ever want to tie my life to someone who puts work first over family. I saw that happen with one of my friend's family when I was growing up and it was dreadful.

"True love is a precious thing. Think about it, Dylan, before you do something drastic."

"I'm thinking, but I always come back to the same solution. I love her and want what's best for her."

"I hope she appreciates the kind of person you are. It sounds as if she does. Don't rush into a breakup, Dylan. That's my two cents' worth."

"That's why I wanted to talk to you about this."

"Keep in touch and let me know what's happening," she said, going to her car as Dylan headed to his.

"You do the same," he called, walking backward. "If you change jobs, please let me know."

"I will," she called, climbing into her car, moving by rote while she thought about what she had learned from Dylan. She didn't want to be involved with Tony in any manner.

One more strike against getting to know Tony Ryder any better. His family would be no more happy with her than they were with Dylan. At least Tony had stood by his sister. Isabelle had to admire him for that.

Sunday afternoon, she looked at her wardrobe to select what she would wear to the Monday interview. Certain she would soon leave Morris, she decided to wear something both professional and a little less buttoned up than usual, something more on the appealing side. Her conservative suits were shades of blue, gray, brown and black, innocuous, all business, hopefully authoritative to offset her age and pale blond hair. Although she was five feet eight inches tall, she wore high heels. She rummaged through her choices, pushing aside the suits to withdraw three dresses, which she tried on in succession.

Tony had forgotten her before and he would again, but she wanted him to notice her Monday and remember her after she was gone from his company. She had to stop thinking of it as Morris and recognize that it was now Ryder Enterprises, a name that gave her a bitter feeling because of Tony and their past, as well as having loved the Morris company the way it had been. Mentally, she had mapped out a rosy future with Morris and then Tony Ryder had brought it crashing down. Unfair a little, because Mr. Morris was also responsible by retiring and selling out.

She finally decided on a deep blue dress with a short jacket and a straight skirt that had a slit on one side. The low-cut square neckline revealed curves while the whole dress clung to her figure. She had matching pumps that would complete her ensemble. Eager to resign and move on with her life, she looked forward to the interview.

* * *

Monday morning she was ushered into the elegant office that had always belonged to a Morris. The thick carpet muffled any footsteps while the early morning sun poured through the floor-to-ceiling windows, spilling across the balcony and into the room. She imagined a smiling Mr. Morris sitting at his broad mahogany desk. Instead, it was Tony, vibrant, commanding, sexy enough to transform what was usually a purely business atmosphere into an electrified ambience. Smiling, he stood, coming around his desk to greet her while another man remained beside a leather chair. A brunette who had been sitting nearby stood.

"Good morning, Isabelle," Tony said, taking her hand to shake it briefly. The moment they touched, her already racing pulse gave another spurt. She withdrew her hand swiftly. His brown eyes were friendly. Unruly black locks curled on his forehead, an unwanted reminder of being in his arms and combing them back from his face.

Instantly, she tried to concentrate on the interview ahead, but when she met Tony's gaze, there was a mocking look, as if he knew exactly what she had been thinking.

He could not possibly know, yet her cheeks grew hot and she turned from him to greet the others.

"This is Mandy Truegood, president of public relations and media promotion," Tony said as the brunette smiled, extending her hand.

"And this is Porter Haswell, our president of operations."

The man smiled, shaking her hand. While he was friendly, his gray eyes assessed her. "I've heard good things about you, Isabelle. It's a pleasure to meet you. I never did get to talk to you at the reception, which I had intended to do."

"Sorry I missed you," she replied. "I left early," she added, without a glance at Tony.

"You've had a spectacular career with Morris, with many awards. Congratulations," Porter said.

"Thank you," she answered. "Morris gave me opportunities. They opened the new hotel chain just shortly before I started, so from the beginning I got to do the ad campaigns. This is a great department with a talented staff. You'll find each person brings a particular specialty. The teamwork is amazing."

"You can tell us about your staff. Why don't we have a seat. We can sit at the conference table," Tony said.

She moved to the rectangular table. Effortlessly, Tony was there before her, pulling out a chair for her.

"Thanks," she said brusquely as he sat to her right. She marveled how he could appear both relaxed and in control at the same time, a puzzling combination. On the table was her own large portfolio, plus a file bearing her name.

Amanda and Porter placed notebooks and papers in front of their seats.

Tony gazed at her with a faint smile. "We've studied your portfolio and impressive file that lists your accomplishments and awards."

"I look forward to working with you," Amanda added. "Morris is a great company and you've contributed to its growth."

"Why don't you tell us about the campaign that you feel you contributed to the most and how you worked with your staff," Tony suggested.

As she talked, she was aware of holding the attention of all three, Amanda asking the most questions, Tony's dark eyes on her while he listened.

The interview went easily. Isabelle tried to inform them of the talent and abilities of her staff. Even though she intended to move on, she hoped they kept her people.

When they concluded, remarks were brief, thanks exchanged

and she left Tony's office, the office she would forever think of as Mr. Morris's.

Relieved to have the interview behind her, and curious what they would offer, she went to her office to clean out her desk. It would be a simple matter to pack her things after she turned in her resignation.

She already had a resignation letter written and copies made, but she wanted to wait and see what Tony offered. She expected far less than she had now. He had a reputation for buying companies, gutting them and keeping only skeleton crews that he moved down the corporate ladder. Some stayed and moved back up in a short time. Most left.

She had no intention of working with him. Their night of passion was a shadow hanging over her, something she had not been able to forget. She suspected from his dinner invitation that he wanted to renew the intimacy. She wanted to bury the memory, but there was no way she could wipe it out.

Her phone rang and she was caught up in business the remainder of the morning.

It was after three when Tony's secretary called to ask her to come to Tony's office. Relieved they were doing something today, Isabelle hurried along the hall to the large corner office Tony occupied. All she had to do was give two weeks' notice and she would be elsewhere, far from Tony Ryder.

Three

When she entered his office, Tony stood in front of his desk, motioning her to a chair. His gaze swept briefly over her, a look that from anyone else would have been impersonal, unnoticed, but when Tony studied her, she warmed beneath his gaze.

He still appeared as if ready for a men's fashion shoot in a navy suit that had no wrinkles and his fresh snow-white dress shirt.

"Please be seated," he said, the words harmless, the look in his eyes not. His dark eyes smoldered with blatant lust.

Aware of his continued scrutiny as he sat facing her, she sat and crossed her legs.

"You had a good interview and made quite an impression this morning." He leaned forward, placing his elbows on his knees. "While I suspect you already have one foot out the door, I want you to stay and work for me."

"I have some very good offers."

"We'll top them," he replied without hesitation. "Here's what I'm offering." He stretched his arm to pick up a sheet of paper from his desk to hand to her.

As she swiftly scanned a neatly typed page with spaces filled in by Tony, her breath caught. She glanced up at him in amazement.

She looked again at the title, reading it aloud, "Vice President of Graphic Arts." She skimmed down the page to the salary that took her breath again. It was higher than any amount she had ever made, higher than what she had been offered by anyone. Shocked, she looked up at him. "You'll raise my salary this much? You would put me over your people?"

"You're good at your job. Seymour Morris praised you highly. You have an impressive record. In addition, you had a good interview. I want to keep you and I think to do so will take a bigger salary. My guess is that you are on the verge of accepting one of those offers you've received, if you haven't already done so."

"You're right," she admitted, looking again at the amount, far more than she could hope to make anywhere else. Too much to resign and walk away without consideration. Too much to even have to think long about it. The title in itself was a promotion. How much had his offer been inspired by her work and awards—and how much because of his memory of their night together and wanting to repeat it? She stared at the figures before her and the title, wondering about his motives. This was not in character with what had been rumored about his ruthless reputation when he took over a company.

"Do you want me in your organization or in your bed, Tony?" she asked bluntly, and one corner of his mouth lifted in a slight smile.

He reached across the narrow space between them to take her hand. Distracting, charismatic, sexy, Tony ignited a fire within her while his brown eyes held her gaze.

"You get to the point. I want to see you outside the office. I want you here in my company. Of course, I want you in my bed,

Isabelle. I haven't forgotten that night with you and you haven't forgotten it, either."

How she wished she could give him a long, cold stare and convey the impression of that night being insignificant and no longer in her memory. She couldn't possibly, which he was fully aware of. "I don't want to rekindle anything. On that front, you'll be incredibly disappointed if I take this offer."

"No, I won't. If you stay, you'll do a good job. I know that much from your past performance."

"I don't socialize, go out with, date, anyone from work. It prevents complications in my life."

"We'll see," he said, running his thumb back and forth on her knuckles. She pulled her hand away.

"If I thought you didn't like that, I wouldn't do it, but I can see the look in your eyes. I can feel your racing pulse. You react as much as I do and we *will* go out together. I'll hold you in my arms while I kiss you again."

"Stop that," she said breathlessly, the command sounding more an invitation than a rejection. "Tony, I'll have to give it some thought. I never expected this offer. As for socializing, even if we do, which we will not, won't that cause difficulty with other employees?"

"This is a private company. I own it. I have a good relationship with my employees. They are a happy bunch in a big corporation. I have married couples working for me. They socialize, eat dinners and lunches together. There are couples working here who go out together. I'm allowed to have a life. So are you."

"It won't be together."

"You're one challenge after another, Isabelle."

"I don't intend to be anything to you, not even your employee, although I may have to rethink that one."

"Let's have dinner tonight. Not a business dinner. It will be strictly social. Whether you stay or go, I'm going to ask you to go out with me."

She was tempted to accept his dinner invitation, except she could see her life tangling in a web woven by Tony until he lost interest. Socializing with Tony, an affair with him—not only would complicate her work life, but it would also be a path to heartbreak no matter how it ended. And it would end. When it did, she would be older with no family to show for her affair of the heart.

"Tony, if I accept your job offer, I will keep my private life separate from my professional life. Thank you, but no dinner tonight."

"Whatever you want," he said, smiling at her, sounding supremely self-confident. "I still hope you accept my job offer."

"It's flattering, tempting and amazing. I'd like to think it over and get back to you."

"Of course. Take your time," he said.

The moment she stood, he came to his feet to walk to the door with her.

At the door he reached out to hold the knob and block her from leaving. When she glanced up, he gazed back quietly. "I want you, Isabelle. We had an amazing night that I've never forgotten. You'll say yes sometime soon because you respond to me. You can't hide it. We both know you respond, just as I do to you."

With every word she was sinking deeper in desire. His seductive ways conjured up their magic. He was right on too many levels, his observations on target. If she stayed, it was simply a matter of time until she was in his bed. Was that what she wanted?

"Tony, that's the strongest of all the arguments for rejecting your offer," she replied.

"Scared how much you'll like your life in the future?"

He was *way* too confident.

"Wisdom says to shun meaningless affairs, as well as office affairs. The only way to do that is to avoid them in the first place."

"See, we could talk over an enticing lobster dinner or a thick steak tonight. We do have things to talk about. We could dance—as I recall, that was a great pastime with you."

"Sorry, no. I see no point. Thank you and I'll get back to you with my answer."

"Excellent," he said, holding the door for her.

She stopped to tell the graphic arts secretary that she was taking off the rest of the day. Gathering her things and the paper from Tony, she left to go home where she could think.

The following morning Isabelle stood in Tony's office again. She had dressed carefully, this time in a conservative tan suit and matching blouse.

"Please sit, Isabelle," he said.

"This won't take long," she replied. "I'll accept your offer. You know I can't possibly refuse. I won't find another like it anywhere."

He smiled, the devilish smile that affected her heartbeat and breathing and was difficult to resist. "Good. You surely will let me take you out tonight and celebrate. An early dinner and then I'll deposit you home. This is a big day in your life." While his brown eyes danced with delight, he smiled at her.

On top of the promotion, his offer was tempting, but some things had not changed. She shook her head and opened her mouth to decline. He placed his finger on her lips. "Wait. I can see you digging in your heels. This is an offer worthy of a celebration. If we didn't have a past, and you accepted my job offer, you would agree to celebrate. You've agreed to work with me, so we're going to be together, Isabelle. We'll work together, we'll be in meetings together, lunches, dinners, conferences, hotels. Stop worrying about one night and one dinner. Celebrate your victory. And this is a victory for you. No seduction. Just dinner."

She inhaled deeply. He had a point. She was going to work with him. She thought of the few times she had been with Seymour Morris, purely business. She couldn't equate Tony with Mr. Morris, but she was going to be thrown with Tony sometimes by working for him.

"I can see the wheels turning," he said. "You'll sit home alone tonight otherwise, will you not? No fun there when you have a real triumph. Stop making a mountain out of a definite ant hill."

"You're persuasive. I'll have to give you that much." She thought about sitting home alone with this fabulous new position dazzling her. One dinner. Maybe she was blowing everything out of proportion. She should be able to have a dinner with him without succumbing to his charm. She couldn't keep from wanting to celebrate this new job. "Dinner it is," she said, wanting to add, *Seduction, it isn't,* but she knew he would stand by his word about that for tonight. She nodded. "Thank you, Tony."

"Excellent. How about I pick you up at your house at seven?"

"Which means you are leaving work early tonight," she said.

"For you and your celebration, definitely. I'm glad, Isabelle. You won't regret your choice."

"Are you always so sure of yourself, Tony?"

He smiled.

She picked up her briefcase. "Now I have to go to Human Resources and fill out paperwork. I've been told I'll keep my same office."

"Yes. You'll get to do it over. We're having them all redone. Soon you can make the selections of furniture, carpet, wall colors, everything."

"Actually, it's very much the way I like it now."

"That's your decision. Welcome to Ryder Enterprises, Incorporated," he said, extending his hand, shaking hers. The moment his hand closed around hers and heat warmed her from his touch, she wondered again if she could cope with working in close proximity to him. She had spent a sleepless night processing his offer. The job was fabulous, a dream position and salary so good it was worth working with Tony. She reminded herself of how little she'd seen of Mr. Morris over the years, yet, she knew Tony would be different. It was just too good an offer to turn down. She ought to be able to work around him without being constantly drawn to him. And he was a workaholic. He would move on to other concerns. He was a deal maker. He didn't sit in one office all the time. She didn't really expect to see much of him after the first few months when he was getting the company set up the way he wanted. Even that, he probably left to others.

Shaking off uneasiness, she withdrew her hand. His enthusiasm was contagious and she smiled at him.

"Thanks, Tony. I hope you're keeping most of my people."

"We'll have a meeting concerning that later this week."

"I'll see you tonight," she said, and left his office.

The day was busier than she had expected and she got home with only a little over half an hour to get ready for dinner.

Was she already making a mistake by going out with him? But she had made her career decision and had no intention of fretting about it. She wanted to celebrate and she had begun to feel ridiculous for making such an issue about avoiding him. She should be able to treat him the same as any other man, Mr. Morris, Dylan, anyone. Just go to dinner, keep a distance, stay composed and cool and Tony Ryder would move on soon and forget all about her. No flirting. No intense reactions. Dinner with a new boss. Nothing more.

After showering, she changed into a red dress with long sleeves and a V-neck. She fastened her hair on both sides, allowing it to fall loosely down her back. Finally she stepped into red high-heeled pumps.

On impulse, she picked up the phone and called Dylan to tell him about her promotion.

"Awesome! That is terrific, Isabelle," he said, his tone changing from enthusiastic to somber. "He remembered who you are and wants to go out with you."

"Yes, he did. Whatever his motive, I couldn't turn it down. It will give me a jump in the corporate world. Even if I just stay a few months, I can get a better job than I had."

"As you told me, think about it. Be careful. His family is also Sydney's family. They won't accept you."

She laughed. "Dylan, they won't have to. Ever. Whatever I do, Tony Ryder isn't going to propose marriage. He's wrapped up in making a bigger fortune. I'm just going to work for the man. Speaking of Sydney. How's it going between the two of you?"

"We're talking. She wants to get back together. I still think it would be supremely selfish of me, yet I keep discussing it with her."

"That ought to tell you something right there. You want to be with her."

"Hell, yes, I do, but I can't be the one to cost her a family split plus losing her inheritance."

"Dylan, stop and think. She's studying to be a doctor and you're successful in graphic arts. You can both live comfortably and well. Multimillions aren't a guarantee of happiness."

"I'm not going to be the one to take her away from her family. Those kind of bitter feelings sometimes last lifetimes and that would be terrible. She's been close to them." He was quiet for a moment, then said, "Want to go to dinner? We'll celebrate your job offer and I'll buy your dinner."

"I'd love to, but Tony asked me if I wanted to go to dinner to celebrate and I accepted. Had I known, Dylan, I would have turned him down. I thought I'd be sitting here by myself. And I didn't want to make such a big deal out of trying to avoid him."

"Ah, sorry I didn't talk to you sooner. Call me on a night you're free and we'll go."

When they hung up, she stared at the cell phone before she placed it on the dresser. She hated to see Dylan hurt and Sydney had seemed like a fine person. She wished she were having dinner with a friend instead of Tony. Isabelle thought about Tony supporting his sister. Perhaps family wasn't as far down his list of what was important as she had first thought. She shook her head. She'd better not fool herself on that one.

When the doorbell rang, her heart thudded. Impeccably dressed, Tony wore a dark topcoat and his charcoal suit with a red tie. Only the thick, unruly curls proclaimed a streak of wildness in the handsome corporate tycoon whose whole life was wrapped up in his work. That and the look in his eyes, indicating his approval as well as his longing, made her pulse beat faster.

"You look gorgeous," he said, taking her coat to hold it for her.

"Thank you," she answered. "I'm excited over my promotion, whatever motives you have behind it."

His smile broadened. "I want you in my company. I want us to work together. I've already told you, I want more than that, but we'll go slowly. Have you told your family? If I recall correctly, you have a large family."

"You really do remember me," she said as they headed toward a waiting black limo. "A limo, Tony?"

"Sure. It's easier."

A chauffeur held the door and she stepped into luxury. Tony shed his coat and asked if she wanted to wear hers.

"I'm comfortable," she said, looking at the fine leather and walnut trim of the interior, realizing what a difference there was between their lifestyles, something easier to forget at the office.

"This is beautiful and makes the evening seem even more

of a celebration—at least to me. You've been riding in limos all your life."

"I'm glad you like it. I didn't remember what you were majoring in when we met. After I recognized you, it came back to me that you were interested in graphic arts even back then."

"Yes. It's all I've ever wanted to do."

"If I had recalled that, I would have known you and Jessie were one and the same. I debated the possibility that you were Jessie and dismissed it. You're more sophisticated now. You've been far cooler, less receptive, not the party girl I recall from that night."

"Responsibilities. Also, some resentment over your buyout of Morris, something I can't help. They've been great to work for and I had a dream staff."

"Hopefully, you'll like your new life even better. I'll see what I can do," he said, his tone conveying a promise that sounded removed from work.

"I'll manage," she replied, thinking he had incredibly dark brown eyes, almost black now in the faint glow inside the limousine.

He touched a lock of her hair on her shoulder. It was a casual touch, yet it was as fiery as a caress and made her wonder whether she was tempting fate by going with him.

"You're decisive—another good trait," he said. "Simplifies life. It's always good to know exactly what you want to do."

"One trait we probably have in common," she answered, thinking she usually was decisive, but she hadn't been around Tony.

Tony's cell phone buzzed and he reached for it, giving her a nod. "Sorry, I better take it."

"Of course," she answered, turning to look at the scenery outside as they sped along the freeway. She heard Tony discussing a business problem with renovations on a hotel that wasn't connected with Morris, so she ceased paying attention to his conversation, surreptitiously studying him when his focus was elsewhere. If she could continue to appear as cool and composed the entire evening, she should be able to get through this dinner, perhaps making him lose a degree of interest in her. She would have a celebration of sorts if she could only ignore the man beside her, but that was impossible. She focused on the new title and job prospect, clinging to it, feeling a tingly excitement over her promotion and trying to ignore who had caused it and why. Finally he put away his phone and turned to her.

"Sorry for the interruption. Tell me, what's gone on in your life during the years between when we met and now?"

"Graduation, getting started in business, gaining experience at my job, making friends. What about you?"

"Mostly business. Nothing unusual. Have you told your family about your promotion?" he asked.

"No. Simply because I was late getting home from work and had to rush to get ready for tonight."

He was staring at her. "I like your hair. I like it best completely down—the way I remember it. Maybe before the evening is over."

"I doubt it," she said. "This is a partial concession. I rarely leave it down and unfastened. As for my family—I'll call them tomorrow night."

"Are they all here in Dallas?"

"Yes, as a matter of fact. Makes it easy for us to get together."

Shortly after, the limo turned into a private driveway, passing a pond with fountains as they drove to a canopied entrance with sparkling lights lending a festive atmosphere. She had heard about the restaurant, a famous one in the area, but beyond her means. Another reminder of the differences between her life and Tony's.

The door was held open for them and inside, the maître d' knew Tony, motioning them to follow as soon as they arrived. They were led to a cozy alcove with a fire burning in a fireplace and a view of the dance floor and stage where a small combo with a bass fiddle, a piano and drums played.

The table was covered in white linen with a bouquet of white gardenias floating in a crystal vase. She could detect the flowers' sweet scent, but her attention was held by the handsome man she was with. A candle highlighted Tony's prominent cheekbones, catching glints in his midnight curls.

A bottle of champagne on ice already waited and the sommelier appeared to uncork the Dom Pérignon. As soon as he received Tony's approval, he poured the pale, bubbly liquid into crystal flutes. Iced shrimp, a steaming artichoke dip and a plate of bruschetta were brought for appetizers. Menus were placed before them.

When they were alone, Tony raised his glass. "Here's to a fabulous promotion in your career and a night to celebrate."

"Thanks to you," she said, thinking he still made it sound as if work was the last thing on his mind even though he referred to her career.

"Actually, both Mandy and Porter were enthusiastic about you and deserve some of the credit for your job offer."

"That's nice to hear," she said, surprised. She had assumed the exorbitant raise and promotion had been all Tony's doing to keep her at Morris. "You can't tell me Mandy and Porter helped set the salary you'll pay me."

The corners of Tony's mouth raised slightly. "No, they didn't. I don't want to lose you. I go after what I want."

Her heartbeat fluttered in spite of the red flags of warning his statement raised. He had made his intentions clear and she hoped she was making hers just as clear, although accepting dinner tonight had to have sent a mixed signal. Though turning down a celebration of his fantastic offer would have been its own announcement of how much she reacted to him.

"Don't read too much into this dinner," she cautioned. "I'm celebrating with you, which frankly, is more of a celebration than sitting at home by myself tonight or worse, working late. As you said, it is not a monumental deal," she added, hoping she sounded casual about the whole evening with him.

He looked amused. "I'm glad you're here, whatever the reason. I want to get to know you."

"Try to keep an employer-employee view. That's all it will be between us. Unless of course, you decide to become a marrying man. I'm interested in marrying in my near future," she added, enjoying herself because she suspected he did not want to hear what she was telling him. She was not only telling him the truth, she was also hoping to make him realize they had no future together. She had no doubt that a woman looking for a husband was the last person Tony would want to spend time with.

"I'm not a marrying man. We can still enjoy an evening out," he replied smoothly, and she wished she could remain as cool as he was. "As a matter of fact, with your attitude, I'm surprised there's no wedding ring on your finger. I can't imagine there haven't been proposals."

"I've been far too busy. The right person has never come along. Where we differ— You don't want to be tied down for years. I do. I want a family, so our association outside of work isn't a good idea."

"We'll see about that one," he said, smiling at her. "I realize you know how to enjoy life. I have a memory."

"I'm older now and life changes," she said, sparring with him. "What are your goals, Tony?" she asked, hoping to change the conversation, which was taking a direction she didn't want.

"I have *a* goal—billionaire by forty."

"Unattainable for ninety-nine point nine percent of the world."

"I doubt if the odds are that bad. What about your main goal? Did your promotion bring you closer to achieving it?"

"No. I want to succeed and have a rewarding career, but I

want a family like the one I grew up in. I love my family. I hope to be married by thirty."

"Married by thirty. That's unique today. Your goal doesn't scare away most guys?"

She hoped it scared away Tony, which was why she was happy to continue bringing up the topic. "I don't tell my intentions to everyone. You may be the first to ask about my goals. You're business oriented."

"Not altogether," he said softly.

"Oh, yes, you are. Time will prove my case."

"Business wasn't my driving purpose the night we met. It's not tonight." She gazed into his dark eyes across the candlelight. In depths of brown was craving that kept her excitement simmering. "Forget business. Let's go dance once before dinner," he suggested.

He held her hand and she stepped into his arms for a ballad. She already knew he was a good dancer, remembering vividly being in his arms the night they met. He pulled her closer and they danced in perfect rhythm. In that moment she realized just how hard it would be to stay away from him in her new role. Besides his handsome looks, he had too much else going for him. He had made it clear he was not into marriage, family, children—commitment—because they would interfere with his focus on business. He had already mapped out his most important goal. If she didn't want heartbreak, she needed to continue to guard her heart.

"Why so quiet?"

"Thinking how strange it is to be dancing with my boss."

"Stop thinking of me as your boss. It's Tony—the Tony you met a long time ago. Forget the office. Enjoy the night."

"I'm enjoying every minute. A limo, champagne, candlelight, a handsome man."

"You're beginning to sound like the Jessie I remember.

I assume you no longer want to be called Jessie by anyone, including me."

"Maybe you most of all. I don't want to explain to anyone why you would call me Jessie."

"I won't until you approve, but I can't keep from thinking of you as Jessie."

He looked into her eyes and smiled. How easily she could fall into his bed. Beware, beware. When Tony spun her around and dipped, she had to cling to him, looking up into his riveting brown eyes. Electricity sparked between them, generating desire.

"You're beautiful, Isabelle," he whispered as he straightened up and they danced together. "I'm glad I bought out Morris. I never would have found you otherwise."

"Tony, let's keep this an impersonal friendship."

"Sure," he said, his expression telling her something else. When the ballad ended, they returned to their table.

After the waiter finished taking their orders, Tony asked, "Where do you go on vacations?"

"I don't take them much. Last summer I kept putting it off and suddenly the year was gone."

"We have to change that. When is the last time you left the country?"

"Tony, I'm tied up in work. I grew up in an ordinary, working-class, blue-collar family. I haven't been out of the country."

"Definitely has to change. When was the last time you left Texas?"

"I did go to a grand opening of one of the Morris hotels in Atlanta two years ago," she said, sipping her champagne. "Unless you've made changes, the company is sending me to a preview before the official opening of an elegant new Morris luxury hotel in San Diego the weekend after next," she said, wondering whether he already was aware of her trip.

"Excellent. San Diego is beautiful and I'm sure the hotel will be grand. What day do you leave?"

"Thursday morning. Three of us are going, two of the Morris vice presidents—Nancy Wrenthorp and George Franklin—and me. On Thursday night hotel officials will show us around. Friday, guests will arrive—mostly media, friends and families of some of the hotel officials. We'll fly out Sunday morning early."

"Do you have any time to yourself?"

"Yes, on Saturday. Friday, I have appointments with media representatives. Nancy and George will deal with hotel officials and look over the hotel and see if everything is ready and running smoothly."

"You should enjoy your trip."

The waiter appeared with their salads, crystal dishes holding greens and slices of tomatoes. Her appetite had diminished and she still felt excitement fizzing in her as steadily as the bubbles in her champagne.

It wasn't long before their lobster and steak entrées appeared, more than she could possibly eat, yet all of it looking delicious. Again, Tony's phone buzzed and she waved her hand dismissively.

"Take your call," she said, understanding that as CEO and owner of multiple companies he was on call all the time. She surreptitiously studied him until he put away his phone.

"I couldn't help overhearing you, Tony. There was a fire on an oil rig you own. I didn't know you had anything besides hotels and the trucking line."

"Ryder Enterprises incorporates a variety of businesses. The oil company is a small but profitable subsidiary."

"Do you need to go? It sounded serious."

"It's serious and costly, but thank heaven, no one was hurt and they're getting it under control already. No, I don't need to go. I just need to be kept informed."

She smiled. "No danger of that not happening." She wondered if years ago he would have gone dashing out. Every moment spent with him drew her back into memories and heightened the attraction to him.

They both ate little and when their dinners had been removed, Tony took her hand to dance again. She went eagerly, wanting to be close in his arms while reminding herself to avoid getting too involved.

They danced to another ballad, followed by a fast number. Tony's coat swung open and his dancing was sexy, bringing back more memories. When they returned to a slow song, he held her closer. "This is great, Isabelle. Thankfully, I've found you again."

"I was never more than a phone call away, Tony," she said, stirring the simmering anger over Tony's buyout of Morris and his not contacting her again. Her anger with him had lost intensity. There were moments now when he charmed her and she let go her past feelings.

"You're in my life now and I'm in yours and I intend to keep it that way," he said and her heartbeat quickened. He wrapped her in his arms and gazed at her, his attention shifting to her mouth and making her heart thud. He would try to kiss her tonight and she wanted him to, but that's a line she couldn't cross. He had been building to that all evening with his flirting, his dancing, his compliments, his casual contacts. Everything he said or did fanned flames between them, even though this was *supposed* to be just a dinner celebration regarding work. Not a big deal, she reminded herself.

Shortly after midnight she told him she should go home. Tony didn't try to persuade her to stay out later.

When the limo arrived at her condo, Tony walked her to the front door. His phone buzzed again. When he ignored it, she said. "Go ahead and take your call."

"I'll get it shortly. Not now. Give me your key and I'll get your door."

She handed him the key, watching as he unlocked and waited

for her to enter. Every second that ticked past heightened her worry. Her insides fluttered.

"Do you have an alarm?" he asked as he followed her inside and closed the door behind him.

She turned to switch off the alarm and then faced Tony. "It's off. This has been a wonderful evening that truly was a celebration," she said, looking up into dark eyes that kept her heart racing. Her words were polite, somewhat impersonal. She intended to keep it that way in spite of wanting to be in his arms, to kiss and be kissed again.

She held out her hand to give him an impersonal handshake. "Thank you, Tony."

"That won't do." He took her hand and pulled her toward him, reaching out to comb his fingers through her hair, carefully removing first one pin and then another. She felt the faint tugs against her scalp, which made her tingle. While her heart drummed, her gaze was locked with his.

"This is the way I remember you and like to see you—with your hair down. Preferably naked in my arms in bed."

"Tony, that night is definitely over and it was very long ago," she whispered, trying to hang on to common sense and avoid getting more entangled with him in spite of her racing heart.

"But unforgettable. You're a warm, passionate, beautiful woman, and extremely appealing." As he talked, he removed more pins and more of her long, blond hair fell freely across her shoulders until all strands were loose.

"Ah, Isabelle, you're gorgeous." He wound both hands in her hair and then his arms slipped around her waist and he drew her to him.

When he looked at her mouth, her lips parted and she was certain he could hear her thudding heart. "We're not ending this night on a handshake. Since I saw you at the reception and realized you were Jessie, I've wanted to kiss you."

"Tony, don't," she whispered, her heart beating wildly. The

moment she had intended to avoid was happening. While his arms tightened to draw her closer, he brushed his lips over hers, a faint touch, but it changed the entire evening. Sparks spun from his kiss, transforming a casual evening into something more, making her forget any handshake. Tony brushed her lips lightly again, then returned to cover her mouth with his.

Isabelle's insides clenched and heated. As his tongue went deep into her mouth, longing swept over her, demolishing worries, igniting fires and rekindling desire. Memories of a night long ago bombarded her. Wrapping her arm around his neck and an arm around his waist, she clung to him, pouring herself into the kiss.

His arms tightened around her. His kiss was even more devastating than she remembered. White-hot, melting, his kiss shook her. How could he be so incredibly sexy to kiss when she didn't want to be drawn to him? She was annoyed with him, determined to guard her heart, yet barriers were dropping away, disintegrating from the onslaught of pleasure.

She ran her fingers through the short hair at the back of his head and then moved her hand across his broad shoulder.

Passion mushroomed, shaking her, driving her to wild kisses that blanked out everything except Tony.

He raised his head. "I want you in my life, in my arms in my bed."

"Never," she whispered, her actions negating her words as she stood on tiptoe and pulled his head down again to kiss him. She felt starved for his kisses, as if no time had passed between that spring night with him and now. Remembering his lean, muscular body, his broad shoulders and hard masculinity, she longed for what she could not have. A night she thought she was beginning to forget poured back, vividly clear.

"Tony, we have to stop," she whispered, even though her actions denied her words as she pulled him close to continue kissing him.

"Why?" he responded before her lips were on his and they kissed again. Passion blazed, consuming protests and reason.

Tony's kisses were beyond dreams, building excitement with lightning speed.

Dimly, she thought she should tell him again to stop, but the notion was fleeting. Giving herself, taking all he gave, she kissed him. She thrust her hips against him, feeling his thick erection, knowing he wanted her and was ready.

Feeling lost in a dizzying spiral, she finally summoned her willpower and stopped. "Tony, that's it," she gasped. She struggled for breath while her heart pounded and her body was on fire for his hands and mouth and loving.

With half-lidded eyes, he gazed at her, brushing long locks of her hair back from her face.

"That got out of hand," she managed to say.

"Not really. We only kissed a few times."

It wasn't *only.* His kisses had been earthshaking, seductive.

He held her waist. "You're special, Isabelle."

Her heartbeat quickened yet more. Words to wrap around her heart and make it captive. "Tonight was a celebration, Tony. I had a wonderful time and thank you. I suppose I'll see you at the office this week."

"Not this week, because I leave town," he said, his fingers caressing her throat.

"Thanks and good night," she said softly, looking into eyes filled with yearning.

"It was a special evening," he said. He swept her into his arms and kissed her hard. Startled, for an instant she froze. It was only seconds, and then she returned his kiss until he released her, watching her intently with both satisfaction and need.

"Until later," he said quietly. He left, closing the door. The lock clicked in place. She looked out the window. Tony was already on his cell phone, his long legs carrying him swiftly to the limo.

"You're a workaholic," she whispered, thinking about the calls he had received. The head of an empire, wanting to keep in touch with his business at all times.

In seconds the limo's red taillights disappeared around a curve in the driveway. She switched off the hall lights and stood in the darkened entryway. Her mouth was dry, and her body was on fire. She wanted him with an intensity that shocked her.

"Good night, Tony. Sexy man," she said, relishing memories of the evening. For the next few hours she was going to pretend Tony was just another guy she worked with and enjoy replaying the night in her mind. Tomorrow she could return to reality. The man was her employer. He was obsessed with work, chasing a goal of billionaire by forty. His true love was power. He would avoid commitment. She had to refuse his next invitation or kiss her own dreams and goals goodbye. She had to resist his kisses, resist him, remember to keep up her guard. Too much was at stake to get deeply involved with him. She promised herself she would hold her own goals always in sight.

At least until her next encounter with Tony.

Four

Tony entered the walnut-paneled study at his parents' mansion to greet his father, looking into brown eyes as dark as his own. It was a typical Sunday evening with a quiet house, the staff at a minimum, his mother at a friend's playing bridge. "You called and wanted to see me. What's up?"

"First, let me pour you a glass of wine. Have a seat."

"Make it a small amount," Tony said, not interested in wine, but aware it would please his father if he would sit and have a drink with him. Tony took a business call while Grant Ryder poured two goblets with white wine from a crystal decanter. He carried one to Tony, who replaced his phone. "How was the Morris party?"

"Fine. Everything went smoothly. I think the transition will be easy."

"You achieved the impossible, Tony, getting Morris to retire."

"I think he was ready and wanted to retire. I was in the right place at the right time."

"Don't be modest. It gets you nowhere." Grant sipped his drink and lowered his glass. "Where's your sister? Your mother and I haven't been able to get in touch with her and she hasn't returned our calls." Grant turned to face his son.

"I think Sydney is studying," Tony said.

"When did you last talk to her?"

"Yesterday, as a matter of fact."

"She has as much told me that she doesn't care what I threaten, she'll see who she wants to see," Grant said, his thick dark eyebrows emphasizing his frown. It always surprised Tony that he was over four inches taller than his father. When he was a child, he thought his father was extremely tall.

Tony nodded. "I'm not surprised."

"She's talked to you, hasn't she?"

"Yes. You know she usually does," he said, knowing from past experience his father was growing more angry. His words became clipped.

"Six months ago I would have urged you to try to persuade her to drop that Dylan person. Now I suspect it might be useless to try to ask you to do anything you don't want to do."

"You're right," Tony remarked with a faint smile, surprised his dad was even hinting at defeat in his attempts to control.

"So, it comes to that. I was afraid it might because you've always been strong-willed." His father sat in a chair and swirled his wine, looking at it for a long time before he sipped.

"Well, you've acquired sufficient wealth to ignore my influence in your life," Grant continued. "I could threaten to disinherit you as I have Sydney, but I'm afraid at this point, you would pay no heed. You'll do as you damn please because you don't need my money."

"That's right, Dad. It's worth every hour of work I put in," Tony admitted, relishing the feeling of being free from his father's attempts to dominate his life. He sat relaxed, enjoying the moment he had relished for years.

"You don't need to look so smug," Grant grumbled. He shook

his head. "I've met my match in my son. If I have to meet it, I can't think of anyone else I would prefer to best me."

"I wasn't trying to 'best you.' I just want to live the way I want to live."

"So what do you think of this artist, this Dylan 'someone' your sister thinks she is in love with?"

"First, my sister probably knows whether or not she is really in love with Dylan. Next, my opinion of Dylan—he's a nice guy. From all indications, he's good at what he does. What's more important, I trust Sydney's judgment, Dad. Dylan hasn't had the advantages I had or you had. Sydney is bright and sharp. Frankly, if I were you, I would trust Sydney's judgment."

"Love is blind, Tony. We don't want Sydney to ruin her life."

"Chances are, she won't."

"How do you know this fellow isn't after Sydney's money? Someday she will be immensely wealthy. That may be his reason for showering his attention and affection on her. Have either of you considered that possibility?"

"Again, I trust her judgment. Besides, Dylan has told her he doesn't want to ruin her life, so he doesn't think they should see each other anymore. He's sticking by that and he wants to cut all ties. Sydney does not want him to. You'll have to admit that's someone who is putting Sydney first."

"Damn smoke screen. I doubt if he means it. It sounds good, but wait and both of you will see. My guess is that he will let her talk him into coming back into her life."

"Maybe," Tony said. "Time will tell on that one."

"I'm glad he's done this for now, but I don't expect it to last. She can't put herself through medical school," his father remarked dryly. "I do have leverage with her even if I don't with you."

"No, Sydney can't put herself through school, but I can help her," Tony said, savoring the moment. His father's head whipped around and his eyes narrowed.

"Damnation. You've already told her you would, haven't you?" He didn't wait for an answer. "So you nullified one of my immediate threats."

"Yes, I did, because I love my sister. And I'm not cutting her out of my life. You and Mom can spend your holidays together as you see fit. I'll see Sydney."

"I never thought I'd see this day. I knew it was possible. Especially these last few years when you've had success after success. Dammit, Tony."

Tony smiled and sat in silence, still reveling in his triumph, recalling dreams as a boy of moments like this.

"So you'll help Sydney. Therefore, my threats are losing their punch. No wonder she's not taking my calls. Dammit, Tony," he repeated.

"If you try to cause Sydney trouble when she graduates—and I imagine you will—all you'll succeed in doing is driving her to move away. You'll lose her completely—and any grandchildren she might give you. She is already looking into where she can live when she finishes school. The places she's considering are far from here."

"I have to hand it to you. I'm impressed. I never thought I would see the day you could successfully tell me what to do and I would have to think about doing it."

"Learned how from you," Tony remarked casually. Silence fell and Tony sat swirling the glass of wine he had barely touched. He let his father ponder the transfer of power.

"Well, it's a new concept to think I might have to back off. You know it's a notion I don't like. Your mother may be another matter. She doesn't want this young man in our family."

"Does she want Sydney in our family?"

"Of course she does."

"I'll repeat—if you keep this up, you two will never know your grandchildren. You'll cut Sydney out of your life. Dad, for years to come, I have no intention of getting tied up in the demands of marriage, so don't think I'll give you grandchildren. You better make that clear to Mom."

A muscle worked in his father's jaw. He clenched his fists and walked to the window to stare outside. As silence filled the room, Tony recalled Isabelle informing him that her goal was to marry by thirty and have children. Her goal would have nothing to do with him except make her reluctant to have an affair, but he expected to get beyond that easily. And soon.

Finally Grant turned around. "You present a good argument. I don't like it one damn bit, but I have to be proud of you. You've outfoxed me, Tony. I suppose I'll have to consider your suggestions. With your opposition, I assume I'll lose a lot if I keep Sydney from marrying this fellow."

"That's good news, Dad. Frankly, I think in years to come, the whole family will be much happier if you accept Sydney's choice."

"If this young man doesn't break Sydney's heart."

"If he does, she will have only herself to blame. Not you or Mom. I better go, but I'm glad you're at least listening. Sydney's your child. You two will really miss her if you go ahead with your threats."

"Even if I capitulate, I don't know that your mother will."

"She will if you talk her into it."

"Go celebrate your victory."

"It isn't a war, Dad," Tony said. "Sydney and I just want to live our own lives now. We're adults. It's time you let go a little."

"If you ever are a father, Tony, you'll understand."

"I hope to hell I learn to let go when any kids I might have reach adulthood, much less in their thirties," Tony said quietly, feeling the clash of wills. He saw the flash of fire in his father's eyes and red flooding his face. "Don't let thoughts of losing control cause your blood pressure to rise," Tony added. "Just let go a little and trust us to make good decisions. Sydney is plenty smart."

"This Dylan person knows nothing of how we live. No telling what kind of life he will give her. I hope you remember that when you look for a wife and get someone from your own kind of world."

"Dad, as far as Sydney is concerned, she has told you what she will do. I've told you no marriage for me for years. You and Mom have to decide what you'll do. We all live with our choices." Tony looked at his watch. "I've got to run. I'm meeting my friends for dinner."

Grant followed Tony across the room. "Think about Sydney, Tony. You may be helping your sister to lose a lot."

"Sure. I'll think about her." Tony left the room in long strides, already making a call by the time he reached the back door, thoughts of family forgotten as he talked to one of his vice presidents about the coming trip.

After he finished his call and drove away, images of Isabelle returned. What was she doing now? He was tempted to contact her, but he expected another business call soon. When he talked to Isabelle, he didn't want interruptions. He called his pilot to arrange to fly to San Diego next Friday. He would surprise Isabelle Friday evening. Next weekend couldn't come too soon.

Twenty minutes later he entered the country club where his family had had a membership since the club's founding. Crossing the thick red carpet in the darkened bar, he joined his closest friends, men he had known from childhood, Jake Benton and Nick Rafford, who greeted him. "Where's your brother?" he asked Jake.

"Gabe should be here any minute. We might as well get our table," Jake said as the two shook hands briefly.

Tony turned to Nick. "Thanks for coming. I know this takes you away from Michael and Emily, as well as Grace."

"Actually, Emily fell asleep early, and Michael will soon. With the kids asleep, my wife will probably be happy for some solitude."

It still surprised Tony that Nick and Jake were married. They had been as committed to bachelorhood as he was. Both men seemed wildly in love and happy with their wives. Nick amazed him the most because he now had two small children. He thought well of Grace, but he saw no plans for any kind of serious commitment in his own life.

As soon as they were seated at a large, linen-covered table, Nick reached into his blazer pocket. "I know you're a confirmed bachelor, Tony, and you're a newlywed, Jake, but you're both going to see Michael's and Emily's latest pictures."

As pictures were passed around of his toddler girl and son, who was almost two, Gabe Benton walked up to join them, sitting across from his older brother with the family resemblance showing in the firm jaws, straight noses, thick brown hair and startling blue eyes. Gabe stood out from the others because he was the only one wearing Western hand-tooled boots with his slacks and dress shirt. All of them paused when a waiter arrived to take their drink orders. As soon as they each had a glass of wine, Tony raised his. The others gave him their attention. "You look like the cat that ate the mouse," Nick remarked to Tony.

"I've already made arrangements with the maître d'," Tony stated. "This dinner goes on my account. We're celebrating because now we have all ended our controlling fathers' manipulations. Nick, you have because you gave your dad the grandchildren he wanted. Jake, you have because you married and settled, and Gabe, you have the good fortune to have escaped, thanks to your older brother."

"Amen to that," Jake said as he exchanged a look with Gabe, who grinned.

"So what's happened with you?" Nick asked Tony. "You just said all of us."

"That's right. I'm including myself. Dad has admitted he has to stop interfering with me," Tony said.

There was mild applause and low cheers. "I'm set to make

more money than he has—in short, I don't need his money, so I can do as I please and he has no leverage to use on me. Tonight he admitted it."

"Congratulations!" Gabe and Jake said together, as Nick reached out to high-five Tony.

"Way to go, Tony!" Nick said, raising his goblet. "Here's to freedom from interfering fathers."

"We'll all drink to that one," Jake remarked dryly. "Mine threatening to disinherit me if I didn't marry—that is the biggest interference of all."

Nick lowered his drink. "I think Tony's dinner should be on us." He paused while Gabe and Jake agreed. "We want to treat you because you've earned it. That's tremendous. Something the three of us have wanted since we were about nine years old."

"Younger than that," Tony remarked and the discussion momentarily ended while the white-coated waiter took their dinner orders.

"I figured we'd celebrate your acquisition of Morris. That's probably what turned the tables with your dad," Gabe said.

"He realizes he no longer has any hold. He can suggest, but not threaten. Unfortunately, now he's focused on my sister."

"Don't tell me that," Gabe said. "Our dad has always concentrated on Jake. I hope he doesn't switch to me. So far, he hasn't."

"I don't think he will," Jake stated. "No habit established. Your investments are going so well, Dad has to be impressed."

"I've never said a word to him about them," Gabe replied.

"I have," Jake said. "I've told him you're handling my personal investments and some friends' investments."

"That probably shocked him."

"Besides, you're the baby and they've always spoiled you," Jake said with good nature, and Gabe's smile widened.

"Don't think I haven't enjoyed it, brother," he said, and the others laughed.

"Will Morris pan out like you expected?" Jake asked Tony.

"Far better," Tony replied, thinking about Isabelle and wanting to cut the dinner short and call her. Tossed green salads were placed in front of them.

While they ate, Nick lowered his glass of water. "This is a monumental day. A time we've dreamed about and I began to never expect to have happen. I insist you let this dinner be on us," Nick continued. "You've accomplished the miracle with your dad and you recently hosted us at a tropical retreat because of the bet you won as the last holdout for marriage." Nick glanced at Gabe. "You would never even enter the bet, so your bachelorhood doesn't count."

"I know that. I didn't want any part of the bet."

"My tag-along brother won't think about marriage," Jake remarked.

"I have no regrets about my lack of participating in the bet," Gabe said.

"Besides, Gabe, you would have had a distinct advantage since you are younger than the rest of us."

"We insist, Tony, on buying dinner," Jake added. "Since we were little kids, all of us have dreamed and schemed to rein in our control freak fathers and we've finally succeeded."

"Thanks. It's a great feeling to finally get free and to best him. Don't ever put Michael in competition with you, Nick," Tony said, thinking about Nick's son.

"Don't worry," Nick said. "I don't think any of us will ever do that to our sons."

"Or daughters," Tony added with his own sister in mind.

All agreed. After dinner they left the dining room to go to a club lounge, where they sat and talked until ten. Finally, it was time to head home. Nick was parked the nearest to Tony and before they parted he turned to clasp Tony on the shoulder. "Congrats, again. I never thought we'd see this day come for all of us. When we were kids we never thought it would happen."

"I enjoyed myself tonight. Maybe a little guilty for doing so, but damn, it was satisfying to hear my father admit he couldn't try to run my life any longer."

"I know it was. With Jake and with me, it all ended peacefully—at least I assume it's ended. I feel sure my dad won't ever interfere again. Besides getting older, he's wound up in Michael and Emily, the grandkids he finally decided he wanted. Who knows with Jake and Gabe? You're in the clear now. Sorry your sister isn't."

"I hate it. I'll pay for medical school for Sydney and I'll see her on holidays, but I can't do anything if Dad goes ahead with his threat to cut her out of his will. I can share what I get, but she'll fight taking it."

"Don't worry about it now. Your dad may change. My life with my dad is so different. Sometimes I can't believe he's the same man."

"Actually, my dad doesn't give up easily. I expect him to think about our conversation and come up with a new threat, but he knows he's lost any real leverage. If I help Sydney, I think he'll threaten to cut my inheritance. I won't be in the least surprised."

"That doesn't worry you?" Nick asked.

Tony shook his head. "I don't like losing a huge fortune, but I'll get along without his money and so will Sydney. He can do what he wants. I'm doing what I want."

Nick shook his head. "I admire you for deciding to stick by your sister no matter what. If it comes to losing your inheritance, let her know what you're sacrificing."

"The realization that I'm free to live my life the way I want to is like freedom to someone who has been imprisoned for a lifetime. No way am I giving in to him. His fortune isn't worth yielding again."

"Maybe it will never come about. Gotta run. See you, Tony."

"Night, Nick. Thanks again for dinner. I really think all of you should have let me treat."

"Forget it. You earned it." While Nick walked to his car, Tony climbed into his.

Tony wanted to call Isabelle, but it was late. "To hell with it," he whispered, and pulled out his cell phone to make the call before driving. The minute he heard her voice, his pulse jumped. He wanted to be with her. Next weekend seemed eons away.

Isabelle planned to spend the week trying to finish projects carried over from Morris. Tony left town after the Monday morning staff meeting and she didn't expect to see him until the following Monday.

She worked until nine Monday before going home. To her surprise Tony called. Several times she started to end the call, but he would always draw her back into talking. In spite of her better judgment, he kept her on the phone for over an hour with his humorous stories about work and interesting conversation. When she finally ended the call, she stared at the phone, looked at her watch and shook her head. "Isabelle, you're losing it. Say no to him," she whispered in the empty room.

Tuesday night when she arrived home, she found a large heart-shaped basket with a mixed assortment of spring flowers on her doorstep. Smiling and shaking her head, she carried them inside to read a card that was simply signed, "Happy Valentine's, Tony."

He called a short while later. "Thank you for the gorgeous flowers."

"Happy Valentine's Day," he said. "Wish I could be there to take you out."

"I'll enjoy my flowers immensely."

"That isn't the reply I was hoping for."

"That's about as personal as it will get, Tony. We don't know each other all that well."

"I beg to differ," he said. "I remember clearly—"

"Stop right there," she said, laughing. "I walked into that one."

"I do wish I were there."

"I'm sure you could come home if you really wanted to," she said, amused because he owned the company and could get someone else to take his place. She glanced at her watch, remembering she was going to cut him short.

"You're right, probably. Maybe I micromanage. I hope to hell I don't though. My dad did enough of that when he ran the business before it passed on to me."

"Tony—" she said, starting to tell him goodbye.

"Tell me what you know about the new ad campaign that was started just before I stepped in. The one regarding the East Texas hotels."

She told him how the campaign was going, what her department had done. She was on familiar ground. Eventually talk shifted away from business and she listened to Tony as she kicked off her shoes and took down her hair.

"You can tell me all about the San Diego opening when I see you. That's a great town."

"I'm looking forward to it."

"Better than where I am in the frozen north. Now if I had you here to keep me warm—"

"Tony," she interrupted, smiling and feeling tingles in spite of trying to avoid them.

"I'm just telling you what's on my mind. It really isn't ad campaigns or hotels. I don't want you hanging up on me when I've waited all day to get to talk to you."

"I know better than that," she replied, remembering all the business calls he had taken the night they had been together. It was over an hour later when she finally ended the call. She stared at the phone a moment, thinking about him. She should firmly end the calls from him. Or even avoid them in the first place, because she had caller ID. She took the call tonight to thank him for the flowers he had sent. But once she was on the phone with him there was no hope of cutting it short, because he always talked her into listening or answering.

Flowers, phone calls, a terrific job so she would stay. Where was she headed with him?

Wednesday night Isabelle waited for her close friend, Jada Picard, a Morris attorney, for their plans to work out at their health club.

When Jada climbed into Isabelle's car, she shook short, straight black hair away from her face and turned gray eyes on Isabelle. "Sorry, I got delayed."

"It's fine. I did, too. I've just been in the car a minute or I would have driven to the door to pick you up."

"After the workout, let's go eat. You can pick the restaurant so we can also celebrate your new job with Ryder Enterprises. How was your dinner last week with our new boss?"

"I'll have to admit, it was a great evening."

"Now that he remembers who you are, I imagine you'll have more excellent evenings," Jada remarked.

"No, I won't." Isabelle stopped for a red light and glanced at her friend. "I'm not accepting another invitation from him. So far, he's been out of town and when he returns this weekend, I'm away on business in San Diego. I'm staying an extra day just to enjoy the city."

"You'll have a wonderful time. I love San Diego. When you return, I predict you'll go out with Tony again," Jada said.

"A relationship with Tony won't happen," Isabelle said, remembering his kisses and being held in his arms, not mentioning the flowers and phone calls.

"Sounds like it could easily happen."

Isabelle moved in traffic, keeping her eyes on the road. "No, it won't. He's not for me," she said, despite how she had been dazzled by his kiss and unable to forget him ever, still recalling the long-ago night in as vivid detail as the recent evening with him. "I just couldn't resist the invitation to celebrate and it was beginning to sound like a big deal if I refused to go out with him. Otherwise, it was nothing and I won't go out with him again," she stated, trying to convince herself that she could say no to him.

"Doesn't sound like 'nothing' to me," Jada remarked.

"He's not my type," she added. "Jada, we're both twenty-eight this year. We've both agreed we want marriage and a family. For me, the time has come. Our new boss definitely does not want marriage or a family to interfere with his ambition. He's already married to his work. Friday night he had calls all evening long."

"Calls are not a big deal. His not wanting to get married—there you may have a stumbling block."

"I promise you, the man's work comes far ahead of anything else in his life. He's every inch the workaholic. I don't ever want to tie my life to one of those. Growing up, I watched my best friend's dad live that way and her mom had to cope without him. He was practically a stranger to his family. That's not for me."

"Yeah, if you grew up around a workaholic, you know what it means."

"Lucy's dad never saw her at any of her games, at recitals, at anything. She had nicer things than I did and a fancier home, but she would have traded some of the comforts for having her father around. My family was really close and she saw that. She loved to come to our house and she told me that was one reason why."

"How sad," Jada said.

"The quality of life is important. Fortunately, Tony is supportive of his sister. Their parents are giving her grief over the man she's been seriously involved with. They don't think he's good enough for her. I've told you about him—my friend Dylan."

"I remember meeting Dylan. He's a nice guy with a good job. What kind of parents does Tony have? In spite of his looks and money, I'd say two strikes against Tony. A workaholic guy with a snobby family. Be careful."

"Don't worry. I've seen the last of evenings out with Tony Ryder."

"I'd still say to watch out. Sounds as if he might be a heartbreaker. He has the looks for it."

"That he does," Isabelle agreed, envisioning Tony's sexy dark brown eyes and his thick, curly hair. "Have you ever gotten your interview appointment with him?"

"Not yet, but I'm not anxious about it. I've got really good offers now," Jada said. "I won't mind moving on."

"That's the way I felt. Having a place to go makes the future look much rosier. I knew you would get some promising job offers," Isabelle said, turning into the fitness center parking lot. "I need this workout."

"So do I," Jada said, climbing out of the car and getting her things to walk inside with Isabelle.

Soon they were both running on treadmills and conversation was impossible. Then each moved on to other machines. After they had showered and dressed, they left to drive to an Italian restaurant.

In spite of the workout and Jada's company, Isabelle couldn't keep memories of Tony from distracting her.

After a leisurely dinner she dropped Jada off at the office parking lot, where Jada could get her own car.

"Thanks again, Jada. The dinner was delicious."

"Have a super time in San Diego. I'll see you next Monday. Bring back pictures."

"I intend to. I haven't had many trips."

Isabelle waited while Jada climbed into her car and then she drove home. As she unlocked her door, her cell phone rang. When she answered, she heard Tony's voice. With a racing heartbeat, she shook her head while she listened to him, even though each phone call involved her more deeply with him.

"How's my most beautiful vice president?"

"Tony! That is so politically incorrect," she chided with a smile.

"First of all, I'm talking to you. Secondly, this isn't a business call and you surely never considered it as such. Third, it's definitely the truth."

She laughed, unable to be annoyed or take the question seriously. "So for now this call is not one between an entrepreneur and his employee."

"Definitely not. A man calling a woman he wants to be with, take out, make love to…"

"Stop right there. You always move too fast," she complained breathlessly, imagining his dark eyes holding their seductive look, aware for this moment she had his full attention.

"Always? Is everything too fast?" he asked, changing her meaning and stirring memories of standing in his arms while he kissed her slowly and thoroughly. "I'll have to work on that one," he said as if talking to himself.

"You know not always and not everything," she replied, knowing she sounded even more breathless than before. "Sometimes I would describe you as slow and deliberate," she said in a sultry voice, drawing out her words and enjoying flirting with him in return, even though she knew better and even though he was far away and not as much a temptation.

She heard his intake of breath. "We *would* have hundreds of miles between us," he said in a thick, husky voice, echoing her thoughts.

"You began this," she replied sweetly. "Maybe we should talk about business. Or far more safe, end this call that I really never intended to take."

"Business is the last thing on my mind now," Tony replied. "I have appointments tomorrow or I'd fly home earlier. Unfortunately, I can't. Why wouldn't you take my call?"

"We're headed nowhere, Tony. This friendship should not be pursued for some basic reasons."

"A minute ago you were enjoying our conversation."

"It was nothing but harmless flirting that you started."

"Harmless is not a good description. You set me on fire."

"You brought it on yourself."

"I tried to call you earlier when I had a break in my meeting. I missed you."

"Sorry, I switched the phone to vibrate and had it in my purse. I worked out and then ate dinner with Jada, one of my friends from work. You probably don't know a lot of the people yet."

"I know some. Jada Picard, lawyer?"

"Right," she said, surprised and wondering how many of the employees he could identify and if he learned only the names of those he planned to retain.

"I'm glad you weren't working late again."

"You did," she reminded him.

"That's also different. If I can get out of here a little earlier tomorrow, I'm going to. Snow is predicted and I don't want to get snowed in."

"No danger on my Dallas to San Diego flight," she said. She kicked off her shoes and carried the phone to a favorite chair to sit and relax while she talked, taking her hair down and combing her fingers through it, promising herself she would end the talk in ten minutes as she glanced at her watch.

It was half-past twelve when she wondered why she couldn't bring herself to cut him short on his calls. Even though she wasn't seeing him, they were getting to know each other better with the long phone calls.

"Tony, I have to say good-night. I was only going to talk a few minutes. It's after midnight."

"So you're enjoying this call as much as I am. We have a great time together, Isabelle. Let me hear you admit it."

"Not now or tomorrow or anytime after that," she replied, laughing.

"Just wait, I'll prove it to you. Let me tell you how—"

"Good night," she interrupted and broke the connection, laughing again. "Unfortunately, Tony Ryder, you're right," she admitted to no one.

Before dawn Thursday she was at the airport, looking for her colleagues in the waiting area at the gate. Since joining Morris she had worked closely with Nancy and George and she looked forward to traveling with them.

It was easy to spot Nancy's red hair and tall George's thick, wheat-colored blond hair. As they waited for their flight to board, she listened to them talk about their kids, thinking about Tony's determination to avoid marriage, preferring his work to a family.

"Lucky you," George kidded her, "you slept peacefully last night while Nancy was up at three with one of hers and my Billy had a basketball game, then dinner, then homework which included a project he needed help with so I had four hours' sleep."

Isabelle smiled with them. "What was the trouble with Molly?"

"Nightmares. She's going through a stage," Nancy replied.

"That's one thing—it should be quiet in the hotel. Nancy and I have dreamed of the few hours we'll be the only one in our rooms and absolutely no demands after midnight," George said.

"Once we're free tonight, I'll bet both of you spend the evening calling home and talking to your families," Isabelle said, knowing they kept in close touch. Their smiles confirmed her statement.

"After a call home," Nancy said, "I'm taking a swim in the pool. We've seen a hundred pictures as they built the hotel and the pool looked gorgeous. Either of you want to join me, feel free to do so."

"I will," Isabelle said, thinking how much a swim would be welcome as a relief in her busy schedule.

While they flew, Isabelle went over appointments and

brochures, names of California people she would meet. When they came into San Diego she gazed eagerly at the blue ocean below. Her anticipation grew. She looked forward to this trip for several reasons, business and personal, thankful for the experience and excited to see the city, the hotel and the ocean.

It was an opulent hotel, with a glassed-in lobby that had glittering crystal chandeliers, a plush deep blue carpet and a waterfall that spilled into a pool made of black marble. They went to the VIP lobby to check in, then headed to their rooms.

She spent the rest of the day touring the hotel, meeting the hotel executives, attending a meeting with them and then having dinner and enjoying a reception that included some VIP guests from the area who got a preview before the next day's activities.

It was eleven when she returned to her suite from the pool. The luxurious suite opened onto its own beachfront. When Tony called, she settled in a chair on the deck, switching off the lights so she could see the whitecaps while they talked for the next two hours.

Later, in bed, she gazed into the darkness while she thought about seeing Tony again Monday. She fell asleep thinking about him and dreamed of him.

Friday, her schedule was booked and included a dinner with media people that ran until after nine. They finally broke up and people left the banquet room.

In her suite she changed to her swimsuit, slipping into a T-shirt, shorts and flip-flops. She headed up to the grand rooftop pool, stepping out onto a well-lit deck with a bar beyond the crystal blue pool. A man near the bar played a guitar, the music clear in the night air.

She put her things on a beach chair and slipped into the water. When she reached the opposite end she turned to see a man enter the area. Her heart missed beats as she paused breathlessly because Tony stood at the other end of the pool.

Five

She was shocked to see him. She watched as he walked along the side of the pool. Her gaze drifted over him, his broad, muscled chest covered with a mat of thick dark curls. His biceps bulged with muscles and his narrow strip of black swimsuit left the rest of him bare, reminding her too clearly of their night of love and his magnificent body.

Feeling hot even though she was in cool water, she continued her perusal. His legs were long, lean and muscled. When he reached the deep end, he jumped in to swim toward her. Her excitement heightened the closer he came until he stopped only inches away.

He combed his hair back with his fingers to get the curls away from his face. While he treaded water to stay afloat in the deep end, she held the side of the pool. Drops glistened on his broad shoulders and she was aware of every inch of him.

Even the spacious hotel pool seemed dominated by Tony, his dark gaze holding hers as if she were magnetized.

"This is a surprise," she said

"I intended it to be, although I didn't expect to find you in the pool."

"I love to swim, but get few chances. The pool is convenient, so I've been swimming both nights," she said, feeling giddy. "You flew here from Chicago?" she asked, still wondering if he had come to look at his newest hotel or if he had a more personal reason.

"By way of Dallas first," he said. "How was your day?"

"Successful. I think they'll have a terrific opening and between our publicity and the media interest, we should get dream coverage. If you came to talk to any of the media, they're scattered all over the hotel."

Tony smiled at her, his eyes dancing. "Isabelle, I didn't fly out here to talk to the media or the hotel people."

She drew another deep breath, finding the air had grown rarefied and she was having difficulty breathing. "You're not here for business?"

"No. That's handled by you and others. I don't have to."

"You may have wasted a trip," she said, seeing red flags of warning waving. He had circumvented her plan to avoid being with him again.

"I don't think so," he said. "We'll swim and then let's go have a drink. We can talk about it."

"Are you trying to complicate my life?" she asked.

"Not at all. You had planned a swim, so we'll swim. Want to race the length and back? You can call go."

Momentarily caught between consternation and excitement, she stared at him in silence until she realized he was waiting for an answer.

"I'll race you. Go," she said, splashing away from him and swimming with long strokes, aware he was beside her.

She relished the physical action, for a few moments trying to avoid thinking about the rest of the evening, yet she kept recalling the vision of him standing at the end of the pool, almost naked except for the strip of black, appealing, sexy, breathtaking.

She pushed herself while he was even with her until the return. Near the end of the pool she gave an extra spurt and beat him, bobbing up as he did.

"You win."

"You let me," she accused, smiling. "Do it again and stop holding back."

"I held back very little. You're a good swimmer. Especially if you haven't been swimming often this year."

"I haven't been in a pool since last July. Race again? For real?"

He smiled. "Sure. You call go."

"Go!" she exclaimed, plunging away from him and stretching herself. He stayed alongside her until they turned in the shallow end of the pool and headed back. Then he pulled away to win handily and wait for her while she swam up to him.

"You won easily as I expected. I concede. I suspect that last race was one of the few times you've allowed someone to beat you at something."

"You're saying I like to win," he said.

"Yes. You're competitive, perhaps controlling."

He hit the water with the palm of his hand, causing water to splash her. "Controlling—I don't want to be that. I've fought that all my life in my dad."

"All your life?" she asked, treading water. "Surely you exaggerate."

"Hardly," he remarked. "That's one thing that drives me to make money when I already have a fortune. If I have more than he does—or he sees I will have, he'll get off my back."

"I can't imagine," she said truthfully.

"It's getting to be less a problem," he said dismissively and she guessed he didn't care to discuss it further.

She broke away from him, swimming lazily, and he joined her as they swam leisurely together.

When she stopped, treading water, he faced her to slip his arm around her waist and pull her closer. Her heart thudded because he was warm, wet, touching in so many places, legs, arms. "Tony—"

"I missed you this week and I've wanted to see you," he said. His brown eyes were dark as night with desire in their depths. Her breathing became difficult again and her pulse raced as she placed her hands on his chest, feeling his heartbeat. She wanted to stop fighting him, to wrap her arms around his neck to kiss him. The attraction between them was mutual and strong, but she saw that as a swift road to disaster. Resistance to Tony was her only hope for avoiding entanglement, which meant heartbreak. Yet right now, she was captivated once again, unable to break away, too aware of his hands on her.

"I wasn't going to do this again," she whispered.

"You want to. I can see it in your eyes," he whispered. He leaned closer. Without thought, she turned her mouth up to him and then his lips were on hers, her mouth opening at the first hot touch of his tongue. Their bodies pressed more closely together and she could feel his hard muscles, his warmth, his masculinity.

Her heart pounded as she kissed him passionately, pouring herself into her kiss, letting go her resolutions. His warm fingers went beneath her swimsuit top, pushing it away as he cupped her breast in his large hand. His thumb played lightly over her nipple,

Pleasure, along with need, burst from his touch. Moaning with relish, she once again responded and gave herself to the moment. She ran one hand across his back, over his hard buttocks, down to his muscled thighs, remembering, discovering him all over again. Submerged in water couldn't cool her because his caresses kept her hot.

She let him for minutes and then wriggled back. "Tony, this isn't a private pool. There's a bar up here—"

"It's private now. I asked not to be disturbed. They're gone. This floor is closed except to us. The elevator is here and doesn't go again until I say so. We won't be disturbed."

She wasn't aware of her bikini top being removed, but she was conscious of his hands cupping both breasts, his thumbs playing with the small buds that were hard, responding to him. She moaned again with pleasure while sensations rippled from each caress. His hand pushed her legs apart and he stroked her inner thighs, his fingers moving beneath her suit to touch her intimately.

Clinging to him, she gasped, arching her back as she twisted against him. Her excitement soared. His thick rod pressed against her and she could feel his readiness.

It was an effort to summon the willpower to resist. "We have to stop. I don't want to cope with the complications this will bring," she said, gulping air.

He opened half-lidded eyes to study her while his hands on her waist raised her slightly out of the water. Her breasts were bare, her top gone. Just his heated gaze on her was a caress that made her ache for his loving.

He pulled her nearer. "Wrap your legs around me," he said in a husky voice. His mouth closed on her nipple with his tongue stroking her.

Wrapping her legs around his warm body, she sighed with pleasure while he lavished kisses on her breasts, first one and then the other.

As he lowered her and kissed her hard, his tongue went deep. She was drowning in passion and complications. She wanted him, yet it would mean disaster in her life and possibly her career.

"We have to stop now," she finally told him, swimming away from him and looking for her top. She found it floating at the edge of the pool. While she pulled it on with her back to him, he swam up to her to kiss her nape.

She turned to him. "Let's get out and go have that drink."

His dark eyes devoured her, making her heart hammer even when she tried to resist reaching for him. She was telling him one thing, wanting another badly.

"Sure," he said, turning to swim away to climb out on the other side of the pool.

Trying to remember the reasons she should withstand his appeal, she swam after him. Now she knew why she had succumbed so easily that college night. He had turned on the charm at the party, his later kisses and seduction impossible to resist.

He waited beside a lawn chair with a navy towel wrapped around his waist. She climbed out, aware of his steady gaze on her, knowing he was still aroused, ready for love and wanting her.

Every inch of her tingled and her pulse still raced. She pulled on a T-shirt and stepped into her shorts, conscious of Tony's fiery attention.

He embraced her. "I want you, but I know how eager and passionate you can be when you lose your reluctance. I'll wait because I want you that way, with no worries about consequences, wanting to love as much as I do. I remember our night together."

She suffered both relief and disappointment with his declaration. He kissed her again and she couldn't hold back. Even though she was on fire with need, she wasn't going to go into a relationship that could tear up her world. If only she could hold to that stance.

Later, she stopped him. "I want to dress and then I'll meet you for that drink."

"Let's go. I'll walk you to your suite and wait while you change. Unless I can help."

Her head snapped around and then she smiled, realizing he was teasing, perhaps trying to lighten the moment between them.

"You can go to my suite with me and wait, but I don't need your help. Or you can go change and I'll meet you."

He nodded, smiling at her, but his eyes still burned with longing, keeping the tension high. "Meet me in the lobby. How long?"

"Give me half an hour."

He nodded. They had reached her door and she unlocked it.

He gazed at her with desire. "I'll see you in thirty minutes."

She closed the door and hurried to shower and dress while her thoughts spun. Still surprised that he had flown to San Diego just to see her, the past hour replayed in her thoughts. He wanted an affair. Physically, she wanted the same. She was attracted to him, more than to any other man she had known, yet Tony would be the most disastrous man to become entangled with no matter how she viewed their relationship or the scenarios she played out in her imagination. She wanted marriage. Tony didn't. Even without marriage, she didn't want to give her heart to a man whose deepest love was his work. A thorough workaholic, Tony was driven to make money. She didn't want any kind of intimate relationship with a man whose thoughts were on his work most of the time. A man whose work came first always. It was a simple situation, but a resolution wasn't easy.

As Isabelle stepped out of the shower, she continued to weigh her options. Have an affair, maybe he would fall in love. For over hundreds of years, how many women had fooled themselves with that reasoning?

She dried her hair and began to dress in a conservative navy blouse and slightly flared matching skirt.

An affair would put off chances of meeting someone who had marriage in mind. An affair with Tony would complicate her life at work. He didn't seem to think so, but he owned everything. It was his company. Even if he succumbed to marriage, he didn't want a family and she did and therein was the strongest reason of all to keep Tony out of her life.

There was no happy solution in a relationship with him except the satisfaction of lust.

Go have the drink, let him politely know his trip was for nothing and get him out of your life, she told herself. She gazed at her reflection in the mirror as she twisted her hair to clip it on top of her head. There would be no politely brushing aside a man as dynamic and determined as Tony. So far, she wasn't getting the message across to him at all.

She looked at herself, hoping she looked poised, cool, reserved. By this time Sunday night she would be back in Dallas and, hopefully, she and Tony *would* part ways except at work.

All the way to the lobby, she kept telling herself to keep their time together short and then go her separate way. Her lips still felt his kisses, as well as his hands on the rest of her. She couldn't forget and there was nothing easy about dealing with him. Right now, her heartbeat raced, because in minutes she would be with him again.

When she entered the lobby he was waiting. His knit shirt and chinos were casual. The look in his eyes was not. Passion was a flame still detectable.

Her heart jumped as she smiled at him. He took her arm to steer her toward the elevators.

"I'm still surprised you flew out here."

"I'd hoped you would be," he said as they went to a small bar on the ground floor of the hotel. A few couples danced to piano music. Tony found a table in a corner. After they had ordered drinks, he held her hand to dance.

The moment they touched, her heartbeat sped up. "This is better," Tony said, pulling her closer. "I've wanted you in my arms and I've waited all week. Isabelle, I've found you again and I don't want to let you go."

"You're going to have to let go," she said as she looked up at him, his words giving her a thrill even as she denied them. His face was shadowed because of the dim lighting, but she could see his expression was solemn.

"Don't say that when we have fire between us. More than that. The first night was magical. You can't deny it."

"No, but that night was long ago. There's no future between us. I don't want an affair and you don't want to get married. When you're talking marriage and children, Tony, then we can spend long evenings together, kiss, see if there really is more than lust between us."

"You're young, Isabelle. You don't have to settle down and become a mother yet. You have years ahead."

"I know what I want."

"You say that to me, but when you kiss me, you tell me something entirely different," he said. "You can't deny it."

She wanted him to kiss her right now. She was fighting herself as much as she was Tony. She stopped thinking and just danced with him, relishing being held and holding him close, moving with him, inhaling the scent of him, clean, soapy, an appealing aftershave, his fresh shirt. Her arm was on his shoulder, her hand at the back of his neck. The vision of him getting out of the pool, muscles rippling, added to her smoldering hunger.

The music changed to a fast rhythm and when she danced facing him, longing intensified. Every twist of his lean body, his heated expression and the sexy twists he made revved up her sensual responses. His impact on her was heightened by the dance and by his concentration on her, which made her feel wanted beyond measure. Black curls fell over his forehead, transforming his appearance from the shrewd all-business entrepreneur to a sexy man filled with a zest for life.

Prudence and wisdom faded, becoming dim voices, melting beneath a burning sun of desire that threatened to consume her caution.

He spun her around and when she turned to face him again, he took her hand to pull her close against him, pausing in the dance.

She couldn't breathe or think. Her heart pounded. Longing suffused her, bringing with it erotic images. Immobilized, she stood pressed against him, forgetting where they were or that anyone else was near. She heard only her pounding heart and, faintly in the background, music. Tony's dark eyes held her captured as completely as his arms around her.

His appeal caused barriers to crumble. She wanted him and it was impossible to stop her reaction.

They were on the dance floor, not moving, lost in each other and forgetting the world, Tony seeming to as much as she. She stepped away and he released her. The music ended and she moved farther from him, yet he still held her hand.

A tango commenced and Tony pulled her, placing his hand on her waist to dance.

She fell into step with him, watching him steadily as they moved across the floor to a dance she always found to be sensual, filled with sexy moves when shared with the right partner.

"You've done this before," he remarked.

"So have you," she said, realizing they were both at ease and familiar with a tango.

"Who taught you the tango?" he asked.

"More a where than a who. I took dance lessons the first two years I worked. I wanted the exercise. Growing up, I had always wanted dance lessons, but my family couldn't afford them. I got a book at the library and tried to teach myself. Actually, I didn't do too bad a job with it. Who taught you?" she asked lightly, curious who had been in his life before she knew him.

"When I was about eleven years old my folks sent me to a cotillion program where I was taught the tango, waltz, lots of dancing, etc. My friends all had to go and we learned manners, as if they were not drummed into me at home. Try placing books under your arms while you eat to learn to keep your elbows off the table. That one was at home. Anyway, it was long ago, like other things in my past, but definitely not forgotten."

His last remark referred to their meeting. He didn't have to say it because she knew from the change in his tone.

They stopped talking, giving themselves over to the dance and to gazing into each other's eyes.

The tango heightened her erotic fantasies. By the time the dance ended, lust was primal. Tony had beads of sweat on his forehead. "I think we came in here for a drink," she reminded him, not caring about the drink but wanting to stop the sexy dancing that heightened tension with each step she took.

"So we did," he said, wiping his forehead with his handkerchief. He took her arm and they returned to their table, where their drinks awaited.

In moments a waitress appeared to take their orders for appetizers. As soon as they were alone, he focused on her. "I've missed you and thought about you all week."

"Nothing is fair about this, Tony, including you and your flirting."

"Let's just enjoy the evening. I know you can. You're all bottled up, fighting yourself and your inclinations because of some imaginary calendar in your life."

"Are you through analyzing me?" she asked, becoming annoyed, wondering whether her irritation was directed at herself or at Tony.

Tony raised his martini. "Here's to finding you again, Isabelle."

Even though she had a spectacular raise and new position, she didn't want to drink to Tony finding her again, yet she raised her piña colada. "To the future, Tony."

They touched glasses and he watched her as she sipped.

"I know the Jessie I spent the evening with years ago is sitting across from me. I'm just trying to figure out how to get her back. I never did forget. I just let go."

"That doesn't matter now. The night you came to see the Morris building, my unfriendly manner was because you bought him out."

"I think in the new position you have, I've made amends regarding the buyout upheaval. As of tonight, your work here is done. You're staying an extra day. Let me show you around. There's no harm in that."

She smiled at him. "Hopeless, hopeless. Your arguments are persuasive. So are your hands and your eyes," she added in a softer voice, and saw him inhale deeply. "All right, Tony, I'd love to have you show me around. Against all better judgment, I'm going to get to know you up close and personal. You don't take no well, do you?"

"Depends on how much I want something," he said. "Also, cancel your plane trip home. You can tell Nancy and George. I'll take you back tomorrow night with me."

"You assume I would prefer this," she said, amused and giving him a look. She was sinking and losing her battle and it was her own fault. If only he weren't so appealing and trying so much to charm her.

One dark eyebrow arched. "You want to fly back commercially instead of with me on my private jet? That will hurt."

"No, I'm delighted to fly back with you. It's just your assumption that I will want to. I think you've had your way far too much in your life."

"I'll have to admit, you've been a big challenge, but an enticing, delightful one."

"Thank you, even though being a challenge to you was never my intention. I just want to move on with my life." She sipped the cool piña colada, aware he still held her hand and continued to brush her knuckles with his thumb. She should pull away, but his touch was casual and she was tired of picking tiny fights with him.

"I seem to be losing the battles, though," she said.

"Good. I'm glad you perceive it that way. And this is much better. Now I'm happy I flew here. For a moment there, I thought I would have to turn around and go back."

"I don't believe you considered giving up for even two seconds," she said, and one corner of his mouth raised in a crooked smile. "And you do move fast," she continued. "I'm flying home with you. You're holding my hand now, plus I'm spending my free time with you. I'd say you're getting your way on a steady basis. For someone I intended to get out of my life, you're pretty well in it."

He leaned closer over the small table.

"One thing that didn't happen that night we met—I didn't get to know you. I can start making up for that now. You're a swimmer and you like dancing and art. What else is in your life?"

As he leaned back again, he continued to hold her hand, stroking the inside of her wrist with his thumb, light strokes she tried to ignore. His fingers had their effect on her, continually fueling desire, a constant reminder of the physical attraction between them.

"I work out at a fitness center, but otherwise, my job takes up most of my time."

"I read your résumé, so I know you grew up in Dallas, went to Tech on scholarships, have a stellar scholastic record and were on the high school debate team."

She held his gaze. "Your facts are correct," she said, surprised he had delved into her background. "All that education was for a purpose. I grew up in a blue-collar family. My folks sacrificed for us. Mom sometimes worked two jobs. Dad sometimes did. From early on I planned to do better and get out of that struggle. I aimed for college from the time I was young. In some ways, I was also determined to succeed. Just not on your grand scale."

"I'd say you've already succeeded."

"I know a bit about you, too. Your history is in the media. Golden boy, born into wealth, old Texas family, on football teams, excellent grades, enormously successful on your own. Not exactly similar lives."

"They say opposites attract. In some ways we're opposites. There were some similarities, too. We both had goals and set out to achieve them."

She laughed. "I'd say we're opposites in almost every way except wanting to succeed at work. Even there, you're far more driven than I am. That is your be-all and end-all, your major focus."

"There are plenty of times my attention is not on business. Right now it's on a beautiful woman. I want to get to know you, make love to you, discover what you like. You'll be more than a memory in my life."

"That promises giant complications."

"But, oh, such delightful ones," he said in a husky voice.

"Tony, stop flirting. Just talk."

"Flirting is far more fun," he replied, and she shook her head.

"Tony—ordinary conversation. Unless you want this evening to end earlier. Tell me your favorite things that do not involve women or your work," she requested, thinking she would steer the conversation to safer, more bland topics.

"Afraid of flirting and where it will lead?"

"I'm just dying to hear you tell me some of your favorites and your preferences," she said in a mocking, exaggerated accent, making him smile.

"Favorites and not involving women or work. I'd have to dig deep there and go back in memory. Way back."

"Surely not," she replied, laughing at him. She sipped her drink while they talked and she lost all track of time with him. The night was forever even while it seemed to be going with the speed of light.

"There's a good song," he said, glancing at the dance floor, which held a few couples who moved to a slow ballad. "Let's dance."

On the dance floor when his arms circled her waist, he leaned close. "Put your arms around me," he whispered.

She wrapped her arms around his neck, barely moving as they swayed to the music. She felt his hands in her hair and then a lock tumbled free. Faint tugs against her scalp as other locks tumbled around her shoulders. She knew there was no use trying to stop him and it wasn't that important. Finally it all fell freely around her face.

When he leaned back to study her, he dropped the pins into his pocket.

"There, that is infinitely better."

"Still changing things to suit yourself."

"Yes, because you're even more gorgeous with your hair unpinned," he whispered in her ear again. He combed his fingers through her hair while he gazed at her with satisfaction. "There. If you had looked like this that first night in your office, I would have known. You're beautiful," he whispered. "You take my breath when I look at you and remember loving you."

How would she ever continue to resist him? It didn't help to have him constantly conjuring up memories of their night of love.

He released her slightly and danced her around the floor.

His total attention, his charm and his flirting all combined to create an illusion that work was not his driving focus. For tonight, he made her feel as if she were the center of his world, absolutely necessary for his happiness. How easily he conveyed the conviction that she held his complete interest. It was flattering, mesmerizing, seductive. She tried to cling to the knowledge that he was pursuing what he wanted tonight, but Monday, his thoughts would be on business and her importance to him would diminish. Beneath his onslaught of attentiveness, it was a losing struggle to stay grounded in reality.

"Holding you in my arms is perfect. I don't want to let you go," he said in a low, husky voice. "Admit you like this, Isabelle."

She opened her eyes to look up at him as they swayed to the music. "You know I do without hearing me say it," she said, and he drew a deep breath. She liked it far too much and could dance in his arms the rest of the night. Tony was magic to her, weaving an irresistible spell.

"Let's go to my suite. We can sit and talk if that's what you want." The offer hung in the air. He sounded casual, offhand about the invitation, yet once again she felt this was the moment to say no. She needed to stop the relationship before it ever started, to avoid it altogether. This was an opening to end whatever this was with Tony.

Why was he so irresistible to her? The man wanted to become a billionaire in less than ten years. She wanted to be married and have a family even sooner. They had clashing goals and if she tangled her life with Tony's she would get hurt and delay or even destroy all hope of the family she sought.

She met his dark gaze, knowing he was waiting for an answer while she was torn between yes and no.

Six

"Let's go to my suite. It's just to sit and talk," he repeated.

"That's exactly what I want, Tony. We can do that right here at our table or while we dance."

"I want you all to myself."

"That goes against all good judgment."

"It won't be anything more than you want it to be. C'mon, Isabelle. It isn't a monumental, life-changing decision. One evening. I'll take you to your suite whenever you want. I just want to be with you a while longer."

"Tony, it goes against all good judgment," she said again, sighing. "Why can't I resist you?"

He leaned close. "We can't resist each other. How many other women do you think I've wanted to spend time with when I know their goal in the immediate future is marriage? You're not the only one who knows better yet can't resist."

Surprised, she studied him. She hadn't thought about their relationship from his perspective. Her goal should send him running, but it hadn't. His remark shook her.

"All the more reason—" she began.

"Shh, Isabelle." He looked her in the eyes. "Live dangerously, as the old saying goes. Spend another hour or two with me."

He brushed a light kiss on her lips. "C'mon with me. You can leave whenever you want."

"Tony." She sighed, shaking her head. "You are a spellbinding man." How many times in her life did she get to spend evenings like this one? She told herself she would just stay a short time.

"Good. Just for a while longer together," he said, smiling and taking her hand as they left.

They took the elevator up one floor and stepped out into a short hallway. He unlocked and held open a door. She entered a suite larger and even more luxurious than her own. From a small entryway, they walked into a spacious living area that held one wall of floor-to-ceiling glass and a staircase to a ground level extension of the room. Through the glass she could see whitecaps. "The view from here in the day must be spectacular."

"I think the view is sensational right now," Tony said in a husky voice, and her cheeks flushed. Desire filled his dark gaze. "I'll build a fire," he said.

She watched as he hunkered down to stack logs in the fireplace and ignite kindling. In minutes he had a roaring fire and she moved toward it. With sundown the temperature had dropped, the air had chilled and now the fire's welcome warmth felt cozy.

A light knock on the door surprised her. She watched while Tony greeted a waiter who wheeled in a cart with a drink and two beers on ice, as well as a bottle of wine on ice. After tipping the waiter, Tony closed the door behind him.

"Before we left the bar I ordered another piña colada for you since you barely touched yours and left it behind in the bar," he said as he brought her drink to her.

"Thank you."

Turning off the lights so they had only the orange glow from the blazing fire, he opened a cold beer for himself and led her to a sofa near the fire. "Sit here and we'll talk." He sat close, turning so he faced her, winding his fingers in her hair while he sipped his beer. "Now tell me about yourself," he said. "Tell me about your family."

For a moment the only sound was the crackle and hiss of the fire. The more details about her life she shared with him, the closer she would be drawn to him and the more deeply she might fall in love with him. His dark eyes were on her and she had his undivided attention. He made everything that involved him too tempting to resist.

"I have two older brothers, a younger brother and a younger sister. In that order they are Josh, Talbot, Trent and Faith. Only Faith is married. There are no grandchildren."

"Any other graphic artists in the family?"

"No. Josh is an accountant in Fort Worth. Talbot has his own construction company in Denton, Trent is a professor at a community college here and Faith is a teacher in Plano. Everyone is in the Dallas area, so we have family get-togethers fairly often." While she talked, he combed his fingers through her hair, so slight, yet still heightening her response.

"My family gets together for some holidays. Sometimes one or another or all of us are scattered because we're traveling," he said.

"What about when you were children?"

"Especially when we were children. We weren't traveling, but our parents often were," Tony replied, caressing her nape, feathery strokes that had a deeper effect and were more sensual. "Do you know a man named Dylan Kinnaly?"

"Yes, I do," she replied, and she hoped he would talk about what he had done for his sister. She had to admire him for that and she wouldn't mind telling him.

"I thought you might through your graphic arts connections. My sister wants to marry him. Dylan is an okay guy and also,

I think my sister knows what she wants. She seems deeply in love."

"He is more than an 'okay guy.' Dylan's a close friend. I think a lot of him."

"That reaffirms my feelings about him. My sister is level-headed. At least she usually is. People in love see the world in a skewed manner."

Isabelle smiled at him. "Don't sound so cynical about people who fall in love."

"Show me someone in love who can think consistently in a clear, rational manner, particularly where the loved one is involved. You won't be able to find anyone. I just see reality."

"No, you don't," she said with a smile. "You're cynical, Tony, when it comes to love."

"Love makes the world go round," he said in a husky voice, and lifted her hair off her shoulders and neck while he leaned close to brush a warm kiss on her nape, stirring a wave of sparks.

"I've met your sister," she said without thought. Her attention was on Tony, his kiss, the faint caresses on her nape, all creating sparks.

"You knew Sydney after you met me or before?"

"I met her afterward. It was a film festival held at one of the local museums. We talked a little because we both are fans of old films. Since then, I've seen her several times with Dylan at graphic arts celebrations or parties. Dylan and I are both members of a Dallas graphic artists' group."

"All this time, Sydney knew you and where to find you? Damn. Why didn't she tell me about you?" His eyes narrowed. "You didn't tell her that you knew me, did you?"

"I didn't see any point in it," she admitted. She would never tell something that might hurt feelings, but she suspected Tony had little experience with rejection from women, and his total self-confidence would keep any hurt feelings from happening.

He studied her with an intense stare. "You really didn't want to see me again?"

"That night was in the past. Since I didn't hear from you, I didn't see any reason to pursue it. You didn't call, come see me—there was no contact. That means you didn't want to see me again. I assumed I would never cross paths with you again. That weekend was magical. Actually, you really charmed me and I had a wonderful time. You brought out a wild side in me that I hadn't shown before or since."

He inhaled deeply. "How I wish I had known all that after our night together. I would never have stopped trying to get back with you. You sound as if you had regrets. I didn't, Isabelle," he stated quietly.

"Not regrets. When you didn't call, I just saw no point in pursuing something that was finished. I've seen occasional pictures of you with society women. You didn't ever call me, so why would I think you'd want to see me?" He slipped his fingers into her hair again. "It no longer matters," she added.

"I just would have found you sooner. How did you get into graphic arts?"

"I've always wanted to pursue graphic arts. I hope to have my own business at some point."

"That may be difficult with all your plans for a family."

"I see my own business as something happening far into the future. At this time in my life, it's just a dream. I've loved my work at Morris."

"I hope you continue to like it. You should, because you have your own department and a lot of authority."

"I'm looking forward to that part of the job and to having my same staff with me."

The corner of his mouth raised in a crooked smile. "So what part are you not looking forward to?"

She smiled in return. "Dealing with my supervisor and trying to keep business and my private life totally separate. So far, I'm failing to do so."

"We're doing pretty well at keeping it separate. Nothing about business has interfered with us tonight."

"You're learning about me. Tell me about you. Other than business, what's in your life in addition to the few things you've mentioned already?"

"When I have time, I play basketball with my friends. I play polo. Travel, swim, play golf. Attend the symphony, the opera. Attend charity balls."

"With your work schedule, I'd say you're spread pretty thin," she remarked, doubting he did half the things he listed on a regular basis. "I think your key words were, 'When I have time.'"

"I make time for the important things. Such as this weekend. This was top priority, definitely," he said, rubbing strands of her hair against his cheek.

"You could have clued me in."

"Would have spoiled the surprise."

"So did all your family get together for this past Christmas holiday?" she asked, wondering what the holidays were like in the Ryder mansion.

"No. My sister went with Dylan to his family's celebration in Waco—not too far. My folks flew to Paris with friends. I went skiing in Switzerland." He glanced at her. "You're looking at me like someone might look at Scrooge."

"Not Scrooge. I guess I just feel sorry for you. I can't imagine a holiday without family."

"You could imagine it if you knew my family. My parents fight when they're home. If they're out doing something, traveling, with friends, then they're okay. Otherwise, they're not the most fun to be around. Plus Dad always has an agenda where Sydney and I are concerned. Until this year. He's backed off trying to manage my life and is now focused on my sister."

"I'm sorry, Tony. I can't conceive of that. Our family times are great fun. I will invite you to go with me to the next big family gathering and you'll see what I'm talking about."

"I look forward to meeting your entire family," he said, but she couldn't believe that he would actually accept such an invitation. She doubted he went home to visit his own family very often. Particularly if his sister wasn't going to be there.

"I'll tell you now—I'm not sure I'd know how to behave in one of those folksy Christmases you see in old movies."

"Then I do feel sorry for you," she said, patting his hand, and he smiled.

"That's a first. I have a lot of firsts with you. You have a few with me."

Her gaze flew to his and they both remembered their night of love when she lost her virginity.

He rubbed his cheek again with locks of her hair. "Temptation," he whispered, his dark gaze on her. "I can't tell you what you do to me. I missed you this week. I'm not even thinking straight. I lose my train of thought at work, something that's never happened before."

Her heart pounded with his confession. She was amazed she had that effect on him. "You're not thinking rationally because of me?" she couldn't resist asking, remembering his description earlier about people in love.

"Don't sound so delighted. No, I'll admit I'm not. Thursday night, I got locked out of my hotel room in the dead of night. After we finished our phone conversation, I stepped out to get more ice and came back to a locked room."

She had to laugh and he grinned. "I got a key from a clerk. You're driving me to distraction, Isabelle."

"I don't believe it, Tony. You're a walking business machine. You're focused on business, living it twenty-four/seven most of the time. You've done a phenomenal job this year, increasing your fortune tremendously."

"Believe me. I'm distracted," he said. "I catch myself lost in thought about you." Each confession placed a tighter hold on her heart. Wisdom told her not to give him credence, yet her heart raced that she was ruffling his ordered, driven lifestyle.

"I don't think as clearly, and locking myself out of my room was a first and totally unlike me," he said, setting his cold beer beside him and turning to her.

"I wish I was having as much influence on you."

She smiled. "I wouldn't tell you if you were," she whispered, more aware of his intent than their conversation. She wanted to close her eyes and raise her mouth for his kiss. She wanted to be in his arms. The culmination of the sexy swimming, dancing and flirting was taking its toll. Just like his effect on her the night they met, his charm, attention and flirting demolished her resolutions and made her behave out of character.

Tony took her drink from her hands and set it on the table.

"Tony…"

He leaned the short distance between them and kissed her, silencing her protest.

Her insides heated while passion overrode all else. She wrapped her arm around his neck and kissed him back. They had been headed for seduction from the moment she had emerged from the depths of the pool and discovered him standing at the far end.

"No seduction, Tony," she whispered as if trying to remind herself to be cautious. Even as she said the words, she showered light kisses on his ear while her hands sought the buttons of his shirt and unfastened them.

"Fair enough," he whispered, peeling away the navy blouse that he had already unbuttoned.

Torn with mixed emotions, losing an inner battle with herself because desire had built to an overwhelming level, she was tossing aside her resolutions. Even though her actions fought her life goals, she had wanted to kiss and caress him since she had watched him plunge into the pool. Now she could yield to impulses that had been storming her senses. As she trailed kisses from his shoulder down to flat male nipples, she ran one hand through chest hair, feeling tight curls against her sensitive palm. Her other hand pushed away his shirt and then caressed his smooth, muscled back. Every touch and kiss, every minute in his arms took her further from her hopes, yet now, tonight, she wanted Tony more than dreams.

She kissed him slowly, tongues intertwined. Always, his kisses were magical, hot, making her want more of him. Mistake upon mistake to say yes, yet she didn't want to resist. Conflicting feelings continued to war. For a few moments she would shut them out and give and take what she wanted. There was still time for no. But for a little while tonight she wanted to live in the present. She could go back to dreams and goals tomorrow.

He slipped off her bra and cupped her breasts while he kissed her. Sensations rocked her. Touching and being touched, again exploring his muscled body. He picked her up easily as he kissed her and set her on his lap, cradling her head against his shoulder, holding her with his arm around her while his caresses heightened passion.

His hand slid beneath her skirt along her bare leg, moving to her inner thigh, light strokes that built the fire already raging. Removing her skirt, he moved her legs apart to pull away her tiny thong and toss it aside. When he caressed her intimately, she arched beneath his touch, gasping with pleasure as she gripped his shoulder. "Tony," she whispered.

Her eyes were squeezed closed while he showered kisses on her breasts, taking her nipple in his mouth. Sensations bombarded her more than ever, driving her to a deeper need.

"Tony," she cried, turning to sit astride and face him. She leaned forward to kiss him while she unbuckled his belt and pulled it away, opening his slacks. Knowing each kiss, caress, move was taking her into deeper involvement, she felt caught in a passionate whirlwind, wanting to never stop, to drive him over a brink of control.

She caressed him until he groaned and held her tightly by her shoulders. Drawing a deep breath, she looked into his brown eyes, to see unmistakable hunger hot and blatant. "A few more minutes, Tony, and then we stop."

"Whatever you want," he whispered while he kissed her between words. His mouth covered hers and he held her tightly against him. Still astride him, she wrapped her arms around his neck.

His hands were everywhere, his mouth taking her kisses. Time and problems didn't exist. Tony overwhelmed all else. Still kissing, he shifted her, placing her on the sofa and coming down on top of her, his thick rod, hot, hard against her.

"I've wanted this," he whispered. "I've dreamed of making love to you," he added, showering kisses, his hand moving between her legs.

His words reminded her of his determination to seduce her, and his hand moving on her intimately was carrying them beyond stopping. Did she want to become Tony's lover? That question cooled her. "Tony," she whispered. "Tony, wait," she said, making an effort to break away, to end the folly. "I can't go on. I'm not ready for this."

He stared at her as if he couldn't fathom what she was telling him. Then he moved away to look at her.

"You're gorgeous. You take my breath. I want to love you again. I remember that night in the smallest detail. I want you, but when we love, I want you to desire it and tell me and show me." All the time he talked, he kissed her lightly and caressed her while she continued to touch him. "The loving was fantastic, Isabelle. I'll wait because that's what I want from you—all your passion."

His words seduced as much as his kisses and caresses. Words

to shake her with wanting him. Words and promises she would never forget and spend hours longing to have happen.

"I can't," she said, moving past him, aware he watched her as she gathered her clothes. He caught up with her, his arm circling her waist, pulling her back against his heated body and thick rod, holding her against him while he stroked her nape with his tongue and his other hand went around her to play with her breasts.

She cried out in pleasure, clinging to his arm, wanting to stop him while hoping he would continue.

"Let me dress. I have to now," she gasped, the words barely audible as her pleasure heightened and her resolve wavered.

"We'll make love, Isabelle. You want to far too badly to keep saying no."

"I want marriage, Tony. You don't. It's that simple. You want to make your billion dollars." She lashed out in the only way she knew would stop both of them.

He stilled and she moved away, gathering her clothes, pulling them on hastily.

He yanked on his clothes swiftly, taking her hand as soon as she was dressed.

She looked up in surprise, thinking he would want her to say good-night.

"Stay and talk. You're good company."

"Always invitations from you that I know I should refuse. Instead, I accept. Talking is almost as dangerous as kissing."

"Not quite," he said, giving her a crooked smile. "Talk is nothing. I talk with Myrtle at great length because she's good company, but that doesn't make it a dangerous pastime."

Isabelle had to laugh. Myrtle Wrightman was the oldest Morris employee, hired by another generation of Morrises. She was an accountant and still sharp and witty and she enjoyed her job.

"That's better," Tony said, smiling at Isabelle. "I like to hear you laugh."

"I'm glad you've found Myrtle and you like her. You do intend to keep her, don't you?"

"Certainly. She's an icon. She does a good job from what I've seen. I wouldn't think of letting her go. Actually, I recommended she get a raise because she hasn't had one in a while."

"I should have qualified my statement and said 'talking to you is almost as dangerous as kissing,'" Isabelle said, sitting in a corner of the sofa, seeing another side of Tony that earned more of her respect for him.

"Want something else? There's a fridge in this suite and it's stocked with drinks and snacks. How about popcorn and cocoa and I'll toss another log on the fire. You don't have to be anywhere in particular in the morning."

"Sounds good, Tony. Let me help."

She followed him to the tiny kitchen and in a short time they sat in front of the fire with popcorn and mugs of steaming hot chocolate while they talked.

As they went from topic to topic without mentioning business, the fire burned to smoldering embers. Finally Isabelle stood. "I have to go. The sun will be coming up in a few hours."

He stood, draping an arm across her shoulders. "I'll see you to your suite—or you can stay here. Either bedroom."

She smiled at him. "I better go to my own suite."

As they headed to her room, he said, "I'll meet you for breakfast unless you want to swim first with me."

"I'll meet you for breakfast," she said, remembering the hot, sexy moments in the pool.

"Great. And after, I'll give you the deluxe tour of San Diego, although I can think of more fun things to show you."

"San Diego is what I really want to see."

At her door, she turned to him. "Thanks, Tony, for a fun evening. I have to admit, I'm glad you flew out here."

"Ah, that makes it all worthwhile," he said. He slid his arm around her waist and kissed her. She put her arms around his waist to return a kiss that soon became *kisses* until she finally stopped.

"It has to be good-night now," she said, breathless, once again on fire with wanting him as if they hadn't spent the past hours together.

"Night, Isabelle," he said in a raspy, husky voice that was seductive. She reminded herself that saying no to Tony was the right decision for her future.

Telling herself to hold to that, she went inside and closed the door, listening to the lock click in place. She had left on lights and in minutes she switched them off and climbed into bed to think about Tony, wanting him, wondering if they were headed for a disaster. Tonight had carried them deeper and closer to an affair. For one brief moment she gave it consideration. Would it interfere so deeply with her goal of marriage? She was still young enough to not have to rush into marriage. She wondered whether she was fooling herself with that argument. Tony was more desirable than any man she had ever known. Would a brief affair be so disastrous?

"Yes, it would," she said aloud. "Get more backbone, Isabelle," she added. For giant reasons, her employer, a man set against marriage, a workaholic, would combine to make an affair a catastrophe. It would be a broken heart for her.

Keeping his promise, Saturday and Sunday Tony showed her the city. He was charming, still flirting, touching her casually: his arm around her shoulders, taking her hand, sitting close beside her, so many light touches that shouldn't have provoked desire, but did. She held to her promise to herself Saturday night and slept alone in her suite.

Sunday night they boarded his plane and flew home with

tension heightening every hour spent together. By the time he saw her to her door, it was midnight Sunday evening.

She unlocked the door and he stepped inside with her while she turned off her alarm.

"I'll always remember this weekend, Tony," she said. "Thank you for a wonderful time."

"I'll remember it, too. Let me take you to dinner tomorrow night." When she opened her mouth to answer, he swooped down to kiss her, drawing her into his embrace and holding her tightly.

All weekend he had charmed her, but she had guarded her heart. Instantly prudence burned away in a blaze of passion that was as passionate as Friday and Saturday nights with him. She dropped her purse and clung to him, kissing him, returning heat for heat, wanting him yet determined to stop.

When she ended their kisses, Tony was as breathless as she was.

"I'll pick you up at seven," he said, and she merely nodded, wanting to reach for him and pull him back.

He turned and was gone, closing the door behind him. She opened it to watch him stride back to the waiting limo and climb inside. She waved, even though she couldn't see him through the limo's tinted glass.

Closing the door, she moved automatically, her thoughts on Tony, wanting him with her. She was falling in love with him.

She acknowledged what she felt in her heart. Loving Tony would be hopeless. An affair with him would be meaningless and disturbing because she never wanted a relationship without commitment and had avoided one all these years. Until now. Unless she moved on and got away from Tony, that's exactly what she was going to get herself involved in. She couldn't exist in a relationship without a commitment. Her heart would be in it totally. And get broken to pieces in the process.

"Move on and save yourself grief," she whispered. She suspected sleep would be a long time in coming.

Since Isabelle would be present, Tony looked forward to the Monday-morning staff meeting with an eagerness he had never had before. All his presidents and vice presidents attended and they went over any significant items for the upcoming week or month.

He was talking to Porter Haswell when others began to file into the room and the moment Isabelle stepped through the doorway, the air became electric. He continued listening to Porter, but flicked a glance at Isabelle, taking in her wine-colored suit with a matching blouse. With her hair pinned up again, she was buttoned up, looking business as usual, except the skirt ended at her knees, revealing shapely calves and trim ankles.

Tonight she would have dinner with him. He suspected she had been about to refuse his dinner invitation when he had kissed away a reply. Sometimes a twinge of guilt plagued him for his efforts to win her over and take her away from her goal of marriage and a family. If someone treated his sister in such a manner, he would be furious. Yet, Isabelle was so damned responsive to him, plus beautiful, sexy and appealing in every possible way. She had made it evident that she desired him and that she had found their night of love together something unique and special in her life. How could he walk away from all that?

He tried to focus on Porter when he felt his phone vibrate. Tony glanced at his phone and saw a text from his sister asking him if he could meet her for a quick lunch. It had their own code for "highly important" with an exclamation point accompanying the message.

He stepped into the hall to send her a quick reply telling her he would meet her and naming a restaurant. Wondering what had happened to cause her request, he returned to the meeting.

He met Isabelle's wide blue eyes and again, the air sparked. He deliberately looked elsewhere, feeling the tension between them. Ruffling through papers on the table, he focused on the meeting, trying to keep his mind off the prospect of dinner with her tonight. When he looked at her or was with her, any slight guilt he felt for wanting to pursue her faded away.

The minute the meeting concluded, she gathered her things and headed out without a glance at Tony.

Thirty minutes before noon Tony left the office for the downtown Dallas club where he and his family, as well as most of his close friends, had memberships.

As he emerged from the elevator on the top floor and walked toward the club restaurant, he heard a familiar greeting.

"Hey, Tony."

Tony looked around to see Gabe Benton in Western boots, jeans and a jacket over a white shirt that was open at the throat. "Going to lunch?" Gabe asked. "I just finished."

"I'm meeting Sydney for lunch. You look in a rush."

"I have a cattle auction to attend."

Tony smiled. "I'm amazed your dad has left you alone about pursuing a ranching career instead of oil. You're a good petroleum engineer, and Jake relies on you a lot. Actually, you're a good investment broker."

Gabe grinned. "What my dad doesn't know won't hurt him. He doesn't hear much about ranching from either Jake or me. I love it, Tony. I'm a cowboy at heart. Too much time with Grandpa Wade when I was growing up."

"Looks like damned hard work for uncertain returns if you ask me," Tony said.

"As if any of the rest of you have certain returns on the deals you make."

Tony smiled. "Go buy a lot of cows."

"Cattle. Tell Sydney hi. Tell her to hang in there if she's still getting flack from your dad."

"I'm sure she's still getting that. I'll tell her," Tony said. "Take it easy." He entered the restaurant as Gabe went striding away.

Tony's thoughts shifted fully to Sydney. Something bad had happened. He could tell from her terse text message. He wondered what his father had done now. Or had Dylan given her a final goodbye and severed all ties? He knew there was no point in worrying or guessing. In minutes, he would know, because he would hear as soon as she arrived.

He was a few minutes early as he had planned. He wanted a table ready when Sydney appeared. He didn't want her to have to wait for him.

He tipped the maître d', whom he knew well, to seat him in a quiet place away from others. The table, in a corner beside a window overlooking downtown, was perfect. He was on the twenty-seventh floor and the view was spectacular, but Tony barely glanced at it as he saw his sister following the maître d' toward him.

With her black curls in a tangle and her clothing rumpled, Sydney looked as if a catastrophe had befallen her. A few feet from the table he saw her tears shimmer and he wondered what new threat his father had given Sydney. He couldn't think of anything else to bring her to the disheveled state she was in. He braced to hear the worst.

Seven

Sydney's sad expression made his insides tighten. Evidently, her news was worse than he had expected. "Dammit," he whispered under his breath, clenching his fists and trying to curb his anger. Not to mention reminding himself again that his father must never interfere with his own life again.

"Hi, Sydney," Tony said, holding her chair, his gaze racing over her. It was a mild shock to see her. In the past days, she had lost weight. Her curls were tangled and she was pale. His worry deepened, and he braced for some really grim news.

"Thanks, Tony, for meeting me when you had such short notice." He sat across from her, waiting in silence for her to tell him her troubles in her own time. The waiter appeared to take their drink orders, returning in minutes with water and a small pot of hot tea for Sydney.

As soon as the waiter took their orders for salads and left them alone Sydney rummaged in her purse. She withdrew a folded envelope and gave it to him. "Here's your money back, Tony. I appreciate that money more than you'll ever know."

"What's bringing this on?"

Her eyes filled with tears and she looked away. He waited in silence, certain she would answer his question when she regained her composure. Finally she faced him as she wiped her eyes.

"I'm sorry. I really loved Dylan. I guess I made a poor choice. I was wrong about him. I'm giving you back your money because everything is rosy between Mom, Dad and me now. I won't be disinherited and Dad will pay for medical school. Dylan is gone for good."

"What happened with Dylan?" Tony asked, feeling a rising tide of anger if Dylan had hurt Sydney, yet still puzzled how he could have hurt her this badly.

She looked away again. The waiter came with salads for both of them and they sat in silence while they were served. As soon as the waiter left, Sydney pushed her plate aside and leaned closer over the table.

"Dylan broke off with me because Dad paid him a lot of money to do so."

Tony clenched his fist, which was in his lap and out of Sydney's sight. Fury suffused him, making him hot. "Damn, Sydney, I'm sorry," he said, as angry with his father as he was with Dylan. "Sydney, if Dylan is that kind of man, you're better off to find it out now."

"Common sense tells me that. I loved him. I thought he loved me," she said, looking away and biting her lip.

"That happens, Syd. It's hard to really know someone else. When did this happen?"

"Last Friday. Dad called me and told me he wanted to see me. When I went by the house, he told me that he would continue to support me in med school and he was not changing his will since Dylan was out of my life."

"We talked a little and then he told me just what you said now, that it was better to find out about Dylan now than later. I told him that Dylan left me because he didn't want me hurt. Dad just smiled as if dealing with a five-year-old. When he did that, I knew something was wrong."

"Dammit, I'm so sorry," Tony repeated, knowing full well the look Sydney had received. His father was always smug when he had the upper hand and had manipulated matters to get what he wanted.

"He told me that wasn't why Dylan left. That it was in his best interests to do so. That's when he told me he paid Dylan twenty-five thousand dollars to get out of my life and stay out." She looked stricken as she gazed at Tony, and his sympathy for her deepened.

"By Dad's standards, it wasn't much money. That's the irony of it. Dad would have paid a lot more." She turned away and put her handkerchief on her eyes, crying silently. "I'm sorry I'm getting so emotional. I've been able to hold it together with Mom and Dad, but I can't with you."

"Don't worry about tears. Dammit, Sydney, where does Dylan work?"

Her head jerked around. "Don't go talking to Dylan. Or worse, don't go punching him."

"I'm not going to hit him," Tony stated, although he didn't add that he would like to. "What did Dylan say when you confronted him about it?"

"I haven't. I don't want to ever see him again. We haven't been seeing each other, anyway. He's cut all ties and won't take my calls. Now I know why. A deal he made with Dad," she added bitterly. "I can't even feel angry with Dad. It's Dylan who tears me up with what he did."

Tony wanted to leave the restaurant and find Dylan and tell him what he thought of him. He knew it was a knee-jerk reaction, but he was furious that his sister had been so badly treated. "I have to agree, Sydney. I can't get as angry with Dad as I do with Dylan for being insincere and cheap. You're so much better off without him. The man you fell in love with obviously wasn't the real Dylan. He pulled the wool over my eyes, too, Syd. I thought he was really a great guy. He seemed as sincere as possible and I'm accustomed to dealing with men trying to fool me."

"I know," she said in a hollow voice. She gripped Tony's hand. "Promise me you won't go see Dylan."

"I'm not doing any such thing. I promise I won't hit him," Tony said, hoping he could keep that promise, because right now he would like to punch Dylan. "Where does he work, Sydney? I won't hurt him. I can find out from someone else if you won't tell me."

"It's over, Tony. Just let it go. I want to give you this check."

"You ought to just keep it, Syd. Now, where does Dylan work?"

She bit her lip and sighed. "He works for L.J. Luxury Yachts. He's head of their advertising department. Tony, don't worry me about Dylan."

"I won't hurt him and I'm not going to worry you. I think you should have talked to him."

"I didn't see any point in it and I…" Her voice trailed away. "I don't know if I can control my emotions. It's difficult enough with you. I don't want to get all weepy around Dylan. Tony, it hurts and it's scary to think how I misjudged him."

"Sorry, Syd. I'm going to dinner tonight with Isabelle. I'm sure she would be happy if you joined us. You two know each other."

"Through Dylan." As she wiped her eyes, she smiled at him. "You're the best brother possible. Thanks, but I'll be busy until late and then too tired for words. That's one thing—I'm too occupied to dwell on this all day."

"If you're going to work late, you ought to try to eat something."

"I don't see you eating," she said, smiling at him.

They looked at each other and smiled. She took a bite and

sipped her hot tea while Tony also ate a little. His appetite was gone, but he knew it would be a long afternoon for him and he hoped if he ate, Sydney would.

"Take the check, Tony," she said, pushing it closer to him.

He pocketed it without looking at it while Sydney took one more bite and then put aside her fork.

"There's one more thing I want you to do for me. I'd really rather you didn't even talk to Dylan. Promise me you won't retaliate or do anything to him, either."

"Sydney, when have I ever done anything like that?" he asked, even though that's what he longed to do. "There's a law against assaulting someone. I don't want to complicate my life with a crime, so stop worrying."

"I'll take that as a promise," she said. "I'm going to have to get back." She leaned closer to him. "And no, I'm not giving you Dylan's phone number or address. I know you can get someone to give it to you, but please, don't bother. Tony, don't even talk to him about this. Don't make me worry and stop confiding in you."

"If that's what you want, I promise I won't talk to him."

"I'm relieved. Thanks for seeing me on such short notice and for brotherly sympathy. Thanks for everything."

"I'm sorry, Syd," he said, standing when she did. She smiled at him, picked up her purse and left.

As Tony headed back to his office, his thoughts were on Dylan.

He entered the elevator, surprised Isabelle was there along with five other employees. In spite of his simmering anger over Dylan, his heartbeat increased at the sight of her. Memories of the weekend were vivid, taunting him. He wanted to take her into his arms right now. Instead, he returned greetings, some reserved, some with smiles and friendly tones. By the time they were three floors away from Isabelle's office, they were the only two people remaining in the elevator.

"Tony, when I saw you before lunch you said you were going to see your sister. Is everything all right?"

"No. Dylan turned out not to be the man she thought he was. Or you think he is, for that matter. I've promised her I won't even talk to him, but I'm not happy about it."

"Dylan?" Isabelle frowned. "Dylan is as straight an arrow as they come. He's up-front, sincere, friendly. I don't know what happened between them. I didn't think they were even still seeing each other."

"They're not, but not for the noble reasons you attributed to him."

"What are you talking about? Dylan decided to stop seeing her so she wouldn't lose touch with her family, or be disinherited or lose your father's support for med school."

"My father paid Dylan to stop seeing her," Tony snapped. "Dylan accepted the money." They reached her floor and he held the close door elevator button. "I don't know which I'm more annoyed with, Dylan or my father."

Isabelle stared at him with a slight frown. She shook her head. "That doesn't sound like Dylan."

"Women are so damn softhearted. It makes them gullible."

Isabelle's frown grew more fierce. "Is that so? I've known Dylan a long time. That doesn't sound like him. Frankly, if he had accepted money to stop seeing your sister, knowing Dylan as I do, I think he would have told me."

"You're that close with him?" Tony ground out the words, beginning to wonder what kind of relationship she had with Dylan.

"No, we're not that close. Dylan is that *forthright* about what he does," Isabelle lashed out, making him realize that in his anger, he had jumped to baseless conclusions about how close she had been to Dylan. He surprised himself because his reaction smacked of jealousy, something he had never felt before in his life. "Has Sydney talked to Dylan about taking money from your dad?"

Tony studied her, lost in thought about what she was telling him, as well as his reaction, and barely hearing her question. "You really think that doesn't sound like Dylan?" he asked, an idea occurring to him that he didn't want to face.

"Yes," she said flatly. "I'm due in an appointment."

"Be a minute late. I need to pursue this a moment. Isabelle, I promised Sydney I wouldn't talk to Dylan. Will you speak to him for me? If Dylan didn't get paid by Dad to leave Sydney, my father made that up."

"Surely not," Isabelle said, staring at Tony as if he had grown another head. "How could he meddle in her life with a lie that she's bound to discover some day? When she caught him, she would be furious or hate him."

"She might discover it and she might not. Sydney and Dylan have stopped all contact. If she's hurt and angry and Dylan has moved on, she'll never know. If Dad—I can't even say it—if he lied about the money, there's a chance Dylan wouldn't ever hear about it. My dad may have been willing to take the risk. The odds are, no one would find out."

"No father would do that," Isabelle whispered, still staring at Tony.

"I didn't think mine would ever stoop that low—he never has, but he's angry about losing control over me. He's furious with Sydney." Tony grasped her shoulder. "Isabelle, I promised Sydney I wouldn't talk to Dylan. Will you ask Dylan for me? Tell him what's happened. I can count on you for the truth."

"You don't even know me that well," she said.

"Yes, I do. Will you do that for me? Hell, do it for Sydney and Dylan. If you and Sydney are right about him, he's getting blamed for something he knows nothing about."

"That's appalling."

"Stop looking at me as if I'm the one who did it. I'm not like my father."

"You're driven and so is he."

"I'm driven to succeed to get him off my back. You can't imagine how manipulative he is." He paused as what he just said made him stop and think. "I never caught him in a lie, but he has gone to great lengths to manipulate things to get his way. I'm not like him, Isabelle, I swear. I would never do something dishonest like this. I didn't think he would. If it weren't for you…no one would know the truth here," he said. "Isabelle and I wouldn't know that Dylan didn't accept the money."

"Tony, I've got to get to my meeting," she said, glancing at her watch. "This truly doesn't sound like Dylan, so I'll talk to him for you and for all three of you. If Dylan hasn't taken money from your father, it would terrible for Sydney and Dylan if they never learned the truth."

"Thanks, Isabelle," Tony said, releasing the button so the doors would open. He watched her walk away, her hips swaying slightly, her skirt ending above her knees, giving him a look at her long shapely legs. She halted and glanced back. "I'll let you know. I'll try to talk to him as soon as possible."

He nodded, still watching her, lost in his thoughts. Anger and shock tormented him. How could his father lie to get his way? Yet Tony could imagine, when his dad lost his power over his son and at the same time had his daughter go against his wishes, taking a last, desperate measure to remain in control. And how was Tony to know what his dad had done in the past?

All afternoon, it was an effort to keep his mind on business instead of his father, Sydney, Dylan—and Isabelle. Once in a meeting, he caught a vice president and close friend staring at him, making him wonder what he had just said in answer to a question he also didn't recall. He tried to focus on the meeting, but in minutes his thoughts drifted back to Isabelle again.

At five he received a text from Isabelle, stating that she would like to see him. He sent a message in return to come to his office.

Within minutes, he heard a knock and looked up to see her waiting in the doorway.

"Come in," he said, standing to walk around his desk.

"Your secretary has gone. Her computer is off," Isabelle said, closing the door behind her.

"She leaves at five o'clock. Damn, I'm glad to see you," he said when Isabelle crossed the room. He met her, taking her into his arms to kiss her.

"Tony—"

His kiss ended whatever she had been about to say. She resisted only seconds and then wrapped her arms around him to kiss him back, setting him ablaze. He wanted to peel off the business clothes and take down her hair, but this wasn't the time or place. She would never let him do that in his office, anyway.

His pulse thundered, shutting out other sounds. He was aroused and tightened his arm around her, wanting to kiss her and not stop. He shifted slightly as he held her with one arm. His other hand slid lower, caressing her throat, easing down to the full curve of her soft breast.

"Tony, this is your office. I don't want to walk out of here looking as if we've been making love."

"We're probably alone on this floor."

"I need to talk to you," she said, walking away and straightening her clothes, winding a few locks of her hair back in place. "I'm going to dinner tonight with Dylan. I'll have to reschedule our dinner."

"Oh, hell," he said, disappointed, torn between wanting to tell her to cancel with Dylan and thanking her for agreeing to question Dylan about the money as soon as possible. "I hate that, but if it helps Sydney, I'll agree. Tomorrow night, then, unless there's hope of seeing you after you leave Dylan."

She smiled at him. "I won't be late with Dylan, but I will have already eaten and it's a work night, so I should just go home then."

"I want to hear from you as soon as you know the truth about the money. I don't want to wait until tomorrow. Sydney looked awful today. She isn't eating, probably not sleeping and studying like crazy. Send me a text or call me when you leave the restaurant. I'll meet you."

"I'll do that. The sooner you hear the truth, the better. I don't know your father, but I do know Dylan. I feel certain about him."

"Either way, I'm going to be unhappy about it. Dad has never done anything like this before. At least not that I know about. If he hasn't paid Dylan, it will make me wonder if he's ever lied about something in the past to get his way. Hell of a deal either way."

"I need to finish a letter before I leave to meet Dylan. I have to go."

He nodded. "I've been looking forward all day to dinner tonight," he said, walking to the elevator with her, catching her for a brief kiss that he wanted to lengthen, but she stepped away. "I'll be waiting for your call after you leave Dylan."

She nodded. "It'll probably be about nine or nine-thirty when Dylan and I part."

When the elevator doors closed behind her, Tony returned to his desk. In minutes he could focus on business because Isabelle had taken over and would help with his family problem. For just an instant, he thought about how important she was becoming to him and in his life.

It was a new experience and not one he wanted to explore, so he forced himself to concentrate on his work.

At six Isabelle entered the restaurant. It was startling to see Dylan, because he had lost weight and had a somber expression she had never seen before. Unlike his usually cheerful optimistic self, he stood and held her chair, barely speaking, appearing intensely unhappy.

"You miss her, don't you?" Isabelle asked when he sat facing her.

He looked away and a muscle worked in his jaw. "I thought I would begin to get over this. Instead, it gets a little worse each day that passes. I've never been in love before, Isabelle, never like this. Sydney has stopped calling, stopped trying to get me to change my mind. I suppose she's getting over it."

He paused as a waitress appeared and they placed orders for water, plus hot tea for Isabelle. "How's it going with you and the brother?"

She wanted to keep the conversation about Sydney going, but didn't want to rush into questions. "He surprised me by flying to San Diego last weekend when I was there for business."

He attempted a smile. "Did you have a good time?"

"Yes. That's never been the problem. But unlike Sydney, who wants to marry, Tony wants to avoid marriage or commitment."

"I doubt if he'll change," Dylan said. "He's in his thirties and has avoided serious entanglements so far."

"His work is his main interest." She paused while their waitress brought water and took their orders. "Dylan, I want to ask something that's very personal and if you don't want to answer my question, I'll understand."

"Ask away. We're close friends. I can't imagine any question you have that I will mind answering."

She sipped her water, wondering if Dylan would still feel that way after she asked him such a personal question. "Did Sydney's father offer you money to stop seeing her?"

"Yes, he did," Dylan said, and Isabelle got a knot in her throat. Shocked that she had misjudged Dylan, too, she stared at him.

"So you stopped seeing her and now you wish you hadn't?"

"Hell, no. He just offered me money this week. I wasn't too

polite about turning him down." His eyes narrowed and he studied her.

"Oh, Dylan!" she exclaimed, swamped with relief. "You told him no, that you wouldn't take his money."

"Damn right. I wasn't nice about it. You thought that was why I stopped seeing her? What's going on, Isabelle? How'd you hear about the money offer?"

"Tony said that Sydney's father told her he paid you to stop seeing her, that his money was why you wouldn't see her again."

"Hell's bells," Dylan snapped, his eyes flashing with fire as his face flushed. "She believed that?"

"Tony told me that she did. At first Tony was shocked when I said I didn't believe it, that you're always so straightforward about everything, and that I was sure you would have told me if you had done that. I think you would have told Sydney."

"She believed him."

"Dylan, stop and think. Both Sydney and Tony were shocked when they heard about it. Tony said his dad had never done anything that dishonest before. I haven't spoken to Sydney, but Tony believed me when I said I didn't think you had."

"So that's why the urgent dinner tonight."

"Yes. Now don't be angry with Sydney."

He blinked and sat in silence. Their dinners were placed on the table, a chicken salad for Isabel, a hamburger for Dylan. She began to eat, trying to give Dylan a chance to think about what she had told him.

"I feel so relieved that you are the person I think you are and Sydney will be, too," Isabelle said finally. "Tony said she has been heartbroken lately and he's worried about her. I'm going to see him when I leave you. He'll call Sydney to tell her."

"I'll tell her myself. That does it. I'm going to see her tonight if I have to knock down her door."

Isabelle smiled. "I'm sure she'll see you. She doesn't know

I'm with you. That was Tony's plan to find out the truth. He promised Sydney he wouldn't talk to you."

"She was probably afraid of what he'd do. I know how I would have felt if it had been my sister." He set down his glass of water. "Isabelle, do you mind finishing dinner on your own? I'll buy your dinner and you can take your time to eat. I'm not hungry at all now. I'm going to see Sydney."

"You don't want me to break the news first?"

"No."

"Dylan, someone has already warned me to beware of Tony because of his family. Sydney is a Ryder, too."

"She'd never do anything dishonest like her father telling her I accepted the money he offered to stop seeing her when that wasn't true. She's ethical and truthful. She's not as driven as the men in the family."

"I'm sure that's true."

"Thanks. Thanks for having so much faith in me and for telling me. I never would have known otherwise."

"Go, Dylan. See if you can find her."

"I'll find her," he said, and left bills on the table to more than cover both dinners. He was gone before she could protest. She watched him hurry across the restaurant and disappear outside.

She called Tony and made arrangements to meet him right away. Her appetite had vanished, too, and she didn't care to linger and eat alone.

When she entered the lot and parked where they agreed to meet, Tony drove up behind her car, reached across to hold open the door. "Get in," he said.

As soon as she had closed the car door, he drove off. "Where are we going?" she asked. "I thought we were going to have a drink here and talk. Mainly talk. I don't need a drink unless it's tea."

"I know a better, quieter place. I've missed being with you. Tell me about Dylan."

"Dylan was shocked. He has not taken a dime from your dad."

"Oh, damn. I'm glad for Sydney's sake." Tony inhaled deeply, unclenching his fists on the steering wheel. After a few moments of silence, he said, "I feel like a kid again, disappointed to discover my parent isn't perfect and the giant I thought he was."

"You dad is human, a man accustomed to getting his way. You, Sydney and Dylan have thwarted him and he lashed out. I'm not defending him, because I think such meddling is despicable," Isabelle answered, turning slightly in the seat to look at Tony.

"You're still lumping us in together. I can hear it in your voice."

"Tony, you're accustomed to getting your way. Have a reputation as a ruthless businessman," she said, not mentioning that he had tried everything to manipulate her into an affair with him. "You're his son. The acorn never falls far from the tree sort of thing."

"Dammit, Isabelle, I haven't ever crossed the line like that to meddle in personal lives or to lie to get what I want. I've bluffed in poker and in business deals, I'll admit, but that's different than what my father did to his child. I've never done anything dishonest like that." He glanced at her while they waited at a red light in a busy intersection. When she didn't reply, he shook his head. "You don't believe me, do you?"

He had to return his attention to the road as the light changed to green.

"It depends on how far you went with it. Poker—that's part of the game and that's nothing. In business, that could mean anything from a harmless exaggeration to something that was totally misleading."

"Ask around. I may have a reputation as ruthless, but I think I also have one as being honest. Where I get the ruthless reputation is for what I'm doing at Morris, trying to streamline and update an old company. That doesn't always sit well with those who have worked there a long time."

"Tony, the main thing here is that Dylan knew nothing about this. He's gone to see Sydney now."

"He won't find her except by cell phone. I told her to wait at my house, that I was bringing you with me and we both wanted to see her."

"That was a little premature, wasn't it?" she asked, surprised Tony trusted her judgment of Dylan that much.

"I think you know your friend. What's more important here than talking to Sydney is that I don't lose your respect. Sydney can learn the truth from Dylan."

She was more touched than she wanted to be. "You haven't lost my respect," she said softly.

"You mean that, don't you?"

Their eyes met for a moment. "I mean it."

He took a deep breath and was silent.

She watched as tall wrought-iron gates opened for them. "So I'll see where you live."

"Yes, you will. I'll take you home when you want. Sydney will fly out of here to see Dylan when she finds out he wants to talk to her. I haven't told her why, just to come out, that I wanted to talk to her."

"I'll be happy to see her again—if I do. I'm sure Dylan has talked to her by now. You do recall this is a work night?"

"Yes. We won't stay late if you don't want to. I've missed you, Isabelle, and looked forward to being with you tonight— all evening with you—but then our plans had to change."

"I'm glad the truth came out." She turned to look at the grounds. Even though it was night, there were lights in the trees and along the driveway, so anyone could see some of the landscaping in the semidarkness. The grounds were tree filled, bare branches in the winter, but she could imagine how beautiful it would be in the other three seasons.

"Tony, this is pretty." They swept around the driveway to pull up in front and Isabelle gazed around when she stepped out of the car. "What a beautiful home you have. I'm surprised. I wouldn't have guessed you'd like one of these older homes. This isn't where you grew up, is it?" she asked, looking at a sprawling three-story stone and wood house with an immense portico to the east. Tall bronze torches flickered at the foot of the steps to the front porch.

"No, not here. I lived in a house like it. It's comfortable, secluded, has good security and it's close enough to downtown Dallas for a short commute." He took her arm to cross a wide porch that held two stately bronze dogs flanking the enormous door with beveled glass panes. Tall china pots with towering banana plants were beside each dog and pots of blooming flowers dotted the porch that held a swing, plus elegant wooden furniture.

The front door opened and Sydney Ryder stood facing them with a slight frown as she glanced from one to the other.

"What's going on, Tony? Dylan has called me several times on my cell phone and tried to talk. I refused to talk to him. I don't know what he wanted. Now here you are, wanting to talk. I'm not sure I want to hear one more disastrous announcement. What's happened, Tony?"

Eight

"**W**hy don't you let us come in and talk," Tony said.

Sydney's eyes widened and she stepped back, motioning to them. "Sorry. Come in, please."

Isabelle smiled, hoping she hid her shock at the sight of Sydney, who was far thinner than she remembered and with dark circles under her eyes. Sydney's hair was an unkempt tangle, and her plain jeans and T-shirt looked as if she had been sleeping in them, and were far too inadequate for the chill in the night air. She held a sweater in her hand that she pulled on.

"Isabelle, it's been a long time since I last saw you," Sydney said.

"It's nice to see you, and part of my reason for being here is good news." Isabelle looked up at Tony, placing her hand on his arm. "Why don't we let Sydney go so she can call Dylan back."

Sydney stared at them. "Why would I—" She glanced between her brother and Isabelle, her expression softening. "Now I am puzzled. What?"

Tony nodded. "Isabelle's right. Go call Dylan and we can talk later."

"I assume as soon as I talk to Dylan, I'll understand all this mystery. Now I'm too curious. I'm going to call him. Sorry to say hello and goodbye in the same breath."

"That's all right, Syd," Tony replied. "We'll see you another time."

Sydney looked at both of them. "If you're in on this, my brother, the news must involve Dad's money. I'm gone. Thanks, maybe, to both of you." She turned to rush down the hall.

Isabelle smiled when she looked at Tony. "I think they're really in love. I've never seen Dylan the way he looked tonight. Or your sister for that matter."

"That's for damn sure. I've never seen Sydney such a wreck. Hopefully, this will work out and they'll be happy again. Now stop worrying about Dylan and Sydney. The staff doesn't live here and they are all away tonight, so we have the house to ourselves. Come here," he said, pulling Isabelle to him while his tone changed, dropping to a velvety note that warmed her.

Switching off the entryway lights, he wrapped her into his embrace. "I missed you terribly."

"We were together yester—"

His kiss ended their conversation. She wrapped her arms around him, her heart racing while she thought *foolish, foolish.* Tony's kisses were addictive, drawing her closer to a relationship.

"You're beautiful," he whispered, brushing feathery kisses on her temple, down to her ear, lower to her throat. "You take my breath away when I look at you and remember loving you."

Every word made her heart pound while she tried to hang on to her resolve. "I thought we weren't going to do this. I came to talk to Sydney and that reason is gone now. Tony, you're being manipulative. I suppose it's in your genes." How would she ever resist him? Her heart raced because she wanted to put her arms around him while she kissed him.

"I'm trying to ignore that one," he whispered. "You can't imagine how I want you."

When he brushed kisses on her temple, she closed her eyes, standing immobile, torn by conflicting feelings. "Have you even heard what I've been saying to you?"

"I've heard you," he answered, his fingers caressing her nape as lightly as his kisses, equally devastating. Did she really want to keep fighting him when she was already in love with him? How tempting to let go and accept a relationship, to see where it would take them and to have Tony's friendship.

He continued trailing kisses to her ear. "Let go of your worries about tomorrow, Isabelle. For this night live in the present and take what you want," he said, echoing her thoughts. His breath was warm on her ear, producing its own erotic effect. "You've got all your tomorrows to say no."

Mesmerizing words. Suggestions her heart wanted more with each passing minute.

His light kisses became kindling for a raging fire, his words even more seductive. She slid her arm around his neck and turned her head slightly as he brushed kisses on her cheek. When her mouth met his, her insides clenched.

His arm tightened around her waist as his mouth opened hers and his tongue won the battle.

She wanted all of him, wanted him inside her. Would he fall in love? She knew better. His heart was already committed to work. Even if he fell in love, work would come first before a family. She never wanted to become deeply involved with a man whose business goal would consume him and now she teetered on the brink of doing just that.

In spite of his manipulative manner, he had become important to her and she could not keep from loving him for his caring for Morris employees, his love and loyalty to his sister, and his generosity with her—all admirable, even if he had an ulterior motive in giving her such a big promotion. His good qualities impressed her. On top of attraction, they were too potent and beguiling.

Letting go, she kissed him in return. His tongue went deep, stirring sensations. She responded with surging passion. This was what she wanted, knowing it as surely now as she had that long-ago night when she'd first met him. The dangers, the outcome, the consequences, all the threats to her peace of mind dwindled away. Barriers and warnings crumbled. She paused to open her eyes to look at him. "Tonight…Tony."

His brown eyes blazed with desire. His arm tightened, recaptured her and he returned to kissing her possessively, demanding a response, eliciting passion so easily.

Her heart thudded as she reacted, winding her fingers in his hair, pouring out all her pent-up longing while desire consumed her. This night would ultimately prove her undoing and break her heart. Even so, she wanted this time together. She would never forget it. She had no idea how long it would take to recover from it. She intended to make certain he never forgot this night with her. There was a depth to Tony and he did care about the people important to him. She intended to become one of them. From what he'd said, she might already be to some degree.

She wound her fingers in his hair while her other hand went to the buttons on his shirt. She unfastened the few at the top and as they kissed, she tugged the shirt from his slacks to shove it off.

While they continued to kiss, she ran her hands across his broad shoulders, remembering and rediscovering, wanting to know every inch, to kiss and caress until he was wild with passion.

While he kissed her, he picked her up in his arms. Kissing him in return, she was unaware where he carried her until he set her on her feet beside a bed.

He shifted her to unfasten her blouse, letting it fall around her feet, followed by her skirt. Slithers of silk and cotton undergarments, fragile barriers removed and tossed aside.

Resting his hands on her waist, Tony languidly looked at her from her chin to her toes and back, meeting her gaze. "I've dreamed of this," he whispered. "Wanting you, thinking how I would like to make love to you, slowly, inch by inch, to pleasure you to the utmost."

"Tony," she whispered, his seductive words working their effect. Clinging to him, she pulled his head close to kiss him ardently. Having made her decision, she let go all caution. She wanted him with a desperate urgency.

Her hands tangled in his thick chest curls and then lowered to unfasten his belt. She freed him from his clothes. She rubbed against him. Warm, bare bodies, soft against hard, light contacts that fueled blazing desire.

He cupped her breasts in his hands, stroking her nipples with his thumbs before he bent to take a taut bud in his mouth. His tongue drew moist circles, each stroke driving her need for fulfillment.

Rocking back, she gasped with pleasure, her eyes closed tightly while she clutched his forearms. Sensations bombarded her, the world spinning into nonexistence except for Tony.

His fingers ran along her hip, his hand slipping between her legs, finding her intimate places. Hidden, private places opening to him. When she gasped and arched against his hand, his mouth came down hard on hers.

She held him with one arm around his neck, her other hand still roaming over his chest and stomach.

His caresses made her moan, the sound muffled by their kisses. Pleasure rocked her. Lifting her again, he placed her on the bed. He knelt beside her, watching her as he picked up her foot to brush light kisses on her ankle.

"Turn over," he said, rolling her slightly until she was on her stomach. His kisses continued along her calf. She dug her nails into the bed, while desire to have more of him increased with each kiss he lavished on her.

Moving with thorough deliberation, he continued trailing kisses up the back of her thighs, his lips warm, so light. The intertwined torment and pleasure overwhelmed. Moaning, she started to roll over, but Tony's hand put slight pressure on the small of her back.

"Wait," he whispered, his kisses lingering on her inner thighs. She tried to spread her legs but was hampered by Tony's legs as he straddled her. "Tony," she gasped, his name merely a hoarse whisper. Need and pleasure racked her. She continued to clutch the bed as sensations showered her.

His tongue was hot, wet along her inner thigh, moving higher, his warm breath another tease, all building desire

"Tony," she gasped, rolling over to look at him as he was on his knees, his thick rod, hard and ready. Beads of sweat gave a sheen to his skin while his bulging muscles were highlighted.

She took his thick rod in her hand, trailing her tongue on him, wanting to stir his passion as much as he had hers.

Closing his eyes and inhaling deeply, he wound his hands in her hair as his breathing grew ragged. He groaned while she continued and then took him in her mouth, her tongue driving him to the brink.

He pulled her up and she looked into his dark eyes. In that moment she felt desired in a manner she never had before—not even that first night when they had both been lighthearted and carefree, just having fun. She had felt desired then, but there was a breathtaking, earnest quality tonight that had not been part of their first night. He wanted her, and the devastating depth of need in his expression all by itself became its own seduction, making her shake and reach for him to kiss him.

Leaning over to kiss her passionately, he wrapped her in his embrace. It was a kiss like none other, passionate, possessive, demanding, consuming her. His kiss fanned her desire into a raging need for all of him, to go beyond caresses and kisses. Her body responded, every inch tingling, aching for him. It was a kiss to never be forgotten, binding her to him this night in an event that would be locked in memory.

It was a kiss that sealed her response to him with no turning back. Her thundering pulse drove out all sounds while she could feel his pounding heart against her own.

She held his strong body, wanting the kiss to never end, at the same time wanting more now. She wanted beyond kisses, wanted Tony with all her being. His arousal was hard against her. He was ready.

She pushed him down to lavish kisses over him, moving to his legs as he had done. Her tongue moved across the back of his knee, up over his inner thigh while he groaned and knotted his fists. Her hands caressed him while she showered light kisses on him. Aware she was in love with him, she ceased to think beyond that point.

His body was strong, hard and masculine, setting her ablaze. Desire intensified while she wanted to prolong their loving, making it last far into the night. She took her time, slowing and doing all she could to pleasure him before he rolled over and she was astride him, gazing into brown eyes that had darkened to midnight while smoldering with desire.

She smiled at him as she caressed his chest and then moved down. Her hair spilled over both of them when she leaned down to trail her tongue over him, more kisses and touches that she hoped pleasured and consumed him. Twice he started to sit up, reaching for her as he groaned with desire, and she pushed him back.

"Wait, Tony, wait, so much more. It has been a long, long time."

The third time she started to urge him to wait, he rolled her on the bed and stretched out beside her to pull her into his arms and kiss her hungrily.

His tongue went deep, his arms banding her. As his fingers tangled in her hair, he kissed her possessively.

"I want you," she whispered, meaning it with all her being, holding back a declaration of love, yet knowing she was hopelessly lost.

He moved between her legs to kiss her, driving her beyond thought, until desire became an aching torment.

"Tony," she whispered.

"Say it. You want me to love you," he commanded in her ear, his breath warm, his tongue hot and wet.

"Yes," she replied, meaning more than he could ever know. Running one hand over him, she held him tightly as she kissed him, moaning softly.

Finally, he paused, his fingers in her hair again. "Do you have protection?"

"No," she whispered. "I'm not on anything."

He moved away to find his slacks on the floor and return with a packet. She watched as he got a condom.

His gaze roamed over her and then he came down to hold her, his arms going around her while he kissed her. "Ah, Isabelle, I've wanted you more than you can ever guess. I never forgot and now I wonder why I didn't pursue seeing you no matter what interfered."

"Doesn't matter now," she whispered, for the moment feeling a bond with him that deep inside she knew was pure illusion. "This moment is what matters. You're in my arms." She pulled him close to kiss him again and he entered her slowly, the brief pain transforming as he filled her and moved.

She arched her back, meeting him, feeling one with him, warm, body against body, each held tightly while they kissed and loved intimately, a union that momentarily transcended reality.

Tension heightened, his control lasting as he pleasured her and she made love to him in return, carrying them higher and higher until they crashed over a summit, a spectacular climax that exploded with blinding lights behind her closed eyes and a roaring in her ears that had to be her own pounding heartbeat.

She held him tightly, imagining her hold on him would last, that the intimacy they had just shared would last even though she knew better.

"This is a special night, Tony," she whispered, clinging tightly to him as they moved together, each gasping for breath, drifting back into the regular world.

"You're a dream come true, a man's fantasy in real life. Ah, Isabelle, seductive, enchantress, perfect."

"Foolishness, Tony. I'm definitely not perfect and I'm no enchantress. Although I'm glad you called me that because I can now tell you that you are a spellbinder, seducing and weaving magic. You are my lover, for this moment all that I want."

He kissed her and she wondered if it was to stop her chatter, to reaffirm what he had just said or simply lust. The lust that had driven them all through the weekend and all this evening. She was falling back to earth, into reality and facing what she had known all along. There was no magic, no commitment, just lust and two healthy lovers who were swept up in passion.

His kiss drove her thoughts away and she clung to him as he rolled over on his side, taking her with him, holding him as close as possible. Their legs were intertwined, and she was in his embrace, pressed tightly against him. His kisses now were sweeter, light and warm.

She hugged him, running her fingers in his thick, slightly damp curls. She refused to think beyond the present moment. Soon enough tomorrow, decisions, choices would intrude, but tonight, she was locked into this time with Tony. That's all she planned to see, think about or acknowledge.

"This is heaven," Tony murmured against her, his breath playing lightly on her temple. "I don't want to ever let you go. You are my dreams. Since I discovered who you are, you've been in my dreams every night."

She laughed softly, winding thick black curls around her fingers. "And did I live up to those dreams?"

He shifted to look at her, smiling and brushing long strands of her hair away from her face. "You more than lived up to them. Reality is far better than dreams. I told you this is perfection, heaven. Would I change anything—no. Not at the moment, anyway."

"*Not at the moment* is the key phrase," she said. "Why does this—tonight—seem so inevitable?"

"Because it was. I always knew you'd be back in my life."

"You knew no such thing," she said, smiling at him, and he grinned.

"Maybe I didn't, but once I found you, I knew you'd be back in my arms."

"That's because you've been aimed at seduction since the night you walked into my office at ten o'clock or whatever time it was."

"How could I not be with the electricity that flies between us? Ah, this has been grand, Isabelle. Move in with me."

She laughed. "Just like that. Move in with me. Tony, what a dreamer you are. Leave tomorrow out of this. Let's just have tonight and enjoy it. We'll get to tomorrow soon enough."

"Sounds like a great idea. So for now, beautiful lady, let's move to a hot tub of water and soak and talk and have a glass of wine."

"I'll accept that invitation."

"I'll carry you." He stood, picking her up in his arms. "I'll start the bath, get the wine and we're set. White, Zinfandel or red?"

"A very sweet white."

He set her on her feet in a large bathroom with a sunken tub surrounded by pots with ferns and tropical plants, some with exotic red and yellow blossoms. She watched him start the water.

As he moved around, she reached out to pick up a thick white towel and wrap it around herself.

Her gaze roamed over Tony's naked body, and desire awakened again. He turned around and she looked up to meet his gaze.

His expression changed as he looked at her. She could see desire flare to life in his brown eyes. He was aroused, walking to her, and she felt as if all the air had left the room. Her breathing became deep and labored, her heart racing. He took her into his arms to kiss her. She felt his hands, felt the towel slip away and then she was pressed against his bare, hard body, his arousal thrust against her, hard, hot, ready.

"Wait, Isabelle," he said, stepping out to retrieve a packet from a table. In seconds while she caressed him, he put on protection. Tony spread his legs, braced himself and picked her up.

"Put your legs around me," he said, lowering her on his thick staff.

She gasped with pleasure, heat suffusing her as they moved together, and she kissed his throat and neck.

"Tony, now, now," she cried, holding him tightly, surging over another brink and feeling an explosive release and climax.

She held him tightly as he shuddered and climaxed, kissing her.

He let her slide to the floor to put her feet down. She wrapped her arms around him. "Ah, Tony, that was wonderful. You are wonderful," she said.

"I'll go get us that wine," he said, leaving the room, and immediately she felt his absence.

He *was* wonderful, she thought, recalling what he had done for his sister. She wondered if the tales about him being so ruthless in business could be true when he would turn around and take such care of his younger sister.

Was Tony really ruthless? So far, he had given her a huge

promotion and let her keep the staff she wanted, giving each of them a raise. She hadn't heard anyone in Morris who had sounded disgruntled or had complaints.

So were those mere rumors about Tony? Or had he reformed? Or had his employees just not seen him do anything yet that was harsh or ruthless, but the time would come when they would see that side of him?

She wondered what was true. She liked Sydney Ryder. Could Tony be like his sister? Or was he like his father? Controlling, unethical if necessary to get what he wanted. She considered all his manipulations to get her into bed, including his enormous promotion and the salary that was almost a bribe. He had two sides and she wasn't sure which one would dominate.

In minutes he was back, placing the wineglasses on the ledge of the tub and picking her up to place her leaning back against him in the deliciously hot water.

Tony was warm, his arms around her while they talked. She could feel the vibrations in his chest against her back as he spoke of his childhood and his closeness to his sister.

"Thanks to you, it sounds as if Dylan will be my brother-in-law soon."

"I don't know whether this will get them back together. It still means your sister will be disinherited and Dylan won't be able to live with that."

"I think they both are really in love. I don't know about Dylan, but Sydney is a wreck and she doesn't need to lose another pound."

"Evidently that hasn't moved your father."

"No, it hasn't," Tony said, and a harsh note entered his voice. "I'm still shocked over what he's done. As I've said, I've never known him to do anything dishonest. I doubt if I will ever trust him as much as before."

"You were probably right about him feeling desperate over losing control of both of you. I can't imagine trying to control others. My family is so far removed from that. We've always supported each other every way we can and everyone does what he wants."

"I'll never get this family of yours straight. Tell me again."

She laughed, turning to give him a look. "Tony, you learned all the hundreds of Morris employees. You call them by name and you really know all the executives. Don't tell me my family confuses you."

"They do. That's different. When do I meet them?"

"I've decided I'll take you home to meet my family when you take me home to meet yours. Which I assume will never happen. Besides, if I took you to meet mine, they would think we're getting seriously involved with each other, with an engagement and a marriage looming. I don't think you would want to deal with that. And then, if they think you're leading me on without serious intentions, I have brothers who take a dim view of anyone messing with their sisters. If you are protective of Sydney, imagine three of you running around protecting her. It compounds," she said, smiling up at him.

"You definitely have a point. So I suppose we don't meet each other's families."

His hands went around her and he cupped her breasts, playing with her nipples, caressing her. "That's better, isn't it?"

She gasped with pleasure and closed her eyes. She ran her hands along his muscled thighs. "Tony—" she whispered, closing her eyes and becoming absorbed in touching him.

"Ah, Isabelle. Beautiful, beautiful," he whispered.

She twisted to kiss him and in minutes she moved over him, holding him tightly with her eyes closed as he caressed her. He climbed out, getting protection and pulling her into his arms to pick her up. They rocked together, climbing to a pinnacle to burst with release. She fell on him, clinging to his broad shoulders while he held her close to carry her back into the warm water.

A half hour later, she climbed out. He came up out of the

water to follow her, reaching to take her towel to slowly dry her, rubbing her from head to toe.

"Now I get to return the favor," she whispered, taking a folded towel and starting with his shoulder, running the towel over his chest and around to his back, slowly inching her way down his back and legs and then moving around in front to work her way up.

By the time she reached his upper thighs, he was aroused, hard and ready for her.

"Come here, Isabelle," he said in a deep, raspy voice. He picked her up to carry her to bed, where he held her and they made love, leisurely at first, then with abandon and finally with a desperate urgency.

"Now, I am far too exhausted to move or think," Isabelle said, sprawled on top of him, her hair spilling over his shoulder and chest.

He ran one hand through her hair while his other hand stroked her bare back. "This is good right now. Just holding you like this, close to my heart, here in my arms for the night. This is perfect."

"I agree," she said languidly, feeling as if she had melted and been poured over him. "So very handsome, Tony. You are handsome, sexy, charming."

"And you, love, are beautiful, sexy, gorgeous, burning me totally when we make love."

"I hope so," she said, smiling.

"This is grand, Isabelle. I wasn't kidding earlier. Move in with me. You want commitment. There's a commitment of sorts."

She raised an eyebrow. She would be hurt if she expected anything more from him. "Tony, moving in with you isn't a commitment in my view. I would definitely be free to move out at any time. No, I'm not moving in with you and we weren't going to talk about tomorrow yet. Not until it happens."

"Oh, sure," he said. "No tomorrows. I'd like to share today

with you. You're already here, but I'd like you to move your things in."

"Definitely not for so many reasons. Not in with you. Not you in with me. I have plans and that would not fit."

"You don't have to stay a long time. Move in for now. You'll be free to go whenever you want."

"Sorry. No. End of discussion." She rolled over beside him and he pulled her close.

"I want you, Isabelle. I don't give up easily or take no well."

"I've already discovered that much about you."

He pulled her close against him and held her. "We'll discuss this some more tomorrow," Tony said.

It was dawn before they finally stopped talking and fell asleep. Isabelle woke, stretched and looked around, turning more to look at Tony sprawled beside her. He was naked, his thick black curls tangled on his forehead. One arm was flung to one side. The sheet covered him from his hips to his feet.

Longing enveloped her as she looked at him, his chest rising and falling evenly. *Tony, I love you,* she mouthed, knowing she felt a love that wouldn't be returned. Tony had gone as far as he would go by inviting her to move in with him. She *could* do that and hope the day would come when he would decide he wanted something more lasting.

In the silence of the room, with the only sound Tony's steady breathing, she shook her head. She wanted so much more of him. She hadn't been able to resist him and had yielded to the temptation of one more magical night with him, but that's all she had ever intended it to be and all it would be.

She gazed at him, memorizing the sight of him, wanting to lean over to shower light kisses on him, certain if she did he would wake.

While she debated getting up, his arm went around her and he pulled her down, opening his eyes to focus on her. The minute she looked into his brown eyes, she saw desire that ignited her own longing.

He pulled her close against him, leaning over her to kiss her, a kiss that heightened her emotions. She wrapped her arms around him to kiss him in return and soon they were loving as if it were the first time instead of a morning after a passionate evening.

Over an hour later she called the office to say she would not be in. She made some arrangements and then broke the connection, turning to Tony, who had been kissing her nape, rubbing against her backside and fondling her breasts again.

"Tony, you need to call the office yourself. And I have to get my car. The bar will think they have an abandoned car in their lot and have it towed."

"No, they won't. I called my chauffeur last night and had him get a tow truck to take it to your house. It's done."

She rubbed her forehead. "You still haven't called the office," she said, surprised he was letting that go. "I don't even remember my calendar for today."

He snagged her wrist as she started to get out of bed. "Forget it. You made your call and you were efficient and if I had been on the other end of the line, I wouldn't have suspected a thing."

"Call the office. You're shameless."

He grinned and she had to laugh. He swooped over her and pushed her onto the bed to kiss her thoroughly. In minutes she held him tightly, forgetting about the office and phone calls and any demands besides Tony's mouth and hands.

Hours later, Tony opened his eyes. Bright sunlight streamed into the room. He turned to look at Isabelle, who slept beside him. The sheet covered her to her shoulders. She lay on her side, facing him, one arm flung out across him, her silky blond hair fanned over the pillow and her shoulder and back, partially spilling over her face. He carefully combed it back from her face to look at her profile. He hadn't told her she was the first woman he had ever asked to move in with him. He had moved in with a couple of women in his life, but the relationships hadn't lasted and he had never expected them to. If he was the one to move in, he could move out when he so desired. By asking Isabelle to move in with him, he was offering an intimate arrangement, but it was far from offering marriage.

It wouldn't be lasting with Isabelle, either. He wasn't ready for commitment and that hadn't changed. He felt driven to make billionaire while he was relatively young. It kept his father from meddling. It would give him all he wanted the rest of his life and he could take care of Sydney if he needed to. Any one of those reasons was enough to avoid a serious relationship for years longer.

At the same time, he wanted Isabelle in his life more than he had ever wanted any other woman. She would never ask him to move in with her, so he had to ask her. This was the only possible way to get her into his arms most nights. She was the most enticing, exciting woman he had ever known. He had let her slip out of his life once before. He didn't intend to let that happen again for a long time. Would he be able to hold her? Would she stay if he couldn't offer marriage?

He had never asked himself that question concerning a woman before. It had always been easy—the question not as important to him. Isabelle was different. The realization of how much she had wound herself into his life and how badly he wanted her around, shocked him. He wasn't in love. He couldn't be. He had guarded against that happening because he intended to reach his goals. Love wasn't something that happened to him and he would know if it did. He had always been certain no one could fall in love against their own wishes. If she just weren't so damned independent and had a goal of marriage by thirty. What woman in today's world had a goal like that? Maybe more than he realized, because most of them probably wouldn't tell. Could he think about extending his goal just a few years? Was it worth losing her to stubbornly stick to his original plan? To his disgust, that inability to yield or adjust did sound like his father's influence and genes.

Tony looked at her, her flawless skin and long, pale lashes, her rosy mouth, the cascade of gorgeous hair that always captivated him. When desire stirred, he was torn between wanting to just look at her and making love to her. He didn't think he would ever tire of gazing at her.

He wanted her to live with him and she wasn't going to. He could feel the resolve behind her refusal. "Gorgeous woman," he whispered, "I want you with me." He pulled the sheet to her waist and drew a deep breath. Heat suffused him, and he was rampant with desire as he trailed his hand over her breasts and watched her stir.

He bent to kiss her. Her arm wound around his neck. Her blue eyes gazed up at him, sleep filled, coming awake, desire igniting. She was warm, relaxed, naked. He kissed her, caressing her and relishing rediscovery, wanting to stretch the day into days with her.

It was the middle of the afternoon before she sat in the bed with a sheet wrapped around her while she braided her hair. "Tony, I need to dress and go home."

He lay with his hands behind his head, watching her. "I vote no to that one. Stay tonight. The day is gone, anyway, so why not?"

"Why not, indeed. Tony, this is sinful. We have been making love since last night. That's just plain decadent."

"Delightful, you mean. Stay now. I'll cook dinner tonight. I haven't shown you my house." His cell phone buzzed, and she was grateful for the interruption in his attempts at persuasion.

"While you take that call, I'm going to shower."

Rolling over, he stretched out his arm to pick up his cell phone from the floor.

"Wait a minute. I have a text from Sydney." He punched buttons, scanned his message quickly and set the phone on the bedside table. "She's made up with Dylan."

"Great for both of them!" Isabelle exclaimed, smiling broadly. "I'm so very glad."

He pulled her into his arms, holding her against his chest. "You're the reason they're together. Otherwise, my dad would have gotten away with his ploy. See what you already mean to me and my sister."

"I didn't do that much. Just told you the truth about Dylan. He did the rest. I'm so glad. I was shocked when I saw how thin and pale and miserable they both were."

"Being in love takes a toll."

"You say that as if it's something frightful."

"They're wrecks. At least, I'm taking your word for it about Dylan's appearance."

"It isn't because they're in love. It's because they're having a rough time not being free to love each other. It's the interference that has them wrecks, not their love."

"That they're together again is very good news. I felt a little guilt because I was the one who told Dad that Dylan had stopped seeing her because he didn't want her to lose her inheritance. If Dad hadn't known that, he could never have told Sydney what he did."

"You never dreamed how he would use the information. Also, I'm glad you're happy they're together. It will mean she will lose her inheritance and that you'll put her through medical school."

He shrugged. "If she's happy, then so am I. I have the money for her schooling. I'll never miss it."

"Don't make me admire you."

He smiled. "Why not? Want to tell yourself I'm an ogre?"

"Hardly. I know you're a workaholic through and through."

"Not quite so through and through," he said, picking up his

cell phone and tossing it to her. She glanced at it and raised her eyebrows questioningly.

"I've just turned it off. Texted the office that I'm not taking calls unless the place burns down."

Surprised, she looked at the phone in her hand to see it was silenced. "You can still get text messages."

"Right, but they're not so intrusive and when I saw that was from Sydney, I thought it would be of interest to you, too. See, I can let go of work sometimes."

"Sometimes, Tony, but it's rare, not routine," she said, unimpressed because it was a temporary fix. Work was ingrained in Tony the same as breathing and sleeping.

"Yes, that's right. I wouldn't have gotten where I am if I hadn't given my full attention to business. Enough on that subject." Tony pulled her close and waved his hand. "I'll give you a tour of the house. This is my bedroom and you've seen my bathroom."

Still thinking about his workaholic ethic, she looked at the bedroom that was large enough to hold her entire condo. "I'm amazed this room is so huge. For that matter, so is your bathroom, although you may have had it redone."

"This is all new. It looks the same age as the original part because I told them to keep it that way—I love the big windows, the high ceilings and wood trim. I have a gym in a separate building. There's a pool and I have a theater room, a billiard room, plus the usual rooms. I think you'd like it here." He rolled over, wrapping his arm around her waist. "I meant it. I want you with me."

With her heartbeat quickening, she gazed into his dark eyes. How persuasive and tempting he was, yet how disastrous it would be for her future. The charismatic, handsome man came with guaranteed heartaches if she became closely involved.

Nine

Incredibly tempted, wanting to say yes, she gazed into his dark brown eyes. "Tony—"

He placed his index finger lightly on her lips, stopping her reply. "Consider living here. Don't give me an answer yet one way or another. I want you to be sure. Just think it through. This is a nice place to live. I hope I'm a nice guy to live with."

Smiling, she ran her fingers through his hair. "I'm sure you're a nice guy to live with. You're definitely a sexy guy to go to bed with," she added in a sultry voice, and watched his expression change, his eyes growing darker with desire.

"I want you here with me," he whispered, magic words that thrilled and tantalized her. The temptation was huge, alluring, filled with promises of so many wonderful moments, fulfillment, excitement, a real possibility of Tony falling in love. Was it worth the risks to have a relationship with him? "I've never asked a woman to move in with me. You're special, Isabelle."

She drew a deep breath. His words thrilled her. One more reason that made it definitely worth the risks to see him more.

Was he falling in love with her? Real love that would bind his heart to her?

She wanted to tell him yes, take the chance on a full-blown affair so that he would fall deeply in love, deeply enough that he would want to marry. Definitely enough to continue seeing him no matter what the consequences. Moving in with him took more thought. The acceptance was on the tip of her tongue, yet the reasons to refuse were strong enough to keep her silent.

He kissed her, pulling her into his arms, her shower forgotten.

It was six the next morning when he drove her home and walked her to her door.

"I have to leave town today. Go out with me Friday night when I return," he said.

She nodded. "Thank you. That would be nice," she answered, standing on tiptoe and wrapping her arms around his neck to kiss him. Maybe Tony was falling in love whether he realized it or not. There was far more chance of it happening if she remained in his life than if she didn't.

Instantly, he kissed her passionately in return.

Minutes later, she ended the kiss. "I'll see you Friday." She went inside, feeling as if it had been a lifetime since she had left home.

Her life had changed and she was caught in the throes of dealing with Tony in all the intimate ways she had intended to avoid. Now she faced the question of the future and whether or not to move in with him. If she didn't, would he continue their relationship?

She decided to go in late to work while she pondered giving Tony an answer. She wouldn't be able to concentrate on her job this morning, anyway. Weighing the possibilities, she always came out wanting more than being a live-in.

At noon she went to the office and attempted to keep her attention on work, finding her thoughts drifting easily. Relieved that Tony had had to leave town, she went home that night to solitude, a quiet night to think things through.

Memories were a torment. She had had a wonderful time with him. His home was beautiful. Tony was sexy, marvelous, handsome—so many great things. She was in love even though she had tried to avoid it. He wanted her, no question there, but how lasting would it be without commitment?

Thursday, she worked out with Jada, opening up to her good friend about the dilemma and coming no closer to a resolution. She missed Tony and wanted to be with him. He had called every night, talking with her more than two hours each time yet never mentioning his offer.

When he called Thursday night she was settled in bed, knowing she would be on the phone a long time.

"I really miss you," he said in a voice that made her heartbeat speed up as much as if he had just walked into the room.

"I miss you, too, Tony," she admitted.

"If it's all right with you, I may change our Friday night plans slightly," he said. "Sydney called me. She and Dylan want to take us to dinner Friday night. I think this is a gesture of gratitude for what you did."

"That's fine," she said, relieved for the young couple. "So they're together."

"Yes, and she sounded happy. I haven't talked to Dad yet. Neither has Sydney. She said she wanted to get her life straightened out with Dylan and when the time is right, she'll tell Dad. She's busy, has her own apartment, so she doesn't see them often. She may be holding back, partially for the same reason I am. I need to get some distance from what happened so I can hang on to my temper with him. Enough about that. Where are you now?"

"In bed," she replied, smiling.

He groaned. "I want to cut this trip short and come home now, but I can't. I don't think we'll be with Sydney and Dylan late Friday. I hope not. I feel I've been away from you a month instead of a few days."

Her heart warmed and she smiled. "I feel the same way." Cautious not to read too much into what he said, she changed the topic to business. "How's the deal going that you're working on?" She listened while he talked at length about the small chain of hotels in Missouri, Arkansas and Louisiana he was thinking about acquiring.

Their conversation moved on when he asked about her work, things at the office. It was after two in the morning before they parted. The calls were getting lengthier and they had more to share.

If she moved in with him, would he fall in love? That was the burning question she kept asking herself. Could she stand to refuse him? Because if she did, she expected him to move out of her life again, just as he had done in the past.

She was on the verge of deciding yes repeatedly, but each time, obstacles arose. If she lived with him, she wouldn't be able to find someone who shared her desire to marry and have a family. Also, if she moved in with Tony, she had to face what it might be like three years from now when she was still waiting for him to fall in love. Or much sooner, if he broke it off. She could be brokenhearted now, but nothing compared to living with him and then having him walk out of her life.

Friday night, as she changed into a bright red crepe dress, she still didn't have a final answer to give Tony. Her heart argued to move in—wisdom cried no. When she opened the door to face Tony, her heart thudded. She had a fleeting awareness of how handsome he was in his navy suit. He stepped inside, reaching for her and kicking the door closed behind him. He wrapped her in his arms, kissing her as she held him tightly and kissed him in return.

Time ceased to exist until she remembered their dinner engagement. "Tony, we have to go."

He released her slightly, "I don't want to go anywhere else. I want to be alone with you." His voice was deeper than usual.

"I know, but we told Dylan and Sydney we would. It won't be a late evening."

"No, it won't," he said. "Let's get this over with."

As they hurried to the waiting limousine, neither brought up the question that had dominated her thoughts all week. She still was undecided, tempted to accept yet always facing solid reasons to say no.

As soon as Tony sat beside her in the limo, he pulled her close to kiss her again.

When they walked into the lobby of the luxurious restaurant, Dylan and Sydney waited. The moment she saw Sydney, Isabelle was relieved. Both Sydney and Dylan looked radiant.

"There they are," she said.

"They look like *afters* in before and after pictures. Thankfully," Tony said quietly to her, and then gave his sister a light hug. "Sydney, you look pretty and, frankly, far better than the last time I saw you." He turned to shake hands with Dylan.

Sydney hugged Isabelle, smiling at her. "I'm grateful to you," Sydney said. "To both of you," she added, glancing between Isabelle and Tony. "That's why we wanted to take you to dinner."

The moment they were seated at a linen-covered table and had given drink orders, Dylan turned to Tony and Isabelle. "We have several things to tell you both. First, this dinner is a token thank-you for revealing what had really happened."

"It's impossible to tell you how grateful we are to you," Sydney added, her brown eyes sparkling.

"We're together again because of you," Dylan continued. "That's one reason for this dinner. There's another." He paused to hold Sydney's right hand. "I've asked Sydney to marry me and she's accepted."

Smiling broadly, Sydney held out her left hand and a diamond sparkled in the candlelight. "Congratulations!" Isabelle and Tony spoke at the same time.

Isabelle felt a lurch as Sydney turned slightly to Dylan. The look they exchanged plainly expressed their love as much as if they had verbally declared it. Suddenly, she knew what her answer had to be to Tony.

She looked at a beautiful emerald-cut diamond surrounded by smaller diamonds on a wide gold band. "It's beautiful, Sydney, and I'm thrilled for both of you," Isabelle said, meaning it. "Dylan, this is wonderful news. Both of you look incredibly happy."

"We are," he said quietly to Sydney, for a moment his smile faltering. "Whatever the consequences, this is what we've decided to do. Sydney convinced me to marry her," he added teasingly.

Tony reached out to hug Sydney's neck, a light, brotherly embrace. "I'll give you back the check, Syd. I meant what I said about putting you through medical school."

Dylan shook his head. "Tony, we'll be married. I'll send her to med school."

Tony shook his head. "I want to do this as a wedding gift to both of you. Also, Dylan, I have to admit, I'm enjoying my freedom from being hassled by Dad and this is a little bit of a payback for what he's done. Let me do this."

Sydney grasped Dylan's arm. "Let him, Dylan. You'll never understand about our father and how he's tried to control our lives."

"No, I don't understand. I'm sure Isabelle doesn't, either. I've heard her talk about her family." He looked at Tony. "Very well, that's an enormous, marvelous wedding present and we both appreciate it," he said, glancing at Sydney, who smiled at him.

"Is a date set?" Isabelle asked.

"We're talking about it," Dylan replied.

"Probably around June. Something small with close friends, and whatever family will be there," Sydney added, her smile fading. "I don't expect Mom or Dad to attend. If they don't, Tony, will you give the bride away?"

"I'd be honored, Syd. If Dad appears, fine. He can do the honor. Have you told him yet?" Tony asked.

"No. I want to wait until Dylan and I have our plans made and I'm not so emotional and angry over it. I'll tell Mom and Dad soon."

"Syd, I don't want to say anything to them until you have," Tony said.

"I'll let you know."

They paused while champagne was opened. Through toasts and through dinner, Isabelle tried to join in Dylan's and Sydney's obvious happiness, but underneath her smiles was a steady hurt. She was glad for them. Their love was unmistakable.

When the evening finally ended as they parted with Dylan and Sydney, Sydney hugged Isabelle again. "Thank you so much. I wouldn't have Dylan back if it weren't for you. Be patient with my brother. He's really a good guy at heart."

Isabelle smiled. "I'll remember your advice," she said, continuing to wonder about the depth of Tony's objectives.

She looked into the female version of Tony, dark brown eyes identical to his, a mop of thick black curls, longer than Tony's. How well did Isabelle really know her brother? Did she have any idea of his ambition to be a billionaire by forty?

"I'm happy for you and I'm glad the two of you are together again. You appear to have truly found love, an elusive commodity it seems."

Dylan turned to put his arm around Sydney's waist, pulling her close against him. "Thanks to both of you again."

"Thank *you* for dinner," Isabelle said, while Tony said the same. The limo pulled up and the chauffeur held the door. They climbed inside and Tony turned to her, pulling her into his arms.

Isabelle came willingly, hungry for his kisses, wanting to love him, wishing she could bind him to her, overcome the force that drove him to put business and success first over all else. "How I want you," he whispered, kissing her again before she could answer him. She held him tightly, kissing him, taking and giving, knowing it was fleeting, meaningless to him.

She lost track of time, but all too soon the limo stopped. "We're at your place, Isabelle. Come home with me tonight. I'll see you home in the morning, but come back with me now."

She nodded and was in his embrace again.

At his house, he released her and they stepped out of the limo to go in through a side door. The minute they were in the mansion, Tony drew her into his arms.

Clothes were strewn all the way to a downstairs bedroom. She glimpsed a four-poster bed, lots of pillows, white furniture. Little else registered with her. She was in Tony's magical embrace again.

They loved through the night and fell asleep in each other's arms. Isabelle was the last to go to sleep. On her side and held close by Tony, she ran her fingers in his hair and then along his jaw, studying him, memorizing his features. "Tonight was special, Tony," she whispered, knowing he was asleep and would never hear her or know. "I love you."

She could not think about *if only* possibilities. She had to accept Tony the way he was and face reality. She studied him as he slept, her heart filled with love and longing. How could ambition so blind him to what was wonderful in life?

Sleep would not come. Speculation was futile. She refused to think about the future and tried to cling to this night, this hour with Tony beside her, one arm holding her close. No one could predict tomorrow.

When she stirred hours later, Tony leaned over to kiss her. Instantly her arms circled his neck and they made love until sunshine spilled into the room over an hour later.

"I'll ask again, Isabelle, will you come and live here with me?"

She sat up, pulling a top sheet close around her, shaking her long hair away from her face, knowing the moment for decision had come. "No, I won't," she answered. "I would love to, Tony, but I want more than I'll get by just moving into your house."

"You want love. Take a chance, move in and see what happens. It's great right now. I would expect it to get even better."

Saddened, hurting, wishing he would set business on a back burner, give it second place in his life and propose, she knew that wouldn't happen. Not until after forty and he had achieved billionaire would his goals change. Business came first.

She sat close to him, the sheet pulled beneath her arms while he had it across his lap. His chest was bare, tempting even after a night of love. She felt as if she were breaking to pieces inside. "Tony, I want it all. I want what Sydney has—commitment. Even more, I want what my parents have, a long, steady love. That's what I've always wanted."

"Live with me. It may turn into love and then into marriage," he said, caressing her nape, playing with her hair.

May. She shook her head. "I want to say yes, but I have to say no. I saw the love between Dylan and Sydney. I want that. I want commitment, your love. I want to be first in someone's life, not to follow a goal to become a billionaire by forty. You might fall in love and you might marry, but you won't give up your driving goals to achieve that billionaire status. And that means putting work ahead of all else. No thanks. That isn't what I want. I'm not sitting home alone week after week, raising children without a father, watching you think about deals instead of your family. You and I have vastly different goals and views of what's important. You pursue yours and I hope you get them and I hope they make you happy. I'll pursue mine."

"You're presuming the worst, envisioning a scenario that

might not happen. Half the world is filled with men and women who don't spend every waking hour together, but they love each other and love their families and raise fine children."

"True, but I've watched my best friend's father, who was a workaholic. They barely saw him and he missed too many big events in his children's lives. It's not spending every waking hour together. It's putting the other person first in your life and the two of you together being more important than business. It's a true partner in the family to help with kids and grow old together. That's the kind of love your sister has with Dylan and you can see it just by looking at them. I'm not moving in with you. Now's the time for the break before my heart is shattered so badly, I'd never recover."

"That's ridiculous. You'll recover from a broken heart if you ever have one, but that isn't what I intend to have happen when you move in with me."

His eyes darkened and a muscle worked in his jaw. She hurt all over, but she was going to stand firm with her decision because she thought any other way would lead to far greater heartache.

"It's been wonderful, Tony. You know I'm in love with you now—"

Tony reached for her.

"Isabelle, come here," he said, his arm circling her waist.

She gripped his wrist and removed his arm. "Just wait and listen. I love you, but I will get over this because we haven't bound our lives together yet."

"Then take a chance on us, dammit," he said, clasping her shoulder with his hand. "Give us some time together and try to see what develops and how deep it goes."

She shook her head again. "No. I already know how deep my love for you goes. I want it all. I watched Dylan and Sydney tonight. They have it. Each one is first in the other's life. They're deeply in love and there were moments when the outside world didn't exist for them. They were barely with us some of the time. There's a unity between them that is a strong bond. That's the kind of love I want. I'm glad they've found it, because I think it's both special and rare."

"Isabelle, dammit, stop. Give us some time together. Two weeks. See if you feel the same after that. You're not giving us a chance. You've got all these preconceived notions. I won't be like your friend's father. Give us a fair chance at this and then stop and take a long look and make a monumental, life-changing decision when you have more knowledge about what you're doing."

"Mr. Logic," she said, fighting back tears. "No, Tony. I already know. You won't change. You can't change. If you'd had any intention of changing, you would have proposed marriage instead of asking me to move in with you. I'm going to dress and I want to go home. You can send the limo to deposit me at home and you don't even have to ride along."

"To hell with this," he said. He pulled her into his embrace, kissing her passionately. She was stiff, unresponsive, but his mouth worked magic and in seconds she kissed him in return.

Her heart pounded and she held him tightly, kissing him, wanting to kiss him into agreement with her, hoping he would never forget her. She loved him and she let it show through her kisses and responses.

He groaned, wanting her, making love furiously, hungrily, while she returned it as passionately, her hands roaming over him.

She leaned back to frame his face with her hands. "I love you, Tony. It might not be marriage with me, but someday, you'll wed someone. You're going to miss the most wonderful part of life while you're out chasing money. You're capable of so much." She kissed him long, slowly, passionately.

He held her tightly, wrapping his arms around her, bending

over her to kiss her as if it were the last kiss he could ever have from any woman. "Damn, I want you, Isabelle."

"And I want your love. There is a difference, Tony." She slipped free and hurried to gather her clothes and leave the room, determined to find a shower away from Tony's seductive kisses.

Tears stung her eyes because it was over between them. She could feel that to her toes and she had seen the look in his dark eyes—anger, hurt, refusal. She hoped he wouldn't accompany her on the ride home. It was over between them and the sooner the break came, the better off they both would be.

She showered, letting her tears flow freely, wiping her eyes as she dried and hung up the towel. She dressed swiftly, rebraiding her hair and dreading confronting him to ask for a ride home.

When she found him, he was in the library. He had dressed in charcoal trousers and his white dress shirt.

"You don't have to come along."

"Don't be ridiculous," he said, smiling at her as if nothing had happened between them. "I brought you here and I'll see you home." He draped his arm across her shoulders.

They rode home in silence and at her door, he pulled her to him for a brief kiss.

"Would it matter if I had told you that I'm in love with you?" he asked.

"Now we won't know, will we? You didn't say you were and you're still not," she replied.

"I know I'm going to miss you like hell," he said, grinding out the words. He kissed her one long, passionate last time and then turned to hurry back to his limo.

"Goodbye, Tony," she whispered, knowing she had lost him now, but that had been her intention. She hurried inside, locking the door and running to her bedroom. She flung herself across the bed to cry. She wanted Tony, wanted to be part of his life, wanted his lovemaking, his laughter, his drive. Instead, she had told him goodbye and he was out of her life.

* * *

The weekend was silent and miserable. She exercised twice as long as usual and tried to do work she had brought home from the office, but her concentration was poor.

Monday morning, she cried silently as she moved through the condo, hunting for clothes to wear to work, knowing she should pick her best to give the image of confidence.

She made it in to work twenty minutes early and headed straight to her office, hoping she would see very few people the whole day. Tony was out of her life and she should start getting ready for it.

How easy that should be, but that wasn't the case.

The day seemed three times longer than normal, the hours dragging, her mind wandering from business.

The worst moments were the meetings, the times she would pass Tony somewhere, the meetings when he was included. The next day was worse and she decided the pain was not worth the promotion, the pay, the move up in her career. Feeling as if she would never be able to concentrate, she called Vernon Irwin to see if his offer for a job with his company was still valid.

The following Monday morning, the sixth of March, she tendered her resignation, putting a letter in a manila envelope and leaving it for Tony's secretary before he arrived at work.

At nine his secretary called to make an appointment for a meeting with Tony.

Isabelle dreaded the meeting, yet it had to happen. She was losing sleep, wondering whether she would look as much a wreck as Sydney Ryder had.

At three, she headed to Tony's office. The moment she stepped inside, her heart thudded when she looked into his eyes.

Ten

He came around his desk and motioned toward an empty leather chair. "Have a seat."

He held her resignation letter in his hand. "I read this, Isabelle. I'm disappointed. Whatever there is—was—between us, I hoped we could keep our personal lives separate from work. I made you a fantastic offer, gave you a promotion, which has enabled you to secure an offer like this from Irwin."

A muscle worked in his jaw and his eyes blazed with anger, yet she could still see desire. She suspected if she told him to tear up the letter and she would move in, it would clear everything instantly. She was still tempted to do so. She wanted to walk into his arms and kiss him, be held and to love him for hours, as they had done not so long ago.

"Why?" he asked.

"I can't work around you. I can't keep my mind on my work. I can't focus. I can't think about the job because I miss you. I remember moments with you, shared laughter, our long phone calls. I miss you every hour of the day and the nights are far worse. I can't stop thinking about when we were together. I can't stop missing you. You asked and there it is."

"Damn," he snapped. "Why are you doing this to yourself and to both of us? Maybe I'm falling in love. You're jumping to conclusions about a future that you really know nothing about. Nobody knows the future."

"I may be, Tony. But this is what I have to do. I haven't changed and neither have you. I want marriage to a man dedicated to his family. I want his main goal in life to be his family—the kids he raises, his marriage. Go make your billions. I want simpler things. I want to love a man who loves me in return and who loves his kids and puts us all first in his life."

"How can you do that and say you're in love with me? Why are you doing this to us? Ambition isn't a sin. Most women would welcome that I'm hardworking and successful. Since when are those two qualities bad?"

"They're wonderful qualities in the right perspective. When they dominate all else, including your love for your family, that's when it's out of balance. That's what I don't want any part of. I've seen what it does to a family. Sorry, Tony."

"Dammit, Isabelle." He pulled her close to kiss her hard and long. She returned his kiss, lost in passion, crying, torn by conflicting emotions of love and loss. He released her abruptly. She opened her eyes slowly to watch him studying her.

"You're crying. You kiss with passion that sets me ablaze. You've told me you love me. Stop fighting what you know you want with all your being."

"I will not. I know what the price might be."

"All right, Isabelle. Take the new job. Go your own way. You don't want me in your life, go find happiness somewhere else," he snapped, striding past her to open his office door and hold it, waiting for her to exit.

She drew a deep breath and left his office, knowing she was walking out of his life.

She wanted him right now even with the harsh words. He was hurt and angry, totally unaccustomed to defeat or rejection. Tears threatened and she wanted out of the office, away from people she worked with, away from Tony.

She hurt all over. She had resigned from a wonderful job. Told Tony she didn't want to continue seeing him. She loved him and those actions hurt, yet she was certain she had taken the only course she could live with. She remembered all the times her friend had bitterly complained about the absence of her father. She didn't want that for herself or her children and she knew she would never be happy with that kind of life and taking a role secondary to Tony's success in business. To become a billionaire in the next few years would take intense dedication. Some women could accept that kind of life. Some preferred it. She didn't. It was personal preference and she had made her decision.

She stepped outside, gulping air, letting the tears come as she rushed to her car to climb inside.

Driving home, she tried to stop thinking about Tony and keep her mind on her driving.

Finally, she was in the haven of her condo. She threw herself on her sofa to cry, trying to give vent to the hurt and hoping she could pour it out and get over it and get over him. Better now than later.

She wondered whether he really cared and how long it would take him to forget her.

She made plans to take some time between jobs to regain her composure. She couldn't start a new job in the state she was in at present because her concentration was gone. She had asked Irwin for time and she decided now to get out of Dallas, far away, with a change of scenery and try to get her emotions under control and adjust to telling Tony goodbye.

Her family knew a little about her problems and the new job and they were hovering over her with good intentions, but she wanted some time alone. Her condo and plants would be fine for a week.

After searching through brochures and talking to a travel agent, she flew to Alabama because of the attractive beach resort the travel agent found. Isabelle rented a small house on the Gulf where she could have solitude and try to get over Tony, wondering if she ever would in a lifetime. She could imagine he would throw himself into work until another woman interested him.

For the next few weeks Tony poured himself into work, traveling and spending the rest of March away from Dallas. The more time that passed, the more he missed Isabelle. The first week of April on a Sunday afternoon he received a text from Sydney telling him that she had seen their parents, who were furious with her. He asked Sydney to come by if she had time, and in an hour she was at his house.

"Come in, Syd. You look great," he said, meaning it. His sister had regained some weight. Her cheeks were rosy and, to his relief, she looked radiantly happy.

"Thanks, Tony. You don't look so hot yourself. Are you sick?"

"No, I'm not sick. Just busy," he snapped, growing more annoyed with each person who asked how he was feeling or told him he looked as if he had caught something. "Whatever Dad and Mom said, you don't look as if it's crushed you."

"I love Dylan and they're not taking that from me again," she replied.

"Let's sit in the family room."

"I can't stay. I'm meeting Dylan, but I wanted to stop by and tell you about seeing Mom and Dad."

"So is Dad still threatening all the same things?"

"Yes, and he's angry that we've learned the truth about what he did. Actually, I think he's embarrassed that he got caught."

Tony shook his head. "He's angry that we learned the truth," he repeated. "He should be apologizing all over the place for what he did and trying to make it up to you."

She nodded. "I thought so, too. He didn't like getting caught. Mom is angry about Dylan, saying I'll never be happy. I'm not marrying someone to please them. Anyway, thank you again for your huge gift to us. We'll get along without the inheritance. That doesn't matter as much to me."

"I don't know that I can understand or agree, but I want you to be happy. You know if I ever do inherit, I'll share it with you."

She smiled at him. "That's the future, Tony. I wouldn't be concerned with it now. You can't possibly guess what will happen."

"True. I haven't talked to Dad yet. I don't think I should until I can cool down enough to hang on to my temper."

"He's probably embarrassed to see you. He knows he's lost some respect from both of us even though he won't acknowledge it. He told me he tried to get Dylan out of my life for my own good and that later I would thank him."

"Damn, Sydney, of all my friends' fathers who were so interfering and controlling, I think Dad turned out to be the worst for his actions with you."

"I doubt if I'll see much of them for a while."

"Can't blame you. They brought that on themselves."

"I need to go, Tony. I just wanted to let you know. You've made the break so much easier for me."

He stepped outside to walk with her to her car and held the door for her while she slid behind the wheel. "I'm glad I can. And I'm glad you're back with Dylan, if that makes you happy," he said, thinking about Isabelle and feeling a knot of anger and loss.

"Hopefully, they won't try to interfere with you seeing Isabelle."

"No problem there. Isabelle and I aren't seeing each other, anyway."

Sydney frowned. "None of my business, but I'm sorry because I liked her a lot. I thought maybe you did, too."

"Isabelle wants to get married. That's not in my agenda."

Sydney smiled. "Ah, my stubborn brother. Well, as long as you're happy and don't miss her, okay." Her eyes narrowed and she slanted her head. "Tony, is that why you look as if you've had a case of the flu? Because Isabelle is gone and you don't want her to be?"

"Sydney, I've been working," he said in a clipped tone, wishing he could sound more casual and less annoyed. "Don't start on me."

She studied him. "You're my brother and I love you, but you can really be mule-stubborn sometimes. You don't look happy."

"Tell Dylan hello for me." He closed the car door and she started the engine.

"All right. I'll be quiet. Now that I know Isabelle has walked out, to me you do look like a man in love. I'm going," she added hastily, revving the engine.

Relieved, he stepped away from her car.

He watched her drive away. Thinking about Isabelle, he returned to the house to continue working. Annoyed by Sydney's remarks, he walked along the hall with his thoughts on Isabelle. He hated to admit it even to himself, but he missed her more each day instead of less and he hadn't expected that to happen.

Marriage? It was impossible to lose sight of his goals. Marriage definitely wasn't in his best interest. If he didn't acquire more wealth and power, he would be back fighting with his father over every big issue in his life.

"Dammit," he said. Sydney hadn't made him feel better. He was glad she was happy, but he didn't need to hear he looked like he had the flu.

When he walked into his office his attention went to the phone on his desk. He wanted to reach for it and call Isabelle.

He shook his head. He needed to get a grip and focus completely on his goal and the business at hand.

Within the hour he gave up and went to his room to change for a run, hoping to shake thoughts of Isabelle and lose himself in physical activity, reassuring himself that within weeks he wouldn't care that she was out of his life.

Isabelle was busy in her new job. She still hurt and missed Tony badly. Whenever she saw a tall man with black curly hair, her heart thudded and she had to look twice to convince herself it was not Tony.

Tralear Hotels had just bought out another hotel chain. They had built a new seven-story office building and Isabelle was instantly busy and working overtime to get brochures, invitations and the graphic art work done for their grand opening reception and celebration. Isabelle was thankful to be constantly busy, hoping all the work would distract her from her misery.

One afternoon when she was getting a haircut, she picked up a local magazine to see Tony's picture and an article about a contribution his family was making to a local museum. Her heart missed a beat as she looked at his picture. So familiar, yet far out of her life.

It was a Ryder contribution, so she wondered whether he had made up with his father since the family was making the donation.

Two nights later, she received a phone call from Sydney Ryder. Tears stung Isabelle's eyes as she heard Sydney's voice.

"I hear you have a new job."

"Yes, I do."

"Congratulations! Guess you didn't like working for my brother."

"That wasn't it, Sydney."

"I called because we've set a date of June twenty-third. We'll have a destination wedding at Grand Cayman. I would love for you to be a bridesmaid."

"Sydney, thank you. I'm honored you asked me," Isabelle said, feeling caught in a real dilemma. "I would love to, but things weren't so good between your brother and me when we parted. I don't want to bring any tension to the wedding at a time that should be joyful. I think if you want harmony and a wonderful time by all, you'll look elsewhere for your bridesmaid."

"I'm sorry, Isabelle. Tony told me, but I didn't know it was a really bad breakup, although he looked terrible when I saw him and he was as grouchy as a bear."

Shocked, Isabelle's eyes widened as she tried to imagine Tony fitting such a description and wondered whether a business deal had gone sour, because she couldn't imagine he had been snarly over their breakup. She tried to pay attention to Sydney. "I really wanted people who are important to me to be in our wedding party."

"That's sweet and I do thank you. I know it's best I decline."

"I understand. I'm annoyed with my woodenheaded brother about this, but I still love you both. Come to the wedding if you can. I'm really sorry. I was so in hopes that Tony was falling in love, which he looks as if he did, but Tony wouldn't recognize falling in love if it bit him. He'd be better off."

"Your brother can certainly take care of himself. Don't start worrying about us now."

"I like you, Isabelle, and I think you were good for Tony. I just hate to see him lose you."

"He knows what he wants. Thank you, Sydney, for asking me. I'm really pleased that you did, but that's a time when everyone should share in your joy."

"Just stay a friend. I'll hear about you and see you sometimes with Dylan."

"I'm so happy for both of you," Isabelle said, thinking about

Tony and feeling as if her loss was growing instead of diminishing as she puzzled over Sydney's description of him.

"Thanks, Isabelle. I hope you get over Tony quickly so you don't even care if he's around or not by the time of our wedding."

"Hopefully, I will," she said. "Thanks, again."

They ended the call and Isabelle cried quietly, missing Tony, knowing she was going to regret her decision for a long time to come. He could be seeing another woman. His bad disposition could be due purely to business. Looking terrible—she couldn't imagine that and guessed Sydney had a different view of her brother than the rest of the female world. Had Tony stopped thinking about her? Only time would tell.

Another week passed and Tony piled on work, knowing that would be his salvation. Always, he had been able turn off his private life and concentrate on the business at hand. Now he found memories of Isabelle were intruding at all hours of each day. He could no longer go to meetings and concentrate on the speaker. Too many times, his thoughts drifted. He wondered what Isabelle was doing. Where was she? Did she miss him as much as he missed her?

He focused on the speaker, following the tables of figures being presented, until he realized his mind had wandered again. Clenching his fist, he tried to concentrate, wishing the meeting would end quickly.

That night Tony stared at the phone in his hand. He missed Isabelle more than he had ever thought possible.

To try to get her off his mind, he read through his texts, including one from his sister. Sydney was coming by to leave something wedding-related. The ceremony wasn't until June, yet Sydney was working on it whenever she had a chance. So far his folks were not participating or even attending. He was undecided whether to talk to them about it, or let it go by because it might be a more harmonious event for Sydney and Dylan if the senior Ryders weren't present.

Tony raked his hand through his hair, tangling it more. It was uncustomary for him to be so indecisive. He seemed to have lost his drive and he wasn't thinking clearly about big issues looming in his life.

Sydney breezed in, heading to his kitchen to spread brochures on the kitchen table. "This is where we're having the wedding. We've rented cottages nearby for the wedding party. I figured you would want your own place because I know how you like your privacy."

As she looked at him, her eyes narrowed. "Tony, are you all right?"

"Sure. Yes, I am. Just busy lately."

"You've been busy since you were eighteen years old." She walked around to feel his forehead and he pushed her hand away.

"Syd," he said in a threatening voice. "I'm okay. Stop that and let's get through this wedding stuff."

She placed her hands on her hips to look intently at him while her foot tapped. "Have you talked to Isabelle?"

"No. It's over between Isabelle and me. We're not talking at all."

"You really are in love with her," Sydney said, a note of wonder in her voice.

"I am not in love with Isabelle," Tony snapped, his temper rising. His sister was annoying him as she sometimes could and had since they were small kids. "Sydney, you're getting bratty."

"You're in love and you won't face up to it." When she giggled, he frowned, his cheeks burning and trying to hang on to his rising temper.

"My, oh, my. I knew this could happen, but I really expected you to make a bargain with some woman and have a marriage of convenience where you both profited from your union. I expected any marriage you would have would be a business contract. Instead, my brother is in love. Face it, Tony, you love her. What's so wrong about that? I know you're not holding out to marry one of those women our folks have picked out for you."

He glared at her. "Syd, you can be downright annoying sometimes. I thought you were outgrowing that, but you haven't. I'm not getting tied up in marriage until I reach my financial goals, and marriage is all Isabelle wants. End of story. We can't possibly be together."

Sydney laughed. "Of course you can be together. Why are you making yourself miserable, Tony? Wait until you see her someday with another man. You'll regret this beyond belief."

"I'm doing exactly what I want to do." He bit off his words, his anger increasing. "I have a goal of billionaire by forty. I have to keep Dad off my back and that will do it for all time. She has her own goal—marriage by thirty. Those goals are definitely not compatible. It's not like you and Dylan—you two *are* in love. We're not."

"I think you won't face the truth yourself." At his glare, she quickly added, "Hey, okay." And held up her hands as if surrendering. "Back to my wedding, then. Is this all right for a place for you to stay?" she asked, holding out a brochure.

"It's fine," he said, barely glancing at it. "You decide, Syd. All this wedding hoopla is not my deal. Do you need help paying for it? I'd be glad to."

She shook her head and gathered up the papers and brochures. "Thank you, Tony. Dylan wanted to pay for it. With you picking up my school tab, it's not placing him in a bind. Now remember, you wouldn't look at the brochures. I'll have to remind you that you told me to make the choices for you. Do you know how unlike you that is? Tony, face the truth. You're in love."

"So what if I am. I might be a little, but I want to reach my goal and that means staying single."

"You're not just a 'little' bit in love. I've never seen you like this. By the way, Isabelle very politely turned down my asking her to be a bridesmaid. She thought it would cause tension at my wedding. Actually, on the phone, she sounds as if she is getting along better than you are. Maybe she's met someone new."

"Sydney, dammit—"

She laughed. "Just pulling your chain. You are in king-size knots over Isabelle. You are in love and blind and in denial." She grabbed up her brochures to dash toward the door. "I'm going. Your choice though about love and marriage. I'll get out of your hair, which, by the way, is badly tangled."

"I didn't tell you how yours looked not long ago."

"That was sweet. Messy hair—mine, yours—both for the same reason."

"Syd—" he said threateningly, and she laughed, reaching for the door.

"See you later, Tony," she called over her shoulder, rushing out. He followed in long strides to watch her climb into her car and turn down his driveway. He waved, closed the door and walked back to his office with his mind on Isabelle and his sister's words ringing in his ears.

He was in love with her and he might as well face up to it. He was thinking about her most of his waking hours. He'd get over it and it wasn't that big a deal. As fast as that thought came, he could remember Isabelle's cutting remark about enjoying his money through the years and what an empty victory he would find it. Were his goals misplaced, blown all out of proportion? Was he ruining his life chasing the dollar when he was already enormously wealthy? The thought of seeing Isabelle with someone else chilled him. Sydney had put him in a sour mood, something she had rarely ever done.

It was even worse when he went to bed. He was lonely, missing Isabelle terribly. He picked up his phone and stared at her name at the head of his list of contacts. He wanted her, yet he always got over breakups, so the feeling of missing her should pass.

Right?

* * *

The following day at the office wasn't any better and then grew worse after the mail delivery. He looked at the thick cream-colored envelope in his hand. It had been opened in the mailroom and he slid out the announcement and invitation, scanning it swiftly, certain it was Isabelle's work.

It was from Tralear with Vernon's signature at the bottom inviting Tony to the Grand Opening Reception of the new Tralear Building under Vernon's new presidency. They would also introduce four new executives, including Isabelle.

Thinking about her, he hurt. How had she become so vital to him? Tony ran his hand over the embossed invitation, looking at the RSVP and then scrawling across it, "Please decline." He tossed it into a stack of mail for his secretary to handle. It was a week from Friday night. He thought about the sacrifices he had made, the long, grueling hours of work he had put in to become wealthy enough to keep his father off his back and to earn the man's respect. Was he sacrificing the love of his life for this goal? *Was* it going to be an empty victory? He missed her more each day. How much worse was it going to get? Was he losing the true love of his life?

He couldn't go back to letting his father constantly interfere with him, yet maybe he shouldn't worry about that and let it wreck his life. He missed and wanted Isabelle in his life. Tony made a mental note to get out of Dallas, go someplace away from work, where he could think straight about Isabelle and his future.

Isabelle couldn't resist stopping at the cubicle of the secretary who was keeping track of the reception RSVPs, and she learned that Tony had declined the invitation. Disappointment filled her even though it was what she had expected.

She missed him and the hurt wasn't lessening. There were moments now she was tempted to call him, accept his offer and forget her plans. She wouldn't meet someone else she wanted to marry. It was Tony she wanted and if not him…suddenly marriage didn't sound all that great.

Before long, the decision would be out of her hands, because he would find someone else. Tony would always have a woman in his life. On his terms.

The night of the reception, she dressed carefully, still wishing Tony would attend yet knowing he wouldn't be there. She had checked again yesterday to see if he possibly had changed his mind, but he had not and they were not letting anyone in who had not accepted the invitation.

She had bought a new red dress for the occasion. She wanted to wear black, but red would be more festive. She didn't feel festive. She simply hurt. She missed Tony and her friends at Ryder Enterprises, which she still thought of as Morris.

Her red dress had a plunging neckline and a low-cut back with tiny spaghetti straps and a straight short skirt. Thinking of Tony, she left her hair down and wore no jewelry.

The reception at the new Tralear Building was being held in a great room that would be used for such events or conferences. The tables were along the walls, covered in white cloths and holding a buffet of delicious food from steamy chicken and chilled shrimp to chocolate pastries and fruits. At one end of the room on a raised platform a band played. Guests mingled, filling the room with conversation and laughter.

She should have been jubilantly happy instead of wishing she were home and finding it difficult to carry on a conversation or even to listen to others.

Every tall man with black curly hair caught her attention. Because of the crowd, she could only see the top of one man's head, and his thick, black curls. She was mesmerized and couldn't look away because his hair reminded her of Tony. The resemblance made her heartbeat race. Would she be the same way about strangers who resembled him five years from now?

Should she rethink moving in with him? She knew it was too late to go back.

Then the man drew closer, the crowd parted and she looked into Tony's eyes.

Eleven

Her heart thudded and she forgot everything except Tony walking toward her, his gaze holding hers, immobilizing her. She smiled, but she was unable to speak. Her mouth went dry and she felt overwhelmed. She wanted to run and throw herself into his arms, but she maintained restraint. This was the time for that if she wanted him back. She felt that intuitively and thoroughly. It was also the time to get him out of her life forever if that was how it had to be.

He walked up to her. "Hi," he said, his thick, deep voice melting her. She couldn't even speak to answer him. "You're stunning," he said, his gaze roaming over her face and hair. "Where can we go to talk?"

"Tony, there's no point. I want all of you. I want marriage to you. I've made that clear and you've made your feelings clear to me. We should just stay in here. I need to greet people."

"I want to talk to you," he persisted.

"I'll be available tomorrow or the next day. I'm sure it can keep," she said, her pulse racing and her insides churning over rejecting him when he kept insisting on talking privately with her. She had spoken openly and frankly about her feelings. She saw no choice, except the one she had to live by.

She started to walk away from him. He pulled her around. When she began to protest, she took one look at his determined expression and closed her mouth.

"I have to talk to you."

"We really have nothing further to discuss."

"Yes, we do. I'm willing to give up my goal of billionaire by forty."

Stunned, she stood in shock, staring at him and trying to fathom what he had just stated. "You can't mean that," she said.

"I do mean it. Totally. I know what I want."

She stared at him, narrowing her eyes. "That is so totally unlike you in every way. I don't think you really can do it even if you think you mean it."

"I mean it, Isabelle, and I can do it if I really want it." He glanced around. "This isn't a good place to talk. The band is playing, people are beginning to dance around us."

She realized he was right. Her surroundings had faded into nonexistence for her. "All right, Tony, step into the hall. I didn't think you were coming tonight. I saw your RSVP."

"I didn't plan to attend and then at the last minute, I wanted to talk to you and I don't want to wait until tomorrow." He took her arm lightly, yet the touch made her draw a deep breath. She wanted to be in his arms more than ever. Her thoughts spun with his declaration of giving up his lifelong goal. She couldn't believe he actually would do so, but she was beginning to not care.

They walked into the hall and she looked up at him. "I have an office two stories down if you'd rather go there."

With his jaw set, he steered her toward the elevators and they rode in silence until they entered her office and he closed the door.

She walked away from him, turning to face him. "Tony, I

don't think you could live up to that even if you think you mean it now."

He closed the distance between them, stopping close to her. "My life is miserable without you in it. It isn't worth the sacrifice to stay single."

Surprised, she clamped her jaw shut tightly and shook her head. Tears threatened. She wanted to believe him, but she couldn't. "Tony, I've missed you, but you've spent your adult life as a workaholic, driven, addicted to work. I don't think you can change. You say you will, but several months after marriage or even a year or two later, your family will slip into second place. And you don't care for kids or really want children."

"Yes, I do. I want you and everything that goes with marriage to you. Kids—" He shrugged. "I don't know, but Sydney is younger than I am and I've always loved her."

"That's entirely different."

"Give me a chance here. I mean it. I want you in my life all the time. I want you enough to give up that goal of billionaire. If Dad threatens to cut me out of their will the way he has Sydney, that's fine. I'm a multimillionaire and I'll always work, but as far as being driven—I'm only driven to keep you in my life. I've put you first in my life." He reached for her, pulling her to him. "I've missed you a hell of a lot. I couldn't think of anything except missing you. When we were together I put you first in my life. You were still first in my life even when you were away from me. I don't want a life without you in it. No billionaire goal. Only family first, and by family, I mean you. I promise, Isabelle." He touched her hair lightly, brushing it away from her face. "I love you. Really love you. I've never been in love before. Nothing like this."

Her heart pounded with his declarations. Could she believe him? The words were magical, what she wanted to hear, but people rarely changed when personality and character and drive were involved.

"Tony, I desperately want to believe you, but people rarely change."

"Of course, they do, if they really want to. Addicts get over addiction. Smokers stop, alcoholics reform, people learn anger management, they get educations late in life when they realize they need them. People can change. Isabelle, I love you and I'll change for you. I'm putting you first right now." He reached into his pocket and pulled out a ring that sparkled in the light. Holding out the glittering ring, he knelt on one knee.

"I love you, Isabelle. Will you marry me and be my wife for all our lives? I promise to always put you and our family first because my love for you comes first."

Isabelle melted. "Yes, Tony," she whispered, her heart thudding as she took the ring with its huge diamond, surrounded by other diamonds. "Tony," she whispered, looking up at him as he stood to embrace her. "I love you. I have for so long."

Tears spilled over and he wiped them away. "Don't cry," he said, gazing into her eyes and then at her mouth. As she stood on tiptoe to kiss him, he leaned down and kissed her.

Her heart pounded with joy as he slid the ring on her finger. She knew she was taking a chance, but was willing to do so because Tony was willing to take a chance also.

"Let's have this wedding soon," he whispered, pausing to look into her eyes. "I don't want to wait until June the way Sydney is."

"I agree," she whispered. "Are you going to let me keep my goal?"

"Definitely. I'm going to help you achieve it."

She smiled at him and then they kissed.

Twelve

At the wedding reception at their country club in Dallas, Isabelle danced with her new husband. She had shed the long satin train to her dress, which was plain lines with a strapless top and a straight skirt. Tony took her breath away in his dark tuxedo, and the look of love in his eyes kept her warm.

It was May with flowers in bloom. The world looked beautiful to her and her love made her smile constantly.

"Your family is nice, Isabelle. Mine could take a lesson."

"Your parents have been nice to me, Tony," she said, glancing briefly at the guests surrounding the dance floor.

"They've given up. Maybe it's old age, maybe hope of a grandchild. They're even going to Syd's wedding and Dad will give her away. They just told her last night at our rehearsal dinner."

Isabel beamed. "I'm so glad."

He smiled. "You are really into families. I've never asked how many kids you want and I suspect I may have to brace myself for the answer," he said teasingly, holding her lightly as they danced around the floor.

"I really never had a set number in mind. I grew up in a big family. It was fun. Let's think about three for a start."

"Start and maybe finish. I can't see myself coaching soccer, but I'm willing to give it a try."

"I can definitely see you doing that, taking charge, making it all run smoothly and helping little kids."

He laughed. "Right now, I want to dance you right out of the door and to the limo and away to where I'll have you to myself for the next three weeks."

She smiled at her handsome husband. "That you can do later. Right now we finish the dance and then I dance with my dad and your father and Dylan and maybe some of your friends and Vernon and Mr. Morris—"

"Stop. I know the drill. Weddings, protocol, ritual, routines—I just want to dream about five hours from now."

A half hour later, Tony stood with his friends.

"Gabe, here's a toast to you. You're the last bachelor, which we knew you would be. You've escaped your dad's meddling and now all our fathers have reformed," Tony said.

"In short," Nick added, "you've led a charmed life. Jake has paved the way for you, helped in some of your fights growing up. What a cushy life you have."

"Beside that," Tony chimed in, "you love that ranch you have and you don't get any flack from your dad. Imagine if any of us had tried to become a cowboy—the blowup and threats would have been monumental."

Gabe grinned and raised the flute of champagne that had barely been touched. "Thanks, guys. I don't know that my life is quite that charmed, but I've been lucky. I still enjoy being single. I definitely enjoy my ranch life, plus the fact that Dad leaves me alone. I do feel a little lucky."

"To the golden boy," Jake said, "my kid brother." They all sipped.

"There is cold beer at the bar if any of you want to get rid of this," Tony said, and Gabe nodded. "If you guys will excuse me, I've been away from my bride a long time now."

"All of half an hour," Jake remarked dryly, and they laughed as Tony left them.

His heart filled with joy at the sight of Isabelle. She had never looked more beautiful than today and he wanted to whisk her away from here and leave for their honeymoon. Before heading to Paris, they were spending four days in New York City and he had no intention of leaving their hotel suite. He was overjoyed to have her to himself, wondering why he had ever thought making a bigger fortune was more important than having her in his life. He watched as Sydney stood talking to her. He was happy for his sister, too, who was so much in love she couldn't stop smiling. He could understand her feelings now.

He walked up to slip his arm around Isabelle's tiny waist.

"Can I steal my bride away?" he asked the group, and without hearing their answers, he led Isabelle away. "Can we leave?"

"Not a moment too soon," she whispered, smiling at him. "My clothes are on your plane and I can just go. I said my goodbyes to everyone earlier."

"So did I," Tony replied, his heartbeat speeding as they headed for a door.

Hours later Tony carried Isabelle over the threshold of their hotel room. He set her on her feet, kicking the door closed while he kissed her.

Holding him tightly, she wound her fingers in his thick black curls. Her heart pounded with joy. She pushed away his tuxedo coat and it fell unnoticed on the floor.

"Tony, there are moments I can't believe all this is really happening," she whispered as she felt his fingers at the buttons of her pale blue dress.

"It's real, love. I'll show you and I'll spend my life trying to make you happy and be the husband, lover, father you want. You're first in my life, Isabelle," he stated solemnly. "Always first. It couldn't possibly be any other way. I can't tell you the joy you give me, but I'm going to try to show you, every way I can."

She smiled at him. "You already have in so many ways," she whispered, fingering the diamond-and-sapphire necklace he had given her as a wedding gift. Her conversation ended as they kissed and she held him tightly. Happiness consumed her. His dark eyes proclaimed his love with unmistakable warmth.

"Tony, I love you with all my heart. My joy is complete in you," she whispered, and returned to kissing him again.

The future looked filled with promises of hope, fulfillment and dreams come true.

* * * * *

LET'S TALK
Romance

For exclusive extracts, competitions
and special offers, find us online:

Or get in touch on 0844 844 1351*

For all the latest titles coming soon, visit
millsandboon.co.uk/nextmonth

*Calls cost 7p per minute plus your phone company's price per minute access charge